DARK MATTER PRESENTS

HAUNTED REELS

STORIES FROM THE MINDS OF PROFESSIONAL FILMMAKERS

Curated by David Lawson Jr.
Copy Edited by Rob Carroll, Jonothan Pickering
Book Design and Layout by Rob Carroll
Cover Art by Olly Jeavons
Cover Design by Rob Carroll

ISBN 978-1-958598-13-9 (paperback)
ISBN 978-1-958598-33-7 (eBook)
ISBN 978-1-958598-34-4 (audiobook)

darkmatter-ink.com

DARK MATTER PRESENTS

HAUNTED
REELS

STORIES FROM THE MINDS OF PROFESSIONAL FILMMAKERS

CURATED BY
DAVID LAWSON JR.

DARK
MATTER
INK

This book is dedicated to all the filmmakers, storytellers, and artists pushing the boulder up that hill.

It is also dedicated to my wife, Cathy, and daughter, Clara, without whom I wouldn't be half the man that I am.

—David Lawson Jr.

CONTENTS

INTRODUCTION
C. Robert Cargill...11

"NATALIE FEARS RECURRENCE" AND OTHER LETTERS THE PSYCHIATRIST
RECOMMENDED SHE WRITE
B. J. Colangelo..14

THE GLOOM
Jay Baruchel..28

DESIRE PATH
Malachi Moore..35

IT STOOD ABOVE ME
C. Robert Cargill...49

A STORY WITH A BEGINNING AND NO END
Aaron Moorhead...54

ILIMU
Wanjiru Njendu...63

THE BEGINNING
Izzy Lee...70

GRIM
Graham Skipper...83

SPELLS
Gary Sherman 96

VOX CANIS
Carl Lucas 132

HOLOGRAM STORE
Brea Grant 148

THE WORLD OFTEN ENDS
Justin Benson 156

FUGAZI
Janina Gavankar & Russo Schelling 171

BREATHE
Nick Peterson 183

THE MAN WHO SAVED THE WORLD
Jared Moshe 190

SPROUT
Jordan Goldstein 200

THE DECEPTION OF YOUTH
Sarah Bolger 206

DEAD NO LONGER
Owen Egerton 215

THIS IS NOT MY FACE
Gigi Saul Guerrero 233

ROLL THE BONES
Ariel Vida 236

WEAVERS
Gille Klabin 252

YEAST
Lola Blanc 259

DETROIT
Michael Dunker 274

MUZZLE
Brett Pierce & Drew Pierce 285

MIDNIGHT: A SERIES OF LETTERS
A. T. White 300

THE FIANCÉE COMES TO TOWN
Cezil Reed 325

IT COMES BACK
Elise Finnerty & Estellle Girard-Parks 333

STRANGE TO ME
Kyra Gardner 340

TOWARDS THE LIGHT
David Lawson Jr. 352

ABOUT THE AUTHORS 361

CONTENT WARNING

This anthology contains content that may be unsuitable for certain audiences. Stories include foul language, disturbing imagery, and graphic depictions of sex and violence. Reader discretion is advised.

INTRODUCTION

C. Robert Cargill

MANY YEARS AGO, my good friend Joe Lynch had his film *Mayhem* accepted into the SXSW Film Festival—a prestigious Austin-based multimedia festival, covering interactive (software), music, and movies. The film track is a huge launching point for independent genre and documentary films, but the popularity of the fest means hotel rooms across the city sell out months—sometimes a year—in advance. Joe was left with a film in a big festival, but no place to stay for its three showings. He reached out, and I let him crash at my place for a week in our guest room.

While there, between screenings, he and I spent most nights out on my porch, drinking beers and telling industry war stories. Our ups, our downs, our inspirations, and sometimes we got deeply personal. Joe called it "porch beers." When he went back to LA. and people asked him about the experience, in addition to discussing the screenings, he told many of them, "If you get down to Austin, make sure to have porch beers with Cargill."

A few months later, someone did just that. A friend reached out and said he was flying into Austin in a matter of hours and was told he needed to have "porch beers." I had nothing pressing, so I picked him and a few of his crew members up from the airport, and we drank on the porch until dawn, once again swapping our war stories, commiserating, and just having a great time talking about work in a purely cathartic way.

He went back to LA and began telling friends: "If you get down to Austin, make sure to have porch beers with Cargill."

And from then on, whenever they were in town, calls and texts came in from filmmakers wanting to have "porch beers."

Within a few years, people began requesting to come over during the three major Austin film events of the year: SXSW, the screenwriter-centric Austin Film Festival, and the genre bacchanalia that is Fantastic Fest. By 2019, I was hosting over a dozen porch beers a year, with upwards of a dozen filmmakers a night sitting on the porch, swapping the stories they couldn't tell at the festival—both terrible and triumphant—all under the auspice of one rule: what was said at porch beers stayed at porch beers. And that held. The stories told there always stayed there. First-time genre filmmakers mingled with A-listers—writers, directors, actors, producers, editors, composers. We were all filmmakers at porch beers, and we learned firsthand that we were not alone. Making movies is fucking hard. Sometimes really fucking hard. It can drain you, grind you down into dust, even sometimes traumatize you. But we've all been there, and the catharsis of talking with your peers about your trials and tribulations can be amazing. Fantastic Fest 2019 saw eight porch beers in a row, one for each night of the fest.

Then 2020 hit. SXSW was the very first major event to cancel. Then Chattanooga Film Festival, a favorite regional festival of many on the circuit, had to cancel their in-person portion. We were all stuck inside, our industry and careers left entirely uncertain, as we all found ourselves inside of a horror movie.

Three filmmakers who had attended several porch beers in the past—Justin Benson, Aaron Moorhead, and David Lawson Jr.—reached out and asked if they could use the name "porch beers" for something they were planning. They'd grown stir crazy during lockdown, and one of the things they lamented missing the most was sitting around and drinking with other filmmakers. So they wondered: What if we did it digitally? I told them I didn't have a trademark or anything on the name, but loved that they wanted to rekindle the experience, if even in a limited capacity.

And thus the Zoom-room version of porch beers was born. Every Thursday night, starting at 8:30 p.m. PST, the room opened, and filmmakers from all walks of life would filter in. Our youngest filmmaker was a twenty-one-year-old fresh out of film school; our oldest was in his mid-seventies and had directed films many of us had grown up on and been inspired by. Over the course of the pandemic, nearly a hundred filmmakers would join the room—some only once, others week in and week out, come rain or shine. Some nights would only host half a dozen for an intimate chat; other nights would see twenty different filmmakers hanging out at once, for hours at a time.

Some jokingly referred to it as "Thursday Night Therapy." Others used it to navigate their current development nightmares, knowing full well someone in the room might have the answer to their woes, all still under that cone of silence. And over the course of three years, numerous deep, close friendships formed in that room. I have over two dozen truly amazing close friends that I hadn't even met in person until years into our friendship.

In 2022, many of us got together for the first time at the Fantasia Film Festival, and then shortly thereafter had a thirty-filmmaker in-person porch beers, reviving the tradition at Fantastic Fest. Somewhere along the line, a discussion was had that we all wanted to do something together. This book is that something. What you hold in your hands is the physical manifestation of numerous filmmakers' emotional survival of the global pandemic. There's a lot we all lost during those years, but for the authors of this book, something wonderful was gained.

These are our nightmares. These are the echoes of the things we've all been through. Horror is catharsis; it is pure, unbridled empathy. This is the distillation of three years of discussing filmmaking, our lives, and what it means to make genre, particularly horror. And we hope you enjoy it.

"NATALIE FEARS RECURRENCE"
AND OTHER LETTERS THE PSYCHIATRIST RECOMMENDED SHE WRITE

B. J. Colangelo

MARCH 12TH

I THINK DR. Paslawski exclusively bathes in peppermint and tea tree oil. I'm going to dread our sessions because every time I enter her office, the smell of menthol slaps me across the face as if I've committed some blasphemous crime in the eyes of the invasive plant community. Tea tree oil *is* an antifungal, so she's only telling on herself.

Why am I starting this way? Probably because I don't want to do this. No, not probably. I really, really don't want to fucking do this.

Okay. So. I'm Natalie. I'm twenty-six. Hi. Nice to meet you—whoever ends up reading this.

My girlfriend brought me here hoping they'd help me or whatever, and now I'm sitting at a desk covered in a layer of film from what feels like hastily applied disinfectant, and my nose is STILL recovering from the sting of cheap peppermint while I play "Dear Diary."

"Natalie fears recurrence," she said to me.

At least she doesn't call it hallucinations.

Someone scratched a pointy looking heart at the top of this desk near the little dip where crayons sit. The linework looks too thick to have been a safety pin. It was probably a paper clip. But…who would need a paper clip? And who would have a casual paperclip at the ready in the middle of a therapy session?

Someone who needs therapy, clearly.

I shouldn't talk shit about the mysterious paperclip carver. They could be very nice for all I know. Or they could be someone who skins cats alive with paper clips and squashes their flesh between their toes. But how did they get it in here? My tits are hanging past my belly button because underwire bras are on the ban list, next to shoelaces and spiral notebooks. A girl who thought aliens were sending her messages through her refrigerator magnets pulled hers out and slit her throat with it a few years back in the middle of the common area, and now my lower back has to suffer.

It's a real crock, but there's nothing I can do about it. Maybe I'm just "projecting my own insecurities onto a perfect stranger." Okay, but in all seriousness, I hate when people say that. Sometimes it just feels good to aimlessly judge someone without it having to be deeply interwoven with my own TrAuMa or whatever. Then again, I'm the asshole on my third 5150 hold in two years, so who the fuck am I to complain?

Okay. So.

Recurrence.

Everyone keeps saying that I'm here for my own safety, but there is no safety. I feel his presence humming through my veins like laying on the floor in front of an amplifier overwhelmed by interference. It just keeps getting louder. He's out there. Waiting for just one millisecond of weakness, and then he'll take me.

If it happens again, it will kill me.

And he's coming.

I want to go home.

THINGS I PROMISE NOT TO TAKE FOR GRANTED WHEN I'M HOME AGAIN

- Underwire Bras
- The Hitachi Magic Wand
- Crunchwrap Supremes
- When I Forget to Close the Curtains and the Sun Wakes

Me Up
- Bad Playlists for Long Drives
- The Way Aria's Hair Dye Stains Everything We Own Red
- Showering Without Shoes
- The Weird Smell of Aria's Ears When She Doesn't Clean Them
- Glitter that Refuses to be Vacuumed
- The Instant Warmth When Aria Nestles Into Me While She Sleeps and For a Moment, Time Stops and I Forget How to Breathe but I Know I'm Alive Because She's Pressed Against Me...
- Lint Rollers

SHE WAS STILL able to see me during intake. I stood there, nude, and she just stared at me through the wire mesh glass. She didn't blink. Not even once. It was her only defense against the tears welling in her eyes. I don't blame her for calling me in.

He was starting to inch inside of me again.

We keep the fan on at night to drown out the constant bickering of our neighbors and their screaming kids. I hadn't shaved in a while so I thought I was just feeling the air current moving around my leg hair or something. Aria was fast asleep and she was wearing these fuzzy cashmere socks my mom gave for her birthday last winter, so I would have known if it was her playing a game of midnight footsie with me.

It wasn't.

It was him.

I looked down toward my feet, just past the rolling hill of my body enveloped in our dingy comforter, to see his jagged smile curling through the cracks around his mouth. The same smile he's been giving me for seven years. I felt him steal the words from my throat when I tried to scream, "GET THE HELL AWAY FROM ME!" so all I could muster was a squeak and a bemused "Help."

He ran through every single hair on my calf and stopped when he reached the scar on the back of my thigh. His touch felt like covering your skin with salt and pressing an ice cube against it—a touch so cold that it burns. I pressed my eyes closed so tightly that the remnants of mascara my cold cream couldn't wash away seared into my tear ducts. My head began to shake something violent.

I heard Aria choke and I panicked. The burning was gone. Somehow, he'd changed targets and he was after her. I knew it. He'd had his way with me and now he wanted the only thing in my life I've ever loved. I couldn't let him. I turned over, the comforter flew off of my body and knocked over the half-empty glass of water on my nightstand. I jolted upright and braced myself for absolute carnage and saw that she was...

Fine.

She had choked a little on the spit pooling in her mouth. I looked back to my feet and he was gone. My heart was beating so loudly I was sure she could hear it, but between the fan and her snoring (she only snores when she sleeps on her back), she didn't budge. She didn't wake up. I sat there and listened to her breath slip through her teeth, to the sound of the fan and the way it jostled the leaves of the Lady Palm in the corner, to the spilled water dripping from the nightstand to floorboards.

Thank fuck we don't have carpeting.

I don't think Aria likes it when I talk about him. Then again, does anyone really like hearing about the people who have been inside your girlfriend before they met you? This would be so much easier if he was someone I let fuck me before I figured out I was gay, but how do you tell someone, "Hey, six years before we met, I was possessed by a demon who called himself Carcirath, and I'm going to spend the rest of my life in agonizing terror, waiting for him to take over my body once and for all?"

Fuck.

They are never letting me out of here.

MARCH 13TH

IT'S 3 A.M. I usually don't sleep the first night I'm admitted. Maybe an hour or so, but it's not the best place for, you know, relaxation or whatever. The woman in the next room is coming down off something. My money's on meth because it's the easiest thing to get in this city. If you can't buy it, there's sure as shit enough tutorials online that teach how to make it. I didn't think it was possible to hear someone sweat, but reality has a fun way of proving me wrong. She's a mom. Her kids must miss her terribly.

I like the night guard. His name's Antwan, and he snuck me a blue Gatorade. He was here the last time I had to be admitted, so he knows I'm good for it. I told Aria on the drive up here that I like this place best because it's connected to the hospital, which means we get food from the hospital kitchen. In the hierarchy of shitty food, I think it looks something like:

- Regular Hospital
- Public School Cafeteria
- In-Flight Airline Meal
- Prison
-
-
-
-
-
- Psychiatric Hospital

Tonight was an embarrassing attempt at mac & cheese. The noodles were mushy, the cheese was powder-based, and it 100% tasted like it was made by a white dude making minimum wage. Maybe this is the kind of opportunity offered to whomever comes in last place on *Iron Chef.* Or like, you know how there are Juilliard graduates who don't turn out to be Viola Davis or Oscar Isaac and wind up as actors in mystery dinner theatre?

Being the head chef at a psychiatric hospital seems like the culinary school equivalent.

Aria took me to my favorite restaurant the night before I got here. It's a small Vietnamese place connected to a Vietnamese grocery store, a hair salon, and a nail salon. A family immigrated to the area and bought an entire city block's worth of storefronts. Walking between Wadsworth and 55th feels like stepping into another world. It's as if someone plucked out a neighborhood from their hometown and dropped it next to the bus station.

There's a beautiful fish tank right at the entrance. Fish haven't lived in the tank since the first Bush era, but that evening, we were greeted by a rainbow swirl of bubbling fins. I guess the grand-daughter of the owner finally got her wish and refilled the tank.

My go-to order is cinnamon beef stew and fried tofu triangles, with spicy peanut sauce as an appetizer. Basic, I know, but you've never had that spicy peanut sauce. If you could make out with God, His spit would taste like that spicy peanut sauce. Unless you're allergic to peanuts—then it's probably just caramel or something.

Our waitress brought us our food, and Aria dove right into her samosas. I grabbed my tofu triangle, fresh from the fryer, and immediately dropped it. I stuck my fingers into my mouth out of instinct and when I ran my tongue across the pad of my thumb, I felt it.

As if granules of salt between my fingerprints had met ice.

Burning cold.

I looked up, thumb still in mouth, and behind the fish tank, just to the right of Aria's left shoulder, Carcirath was staring directly at me, his smile wider than the last time I had seen him. I stumbled out of my chair, unable to pull my thumb from my mouth, unable to unlock my jaw.

"Baby, baby, what's wrong?" she pleaded with me.

But I couldn't answer.

I inched away, my eyes locked with his, and stopped only when the back of my thigh bumped into the table behind me, where an elderly woman was trying phở for the first time (my intrusion knocked her face into a spoonful of the hot broth).

"Natalie. Answer me. Please."

I fell to the ground, my eyes never losing focus. He knew I could see him and he loved it.

He slithered beneath the table that held the fish tank, and crawled closer. The carpet turned black, and the fabric disintegrated the moment his prolonged digits made contact. I watched as the fish began to turn belly-up one by one and float slowly to the top. I was overwhelmed with an unbearable stench of rot as every meal immediately spoiled and started to decompose. Carcirath is a harbinger of death, and he had an overdue debt to settle with me.

Aria dove across the table, grabbed my shoulders, screamed "NATALIE!" and put her face in front of mine, forcing me to break eye contact with him.

I snapped away and looked around. Everything was fine. The fish were swimming. The food was fresh. The carpet untouched. To everyone else, all I had done was caused a scene, knocked over an old woman, and embarrassed my girlfriend. He was there. I know he was.

Artwan is coming for my crayon.

I should probably try to sleep.

MARCH 13TH (still)

IT'S A QUARTER till 2 p.m. now. I managed to get a few hours of sleep, but Artwan woke me up at the ass-crack of dawn for breakfast. If you're not up by 7 a.m. for breakfast, you won't get it. They like to get us out of our rooms early so they can lock the door behind us as soon as possible. That's the thing no one ever talks about in psychiatric hospitals—there's no real alone time. We're all labeled as high-risk the moment we're admitted, so I get it. I dozed off in the common area for a hot minute only to be rudely awakened by this girl who was smelling my hair. The shampoo here smells like a retirement home after they disinfect a room someone died in, so I don't know what she was getting out of it.

Our enthusiasm (or lack of) toward showering can influence whether or not they keep us longer than seventy-two hours. Swear to God. If you try to fight showering, you won't get to go home. I've developed a habit of singing. I sing really well, actually. But I'll be damned if I'm gonna let these assholes appreciate my gifts for free. Nah, they're getting my full nasal, deep vibrato, off-key Miss Hannigan finest. "Easy Streeeeeeeet!" I haven't decided if it's a good thing or a bad thing that I'm completely unfazed by people watching me shower.

I think I prefer it.

Aria and I's apartment has this big, vintage, claw-foot bath tub. It gets so damn cold in the winter that before it's comfortable enough to take a bath, we have to dump in a pot of hot water big enough to boil a Thanksgiving turkey before ever turning on the faucet. Our hot water heater sucked shit trying to fight frozen Midwestern pipes, but we made due.

When we got home from the Vietnamese place, Aria had set the whole bathroom up for me. She lit a few ghost flower candles (my favorite), prepped the warming of the tub, added some epsom salt, queued up a playlist of stuff like *Massive Attack* and *Portishead*, and atop the bathtub tray, laid out a glass of whiskey and a bath bomb in the shape of a heart.

No one has ever shown me that kind of affection.

She tried to walk away and leave me to it, but I reached out and grabbed her hand to pull her back to me. I twirled her back to face me and pressed my forehead against hers. Lifting her chin to meet her mouth to mine, I kissed her as I shimmied out of my pajama pants. They fell to my ankles, and I wrapped my arm around her waist, pulling her body against mine so she could feel that I was disrobing.

"Stay with me?" I asked her.

She skimmed her hands down to the hem of my tank top and lifted it over my head, pressing my flesh against her still clothed body in the process. Her lips burrowed between mine, the barbell of her labret guiding my jaw open as she whispered into my mouth.

"Is that what you need?"

I slid my hand across the small of her back and crept my hand up her spine. The clasp of her bra melted between my fingers, and the straps dropped down her shoulders and through the sleeves. I pulled the straps down her arm, pulling her wrist through the loops, and watched as her bra dropped from underneath her oversized *KISS* t-shirt on top of the pile of clothing strewn across the bathroom floor.

Aria slinked into the bathtub and slowly descended into the water—her red hair bleeding dye and turning the clear water a subtle pink. She lifted her right eyebrow and pouted her lips at me. The siren wail of Beth Gibbons' voice bounced off of our walls, and as Aria's muscles relaxed from the warmth of the water, a moan escaped from deep inside as if her very being was calling me toward her. She loved me. Even after everything that had happened, she still desired me and deemed me worthy. I lifted my leg and stepped into the tub, my toe rolling the epsom salt across the bottom until I felt it. The frozen fire.

I yanked my leg out of the tub, kicking over the bathtub tray and spilling whiskey onto the floor.

"What the fuck, Natalie?"

Aria stood in the tub, water flipping off of her skin and leaving little black specks all around the bathroom. Every water droplet immediately singed through wherever it landed, the blackness spreading and sprawling as if they were trying to grab hold of something. I watched the blackness twist toward my toes.

"Natalie, answer me!"

I snapped my head to look toward Aria only to see Carcirath standing behind her, his arms outstretched like the twisted limbs of a rotted tree, his darkness cloaking her in shadow. I dropped to the floor, my naked body curled into a fetal position, eyeballing the void worming toward me. Aria took a step out of the tub, and Carcirath followed in synchronicity.

"DON'T YOU FUCKING TOUCH ME!" I shrieked.

I laid on the floor and screamed myself hoarse. She kept her distance and stood in bewilderment, completely unaware of the horror that surrounded her. She couldn't see him. She couldn't fucking see him! I slammed my hand against the floor, cracking the tile beneath my palm. Crimson dripped down my fingers, and when my blood met the rot on the floor, it stopped crawling toward me.

That's when I blacked out.

I woke up in the front seat of the car, my hand wrapped in gauze, Aria in the driver's seat, eyes locked forward and staring straight down the road.

"You need more than what I can give right now," she muttered.

My hand was throbbing, and my abdominal muscles stung. She told me that I couldn't stop screaming about needing to protect myself. I had slammed my hand into the broken tile over and over again until I was gushing pools of blood onto the floor. Apparently, I rubbed it all over my body and screamed, "it's the only way he can't get inside of me again."

"Please, Aria, don't let him take my body this time," she repeated back to me.

I asked if she saw him. She said no. I asked if the bathroom had been consumed by the void. She said no. I told her I didn't believe her and I knew what I saw. She threw her phone at me, told me to unlock it, and still on display was a photo she had taken.

No Carcirath. No rotted walls.

Just spilled whiskey, a half-melted bath bomb, a broken tile, and me laying in the fetal position, covered in my own blood.

Artwan said it's time for group.

MARCH 13TH (YES, AGAIN)

DINNER TASTED LIKE resentment. Group was fine.

Dr. Paslawski asked me to share my story, and I told her I didn't need any more people in this world thinking I've got bats in the belfry. I don't like talking about it because I know how fucking insane it sounds, but it's real. Okay?

I was possessed by Carcirath when I was twenty years old. Some wannabe exorcist my college roommate found online got him out of me, and then I moved to a new city and tried my best to start a new life. The thing people don't know about demons is that they aren't some supernatural entity that can only be flushed out by the "Glory of God" or whatever religious bullshit people have been peddling as a scare tactic. No. Demons are a part of us no matter what we believe. Most of us learn to live alongside them. Some of us are lucky enough to beat them. As for the rest? The demons take hold and they never let go.

I think it's because he knows I'm finally happy—that's why he wants me now. And I see him. Everywhere. I watched him slip in while the orderly had me squat and cough. He knows I know, too. He's been taunting me. I've seen that fucking smile peering around the halls, lingering above the TV in the common area, and making a home in the communal shower.

But why? What did I do to attract this? Is it because of where I grew up? Genetics? Too much red meat? What is it? I've been racking my brain trying to figure it out. I know that if I can figure out what brought him to me in the first place, I can figure out how to avoid him.

If he takes me again, he will shred me from the inside out. Carcirath comes not to inhabit, but to annihilate. He takes over his host and slowly destroys it, reveling in their pain and suffering and the misery that it inflicts on everyone who loves them. I know the catastrophe he brings because I've felt it, and I wouldn't wish it upon even my worst enemies. But he just keeps coming back. And I'm scared, alright? I'm scared. I'M FUCKING SCARED.

I'm scared of every molecule in my body feeling like a fiery tundra. I'm scared of my body withering away in front of me, unable to stop it. I'm scared of feeling my organs decompose while the rest of me is fighting to stay alive. I'm scared of going to sleep convinced that it'll be the last time I ever shut my eyes. I'm scared of how much pain my dying will cause her. I'm scared that when I'm gone, she won't feel any pain at all. I'm not afraid of recurrence. I'm afraid of dying.

There is no comfort in knowing you're going to die, just anticipation.

MARCH 14TH

THE GIRL WHO smelled my hair yesterday is gone. Her body is still here, walking around and acting as if all is well and good, but she's gone. Her name was Jeannie, I learned.

She was walking the halls late last night, repeatedly proclaiming that something was under her skin and that it needed to be washed away—some real Lady MacBeth shit. Her pleas started off like a standard psychiatric freak-out, but her voice randomly turned deep and guttural, as if her voice was trapped in a tin bunker. There was no way any of us were going to get any sleep with her manic episode reverberating up and down the empty halls, so we all peeked our heads out of our rooms and tried to decipher what was going on between her incoherent ramblings and the hushed tone of the nurses on staff. Her feet tripped over one another, and she stumbled right in front of my door before stopping.

"My blood is burning cold," she screamed at me, compulsively rubbing her forearm raw.

The orderlies did their best to de-escalate her. Kind words, prodding questions, anything to get her to stop rubbing her calloused hands against her soft flesh. Dead skin rolled off of her palms like sprinkles of decay and stuck to the sweat that glazed her arms.

"He's swimming in my veins!" she cried. "He's here!"

Her gaze never left mine. A nurse sedated her—probably Haloperidol—but even after the medication took hold, she kept talking. Her words were a tsunami, and I was going to drown.

"Carcirath. Carcirath. Carcirath. CarciRATH. CARCIRATH! CARCIRATH!!!"

You can pump someone with as many anti-hallucinogens as their body can handle, but if they're not hallucinating, all you're doing is shutting down any defense system they once had to fight what they're seeing. Her muscles relaxed and she lost the ability to hold her head up on her own. She slumped to the floor, limbs loose like a marionette without a puppeteer, her box-dyed black hair covering her face like a shield. But her eyes still gazed up toward my window. Fetal position—it's a position I'm all too familiar with.

"Show's over," a nurse bellowed. "Get back to your beds!"

The hallway echoed with the symphony of bare feet against linoleum flooring, hollow doors latching and locking, and a dozen or so bodies flopping onto vinyl covered mattresses. The nurse called for an orderly and mumbled something about leaving her there until they could bring a wheelchair to cart her back to her room. I crouched below the window in my room, eyes fixated on the torpid figure across from me. Her hair began to writhe across the floor, crawling toward my room and sliding through the crack under the door. I was entranced as her body edged closer and closer toward my room, her face dragging across the tile and collecting dust. I felt a shriek building from deep inside my throat, but when I tried to scream for help, all I could choke out was "Hi."

Her head SLAMMED into the door and her hair began to climb up the side toward the knob. Her hair couldn't reach. It just flailed and slapped against the door, pulling her head into the wood frame over and over again. I backed away and pressed my back against the wall as I saw an orderly grab her off the ground and try to pick her up. Her hair desperately tried to cling on to my side of the door, but eventually he got a hold of her and pulled her away. He yanked her with such force that her hair flipped back over her head to reveal her face and for a brief moment, I saw what I knew to be true the entire time.

Carcirath's face—that jagged smile—slapped across where her mouth should be. A small yelp peeped out of my mouth and just like that, she was back to being a very, very ill woman in need of serious help. They transported her to the quiet room, a clump of her hair remaining underneath my door like the connective tissue between the safety of my dorm and the vulnerable danger of being anywhere else.

I tiptoed toward the nest of hair and held it between my fingers, the same hand I had brutalized days before in my bathroom. I clenched my fist and felt the inside of my knuckles blister—her hair, like the blood she was screaming about, was like squeezing liquid nitrogen. When the pain became unbearable, I unlocked my paw and watched as her hair dropped to the floor, disintegrating into nothingness before it even reached the ground.

After all these years. Seeing him everywhere. Feeling his eyes on me. Watching him destroy everything around me only to restore it to normalcy like a sick joke. And for what? To take over an innocent person right in front of me? To hurt someone, knowing full-well I can't do anything to help her without making myself look even more insane than I already feel? I've sacrificed jobs, relationships, and my own sanity trying to keep myself protected and now?

He doesn't want me anymore.

Most of today has been spent trying to figure out what changed. Like, why is he suddenly uninterested in me? I'll never get an answer, and I think I'll spend the rest of my life trying to make peace with that. He didn't kill me, but he took me over once, and no matter what happens to him or who he takes next, I'll never be able to un-experience that. I survive, but his looming presence keeps him immortal. Maybe that's his power. I don't know. I just know that I wear him on my flesh like a permanent stain. My scarred hand, my increased heartbeat, my anxiety. He's done with me, but I will never be done with him. I've spent so many years trying to figure out how to stay alive, I'm afraid I don't know how to actually live. What if I don't know how to do that?

They're letting me go home today. I've proven not to be a danger to myself or others, and Dr. Paslawski's minty ass thinks it's normal for me to be afraid of past trauma, conveniently ignoring the fact my trauma is being fucking possessed. But I'm returning to Aria with a fresh new prescription, three bottles of blue Gatorade, this journal, and a brand-new pair of ugly brown non-slip socks.

I hope she still loves me.

THE GLOOM

Jay Baruchel

HE TOLD THEM about his time in the war, and this excited them. And they were proud of their excitement. This was a new era. Shame was a thing of the past. Strength and confrontation were to be the defining values of the current culture. No more need for excuses. This was their time, and the world belonged to them, and if they felt a primal connection to his anecdotes of soldiering and murder, they were not going to hide it. They wanted him to know as they wanted the world to know: This was Germany, and they were Germans, and this century was theirs to devour.

Their invitation was not accidental. Tom was a veteran from the other side of the fight, a remnant from a war he still didn't understand, mostly because he never had to. Understanding was never part of the job. He had lost a lot of himself after the war, had lost context, and he fell into the ranks of the countless living ghosts scattered about Canada after Armistice. He hated himself, and he hated the neighborhoods of soft, ruddy-faced men who never left home for the exhausting, meaty ardor of the Somme, or the tendrilled, yellow hell of the gas attack at Ypres. His resentment was matched only by his jealousy of their cleanliness and ease. They weren't ruined men like he was. They weren't damned to a lifetime defined by one half decade of seasonal violence.

Tom had nowhere to be, and every day gave him less to live for, so when he received their invitation postmarked from Berlin, which contained a ticket for passage aboard the City of Liverpool and real money to be spent on food and liquor, he was quick to take them up on their offer. He was hungry and bored and suicidal, and this kind of adventure would provide him some reprieve. He had something to do and someone to be now. He once again had a spine for his soul.

They wanted to hear Tom describe how it felt to kill their fellow Germans. They enjoyed it, but Tom didn't understand why. Still, he obliged them—after all, they had paid for him to come to Berlin and provide the service requested. Tom still wasn't sure who "they" were, or whether there was more to this invitation than what was expressly contracted, but he had a contingency plan if things went south: He would kill them all.

He ran the tips of his fingers across the scar on his cheek and eyed the room for the strongest and weakest among them.

"Herr Cameron?" It was the voice of the "fancy one," with the pince nez and scurvy skin, who looked like a university professor. "Have we lost you to the clouds again?" He took a drag of his cigarette and laughed as he exhaled the smoke.

Tom scratched at the unpickable contours of scar tissue. "No. Sorry. I was just trying to remember specifics."

"Splendid. As you know, we adore specifics. Please, continue." Fancy played with the hair of the old fortune teller sitting next to him, looping her gray hair around his bony finger and tickling the pale scalp. She smiled lovingly back at Fancy and used the dying ember of his cigarette to light the one dangling from her lips.

"I have a question," she said. "When you were out there, on the battlefield, did you dream of the violet in the mire?"

The room quieted to a whisper.

Tom's blood ran cold. Yes, he had dreamed of the violet in the mire. It had happened during one particularly restless sleep in the tunnels beneath no man's land. But how did these people know that? Was it safe for him to admit it to them? There was a subtle game to the way the question was posed that told some part of Tom that these people already knew the answer.

Behind the Fortune Teller stood the Steel Helmet, a vulgar cartoon in neatly pressed khaki, flexing his fattened bicep under an armband emblazoned with a crooked cross they called the swastika—the same crooked cross that Tom had seen on the arms of legionnaires and the fascinators of rich ladies. The crooked cross he saw more often the deeper he traveled into Germany.

Steel Helmet wasn't so different than Tom. They were both hardened shells of a man, broken by the brutal war they survived, but there was an important distinction, something palpable, that separated the two sides they fought for—beyond just the chasms of geography and language. The Germans were wide-eyed and impatient, and the entire country practically shook with the kind of pent-up anger and emasculated desire for vengeance that can only come from defeat. Germany had suffered an economic and infrastructural death, but it could not survive a psychic one. Three hundred years of Prussian militaristic obsession could have yielded no other outcome. Germany had to kill or else it would die. And so there was no pragmatism to be had, only the vivid, white-knuckled angst of slighted men and the ironclad belief in their own supremacy. Canada had been beaten to shit and traumatized and profoundly altered, but the nation would be resurrected.

Which was why Tom couldn't understand why this particular group of Germans were so interested in hearing him describe killing their soldiers. Somewhere inside him he suspected that all was not what it seemed, that he was being had. Somehow, in some way he couldn't yet divine, Tom felt that they were getting the best of him, that this whole interview was a ruse. But he had been trained to face danger head on and reject any desire to retreat, so the only possible reaction he could have at this moment was to stay and meet the enemy where they stood.

"Yes," Tom admitted. "I dreamt of the violet in the mire."

A chorus of excited whispers trickled through the crowd. A chair made a terrible scraping sound against the floor as Fancy quickly shot to his feet.

"And was there anything else?" he pressed, his eyes sharp with intensity. "Do you remember anything else about that dream, Herr Cameron?"

A disdainful tongue clucked its disapproval. "This is inter- ference," said a new voice. "These leading questions serve only to taint the purity of our exercise." The speaker was tall, broad-shouldered, and well-groomed. His suit was tailored to fit perfectly. Tom had overheard him bragging before the exercise about being a self-made man—a capitalist.

"Don't listen to him," the Capitalist said to Tom. "He's an intellectual. He's like a Jew, forever nudging, inch by inch, until he gets his way. Please tell us only what you remember."

"I couldn't see a fucking thing," Tom continued. "And we all had to be quiet. We always had to be quiet. The boom of artillery, the screams of mutilated men, it didn't matter. We *had* to be quiet. We were right underneath them, you see. We were underneath all of it, tapping away, chipping away, digging like rats under no man's land. Rats who couldn't scurry. Rats who had to crawl slow and quiet while the thunder above never stops, and you're always wet, and you know you deserve to die, and all you want to do is just scream, but you can't. So, you scream on the inside. You shiver. It's a cold that never leaves, even when you're sweating through the same filthy clothes you've been wearing forever. And you hate your own men for it. At least, I did. I hated the men that put me down here. But more than that, I hated the men we were digging towards. I hated the Germans. I hated you. I hated your countrymen and killing them was the closest I ever came to feeling fulfilled. And we could hear them—the voices of your vile compatriots—when they weren't being as quiet or as careful as we were. When they didn't know we were nearly upon them, slithering on our groaning bellies, only a thin layer of rock and mud between us.

"We slept in shifts. Most couldn't sleep no matter how hard they tried, but I could. I was lucky like that. But when you force yourself to sleep like I did, you dream differently. The dreams down there beneath the constant warring above were like when you're sick, like being kicked in the head. They're just there. And they're sharp. And mean. And I'm helpless. And I think of home, but I know I'm just thinking about it—not pretending or believing I'm there. Like my dream is making fun of me. My dream wants to break my heart. And so, it shows me the muck. Blood and piss and shit, and it's everywhere. Shows me how the muck is the world. But at least I know it. And at least I know to hate it. The muck doesn't expect anything of me, even if it asks everything of me. And that's all right. That is something I can understand. But the dream wants to break my heart, and so it shows me something beautiful. It shows me fragile things of beauty and then corrupts them. One night, it shows me a flower. A beautiful flower. The violet. Growing out of everything awful. But before it could be corrupted like the rest, I awoke to find the big Irishman from Quebec on top of me, his big hands pressed against my mouth to shut me up.

"I could hear the Germans on the other side of rock, working at the wall with hammer and tongs. An explosion topside shook the entire tunnel. The Irishman and everyone else on our crew were fixing bayonets. Apparently, we were expecting the Germans at any moment. The Mennonite from Kitchner could speak German and he was whispering his translations of what he heard. 'One of them is talking about his dreams…says he dreamed about a flower…'

"And that's when the thin layer of rock between us crumbled to reveal four startled Germans, eyes wide like terrified little kids.

"Then, in the gloom, I saw him, and he saw me, and it was like looking into a mirror. And I'm not trying to be poetic. I mean he physically looked like me. Not similar, not the same. Identical. And I could see that he was trying to make sense of me as well."

Unglaublich," whispered one of the listeners.

"And as the Irishman and the Mennonite and the rest of my crew bludgeoned skulls and ran their bayonets through the eye sockets of these helpless Germans caught by surprise, this man and myself, we just looked at each other. We looked at ourselves. And even though I knew he was me, I also knew I had to kill him, and I could tell he was feeling the same…"

Tom paused. "But that's where the memory ends. I've tried to remember what happened next, but I can't. The next memory I have was waking up in a hospital and learning the war was over."

"And have you been happy, Herr Cameron?" Fancy asked. "Have you been happy in Canada since the end of the war?"

"No. Of course not. You know I haven't been happy."

"Well then," said the Fortune Teller. "Perhaps we can provide you some catharsis." She pointed with her eyes to a shadow standing in the doorway.

The shadow stepped hesitantly into the dim, smoky light, and revealed himself to be the German soldier from the tunnel—Tom's doppelganger from the gloom. The double seemed to be as confused as Tom was.

Fancy smiled at him and gestured at Tom. "Please. Join him."

Tom clenched his fists and readied himself for a fight as the double approached and took his place beside him.

Soon after, a valet entered the room, pushing a small medicine cart like the ones the nurses would use to bring the soldiers their painkillers and rations of chocolate pudding. But this cart carried something different. Glinting atop the tray was a Luger and a bayonet, the virgin blade yet to spill blood, its serrated teeth sharpened, ready to rip and tear.

The Valet wheeled the cart to the center of the room, only a few steps, or one determined lunge, from Tom and his double. It was obvious now what the crowd had planned. The men would have to fight, and one would have to die.

The Fortune Teller slid her hand between the Capitalist's legs.

Tom kept his eyes locked on the most familiar eyes in the world has he inched towards the weapons, and his Double did the same. Tom didn't have to look to know the Fortune Teller had slid her other hand through Fancy's legs and that the Capitalist was happy about it. He could hear all three enjoying themselves.

The closer Tom got to the weapons, however, the less he felt like killing his Double, and the more he felt like killing the ones who had brought him here.

Tom looked at his Double, and his Double looked back at him. Tom saw the man's eyes flick anxiously to the weapons on the cart, so without hesitation, Tom lunged for the Luger. He grabbed the pistol, and his Double grabbed the bayonet. His Double slashed at him with the serrated knife, but Tom dodged the attack and kicked the man backwards with his boot. He aimed the Luger at his backpedaling opponent and...

Fancy ejaculated with a loud, ecstatic moan.

Disgusted, Tom turned the pistol to Fancy and pulled the trigger, causing Fancy's chest to explode with blood mid-orgasm. The Fortune Teller recoiled from the bloody mess and let out a terrified scream. The Capitalist, still hard, struggled to pull his pants back up so that he could escape.

Tom's Double smiled devilishly at Tom, and his grip tightened around the handle of the bayonet. Fueled by pure adrenaline and an unquenchable rage, he slashed at the Capitalist's throat and sent his blood spraying across the room. The Capitalist grabbed at his bloody neck with wide, terrified eyes and collapsed to the floor, his genitals still on display.

Tom turned his pistol to the Fortune Teller and shot her in the face. Her head flew back in a burst of red, her screaming mouth now silent, but still agape.

Steel Helmet rushed Tom with the intensity of a bloodthirsty killer, but before he could reach him, a whetted bayonet was plunged into his gut. Steel Helmet groaned, the sound a mix of pain and fury. Tom's Double stared Steel Helmet in the eyes as he twisted the blade and wrenched it from the man's stomach. Blood and guts spilled out everywhere.

Tom kept firing, and his Double kept stabbing.

Once Tom ran out of bullets, he used the pistol's handle as a bludgeon and beat in as many heads as he could. The killing continued until everyone in the room was dead. Even the Valet received a violent end.

Outside it was morning, and the streets were crowded with happy citizens, all laughing and smiling and cheering for an approaching parade. The parade was an orderly regiment of khaki-clad teenagers and middle-aged men desperate for a fight they could never win, marching as if to war. All of them were wearing armbands with the crooked cross.

Tom and his Double looked at each other and grinned. They knew what they had to do. Tom's Double gripped his blood-soaked bayonet tight, and Tom readied the Luger like a hammer.

DESIRE PATH

Malachi Moore

IT WASN'T WHAT he could not discern or make sense of that frightened him about the world, but of the thought that human beings, mankind as an entirety, were satisfied with the shallow demarcations it inherited of the physical, nonphysical, and uncanny phenomena of its time. That we had become so satisfied with simplifications to the obscurity in our minds, and that any explanation not yet to be found within the archives of science or religion would simply be found as either a medical symptom of the disturbed, or far worse. There were too many before him whose lives were destroyed from the limited perspective of man, too many souls governed under the Dionysian eye who were convinced of their demonic cultivation and subsequent perdition. He knew these things, not only because the young man fancied himself as an intellect, but because he saw firsthand, through the collective diagnoses of his own father's eccentrics, what horrifying images our minds can conjure in making sense of the unknown. And if there was anything that frightened the Black adolescent more than being misunderstood himself—the apple not falling too far from the tree—was the perverse, inexplicable drive towards the profound and the feeling that perhaps, beyond the fear, there was something worthwhile to discover.

Elijah Wright found that the only thing he had in common with his fellow classmates was their pursuit of higher education. The consensus from generations past was that college was the best place to discover obscure agencies of the self, but it did not appear to Elijah that his own social structure allowed the same perspective on *purpose* as it did for those—of the same ethnicity and those for whom the system was originally designed. It was more than just the color of his skin; he was far too disillusioned by the contradictions of his suburban upbringing—a vast area of compressed burdens one would never know unless made privy to by some serendipitous chance or terrifying ordeal—to believe that any mundane vocation could weather the perpetual storm that is the mind of mortals. That was the first time he heard secrets carried through the wind, the suppressed regret and energy of negative emotions that never quite made it to the surface; they all arise and find their place in the tangible world sooner or later.

It was early during his first semester at The University, in the midst of a brisk New England fall, that Elijah found himself strolling along the narrow, brick pathway, lined by lush Dogwood on both sides. The thickets swayed in the subtle nor'easter breeze, sporadically casting the golden-hour rays on the accumulated sweat above his brow. The straps on his overburdened JanSport clung to his thin shoulders as he continued to walk down the promenade towards the campus' oldest library, one that most undergraduates—let alone the wide-eyed, unseasoned freshmen class he belonged to—would never care to visit before finals came around, or rarely ever at all. The trek was simply too inconvenient for most to go out of their way now that there had been several new additions to the refinement of the school, where one could find everything but the silence and solitude Elijah so craved. No, it was the aged timelessness of the library that called out to him, like the whispering Cornus leaves that carried with them their foreboding secrets. For a moment, one could have sworn that there was another nearby with a propensity to shadow, but paranoia was a feeling Elijah was all too familiar with; he was convinced that as long as he didn't turn around, whatever it was could not be made real.

Oftentimes the young man found himself sensitive to the energies put forth by those around him. Whether the uninvited impressions came to him as clear as day, or in a rebus scramble of the psyche, what laid beneath his long, statuesque frame were the ethereal sensations that created tension within every limb—a numbness to the senses whenever he found himself around those whose anguished, inner-selves were bursting at the seams. The constant heightened forewarnings of an unknown danger approaching made Elijah anxious himself, but was not a feeling he could ascribe to nor define within the family that raised him. And so, he was just like everyone else, and yet the only one to both recognize and reckon for the solidarity of lost souls. Perhaps, then, one might have seen Elijah as an empath of sorts. *But what side of the Divine would gift him with such cognizance?* he wondered. *Where had his forefathers, cursed with the same bestowment, landed on the genealogy of Genesis?* Elijah discerned that his father's own self-inflicted mark of Cain was the result of his existential disquietude, and panicked at the thought of the comparisons. He shuddered a little in the hot, setting sun, then folded his arms and shook the thought off entirely. He figured the best remedy to such apprehension was to disappear into the multiple worlds that books had to offer.

The safe haven—now just fifty yards left of the shaded walkway, to the right, then another seventy-five down what was once an elegant esplanade of milky, meandering stone, reduced now to a desire path of pea gravel—took on many names, but the one that most accurately described its peculiar aura, the one that accumulates with arduous time passing and graceful aging, was "The Old-Soul Library." Its weighted wisdom was commanding. Like the resounding chime of a grandfather clock at the top of each hour, Elijah could feel its presence long before reaching the article of virtue. Built in the early twentieth century, it was originally constructed as a summer estate for a wealthy mercantile couple, long before it was conveyed and established as an aesthetic staple to the University. William and Marie Valdemar were those individuals unlike any other who were stirred by the accursed reverie of the American Dream, the thought that one's monetary stature and constant striving for a higher, social pedestal would result in (at some point) a sense of belonging and contentment. They were *nouveau riche,* and despite their aristocratic façade—keeping the less affluent around reminded them of their prestige—the encumbered blue bloods knew that the Valdemars were born of a different color, and they would not let them forget it. Because of this, The Valdemars suffered a great, cerebral pain within those bedrooms and hallways, their silent anguish bleeding into the walls.

Elijah read a great deal about the second owner of the estate, both from the confines of The University's warped history of a Mr. Thomas Landor, and the subsequent, thorough search spurred by Elijah's own fervent curiosity and inability to accept the proposed idea of a common mortal. He found it peculiar, despite the school's acclaim for the many neoclassical, artistic contributions, that there was nothing mentioned of Landor's agency in investing his entire fortune in European art, or the decision made to live a solitary life within the imposing mansion fit for a multitude. From what Elijah found, it appeared that the man did in fact come from wealth, had a family, and no signs of a physical impairment that would hinder anyone's own lust for life. Instead, however, Mr. Landor spent his days renovating his stately home in the countryside, surrounding himself with novels, emblematic paintings, busts, and sculptures alike, occasionally writing narratives of his own that could now only be found within the online archives of The University, for the unenthused and—frankly, otherwise preoccupied—students of The Information Age. It didn't matter; the estate was Thomas Landor's magnum opus, and it wasn't until that Black Tuesday, after the capitalist-governed society deemed his life's work meritless, did the man disappear entirely without a trace. Headlines consolidated his presumed suicide with the rest of those that placed their existence in tangible worth, and it appeared to Elijah that one really had no say in the final historical consensus of his life; it made him itch, thinking about the irrelevancy of it all.

It was no later than nightfall when Elijah arrived at the entrance of the estate, when the split between the apocalyptic skies and the darkness that fell below the tree line made them their own. He brushed the thick slab of tarnished marble, where the wrought iron gates of the Valdemar's had since been removed and placed elsewhere, and for the first time, realized just how fatigued the walk had made him. It was true that the young man already lacked a certain exuberance given to those who were not conscious of every pleading prayer of the witching hour, but as he gathered himself and stepped further onto the crunchy gravel of the perennial property, Elijah felt the weight of an exhaustion far greater than his own. The foreign wave of energy struck him like the warning gusts of an approaching storm, suddenly aware of the black, abysmal path that stretched out ahead, and the fear that stifled his desire to progress any further. Anxious winds matched the swirling of his own thoughts, oscillating between original conviction and an apprehension of such a place ever existing. It was then that rows of motion-sensor lights symmetrically placed along the path were alerted to his presence and promptly awoke. There in the distance, in all it's great splendor, Elijah could see exactly what he came for, and then some: the three-storied, Beaux-Arts-mansion-turned-student-resource, and a silhouetted, solitary man standing on its large porch, his hands on his hips. By the looks of it, he had been waiting for Elijah to arrive.

Suddenly, the thought of Death trudged through Elijah's mind as he contemplated the source of impetus that propelled his feet to do the same, towards the shadowed man directly ahead of him. The perplexity brought him back to the suppressed memories that would not stay buried, the memory of requiem, trudging the nave to the altar far ahead where the Wright patriarch's casket encased the vessel of a tortured soul. Perhaps it was the frantic way in which the figure in the window moved that reminded Elijah of his father whenever the man was clearly under the spell of some debilitating scrutiny. Even at a young age, Elijah knew the thoughts that brought his father duress were not the man's own, but rather the world's own anxieties given voice, then recited and interpretively performed like some horrific marionette. Elijah dismissed the terrifying apprehension of a curse not yet bequeathed and, with it, the administered paternal love of a father to a son; it was his own secret left to the winds, leaving nothing within his exposed consciousness but feelings of reproach, to which his father heard without a doubt. And now, as the man stopped to look at Elijah—the faintest glimpse of compassion from a distance—then carry on inside, Elijah knew what it was that caused him to fear moving towards the unknown: the guilt of a son, longing for his father's understanding of such an esoteric burden, and forgiveness.

Elijah arrived inside the light and airy entrance hall with heavy legs and feet, conscious of the sapped energy he once possessed that now seemed like a distant memory. He stepped down to the sunken entryway, eyes fixed on the high ceilings and the immaculate chandelier with incandescent bulbs that lent itself well to the gleam of the walnut-paneled walls. He could feel that whatever emotion stirred within him—an eagerness of some kind—was being heightened by his presence here. Further ahead was the first sign of modernity: a tall, curved desk of a different shade. Without having to get any closer, seeing the messy bun on top of a young woman's head peer over the top translucent tier, Elijah could feel that he was not alone. Her scattered, fretful impressions caused him to feel on pins and needles as he continued down the weathered tile floors, tensely scratching the inside of his forearm. Elijah's mind voiced the 'Welcome' sign fixed to the middle of the desk while he approached. For a moment, he thought that the toiling individual whose face was still hidden had done the same for all but two of them to hear. But this was not the voice of a young woman that Elijah heard, nor of his own; instead, the faintest, calming, baritone seeped through one ear and quickly out the other.

"What?" Elijah said nervously. Only one who was closely watching could see the slight tremble of his lower lip. The abrupt nature of his tone shocked the young woman out of her strained concentration, and for a moment, his mind felt less crowded. She looked up at him with swollen, alert eyes. Her limbs looked as though they were vibrating, undoubtedly from the influence of some abused amphetamine cocktail, voice hoarse and distinct. In any other setting, this would be cause for concern, but this was University; she was simply the embodiment of a stressed-out college student.

Elijah quickly looked around his surroundings for the voice that greeted him, noticing a graceful, spiral staircase in the adjacent hall to his right. He asked the young woman if anyone had walked in just before himself, to which her contempt then weighed down her brows.

She finally spoke. "Great. My train of thought is lost. No one ever comes in here, especially this close to closing. I've only got about an hour or so."

Had that much time passed? Elijah continued to scratch, comforted by the familiarity and ascendancy of his own internal voice over others, though anxious by the apparent duration of his walking reverie. He could also not, for the life of him, shake the feeling that he was being watched. These agitations at times were both internally clamorous and the entire purpose of his many visits to the library in the first place. The remedy to such was to fix his attention to any tangible form of written literature. Craving anything but his own thoughts, he settled on a brochure of the grounds and was immediately made known of something he swore was never there before.

"There's a third floor here?" he said to the young woman. She looked up again, this time more slowly and passively. It didn't take a clairvoyant to discern her frustration growing more and more intense, but whether her shaking head movement was a response to his inquiry or to his presence in general was less obvious. Elijah continued to examine the floor plan of each level, noticing that most bedrooms and quarters had been repurposed for private study on the second floor. *So, what could possibly be up there on the third and final floor?* "You're not the least bit curious?" Elijah added, attention fixed on the vague pamphlet.

"I don't have time." Her voice sounded different, less distinct—translucent and fleeting like the passage of time. And when Elijah looked back up to ask for her response again, the young woman was gone.

It had struck a quarter past the eleventh hour when Elijah pressed the tarnished call button to the elevator concealed within a room the size of a tall, rectangular prism located beside the staircase. Elijah knew the time by the distant Westminster chimes, the sound of which were joined now by the irregular breaking of silence by the turnings of a page elsewhere in the library. The elevator's motor lamented from its sedentary state, the rusted cables singing their own horrific tune as well, roughly scraping against the metal pulley whose actions were both concurrent and no less harsh than Elijah's nails to his own skin. It felt as though the library was coming to life, or perhaps waking after an extended rest, eager to wear down the frayed line of defense to Elijah's vital force. *To give it more thought*, he told himself, *means to give it validation.* These were the words his own father pleaded to himself for all to hear. *Keep your head*, he would say. It was true there was nothing tangibly within Elijah's surroundings that would suggest any danger of sorts, but as he waited for the car, staring at the base of the adjoining staircase, he was convinced of a higher existence's insatiable gaze looking down from the top, that circular bullseye, to the ground floor, just waiting for Elijah to wander in its line of vision. Elijah did exactly that just as the elevator arrived and was met with great relief as he looked up and saw nothing but the spiral staircase ascending toward the abysmal ceiling. He turned once more and entered the claustrophobic confines of the elevator cart, noticing that there was no button available for this apparent third floor. Rather than give any more attention to his ongoing angst, Elijah mustered what energy he had left and pulled himself up the steps.

Keep your head... Keep your head... Keep your head.

Little by little, the resonance of sound ceased as Elijah ascended the worn, moaning stairs of Persian texture. He could smell the perennial, musky sweet scent of old literature that pleasantly lingered in his nose, and he could tell that what he had come for was near. The second-floor stairwell opened up to a short hall that had very little renovations done to distinguish itself from early twentieth-century decor except for the buzzing, fluorescent lights that hung above. It was like stepping into another time, shelved and forgotten, simply there to collect dust. It was this that caused the stuffy ventilation system, Elijah told himself; the ventilation that served as the source of what sounded like an individual's stifled breathing, and that created the subtle, warm air he could feel on the back of his neck. The brochure in Elijah's hand, when not used as a scratching apparatus, ushered him further down the vestibule of faint, elaborate wallpaper, until he reached the end. There, to his left, were the endless shelves of fantastical publications that brought his anxious mind an abundance of ease.

Finally. Peace of mind.

A Comedy so Divine, Passions of the Soul, Shelley, Baldwin, and Coates. The mystic carillons chimed while Elijah fell deeper into an interminable place, where time was irrelevant and the only thing to occupy his psyche were the traumas turned philosophies of those who lent their own voices to immortality. He was lost in a labyrinth, weaving through rows and columns of colorful, paperback prints, holding in his trembling arms all that he could carry in his forgotten, weakened state, drifting further and further into the belly of the whale that was "The Old-Soul Library." Every step became more difficult, wearied down by some uncanny force of nature, and for a moment, he believed himself to be weeping. He reached an area where the doors of what once looked to be a large study had been removed, then timidly peered inside at the modern work surfaces of the University's doing—a chaise lounge and mantlepiece surrounding a closed fireplace. He decided then to rest for the little time he had left before the library closed for the night. His body nearly collapsed into the chair, and he clenched his eyes shut from the deep, guttural yawn that ensued. When he opened his eyes, the number of books Elijah accumulated had increased by one: a leather-bound journal embossed with the name of a Mr. Thomas Landor. His thumb brushed against the cover, confirming the existence of such a memento, but he then fell into a deep, hypnotic sleep.

The mind of Man belongs to no one but to those who came before him.

The full-hour chime rang three, the harsh, weeping sounds against celestial bells unmistakable. These were not the cries of a young man waking from his untimely slumber, but that of a woman settled in her anguish. At this precise moment, Elijah thought he had never felt so miserable in his entire life. His head ached as it rose from the desk, throbbing in tune with the lurching thumps of his heartbeat. The strain to open his heavy eyelids was arduous, but not more difficult than to perceive what laid out on the chaise just five feet to his side. He turned his body in his chair and faced the vision directly.

"M-miss?" he muttered. "Are you alright?"

The pale woman's head rested on the upholstered arm and her own. A thin, black evening dress made of silk gripped her thin shoulders, and a long string of white pearls hung down from her neck all the way to the edge of the chaise, swaying from the movement generated by her deep, growling cries. Dark blotches of eyeliner ran down her shriveled, worried face, and no sooner had she revealed her distressed, panicked expression did it turn into something of rabid anger. A sharp vibration imbued the floor and gathered inside the woman like an intense electrical current. She shrieked, eyes and jaw wider than humanly possible. Elijah gripped the backrest of his chair and recoiled, falling hard to the floor with a massive thud. The woman's screams echoed in his head like a mallet striking a gong. He immediately rose from the hardwood floor and frantically sprinted out of the study towards the rows of bookshelves from where he came. Everywhere he looked, the library came to life, manifesting the pained, anguished souls of students past. The chorus of wails created disarray within Elijah's mind, making the once-illusory labyrinth of intellect a maze from Hell. Not a single thought was his own. He was possessed by his impulse to escape.

As he quickly approached the exit, a thought ran into his mind that his stay here at the library might be perpetual, and for the first time, he was worried for his own well-being. Panicked thoughts followed like a magnificent lightning storm. Money, happiness, poverty, solitude, purpose—each apprehension took on its own voice, and despite his hands pressed firmly against his ears, it appeared as though the library knew that he was trying to get away from it all, reflecting a phantom whose image was befitting of his internal quarrel. Elijah no longer cared about the delicate prestige of the building. He would have broken the hinges off the closed exit doors before him had they been locked. And as he sprinted forward, bursting through the exit, then leaping onto the hard, crunchy gravel outside, his heart sank even further at the sight of the tall, wrought iron gates locking him inside the estate for what Elijah was now sure would be forever.

He gripped the cold bars, shook them like the frantic, caged animal that had consumed him. He was trapped. It was then he realized that freedom was what he had wanted all along, freedom from the fear and the pain of the unknown. He had assumed that by facing the unknown, he would be able to escape it. but he was simply trapped in it. With this clarity, he took a deep breath and began to hear the crickets and their longing cries for companionship, and he felt the same. He turned around and leaned against the phantom gate. He stared at the library and perceived a faint light coming from the third floor, blocked by the imposing stature of the shadowed man he saw hours before. It was the first time Elijah's own internal woes were not only heard, but countered by another in a soft, baritone voice:

Climb higher, Elijah. I know how you can be free.

The library grounds were back to their usual, abnormal silence that Elijah had originally intended on relishing. It was even quieter than normal, like the building was exulting its victory over the ignorance of anyone who thought they could withstand its faculty. He approached the stairs as he did before, and ascended, looking up to the ceiling above and expecting the same dark abyss to stare back at him. But instead, he was met with the lively, eager expression of a man breaching through the gloom. The man beckoned with one arm, smiling, then glided back behind the railing. On the final step, Elijah turned his attention to the rope that was stretched across the entrance of the hall, and a red sign with white lettering that warned, 'OFF-LIMITS.' He brought one foot over just before the next. The shadowed man was no more, revealing himself to be the previous tenant of the estate: a Mr. Thomas Landor, not a day over thirty.

"Hello, Elijah. I've been expecting you." An uncanny wave of familiarity suddenly hit the boy's conscious, as if waking from an immersive dream, immediately being made aware of one's comforting surroundings. He was dumbfounded, yet knew everything there was to know.

"Mr. Landor?" he thought as he hesitantly approached. Just then, there was a glimpse of sourness in the man's serene disposition as if for a moment he forgot who he was.

"Landor, yes. Indeed, in a previous life, having since reached greater heights of being. I think it's time I showed you something. Please." He motioned Elijah to walk with him down the hall towards a room at the end, its light cut off by the angle of the door being slightly closed. *"I've noticed the two of us share something in common, something that has allowed myself to persevere throughout the time that's succeeded me."*

Elijah tried to speak, but was hindered by his sore, withered larynx. He wasn't even sure if the man to his left was speaking. He could only be certain of the creaking hardwood floor as they approached their destination.

"Libraries are peculiar, aren't they? Such an alluring, raucous clubhouse of tangible thoughts, where ideas and emotions can come to life. Over the years I've noticed that individuals come here, burdened by their own thoughts, though none quite like yourself. I have always been gifted with an acute perception of the world around me. And so, I possessed the things that made me feel like I could endure—the arts, the literature, the beautiful interior of my home, until... Well, until I withered away and became an extension of its foundation. Despite the accumulated pain and anguish of years past from those who have taken refuge here, there is freedom in the midst of chaos."

Elijah slowed his pacing towards the door, uneasy, attempting to painfully swallow, and cleared his dry throat. "Please," he murmured, "I just want to get out of here."

"And struggle through life with your gift? I can hear your thoughts, Elijah. Your disquietude is tumultuous. Why feel dulled by the incessant apprehensions of those you owe nothing to? Why not join me in immortality?"

"What is it that you want—"

What I want is to simply move forward, like yourself. The same reason anyone seeks higher education, no? To find new methods of metamorphosis, to reach our highest selves. Why, how could you do such a thing when you allow other people to cause harm to yourself? All I'm suggesting is that you simply let go of it all and allow this place to bear the weight—to become a part of something greater, as I have. Or is your destiny written the same as your father's?

Elijah stopped, now mere steps away from the door, and watched Mr. Landor proceed. He gripped the doorknob, then turned back to face the young man's panicked expression.

"I'm nothing like my father!" Elijah screamed. "My mind is my own."

"The mind of Man belongs to no one but to those who came before him, Elijah. And I'm afraid that despite your best efforts to suppress such feelings, you are in fact just like him. It's the reason you're here. Why you've heard my calls, carried by the winds."

He pointed at Elijah's forearm, to the blood that dripped from the panicked scratches on his wrist. It dripped down from his hands to his fingertips, down into the dark crevices of the floor.

"The transformation has already begun. It has been for quite some time." Mr. Landor opened the door. Inside, stood the resplendent Forefather of Time, swinging its massive pendulum in a hypnotic trance as the floor below began to shake, bend, and contort. Something was growing out of the floor, revitalized by the blood of Elijah. It was a wooden body, grotesque and unrefined. Elijah's blood streamed towards the unsightly being which continued to grow in size as it drank more of the red fluid. Its brown, hardwood exterior softened like skin, then sprouted limbs and formed a face with features no different than Elijah's own. Paralyzed with fear, Elijah could do nothing but stare back at the eyes of a creature that he was sure of knowing so well. It was himself.

All that I am asking is for you to simply let go.

The sun of a new day breached the horizon, glistening the morning dew on the freshly cut grass of The University's oldest library. Its wrought iron gates creaked open, and the sound of an individual's footsteps approaching was heard on the crunchy, pea gravel. It was Elijah walking down the Desire Path, standing tall with glowing, healthy skin—not a mark, self-inflicted blemish, or line of worry in sight. He smiled at the road ahead, feeling as though it was the first time he'd ever made the trek, and lost himself within the blissful, morning silence.

IT STOOD ABOVE ME

C. Robert Cargill

IT WAS DARK. Black. A pitch so deep it seemed to move and swirl on its own. Like something had swept in and filled the void of night with something far, far worse. And it was cold.

Freezing. Not the mere absence of heat, but like the touch of ice to the skin, a cold that seemed to huff and wheeze as crystals froze up and dropped from its breath.

I pulled the covers around me, balled my hands into fists around the edges to draw them as tightly to my chest as possible. But nothing abated the chill. Nothing chased off the grasp of the cold dark around me.

My body was rigid against the night, unable to move, unable to do anything but shiver in place. My eyes darted around the room, desperate for light, only to find an ever-present dark in its place.

And then I saw it—slithering out of the nothing like tendrils of mist settling into a roiling figure. Head. Shoulders. The hint of a torso. Not quite human, merely close enough—a haunting half-dream made flesh. It didn't speak. It didn't move. If it had eyes, I could not make them out.

It was there. Looming in the dark.

And it stood above me.

And it waited.

I cried out, but my voice didn't work, the nascent scream caught in the back of my throat. There it howled silently, trying as it could to tear its way out, the note fading before gripping tight my tongue and sliding back down into my belly.

Where were its eyes? I couldn't see its fucking eyes. I could feel them staring deep into me, but I couldn't see them.

Where were those fucking eyes?

Sleep paralysis. Anxiety. Lucid dreams. Everyone had a diagnosis. But no one had an answer.

What do you see when you sleep? they would ask.

"I wasn't asleep," I would answer. "That's the point."

But science only believes what it can see. And it can't see what I see. It can't see through my eyes, and my eyes seemed to be the only things that could see it. Some would ask me to draw it. But how do you draw black on black, a dark so deep that it eats the light, swallows it whole, and shits out something blacker?

Well, what did it do?

"It stood above me," I said.

It just stood there?

"What else would it do? It stood above me. And it waited. That's all it ever did. That's all it ever needed to do."

I wish I could say the first night was the worst, that I would get used to the dark, get used to the cold, get used to staring eyes that weren't fucking there. But there's no getting over that. No getting past the way the chill seeps into your bones, the way your eyes never quite adjust, the way the figure never comes truly into focus.

You try to explain. You try to paint them a picture. You raise your voice when they don't believe you—when they use words like diagnosis, disorder, psychosis. And your voice gets louder still. And they give you that look. That sad, pitying look like you're the crazy one.

So, you ask for a second opinion, and after you raise your voice again, and they look at you the very same way, you realize science can't help you.

A sleep demon, a spiritualist would tell me. *Night Hag. Night Mare.* It has a dozen different names spread across a hundred different cultures. But it is all the same black beast, the same dark thing that has come to ride me into oblivion.

What has it done?

"It stands above me. And it waits."

And what, pray tell, do you think it is waiting for?

That question haunted me awake as the beast did when I tried to sleep.

I had completely abandoned science now and spoke only to the spiritual. Priests. Rabbis. Woo woo crystal bitches with tarot cards and burning sage. But the responses were always the same. For a time, I stopped at every storefront with a neon hand and the promise of *Fortunes Read Here,* praying each time that this might be the one with the answer. They read my palms, my aura, my cards, my tea leaves. The charlatans showed their hands pretty early. But the real ones, the real ones could see it behind me. Its cold made them shiver. Some refused to let me in the front door.

And the real ones all said the same thing.

Whatever you do, do not tell it your name.

"What?"

Never tell it your name. It needs your name. It found you in the night like a campfire in the wilderness, and it wants to huddle around you for warmth. Whatever you do, never tell it your name.

Every night, I plunged once more into the cold, dark abyss of my night terrors. I tried in vain to peer through the dark, but I only felt the absence of love, the absence of joy, the absence of God. And so once again, I turned back to science.

Different doctors put me on different cocktails of drugs. I endured the words diagnosis, disorder, psychosis. Every night, I downed their pills, prayed to a God I could not feel, and every night, the cold dark crept back into my room.

It stood above me.

And it waited.

I could feel myself wasting away from the inside. For a while, I tried not to sleep at all. Then I tried edibles—tried floating away on fuzzy-headed clouds of THC-fueled delights. Ultimately, I drank myself to sleep. But the black always returned. It stood above me. And it waited.

It waited.

It waited.

And it waited.

And every morning, I shook off the shivers and tried to warm my bones in the sun, clutching a scalding cup of coffee and the dream that I might get to see a time without it staring down with its nothing eyes.

Then one dark night, plunged deep into the frozen hell of its gaze, long after I had exhausted every pill, tried every drug and booze, and found the very last tiny bit of hope burned out of me, I finally saw its eyes. A pair of desperate, pleading eyes.

And in a moment of panic, I found my voice. I could at last scream, beg, plead, yell, curse, swear, malign. The words would no longer die in my throat.

I looked into its eyes.

I opened my mouth.

And I blurted out my name.

For a second it looked at me, its eyes thankful. Then its hand reached into my open mouth, its arm forcing its way down my throat, past all the dead words and screams, and it snatched my soul from inside of me, tore it out, and flung it deep into the hellish frozen void. And as my soul pinwheeled wildly out into the vast nothingness, I looked back and watched as the thing that had for so long stood over me crawled inside of my body and took my place.

And that's when everything became cold. Nothing but dark. Nothing but absence.

My life became like a dream, slowly fading, its details growing fuzzy, names and dates vanishing in seconds, memories feeling nonsensical, like they never could have really happened. Not to me. Not to anyone. Had I ever lived at all? Or was it a lie I told myself to cope.

No, it was real. Warmth, I remembered warmth. I remembered what it was like to be out of the cold. This wasn't life; this was something else. This was the dream that wouldn't fade, that wouldn't let go, that seemed like mere seconds stretched out across eternity.

My name, gone. My job, my family, my loves. I couldn't remember any of it. My life had become a distant star, cold and unremarkable against the void. A speck of light that emitted no warmth and illuminated nothing.

I wandered, aimless, through an inescapable expanse. I stared at all the distant stars, all of them so cold, so far away. And I pined for their warmth. Their comfort. Their name.

I don't know how long I was out there. A second is a year is a lifetime. I just wandered the stars, looking for any way out.

And then I felt it. The memory of warmth. It did not chase the chill from my bones. It did not wipe the dark from my sight.

But it promised to. I had no eyes to see. I had no mouth to beg, to plead, to scream. But I could feel it. The warmth radiating from her body.

I looked down at her. She was so beautiful. So full of life. So warm. Her heat chased away the hint of my loneliness.

She was the brightest thing I had ever seen.

And she looked up at me, her eyes full of terror, as if she knew exactly what I wanted. That I wanted to tear her soul screaming from her body, fling her into the void, crawl into her very flesh, and feel the warmth of the sun once again. If she wanted to scream, she couldn't. She just stared, eyes pleading.

So, I did the only thing I knew to do.

I stood above her.

And I waited.

A STORY WITH A BEGINNING AND NO END

Aaron Moorhead

HELLO,

I'm the child of the woman you killed.

~~The worst day of my life was~~

I teach creative writing to kids. In an elementary school classroom there isn't a day I don't want to punt a few misbehaving maniacs through a window. But I tell myself I don't know their whole story. Maybe there's something else going on. Maybe they're having the worst day of their life.

When I was five, my ~~d~~Dad took me to Disney. I was too young to remember it, but a single memory remains, and I've reconstructed the rest from context and the occasional oral history from Dad. When he tells his side of it, he's laughing, as if I want to hear this old yarn. But it's a sick laugh, and I've never gotten the joke.

I was too young for half the rides, but just being at the Happiest Place on Earth was the most exciting thing I'd ever done in my five years on the planet. I don't remember why we went – it was springtime for sure, so he couldn't have taken me there for my birthday. He must have done it for the special occasion of him waking up one day and remembering that I'm his child and he loves me. His idle mind never goes to sports lineups or his empty stomach or some entrepreneurial project. It only ever thinks of others, of me, wondering if I'm happy, and if not, scheming different ways to fix it.

I'm so certain it was springtime because I have a severe allergy to tree pollen, an allergy that blooms once a year, every March-April. As soon as we got out of the car, my nose filled with snot, and I was sneezing a hundred times a minute, the Florida humidity and pollen conspiring to ruin my day.

My eyes were so red and itchy, I could hardly see, and my nose was raw from wiping with recycled bathroom towels. I looked like I had been crying, but I told myself I wasn't upset, it was just the allergies. But just knowing that I looked upset was enough to upset me for real.

But since my dad's entire day was focused around My Good Time, he took a calculated risk and slipped me a potentially fatal dose of Benadryl in hopes it would defeat my allergy attack without sending me into renal failure.

Always smiling, he crouched to wipe my nose outside Mr. Toad's Wild Ride. I hated it—how can he be smiling when his child is in hell? ~~(did you know Mr. Toad goes to hell in that ride too?)~~ *I ran away from Dad as if he were the source of my pain, clutching a Goofy-shaped funnel cake he'd bought to distract me from my streaming nose. I ran toward Mr. Toad, tripped on my own feet, and planted that nose into the blazing hot cement.*

I skinned my knee and road-rashed my face. The funnel cake splattered all over my favorite shirt, Mickey and Minnie kissing in a giant green heart. Now I cried for a more primal reason.

And beneath the sobbing, I couldn't stop sneezing.

It wasn't just the physical pain. Not just the humiliation. It was that my expectations of a perfect day were demolished in that moment. I looked to Dad, a man so ready to deliver his child a glorious memory, a man who I thought had no problems at all, smiling through all of it. And I was the opposite. To him and all around, I was the joke.

I answered his smile by escalating. Wailing like I wanted my vocal chords to feel the same hurt as my raw face, like I wanted every onlooker's ears to taste my sting. And I wouldn't stop, even long after the throb in my knee and face faded, long after the Benadryl did its magic, long after my father called it quits and put me back in the car to take me home. It was only noon.

Despite being a public school teacher, my students think I'm infinitely rich because all kids think all adults live like sultans. I now get that Dad was not a wealthy man, and throwing away two tickets to Disney World Orlando after a couple hours would be a big pill to swallow. I'd ruined his day. Knowing him, he never even ran the cost/benefit of leaving vs. staying in his head. He did it instinctually. The smile that drove me to rage was a mask he wore for my benefit. He was walking through hell with me.

Once, after being carefully honest with my students about what happened to my mother, one of them finger-painted a portrait and proudly gifted it to me, like a cat presenting a dead bird to its owner. Mom was a haloed angel with X's for eyes. We shield our children with lies that make the world less painful, but they demonstrate over and over that it's usually adults overcomplicating things that are simple. Dad's a master at hiding his pain. He'd never burden someone else with the world he holds up in his head. But for a moment, the vibrant image of life Dad was always speed-painting in real time for my benefit was dulled, his primary blues and reds and greens accidentally mixed to make brown.

After an hour of my banshee freakout driving back to Tampa Bay on I-75 with the A/C on full blast to try to clear out the pollen, he gave me a look.

That look is the single tangible memory I have of this whole event. I could draw the look if I had the talent or the masochistic drive, but all I have are these letters I string together into words. The mask slipped and he failed to hide a sardonic meanness in his close-lipped smile, a cutting, cruel crease in his brows. If I think about it too hard nowadays, I analyze it into a look that said "You think you've felt pain? Try having your wife murdered and having to raise a kid alone."

All the look really said was "You're being ridiculous."

He saw me notice it, caught himself, buried the look back into his soul, cracked a joke as a smokescreen. Something like "Ah no, worst day of your life!"

Outside looking in, I don't blame him. But he had failed me. Not because of the crack in his veneer, but because he was wrong. He couldn't grasp that I wasn't, in truth, being ridiculous.

He knew I was five years old, but he didn't understand how insubstantial five years of life experience really was. In those years, I was still bobbing in the shallow end of emotion with floaties on. I had never once experienced euphoria or romantic love. I had no concept of bone-hurt, forever loss, true pain. That lesson lay in the years to come.

When you killed Mom a few years before that, I was miles away, not yet capable of understanding human speech. I have no memory of it at all. I had no reaction to the death of my mother, except however a baby reacts when one of the two murky figures that occasionally wander into its field of vision disappears and the other makes a lot more crying noises (just like the ones I made). Maybe that was a way I connected with Dad early on. He cried, I cried, he cried, I cried, we cried.

Hell, lots of strange things like that happen when you're a kid and you don't even notice because you don't have a reference level for "normal" yet. Maybe the loving kissing hugging holding feeding figures around me are supposed to come and go. Since I didn't yet have a sense of object permanence, I lived in a magic world where things disappeared and reappeared around me on a regular basis. That was my normal. ~~Sometimes it still feels that w~~

So that day at Disney was supposed to be the greatest joy of my short little life, and the destruction of that expectation sent me plummeting to depths I'd never felt before.

At the time, it truly was the worst day of my life.

Since I never had an opportunity to grieve Mom, all I know about grief is what it did to Dad. I'm going to assume you've spent some of your years on death row thinking about that, so I won't torture you with it. But he did a great job with me, and I don't feel messed up. Well—I guess being a little fucked in the head from it is some kind of factor in the primordial soup of who I am, since my therapist suggested I write this letter. Even having a therapist at all implies there's some damage there, right? But most of the time I think everyone should have a therapist if it wouldn't put such a strain on the healthcare system, so maybe I'm fine. The point is, I want you to know that you didn't mess me up.

I've read the court records, but I won't pretend to know who you really are. So I'm going to give you the benefit that I give my students. I assume you weren't born to kill my mom. I assume you didn't want to mess me up. I assume that when you did it was your lowest moment, your most horrible day.

~~I forgi~~ It's not up to me to forgive you. But if it helps, I hold no ill will towards you. I assume you were a ~~good~~normal person who got handed terrible choices, and because of the life you had before that day, you made the worst one. And I assume that if you had the chance to go back, you'd make a different choice.

~~Violence Trauma~~ *The awful things we do to each other is a* ~~circle cycle~~ *story with a beginning, but no end.*

I believe it's our human duty to try to put a period on the final sentence.

This letter is my effort.

"AND THEN I signed my name, and the date which is about…seven years ago. And I'm sorry I never sent it."

I can't see his eyes. The fluorescent lights are extra bright on my side, the bulbs are out on his, and he's leaning back in shadow. I'm mostly seeing a scuffed and foggy distortion of my own reflection. He's a hazy double image silhouette of an old man, hunched in the plastic chair, holding the receiver to his ear. On the counter next to the glass, his other hand is the clearest feature I see, aged and broken porcelain. A green vein pushes back out of his thin eggshell hand toward his wrist like a trapped worm, then the detail fades into a blur.

Is he even looking at me? This setup must be torture for loved ones, not being able to clearly see the human on the other side, but it's a relief for me. I wonder if he's leaning back in the manner of a snake, preparing to strike. Or maybe, to him, I'm the viper, and he's readying his aged body to run.

He'd listened silently as I read.

I tap my fingertips together rapidly, waiting for his response. It comes after an uncomfortably long time, his voice sounding thin with treble through the cheap phone.

"S'okay."

that's all he has to say?

I remind myself that this isn't about me. He can react however he wants. Isn't that the point of what I wrote? But I wrote it so many years ago, as part of therapy I didn't really need, and it just doesn't feel as real or necessary anymore. It wasn't particularly painful to write *then*, and the whole damn thing was *about* how detached I was from the experience.

why am i here then?

"What, um…" I clear my throat. I'm crawling out of my skin to be done with this non-conversation.

"What…did you ask for your last meal?"

"Couple Whoppers. Fries. Sprite, uh…"

"That's a good pick. Great pick." Terrible pick.

I'm certain he's staring at me, as if waiting for me to recite some momentous statement I came here to make. I'm always on autopilot when looking someone in the eyes. I can't look at people and think critically at the same time. But people think I'm being disingenuous if I don't look them in the eyes, so I'm in the trolley problem where I'm both controlling the train and I'm everyone tied to the tracks.

"You know, no matter how I felt about it, I can't…it's not in my power to…get you released or appealed or anything. That's up to the state, that's not a me thing…that I can do."

"I know."

"Okay. Thanks."

why did i thank him?

"But, um. This ridiculous…ah, truly awful thing happened. I'm sure your lawyer already guessed about this and told you, but if you care, the prosecutor was really young, and she had an easy case against you. And there was, um…a lot of focus on the family, I guess, for…"

I've lost my train of thought and I'm talking in circles because I'm trying to hold eye contact.

"For…for the…"

He doesn't help me. He lets me sit in wretched, creaking silence as I figure it out.

I shift my focus to the scratches on the plexiglass. Someone has carved a rudimentary, geometric heart into a divider that was meant to be invisible. How did they cut this into the glass with guards standing around, how deeply important must marking this expression of love have been to risk it in this place? I fixate on the heart and let my mouth run.

"We were pressured, hard, into pursuing the death penalty, and even then we didn't want it, but the DA needed a big win to prove herself and you were it. My dad was frustrated and sad and mad but he's not…he was way too broken to want anyone else to be hurt. They were relentless. They even came to me about it, and I was too friggin' young to read. You already guessed this I'm sure, but just, you know, so you can get a look into our side of it. We didn't want this either. Even though we didn't say yes, um, in the end we didn't say no either, so…"

He's silent.

"So I thought this morning I should be here as a witness because maybe Dad woulda wanted to be here. But he wouldn't. He wasn't a vengeful guy. He wouldn't have wanted any of this."

I measure my next words. I don't want to get this wrong and have one of the last things he ever hears be something poorly considered. I can feel his eyes blazing through the plexiglass.

I look down at my hands for comfort and let the dam break.

"I think it's 'cause I never sent the letter. It was just a stupid friggin' therapy exercise and even Marla—she's my thera—nevermind. She said I wasn't obliged to mail it and just writing it was the whole thing of it, but I knew it might mean something to you, so I said to myself, I said, I'll do it next week, then next, but actually mailing it never happened because it felt kinda freaking awkward, you know? Like, you'd answer and I'd read it and have to answer that—I mean, I'd *want* to, but I'd also *have* to, you know—but then also I'd have to tell Dad I was goshdarn penpals with Mom's…you know? And I didn't want that in my life, but you also probably didn't want it in yours either. But I came in today because I thought you should hear the letter. Because I might want to hear it if I were in your shoes. Before the…the thing today. Kinda like in the letter. I just thought it could help on…you know, on the worst day of your life."

My mouth is on a different set of tracks that never intersect my mind. The mouth and the heart are more connected to each other.

I'm still looking down, comparing the freckles on my left hand with the ones on my right, and I don't know how I hadn't noticed before—there are twice as many on my left from the commute to the school every day, driving south in the AM and back north in the PM, the sun always warming only that one arm leaning out the window, in a cumulative effect of the ravages of time and UV damage, and I realize with horror how much time has passed and how I can't undo it, the freckles are there forever, but it's fine because I like my freckles, I just don't like skin cancer because it reminds me of getting older and dying.

I can't help but compare my skin to his, pale as cauliflower. What a privilege having these spots is. How badly he surely would like to earn them with a life well-lived in the sunshine.

But didn't he earn the life he has?

I rub at the patch of freckles below my knuckle.

He remains silent.

So I look up.

He's crying. Jesus. I uncorked him on the day they're gonna put acid in his veins. I'm a horrible person. He's keeping it quiet, but tears are flowing.

"I'm really sorry. This was all selfish. You don't need to see my face and relive it all through my therapy exercise on today of all days…"

I reach for my jacket—

"I would'na answered."

He has a thick Ozark accent and a goopy rasp from a throat that doesn't get much use anymore. I look up and he moves closer to the scratched-up dividing glass, and his features come into definition. I hadn't seen an image of him since his mugshot was taken. Pale—pallid—from more than half a life indoors. The loose skin of his neck is covered in shaving cuts. The cracked hollows above his cheeks tell a long, tedious story.

"You said it. It was nice. Story with a beginning, no end. If I answered, that woulda…kept the story goin.'"

He leans in a little further, the tip of his nose almost against the glass now, his breath making an oval of fog on the window.

"But you ain't right. You wrong."

I swear to myself I'll stay silent and maintain eye contact. Accept the verdict he is about to hand me. He's about to go meet the greatest Judge, be it Him or Nothingness or the Bardo, so the least I can do is humbly bow to his justice. My breath hitches in my throat as we lock eyes. He's carefully turning a thought over in his mind, handling it like a prospective vase purchase at an antiques shop. I'll give him the space to figure it out, as he did for me.

"In here, no one chums up to the guy that killed a mama with a newborn. Here, they just puttin' me in the hole all the time. They ain't never give me a cellmate. An' no one to talk through the walls, pass notes like in the movies. If'n I'd a family, I reckon the whole thang woulda gone differently with yer mama, but they gone. All my friends turned tail when I got put in here. Don't blame 'em. 'N I sure wish I had a relationship with a god. But I just plainly speakin' don't. That been my life after the day."

He pulls back and looks up at the ceiling, at the broken fluorescent fixture above him. The light that should be on but isn't.

"Th' thangs that lead up to the day that got me placed in here… they were dark. Awful. Awful. They was never happy days. Not one. They was…" He pauses, finds the words… "a downhill slide from birth that already done started at the bottom."

i can't move

"So, I figured yesterday that I found my peace. Prepared. To disappear. Die alone. End the darkness. I was ready for a bad end to a bad life."

He swallows, hitching sobs making his words rocky when he breathes in.

"Then you show up."

I've ruined his death. He's condemned me. I'm guilty.

"You. Comin' here. You coulda let buckets a' hate out on me. You coulda screamed at me, hurt me, told me…I should die alone." He takes a sharp intake of breath, his voice trembling on the exhale, "An' it still woulda been better…than dyin' alone."

i won't blink

"Instead, you come here today an' become the person to show me the most of anything near tenderness in my life. I don't think you did it for you. I think you did it just for me. Somethin' it sounds like your dad'd do. I believe that's called grace. So, you ain't right. You're so wrong."

A guard enters the room to lead him away. He gives me his final words:

"This is the best day of my life."

ILIMU

Wanjiru Njendu

RUNNING FOOTSTEPS IN a forest. Panicked or in pursuit? Deep, panting breaths.

The bushes and trees are brushed aside as the pace is increased. The moonlight peeks through the foliage where the branches are shoved apart.

A guttural, feral growl. A slash and then...

Effia wakes up startled in a California King bed. Kenyan-American, beautiful, dark-skinned, with short hair, her eyes appear dark, then quickly turn back to a soft brown. She is drenched in sweat, her sleep cap askew on her head. Her hair is matted to her forehead. The bed sits in the middle of a tastefully furnished New York City loft.

Kunal—Indian-American, good looking, Wall Street type—pops his head around the bathroom door, damp hair falling into his eyes. "Babe, you okay?" Effia takes a moment to slow her breathing, and Kunal comes into the doorway. "Eff? Babe, are you okay?" he asks again.

The light of dawn and the sounds of the waking city outside pour in through the open loft window. The loft is spacious and luxurious.

"Yeah, yeah I'm okay," she answers. "Just had a weird dream... Well, nightmare... Felt really real."

Kunal comes over and wraps his arms around her.

She flinches. "Sorry honey, I'm really sweaty. Maybe after I shower?"

He smiles and gets up. "Bathroom is all yours, I'll get started on breakfast."

Effia grabs his arm, stopping him. "Join me in a few?" she says, managing to force a seductive smile.

He grins back at her. "Definitely".

In the bathroom, Effia pulls off her slip in front of the mirror and notices she has clawed her skin on both sides of her shoulders. She touches one side and flinches in pain. She hops into the shower. The water is scalding, but she barely flinches.

In the kitchen, Kunal takes a pinch of power from an ancient looking bag, then drops it into a cup of coffee, stirring until it dissolves.

Effia grabs a robe off the door and belts it tight just as Kunal comes into the bathroom. She smiles brightly at him. "Sorry babe, just realized that I have an early appointment this morning. Next time?" She kisses him on the cheek and brushes past him on her way into their walk-in closet. Kunal glances at the empty space next to his towel, then at hers shoved into the laundry basket. He frowns. He picks something up from the bathroom counter and follows her.

Effia is in the closet, tucking her shirt into her pants, dressed in record time. The shirt sticks to her damp skin in some places. She turns to Kunal while pulling on a casual safari-style jacket.

"You left this in the bathroom last night. Didn't you promise your mum you would never take it off." He messes with her for a moment, holding the object from the bathroom higher than she can reach, and then hands her an amulet. It looks old, and it hangs on an aged leather necklace. There are some kind of letters or characters inscribed on the amulet's exterior.

"Thanks." Effia tries to put it on, but flinches from the pain of the scratches on her shoulders.

Kunal steps up to her. "Here let me help you." He slips it around her neck and kisses her behind the ear. Neither of them notice something ripple beneath her skin. Kunal's kisses begin to hint at something more, sex perhaps, but then...

The doorbell rings.

"That's Marisa. Gotta go."

Kunal had already poured the coffee into a to-go mug, which he places firmly into Effia's hand as she leaves.

Effia gives Kunal a brief hug, then hurries to the front door to let in Marisa, their cleaning lady. The two women exchange quick pleasantries, and then Effia grabs her stuff and sails out the door.

Once in the apartment hallway, she nearly crashes into her neighbor Mrs. Dobson, who always carries a poodle in her arms. Effia cringes, then forces a smile. "Hi, Mrs. Dobson. How are you?"

Mrs Dobson sighs. "Baby here had a rough night," she says, kissing the dog on the forehead. She starts to walk with Effia, who is now forced to slow her pace to let her keep up. She sips on her coffee.

Mrs. Dobson continues to chatter away on the elevator ride to the lobby, and then from the lobby to the building's front door.

It is here that Effia makes desperate eye contact with the doorman, Miguel, who understands her and intercepts Mrs. Dobson before she can exit onto the street. "Why don't you let me take Baby out for you? It's a bit windy today." Mrs. Dobson smiles at him and hands over Baby. She then heads back to the elevator and takes it back up to her floor.

"Thank you, Miguel," Effia says. "I thought that she was going to follow me all the way to work." She gives the doorman warm smile and starts to leave.

"Miss Effia!". Miguel points to the lobby desk, makes his way over to it. "You have a delivery. It was delivered late last night, left with the night doorman."

As he reaches over the desk, Effia notices the bracelet around his waist. It looks old. Two symbols, an eye and a dagger, are engraved on the metal . "Is that new?"

Miguel smiles. "Yes, it is. My grandmother is visiting, and she gave me this."

As he hands over the package, his hand brushes Effia's, and something moves beneath her skin. Miguel pulls back in shock, but Effia is too busy juggling her bags and this new mystery package to notice.

Baby growls and yips sharply, squirming to get out of Miguel's arms. She nips at him hard, draws blood, and he drops her. She hits the floor running, and darts back across the lobby to the elevators.

"Are you okay?" Effia asks. "Did she draw blood?" She frees one of her hands and reaches out to help inspect.

Miguel recoils from her touch. "I'm fine. Please go!"

Surprised by his tone, Effia pauses for a moment before gathering herself and heading out.

EFFIA'S VETERINARIAN PRACTICE is a pristine space decorated with bright African artwork. A few owners and their pets are in the waiting area when she arrives. The animals cringe and pull back as she walks by; some even hide beneath the chairs.

A powerfully built West-African man, with a large dog, stares intently at the amulet around Effia's neck. His wife elbows him sharply to break his stare. Effia ignores them and hands the mystery package to her assistant. She motions for the employee to open the package and calls the first patient back. Her assistant opens the box to reveal a strange looking plant, with purple petals and white flowers. The African man looks frightened by the sight, but after a silent argument with his wife, it's clear she's not leaving until her pet gets treatment. Effia's assistant sets the flowers on her desk.

A short time later, the African couple with their large dog are called back to the exam room. The man sits on the chair farthest from her. Effia coaxes the dog onto the examination table. It growls softly at her.

"I am so sorry. I don't know why he is doing that. He is usually so easy-going," the wife says. She smiles at Effia, attempting to ease the tension in the room.

Effia notices the dog acting strangely, notices how it growls softly at her. She's about to dismiss the behavior when it suddenly breaks free of its leash and sprints at Effia in attack mode.

Effia's assistant screams, but the dog's owner is able to grab the animal and subdue it before it can jump the waiting room desk.

"We are leaving right now!" he tells his wife. He lifts the dog with one arm, and grabs his wife with the other, nearly dragging her from the office. Effia and her assistant stare at each other in shock. Neither of them notices that one flower on the plant has turned black.

Effia suddenly clutches her stomach and heaves up her liquid breakfast into the nearest waste basket. Her assistant rushes over to help. "Are you okay?"

Effia nods, but she looks queasy.

"Let me grab some tums," her assistant says, then exits in a hurry.

WHEN EFFIA ARRIVES home later that day, she finds Kunal in distress. The look on his face makes her drop everything and rush to his side. "What's wrong?"

"I just got off the phone with your uncle from the village. I'm sorry, babe. Your grandmother is dead, and your mother is missing." He envelops her in a bear hug. "I've already reached out to my travel agent, and he is booking us flights for tomorrow. I've already called your assistant, and she is having the on-call vet handle the rest of your appointments for the week."

Effia is on the verge of hysterics. "Wait... slow down. What do you mean my mother is missing and grandmama is dead?"

Kunal walks her to the kitchen and sits her down at the table. He hands her a glass of water, sits opposite her, takes her hand into his. "I don't know, babe. He didn't say much else, and he got off the phone quickly."

"I need to call my mum." She gets up and moves swiftly to her bag. She pulls out her phone and dials the first contact.

"I already tried, babe," Kunal says. "I think her phone is dead. It goes straight to voicemail." He tries to hand her a glass of water, but she pushes the glass away. She does not notice a slight powder residue on the glass bottom.

Effia's call goes straight to voicemail. She hangs up and dials again. Nothing. Tries again. Nothing.

Kunal gently takes the phone from his wife and allows her to break down sobbing in his arms. "Look, all we can do is pack tonight and try and get some sleep. Hopefully we can learn more tomorrow."

THE CLOCK ON the wall reads 11:55 p.m. Effia moans in her sleep, troubled. She is sweating profusely.

Running footsteps in a forest. Panicked or in pursuit? Deep, panting breaths.

The bushes and trees are brushed aside as the pace is increased. The moonlight peeks through the foliage where the branches are shoved apart.

A guttural, feral growl. A slash and then...

Effia is jolted awake. The plane is trembling. The seatbelt sign lights up, and the pilot's voice comes on over the speaker system.

"Ladies and Gentlemen, we've hit a bit of turbulence, so please fasten your seat belts. We will be landing shortly."

Kunal smiles softly at her. The stewardess comes by and hands Effia a warm towel to refresh her face.

Effia excuses herself and goes to the bathroom. She rinses her face and then vomits into the sink. She stares at herself in the mirror, then cradles her abdomen. She put a small item in her bag.

WHEN THEY ARRIVE at the airport, the customs and immigration officer stares at both of them. Effie hands over three passports: one American for Kunal, and one American, one African for herself. The officer opens her African passport. The picture is of a very young Effia. "You haven't been back for a long time."

Effia stares back, defiantly. "I haven't had a reason to come back."

He narrows his eyes and then stamps the passport. He barely looks at Kunal's passport, just stamps it and hands it back to him.

From the line next to them, an old woman stares at Effia. When Effia bends down to put the passports back in her bag, the amulet slips from the neck of her shirt. The old woman screams at the sight of the jewelry and turns away in fright. Her adult children gather around her so as to block Effia and Kunal from view.

IT'S DUSK WHEN they arrive at her late grandmother's village, and every person they pass stops what they're doing to stare at the car. They whisper among themselves. The car drives into her grandmother's compound. Her uncle and a few older men are standing at the entrance of the home. The men are all wearing bracelets made of the same beads as the man in Effia's veterinarian clinic. Sober looks are on their faces. Effia and Kunal get out of the car to greet them.

On one side of the compound is an old hut that has been reinforced by modern engineering. The reinforced steel door has large dents in it. Behind the hut is a freshly dug grave. The same purple plant with white flowers that Effia was gifted back in the United States now grows wildly around the exterior of the hut.

"Where is my mother?" Effia asks the men. "What happened to my grandmother?"

The men slowly form a semi-circle around her. The eldest man steps forward and starts to chant.

Kunal steps in front of Effia to protect her. "You heard her. Where's her mother?"

The eldest man sighs "She is in the hut."

Kunal grabs Effia's hand and together, they head to the hut. But neither notices a man come up behind Effia, brandishing a large knife. With one swift motion, he cuts the necklace and rips the amulet from her neck.

Effia cries out as her eyes turn black. Dark veiny lines run up her arm, toward her neck. Kunal freezes in terror. The flowers on the plants around the house all turn black. Two men grab Kunal by the arms and pull him away from Effia. Two different men grab Effia, her skin continuing to turn black, and push her inside the hut. As they drag her, she drops her bag, and a positive pregnancy test drops out. Kunal spots it and struggles even harder to get to her. He is hit over the head and passes out, dropping like a rock to the ground.

The door slams shut on Effia.

As her eyes adjust to the pitch-black darkness, a growl emanates from somewhere deep inside her.

THE BEGINNING

Izzy Lee

AN IMPROBABLY LOUD *CRACK*—a sonic ear punch that almost gave her a heart attack—forced Lex upright and out of her dreams, nearly sending her tumbling to the floor, heart thudding way up in her throat. She'd never been one to sleep particularly well, and tonight's dream had her conversing with an intriguing actor from a bizarre film she'd just watched, a guy with low-set eyebrows pushed down against secretive eyes. The movie had taken several strange turns, culminating in a kinetic car accident and oddly ambiguous epilogue that was nothing short of cosmic.

Violet light flashed from the edges of the curtains, and Lex kicked off the sheets twisted around her ankles and rushed to the window. She peeled back one of the curtains and peeked out.

The yard below looked like it always had, her daughter's bright yellow tricycle and other assorted toys askew on the dirt. *It's not even raining.* Wiping the sweat from her forehead, Lex wondered where the sound had come from. Perhaps one of those weird, dry thunderstorms. The arid summer months had made living in the desert town feel like an actual, earthly version of Hell. The only thing keeping Lex in town was the old house she'd inherited and some family that lived nearby. She'd never be able to afford a place in a big city, especially with a four-year-old. And for what? A run-down, overpriced apartment in a shitty neighborhood?

She turned and padded down the hall to Kira's room. Strangely enough, the girl hadn't screamed or cried out at all. There'd been no frantic child running to Mommy's bed with terrified eyes and a face slicked with tears to console.

"Kira?" Lex called, entering the room. The girl's bed was empty, the unicorn-print sheets thrown back like her own, as if she'd leapt from the mattress.

Don't panic, she's playing, hiding somewhere.

But Kira wasn't under the bed with her toys, or in the closet. She wasn't under Mommy's beat-up, old bean bag she'd sometimes use as a shell, pretending she was a turtle. The girl wasn't in her room at all. It was 3 a.m.

Lex rushed through the house, checking every nook, both upstairs and down. She tried to quell the rising fear that her daughter was somehow suddenly missing from their home on the edge of town, in the Middle of Nowhere, Nevada.

When she stopped pacing in the living room, sweat rolling down her spine, she realized that the front door was wide open.

As soon as she went outside to check the porch—again, no child in sight—a strange odor hit her. It was similar to the scent of rain—though there was none—mixed with something at once electrical *and* decayed. The scent of something impossible and wrong. Not a single cloud hung against the canvas of black night.

Nothing seemed to be amiss down the long, barren road in front of the house, either. As Lex lived in a more-or-less inhospitable environment to most living things, there wasn't much around but dirt and mountains.

The sound of a murmuring child pricked up her ears, and she followed the sound to the back of the house.

There in the backyard, Kira knelt by a hole in the ground that hadn't been there before. As Lex approached, she saw that Kira was mumbling something to an object in front of her, some kind of black box emanating the same violet light she'd seen in her bedroom. The box's open lid promptly snapped shut on its own, squelching the light.

"Honey?" Lex crouched down next to her daughter, filthy in her tiny nightgown. Had she been crawling in and out of that hole?

Kira kept talking to the box, but it wasn't in English. Lex didn't know what the hell language it was, but it was unlike anything she'd ever heard.

"Baby?" She placed a hand on her daughter's shoulder, which felt oddly cold in the nighttime heat. "You okay? What are you doing out here?"

The girl stopped muttering at Lex's touch. She looked up at her mother with vacant eyes and a… faint spark of violet in her irises? Nearly imperceptible, the glint vanished, and Kira fainted, falling backward into her arms.

Forgetting the box, Lex scooped up her daughter and brought her inside where she held the little girl on the couch until she passed out, too.

LEX AWOKE TO the familiar sounds of loud cartoons. Kira sat in front of the TV set, legs crossed, cuddling her favorite stuffed animal, Miss Kitty—holding it against her cream-colored, rose-print nightgown, still covered in dirt. Had it not been for that detail, Lex would've been convinced that this morning was like any other, and that the strange occurrence had been a particularly weird dream, perhaps influenced by a block of late-night cheddar.

"Hey Kira," Lex sat up and approached. "Do you feel okay?"

The girl looked up and smiled. "Yes, Mommy."

Lex chuckled. The girl had always said *yeah* instead of *yes*.

"Want some breakfast?"

"I ate already. Me an' Miss Kitty had tea and biscuits."

"Well, isn't that fancy?" Lex couldn't help but put a hand on the child's forehead. Thankfully, her temp felt normal, though it was already starting to swelter in those early July hours. She stood and flipped on the standing fan, positioning it so that it oscillated a cool breeze back and forth over her little one.

"Mommy's gonna get some iced tea and a biscuit, but when you're done with cartoons, it's bath time. Got it?"

Already entranced by the old-school, dancing skeletons on screen, Kira nodded.

Lex ruffled the kid's soft, sweet hair and made her exit, but paused at the doorway to glance back over her shoulder. Kira remained entranced by the animated images jumping around on the TV like any other young child.

OUTSIDE, THE HOLE in the ground gaped, the brilliant blue skies still clear of clouds. Squinting against the sun, Kira approached the hole. It was surrounded by what seemed to be an improbable amount of dirt. The opening looked awfully deep. Lex thought of the sci-fi films she'd seen, searching her mind for any with plots similar to last night's events. The movie plots with meteors falling to Earth always started with a violent impact, but she was no expert on rocks plummeting from the sky. She wondered if there was anyone in residence at university in Reno who could explain last night's strange odors and the new gorge in her backyard.

Lex edged closer and peered into the hole. No discernible end, just…darkness. Lex pushed some of the upturned dirt into the cavity with her shoe and listened. No sound. She kicked a pile of rocks with more force, watching as they disappeared into nothing. But after the initial, ordinary sound of her own movement, there was nothing to signal that the rocks had hit bottom.

She remembered the time a guy in a white van had chased her car through the desert when she was alone and just eighteen. He'd accelerated until he'd gotten a good look at her, bringing the van up to her sedan. When he was close, he'd shouted to her and asked if she'd wanted to party. After she shook her head, he swore at her and called her a variety of horrible things, then followed her as she nailed the accelerator to the floor. It had taken forty-five minutes to lose him. She wasn't sure if she'd live another day if he caught her, if he smashed into her and dragged her from the wreck.

Staring into the hole had felt like that.

The faint remnant of a strong right angle marked the dirt, along with some bizarre scratches and swish marks she hadn't seen in the night. The nearby brush—what was left of it—was blackened and burned away.

The box was gone.

Lex shivered as the hairs on her arms rose, even in the glaring summer sun.

BY LUNCHTIME, LEX had managed to quell the sensation of everything inside her screaming. She'd pushed a fair amount of dirt back into the hole and had cordoned it off with some rope and branches scattered about. It wouldn't entirely prevent Kira from falling in, though, so she'd have to work at it for days or hire a handyman to come fill it up with a bulldozer.

Lex wondered if she could somehow make the place more livable with a good set of sprinklers and sod installation, though money was tight, as always. The yard was a damn eyesore in any case, and a nice patch of green would be wonderful. Maybe with a few more web developer gigs, she could also afford a nice patio set, get some shade. It'd be wonderful to have a decent place to read a book while Kira splashed in the relief of a kiddie pool.

Come to think of it, Kira's birthday was next week, on a Saturday. Lex could simply burn up a credit card and make it happen. They could have a small party with some of her favorite preschool friends. They should've had a nice space like this long ago. They nearly had…if Greg hadn't been so irresponsible.

Lex tried to punch the memories of her late husband in the face. How he'd gone and gotten addicted to meth and lost his job. How he started selling his things, then hers, then the family's (like their previous patio set), and finally, how he'd resorted to thieving. Then he'd overdosed on a park bench one stupid afternoon and never came home again. She learned from the police that he'd graduated to heroin, and that it had been the veritable nail in his coffin.

She cursed and swatted away tears. Lex's heart hurt whenever she was reminded that Kira would grow up without her biological father, but she was also grateful that her daughter had been too young to have been hurt by him.

Her fists curled into angry, dusty balls. Lex was going to create that tiny oasis of a backyard. She'd pay it off later, like most Americans. She'd find someone who didn't do drugs, who was responsible, loving, and kind—someone who wanted a ready-made family.

But today was not that day. Today was for shoveling dirt into stupid holes and making sure her kid was all right.

AFTER DINNER, LEX tried to get more information out of her daughter, but Kira had no recollection of being awake and outside in the middle of the night, nor of the violet light or insanely loud crack of thunder (or whatever it was), so Lex moved on to the next question. "Do you know what happened to the box that was outside?"

A flicker of recognition flashed in the four-year-old's eyes, but then she shook her head.

"Are you sure?" Lex prodded. "That was a strange thing to show up for no reason, huh?"

A slight downward movement of her head—barely half a nod—then nothing. She'd almost caught Kira agreeing. Lex watched the girl and changed tactics. She snatched the crayon caddy and a construction-paper pad and sat down on the floor next to Kira. She selected a black crayon and drew a box shape.

Kira looked up with questioning eyes. "What's that, Mommy?"

She began coloring within the lines, making a dark rectangle. "That's the weird box we saw outside by that hole last night. Remember?"

Kira studied the drawing, then chose a purple crayon of her own and began moving it around the picture of the box. The scribbles resembled some kind of light or smoke. Lex let her keep going.

Next, Kira picked up the black crayon Lex had set down. Her tiny fingers drew black squiggles and ant-type things near the box. She sat back to look at her work and sighed, sounding resigned. Lex muffled a giggle at her child's mature reaction.

"What's up, kiddo?"

Kira's lips twisted in a bothered way. "It's not right." She ripped another piece of paper from the pad and drew a new box. Watching, Lex grinned, proud.

But in the second drawing, the box's lid was open.

The purple light was there, and so too were the black squiggles—only this time, they were flying out of the box. Lex's grin faded. She bit her lip, resisting the urge to ask questions as Kira continued coloring.

The child drew the ant things, but now they were green and much thicker. Following that, the girl created a small human with long hair, in a nightgown with little red marks on it... roses?

Kira had created a not-so-subtle nightmare version of herself from last night. In the finished drawing, she was laying on the ground, green spiders or insects crawling beside and over her.

"What are these things?" Lex pointed to the insect-like creatures, gut clenching.

"Crab aliens," Kira answered, matter-of-factly, like it was the most obvious thing in the world.

Lex stared at the black squiggles around the drawing of Kira's body. One squiggle appeared to be going into the mouth.

It was hard to find the words, but when Lex did, she pointed to the mouth squiggle. "What's that, Kira? What is happening here?"

"I don't know what the black worms do, Mommy. They just go inside."

"They...what, sweetheart?" She swallowed, desperate to wet her drying mouth.

Kira shrugged and sighed. "Can I play with my sticker book?"

Lex wasn't sure what else to do, so she smiled and obliged her daughter's request.

THE NEXT DAY, a local landscaper filled and leveled the hole, then installed several massive rolls of sod, brimming with vibrant green grass. Their own tiny piece of heaven set against the desert backdrop. They deserved this.

Brand-new patio furniture—not the rusted, broken-down crap Lex was used to—was delivered and set up, all by sunset. Lex and her wine glass settled into a swiveling mesh chair beneath the matching table's fully extended umbrella, while Kira ran around breathlessly excited, making up new adventures and party plans with an invisible friend.

The cool sauvignon blanc slid down Lex's throat, a simple comfort after a day's work in the heat. Though she'd gotten an amazing number of things done already, she kept on working, now tapping away on her phone, sending invites to Kira's fifth birthday party.

Everything would be just fine.

SKITTERING.

Lex opened her eyes, listening in the dark. The clock read 3 a.m. But as soon as she closed her eyes, the skittering continued. Was Kira playing a silly game?

Lex sat up, eyes adjusting to the moonlight coming in through the partially open window. She touched her feet down on the rough-hewn wood floor to get off the bed. Something angular and sharp ran across her toes. She gasped and yanked her feet back up.

With one click of the lamp, she was shown sights that made her scream.

Dark, crab-like creatures scrambled to the darkness beneath her bed.

"Kira?" she shouted, panic clawing in her throat. The things rustled, skittered, and scraped—then fell silent.

Lex dared herself to look under the bed, her mind conjuring the wildest of possibilities. What if there were a thousand of those things? It didn't matter. She had to face whatever threat there was to protect her daughter, no matter how much her flight response fought against leaving the safety of her bed.

Cold sweat dribbled down her skin.

She forced back the fear and swung her face down, right below the bed frame.

The things were gone.

She got up and pushed the bed aside. The heavy, mahogany frame groaned against the floor, an affront to the quiet of the night. Almost there. Lex put her weight into it and shoved the bed again to reveal a hole in the wall roughly the size of a grapefruit. It reminded her of the mouse hole from the cartoon *Tom and Jerry*. That wily mouse was also an agent of chaos.

She shook the childhood memory from her thoughts. This was silly, absurd. She was overwhelmed and had conjured a nightmare from something ordinary, like an insect or scorpion. She'd call an exterminator in the morning. For now, time to check on the kiddo. Lex crept down the hall, hoping she didn't have to explain why Mommy was rearranging furniture in the middle of the night.

Kira was out cold, safe in bed, and for that, Lex was glad. A glance out the window told her nothing. Parenting was rife with little sleep and no answers.

Danger now over, Lex huffed and went back to her own bedroom. She plopped down on the askew mattress but found sleep to be impossible.

IN THE MORNING, Kira was pale and groggy, even a little green, so Lex kept the girl home from her summer playgroup. Being sick is never fun, and to Lex, it seemed that the worry of what *might* happen to Kira was probably much worse than the child's actual sickness. A muted version of Kira fumbled with a toy, dropping it with a clatter on the wood floor. Her movements had become sluggish, and this upset Lex more than it normally would.

In an attempt to shift emotional gears, Lex put on a hopeful smile for the sake of her child. She built a makeshift fort with a sheet and pillow in front of the TV and left Kira to watch cartoons with crackers and a juice box.

When the exterminator arrived, Lex told him what she thought she'd seen. She tried to make light of the events with sheepish laughter, though she felt more on the verge of cracking up in a mental sense. The stained name tag on the exterminator's uniform read "Bob."

Bob had no sense of humor whatsoever, and Bob wasn't convinced that monstrous crab-insects from space had woken her up in the dead of night. He did agree that the hole in the wall was indicative of an infestation of *something*, so at least the house call wouldn't be a total waste of time.

Lex gave Bob a tour of the property, and the exterminator kept an eye out for any other damage or signs of infestation, like animal droppings. In addition to the opening under Lex's bed, they'd found a fresh crack in the foundation, as well as a rip in the new sod, right where the pit used to be. After investigating the sod for pests, Bob had been decent enough to help her push the soil and grass back together, but it didn't nearly look as professional as it had before.

The place was sprayed for vermin, and again, Lex tried to make the most of the situation. She and Kira went out for her favorite ice cream—birthday cake flavor, with rainbow sprinkles. On the way home, they passed the park where Lex's husband had breathed his last breath, where he saw blue skies for the last time before blinking out and into the void. Kira begged Lex to stop and play. Lex suggested other activities, but Kira wouldn't have it. Ultimately, she relented and pretended her skin didn't prickle every second they spent there.

While she pushed Kira on the swing, Lex trained her eyes on the back of the child's silky head of hair—anything to avoid the nearby bench on which Greg was found pale and dead.

She imagined creeping out some dark night with a can of gasoline and a book of matches, gritting her teeth in a sort-of crazed devil grin. She'd watch the fucking bench burn in furious yellow and Halloween-orange flames. Maybe she'd even let a little of that inner madness out, those suppressed primal urges in everyone that civilized society had tamed. That'd feel so fucking great. She'd cackle while the thing burned, and then she'd get in the car with Kira, who'd be asleep in the back seat, and leave the burning bench and this shithole of a town in her rearview mirror, forever.

Soon.

But first, mediocre pizza with Kira, and Tuesday family night at the drive-in. Still pale and weary, Kira had conked out early, slumped in the passenger seat with a blanket and pillow. Lex gazed at the sweet girl, wondering how she could protect her from the heartbreak of the world. It was an impossible task.

Lex stayed for both features at the drive-in simply to avoid the depressing motel room she'd moved them into for the night. As she sipped a little juice box of wine, she tried to push away the thought that Kira would have to grow into an adult.

THANKFULLY, THE GIRL'S vigor improved within the week. Playgroup resumed while Lex worked from home, and there were no more weird nighttime incidents. Lex even managed to score another freelance gig, one that'd last for at least three months and would pay off the home improvements. By Saturday afternoon, Lex's mood was as light and airy as the balloons she'd tied around the backyard.

In fact, she'd decorated the whole place in an explosion of color. The change from drab dirt and emptiness to a colorful cheer made her so happy, she teared up. It was made all the more vibrant by the kids and parents now mingling and playing in the gorgeous sanctuary. Gifts torn open with glee and surprise. Lime and strawberry cupcakes. Crepe paper banners and a cookout. Kids' books and laughing parents, their joviality aided by Lex's very-adult iced tea recipe, which was sauced-up with peach bourbon.

One of the men had volunteered to grill. His name was Todd. He was handsome and newly single, and he stole glances in Lex's direction as he turned the meat and sipped his drink.

Kira was having the time of her life.

Lex breathed the humanity of it all in deeply. Maybe she could do this, really do this right.

"MOMMY, CAN I share my other toys?" Kira asked, tugging on Lex's sundress. The girl was referring to the new plastic toy chest Lex had added to the outdoor patio.

Lex ruffled Kira's soft hair. The bright yellow toy chest was already open. "Of course," she smiled. "Do you need help?"

The birthday girl shook her head and ran to the toy chest, followed by the rest of her tiny, happy friends. Lex felt lucky to witness such simple joy.

The parents watched the kids play, on guard for mini meltdowns or scuffles. Gradually, they relaxed. They commiserated, drank, and made plans for more gatherings. Lex was thrilled. The party had gone so much better than she'd ever hoped.

But at some point, they stopped hearing the chatter of children. All the adults heard were their own voices, which fell to a hush as soon as they realized what was happening. Anyone who's ever been a parent, older sibling, or an authority in charge of children knows a problem is likely on the horizon when the wee ones are too quiet.

Collectively, the parents turned toward their kids.

The unmoving preschoolers were kneeling, hunched in a circle. Lex couldn't see what they were doing.

"Kira?"

The girl didn't respond, didn't move. She and the rest of the children were too preoccupied with whatever it was they were doing or watching.

Lex approached. The center of the children's circle was bright violet. The box was there, and it was open, its light shining on the kids.

They were still as death, kneeling. Their eyes were rolled back, white, like feeding sharks. Slinky black worms slithered from Kira's mouth and nostrils, moving in waves to the other children's mouths and noses.

Lex's scream overpowered the scuttling sounds behind her as she ran to Kira. She snatched her up and pulled her close.

"They go inside, Mommy," the girl whispered.

A chorus of shrieks and hostile commotion.

Lex turned to see the crab-things fleeing a widening rip in the sod, darting up and spinning webs around the other horrified adults. But they weren't crabs. In the daylight, they resembled spiders made of strangely flexible metal. Their horrible webs were made of a silk that was strong like fishing line, but barbed. The webs cut into the flesh of the adult partygoers and turned their clothes red.

One of the spiders shot toward Lex.

Darkness.

Then blinding violet, an ear-sucking sonic boom, and a rush of wind—the sensation of rocketing through the air like a roller coaster.

Still clutching her daughter, Lex and Kira were yanked upward through the air, above the house and into a vortex of light painful to her eyes.

"MOMMY, CAN I share my others toys?" Kira asked, tugging on Lex's sundress.

Lex ruffled Kira's soft hair.

"You can do whatever you want," it said. It watched the spawn assigned to her run to the toy chest with the others. It looked like Lex, but it wasn't Lex anymore. In fact, it wasn't even an Earth woman, but it would pass for one. It surveyed the others who now looked human like it, in some form or another. In concert, they all looked back at it and nodded. They had much to do.

This was only the beginning.

GRIM

Graham Skipper

DATA ENTRY: NEW ENTRY: DIARY: AUTOSAVE ON
DESIGNATION: PRIVATE ENTRY: DO NOT SEND UNLESS INSTRUCTED
BY AUTHOR

DAY 1

THE WEIRDEST PART of these long-haul flights is waking up to a
captain several years older than when you left. It gets more
noticeable the older they are, but when you first come to, you
feel like you're in a dream, and the guy waking you up is almost
the guy that put you to sleep. But not quite.

I met a guy once that used to be one of these long-haul pilots,
the poor soul tasked with ferrying goods and materials—and
sometimes people—from Earth to the more far-flung stations
in our solar system. The farthest I've been is Jupiter Station,
which orbits our biggest planetary neighbor, and that offers a
lovely view of the Earth-sized storms on its surface. That station's more of a tourist destination; the cabins are nice (some
are bigger than my apartment back on Earth), the food is tasty,
and you feel more like you're aboard a cruise ship than a space
station. I was a bus boy in their big restaurant there. It was my
first off-world job.

Where we're heading today is a far cry from that kind of luxury.
You'd think Saturn Station (I wish they'd be more creative with
their names for these places) would be like Jupiter. I mean, it's
Saturn, the most beautiful of the planets—definitely one of the
spots in the system that rich folks would want to visit. But the

additional years of travel time is a big turn-off to regular folks. See, it only takes around a year for a well-timed flight to Jupiter, so the big cruise liners can make deals for speedy two-year round-trip voyages. But to get to Saturn, you have to tack on another six to eight years on top of that. A fun trip for a couple of years is one thing, a decade is another.

That's why Saturn Station is more practical. There's a handful of bunks, a mess hall, a bar (of course) and one legendary son-of-a-bitch named Dewey who runs the place. I've never been to Saturn Station before, just heard about it. My captain tells me it can be kind of a rough place, but I'm looking forward to the layover regardless.

We have to refuel there en route to Pluto. Turns out Pluto is way the fuck out there. I knew the length of the trip before embarking, but to think that we've already been flying for about seven years and still have five more to go… it's kind of wild. I'm sort of regretting my decision to have the captain wake me up for the stay at Saturn. The distance now feels farther somehow.

DAY 1…AGAIN

I'M RESTARTING MY calendar. We arrived in orbit at Pluto today. Captain Mac (that's what everyone calls him, but I can't imagine that's his real name) popped open a bottle of champagne 'cause this is the farthest from Earth he's ever been. He's a weird dude, a lifer on the shipping lanes, just doing a decade here, a decade there. People in this line of work don't have families, and all the ones I've met have said that they just felt like Earth wasn't home to them. They prefer the cold and the dark. The creaking metal. The shitty engine whiskey. Captain Mac's that type of guy.

We're going to orbit for a day to get in the right position for dropping me down. I guess I'll have a little of that engine whiskey after all, once this champagne has disappeared into my gut.

DAY 2

CAPTAIN MAC DROPPED me surface side on his remote shuttle. I docked with Point Grim (now there's a creative name for a station, finally) at about noon Pluto time. At the brightest point in the day, it looks sort of like an hour after sunset on Earth. The sun is about as bright as a full moon, or a lamp post a few blocks away. I actually like it—I'm a winter guy, never liked summer much. Beaches never did it for me, but I love a good Scottish seaside tavern. Cloud cover, storms, you know.

I guess that's why I didn't really balk at this gig. Twelve years to get here, ten-year contract, twelve years to get back. By the time I return, I'll be damn near sixty. The cryo-sleep ages you a lot less though, so I'll still be looking forty-five. I'll also be able to retire at that point, with an insanely fat pension for really only having done ten years of work. It's a pretty sweet deal when you think about it. My mom was sad, and saying goodbye to her was weird and intense. Just knowing that I was hugging her for the last time was a strange sensation. I cried; I'll admit it. But Dad's long gone, I have no girlfriend, no pets, none of that stuff…seemed like this was the right thing to do.

It's great, too, 'cause I don't have to actually know much. See, they don't send scientists out this far, they send grunts like me. Engineers, roughnecks, people that can fix stuff. The whole station is automated. I don't need to know how things work, just how to repair them.

Point Grim is the furthest telescope in the solar system. It's actually two massive telescopes: one is a Cassegrain Reflector and the other is a huge radio telescope that's about a mile wide. They built this station about thirty years ago using an army of AI. It was all over the news. The budget was damn near a trillion dollars and there wasn't even necessarily a mission, aside from "it's super dark out there and really far away, and it will give us the best view of the universe we've ever had." So, I guess the mission is "look for stuff?" Anyway, it's all automated just like the shuttle I was on. I don't even think I could look through the telescope if I wanted to. I'm just the janitor here.

I'm replacing this guy, Vince. Met him super briefly on my way in. He walked up, looking like he had drunk about fifteen cups of coffee, handed me my manual, shook my hand with these wild eyes and said, "good luck." Then he was out the door and on to the ship. Weird guy. Must be stoked to get into that sleeping chamber and wake up back on Earth.

They warned me about how lonely it would be out here. I'm not too worried about that, though maybe I should be. They put me through a ton of psychiatric tests and said I was fine. I feel fine. I'm actually feeling excited about all the time alone. I spend most of my time alone anyway. Maybe now I'll actually finish reading *Dune*.

DAY 21

I FINALLY GOT my last poster hung—they let me bring my Godzilla poster collection, which I appreciated. Fifteen vintage posters, all original. They're really the only possessions I care about. I'm such a weirdo, I learned woodworking in the months before I left so that I could build my own custom frames for them when I got here, using the synthetic wood I could make on the station (no way they'd approve something as heavy as framed posters for the journey out here). So, I've spent the last few weeks doing that in my spare time, which I have a lot of. I essentially just get up in the morning, make some coffee, check to see if there were any alarms overnight (there haven't been), do a walk around the station to see if everything is still turned on, then I'm done. Vince left a still of good whiskey (good being a relative term), so I've been partaking in that and reading up on how to run a still. Might try my hand at making some myself. So yeah, that's been my days so far, just a little under a month in: Wake up, do my rounds, get drunk, jerk off, then build some picture frames.

Still haven't even cracked open *Dune*.

DAY 104

MAN, ALARMS WENT off last night like crazy. First time it's happened since I've been here. About damn near gave me a heart attack. Ran to see what it was, and it looks like both the optical and the radio telescope detected something off-the-charts huge, about 100 AU away, out in the Kuiper Belt. Stacy, the scientist that I think they've assigned to me, was freaking out saying it was reading as incredibly massive, like as big as a planet, and it wasn't anything they've seen before. Problem is, it was too dark for them to actually see what it was with the optical telescope, and all the radio is reading is weird X-rays and other things I didn't understand. But still, Stacy was losing her shit over it. Guess they'll focus the telescopes on whatever it is over the next few months.

DAY 199

BIT OF A breakthrough on "Planet X" last night. The optical picked up an image finally, and to everyone's shock and surprise (Stacy looked like she was going to have a coronary) it appears that what we have on our hands is a miniature black hole. On black hole scales, miniature means planet-size, I guess. So, it's still a pretty remarkable thing. Stacy tells me it must be a "wandering" black hole, and possibly very old because it's so small. I guess big ones get big because they eat a lot of matter, but small ones used to be big because now they've spent billions of years shedding matter if they haven't been eating. I asked her what would happen if it got any closer to me, and she laughed and said that if it got anywhere near me, I'd be dead. I asked why she was laughing about that, and she said it was extremely unlikely it would come anywhere near me, as it's on a much different course. About as unlikely as encountering one of these in the first place, I guess.

DAY 225

IT'S BEEN A few weeks since the discovery of the black hole, dubbed "Scylla" by the team in Houston. I appreciate the creative name. Originally, they were calling it Unknown Object 72-A, which was awful. Scylla has a much nicer ring to it. They're telling me they announced the discovery on Earth, and that they gave my name as the "researcher" who made the discovery. I laughed and said my mom must have been proud to see that.

DAY 260

WOKE UP TO a message from Stacy. They've been tracking Scylla's progress and it seems to have stopped. Which she says is really weird and should be impossible. She said one explanation might be that it's been hooked on the gravity of some other huge object in the Kuiper Belt—something even bigger than Pluto, which is also possible but would be surprising that they didn't know about it yet. Pretty weird.

I admit I feel a little creeped out. The station feels super empty. Like incredibly empty. The only time I've ever felt this alone was when some friends dared me when I was twelve to go into one of those abandoned shopping malls, where people used to go to buy stuff, and the place was vast inside. And it was so weird because you could almost feel the people that used to be there. Like their ghosts or something. And I had to walk by myself through the whole mall and walk out the other end to where they'd be waiting for me. And I just felt incredibly alone.

For the first time since I've been out here, I feel like that.

DAY 295

I HAD A nightmare last night.

I've had a few nightmares since I've been here, but this was by far the worst.

So, Scylla is still just hanging out, not moving. Stacy says the team is baffled. She's wondering if the instruments malfunctioned somehow. It's so strange.

But in my dream, I could see it.

Out past Point Grim, where the sun is even dimmer and the rocks even colder, I could see it just floating in the black.

It was a perfectly black sphere, just the absence of existence, massive and endless and impossible. And skirting the edge of it, just barely visible, was a thin ring of starlight from the stars light-years away.

I was floating in space, and I was crying. I couldn't close my eyes. I just stared into the void, and somehow tears were flowing down my cheeks in violation of reality. My mouth was open, and I was trying to make noise, but nothing was coming out because I had no breath anymore. I had nothing anymore.

And I could hear it—a deep moan like two tectonic plates grinding against one another. Echoing infinitely and building on itself, somehow getting deeper and deeper, almost musical, like a thousand bassoons all playing their lowest note at once. Beautiful. Terrifying.

And although it was pure black inside, I felt like I could almost see something in there. Something with eyes as black as the nothingness in which it resided. Squirming, and writhing, and vibrating, with what I can only describe as anti-life. I was home in that place. That impossible place.

The groan emanating from its lair grew. Not louder, but more intense. My teeth shook in my head, and my eyeballs felt like they were going to implode. My entire body suddenly got so cold, and the tears on my face started to freeze. Oh shit! I was going to die! Whatever magic that had been preventing me from being taken by the cold universe was suddenly powerless, and oh fuck WHAT IS THAT THING? I SEE IT! I SEE IT!

And then I woke up.

Scariest dream I've ever had.

I made an appointment with their psych dude back home. It won't be much help cause of the transmission delay, but it'll feel a little bit like a lifeline.

I don't want to go back to sleep tonight.

DAY 333

OVER A MONTH of no sleep. Or little sleep. My body gives up after so long, and I crash out for an hour or so. But the dreams start again. They sent a synthesizer recipe for some drugs to help, but I'm afraid to take them. I don't want to be trapped in there.

I have this uneasy feeling that if I don't wake up in time, it'll get me. Whatever it is that lives inside of Scylla.

Or is that Scylla itself?

DAY 362

COMING UP ON a year here. Thank God I started taking the sleeping pills they were having me synth, because I'm finally getting a night's rest now and then. And they suppress dreams, too. Somewhat.

The weird thing is, I'm starting to daydream.

At least that's what I think it is. I'll be just sitting around, and I'll hear…whispers. Not exactly whispers, 'cause they're not saying any words, it's just slightly audible hushed voices saying nonsense. Right behind me, down the hall, up in the vents. In my manual, it says auditory hallucinations are a thing and that they're a thing even in non-crazy people. So, I haven't told anyone back on Earth about it.

They'll think I've started to go mad.

But I'm not.

DAY 366

DRANK AN ENTIRE bottle of whiskey last night to celebrate a full year. Being smashed helped with the whispers and the general uneasiness. I feel like shit today, but the headache actually helps. Feeling something familiar is way better than feeling what I've been feeling—that there's something totally unknowable out in the dark, and that all I want to do with all of my being is float into it.

DAY 396 OR 397

I THINK IT'S 396 or 397. I've stopped keeping an entry every day. I'm sure there's a log on the main computer that could tell me what day I got here, but the main terminal is located in a room with a gigantic bay window that looks out over the Plutonian landscape and the sea of black above it, but space doesn't feel exciting anymore—it doesn't feel like there's something out there worth discovering. It feels like some giant mouth that's just open, waiting. Beckoning us with the promise of something new, when really, it's merely nothing.

DAY ?

MAYBE TODAY IS Day 400. I don't know. I've been sleeping for what feels like days—I checked-out a long time ago.

There's a constant hum. All through the station. A deep, incessant hum, like a bunch of monks singing.

Reminds me of the groan from my dream.

...From my dreams.

When I put my hand to the wall, I can feel it vibrating. I've walked the miles and miles of corridors, and I've put my hands on every inch of every wall in this place, and I can feel it every-where. I can even feel it coming through the keyboard at the monitor stations, through the glass on the windows, and from the inside of the toilet.

I wanted to see if I could feel it on the top of the observation dome. So, I took off my weighted boots and just jumped, and I went up to the glass ceiling like in *Willy Wonka,* and of course I felt the hum there, too.

I'm not afraid of the black in the sky anymore. To tell the truth, I'm more afraid of the faces of the people on the screen when they call. They don't seem right to me, their faces. Or their eyes. So, I just turned it off. I lied and told them the video communicator was malfunctioning, and that it would take me a while to fix it. But really, I just can't look at their faces. It feels like an unnatural mirror looking back at me.

So, I look up into the black instead.

I wonder if Scylla has a face.

DAY ?

I PUT ON a suit today and went for a walk outside. They discouraged me from doing that unless I absolutely had to, but there's something different about being out there and staring up at the black versus being inside that dome. At least out here I feel like I'm more connected with Scylla. With her big yawning expanse.

I wish I could take off my helmet and look up without this glass between my eyes and the black. I wish I could feel this cold against my bare skin. Sometimes I wish I could just take this suit completely off, be naked in the unending night.

DAY ?

I SPENT SEVEN hours outside today, just lying on the icy ground and staring up at the cosmos. That tiny fuzzy star that used to feel so hot and oppressive back on Earth, but it's just a distant memory now, floating above as if calling out for its lost child.

But it's too far away, and this child likes being lost.

Charon looms in the sky like a monster about to smash into us, massive on the horizon, like Mount Everest slowly swimming through midnight waters, watching and waiting.

I love looking at Charon. Perhaps there's another me there, looking back.

I know I'm alone.

Except for Scylla.

DAY ?

SHE SPOKE TO me today. I call her she, but she is beyond gender. She is beyond any physical constraint.

She told me she has chosen me. She trusts me. She believes in me.

She loves me.

She is infinite, from boundless time and space. She has existed since before the beginning. She will exist after the end. After the universe has expanded too far, after all its physical delights have evaporated and all is as cold and dark as she, she will be floating aimlessly through the void, smiling and basking in her infinity.

I ask how I can pay tribute. She says my faith is enough.

She asks if I will be her emissary.

I weep and fall prostrate.

My love, my God, my nothing, and my everything.

Yes.

DAY ?

SHE SHOWED ME a vision

floating now in the void unafraid as i once was
i am so cold but i am filled with love for her
i see the doorway the cold black the orb the ring of starlight
she beckons me

i cannot see her eyes for they are black in the black but i can see her eyes for they are her eyes and she allows me to see them

they burn with madness with delicious madness unrestrained by logic or laws or purpose or duty they are burning so bright so bright so bright

oh my god my great god

i near the orb the perfect line of black against the darkness starlight bending further as i near it what is inside i ask myself i know i should die i should be dead but she wont let me she will protect me

i feel nothing as i slip beyond into the black but instantly all around is chaos light and chaos and sound and streaks of infinite colors of light white-hot light all cascading like a waterfall down down down to a single point a single atom a singularity where all of this becomes nothing because that is what she wants she wants for nothing at all

and i see her in the black her body black and unfathomably huge arms and legs and other things i have never imagined writhing in the dark her pure black teeth bared as she smiles at me her black eyes blessing me with their madness that bows to no man or god or rule of reality

she speaks to me she says go and tell them i am coming i am hungry i am all things and i am nothing and i am coming for them tell them spread the good news

i will do as she says and then i will join her in the black

she is coming

she is coming

she is coming

rejoice and be glad in it

TRANSMISSION: DIARY ENTRIES: ALL:: SEND
TRANSMISSION: SENT
**
**
**
NEW TRANSMISSION: AUTO-ALERT: TELESCOPE "CASS"
OBJECT "SCYLLA" MOVEMENT DETECTED
COURSE CHANGE FROM PREVIOUS ORBITAL PATH

CHARTING BASED ON NEW DATA...
CHARTING BASED ON NEW DATA...
CHARTING BASED ON NEW DATA...
NEW COURSE DETECTED: INWARDS TRAJECTORY: 1 AU/1 SOL
FIRST OBJECT ENCOUNTERED: DWARF PLANET "PLUTO" AND SUR-
ROUNDING BODIES
OTHER CELESTIAL BODIES IN PROJECTED PATH: SATURN, EARTH,
VENUS
FINAL DESTINATION: STAR DESIGNATION "SUN"
TRANSMISSION: SEND
TRANSMISSION: SENT
**
**
**

SPELLS

Gary Sherman

ABSOLUTE DARKNESS. A low, howling wind. The constant patter of a drizzling rain. Flashes of lightning ignite the blackness, transforming misshapen branches into macabre tentacles, hungrily reaching down to snare some unsuspecting prey.

A cacophony of noises. Voices? Distant. Barely distinguishable. Rhythmic. A roar of thunder obliterates all other sounds. It fades. Only the rain. The droplets. Silence. A pinpoint of light appears. Slowly approaches. Grows. Begins revealing itself. A lantern of some kind. Its beam creates ghostly shapes in the drizzle and mist. Whoever or whatever is holding the lamp is only a vague shadow beyond its blinding glow.

The light gets closer, illuminates the ancient trunks of vine-encrusted trees that line the path. Closer. Its beam searches. The clinging vines writhe to escape the light. Closer. The harsh light defines footprints in the mud. Closer. Squishing, careful footsteps approach. Out of the darkness, from behind the light, a face appears. Another flash of lightning reveals a surprisingly pleasant face. Youthful. Gentle features. A large halo of long curly hair. Aron Schneider seems out of place in this environment. His intense expression of fear and anticipation is palpable. He stops. His stare is locked onto the darkness beyond.

In front of him, beyond this primeval forest, straight out of a Grimm's fairytale, a strange little cottage. Windows covered by overgrowth. The faintest hint of a flickering light from inside. Its diminutive doorway only a scar.

Aron listens. Is it just the wind? Or his imagination? A rhythmic chanting whispers out from within. After a deep breath, he takes a tentative step forward. Stops.

SLAP! From out of nowhere, a spindly, aged hand, with long, unkempt nails clamps onto his face! Violently yanks him down, disappearing into a pool of blackness.

MOMENTARILY BLACK, THE darkness is shattered as Aron bolts up out of a deep sleep. Startled. Confused. For a moment, lost. Then realization. Lit only by the big city glow leaking in through the old casement windows, the twenty-four-year-old looks around.

His bed is adrift in a sea of cardboard boxes. Asleep next to him is his wife, Chloe. Long, dark hair frames her delicate features. Without awakening, she pulls the covers up around her. Aron remains still until she is peacefully back to sleep. He stares lovingly. Gently kisses her head. Silently eases out of bed. His *Steppenwolf* T-shirt and tie-dyed pajama bottoms, and his hair styled like Jimi Hendrix scream 1971.

Aron wades through the piled boxes to a baby's crib. He stares lovingly at his seven-month-old daughter, Mimi, sound asleep. Straightens her blanket. Blows her a kiss. Tiptoes to the windows. Looks out. A commanding view of London. Seven stories below, the vast city, asleep, glistens beneath a light rain.

After a long moment, he eases to the door. Emerges into the endless, winding, door-lined corridor of this huge turn-of-the-century penthouse flat. Painters' scaffolds, drop cloths, paint cans, and mounds of decorating equipment scattered about. Carefully picking his way through the debris, he disappears into one of the doorways. The door closes behind him.

CLICK! The harsh light of a naked bulb floods the large sitting room. A huge expanse of windows. An elaborate fireplace. More boxes. Everywhere. Piled high. Near the windows, an easel holding an exquisite, half-finished abstract, sits surrounded by an artist's accoutrements. Across the room, peeking out from more boxes, is a desk chair and small folding table. Aron sidles through the labyrinth toward the table. On it, a portable manual typewriter. To one side of the typewriter is a stack of typed script pages. To the other, blank paper awaiting ink. In the typewriter, a half-finished page. Sliding into the chair, Aron reads. Thinks. Begins to type. CLACK! CLACK! CLACK!

LONDON IS AWAKE before the late-rising sun again loses its battle to penetrate the gray mass hanging over the city. A typical January morning 51.5° north of the equator.

Splash! A foot sporting a heavy Oxford hits a puddle. It belongs to Daniel Cooper-Benson, a stout yet handsome man of fifty-six, swathed in the trappings of the British privileged class. Burberry Gabardine Trench Coat. Saville Row three-piece suit. Regimental striped tie. And, of course, an umbrella. He approaches a building in Soho Square emblazoned: BRITISH-AMERICAN STUDIOS. With practiced aplomb, he collapses the umbrella and gives a sincerely friendly nod to the elderly concierge at the door. In perfect Etonian parlance, "Good morning, Mr. Fellowes."

"And to you, Mr. Cooper-Benson. How are you this morning?" is returned with a slight tinge of Cockney.

Daniel smiles, "Better than I deserve, old chap. Better than I deserve." Disappears inside.

HOLDING MIMI IN one arm, a mug of coffee in her free hand, Chloe maneuvers the chaos of workmen busily transforming years of neglect into livable luxury. A workman graciously opens a door for her. A smile and sweet, "Thank you." Her accent is, charmingly, quite Irish.

Aron is sound asleep, slumped over his typewriter.

Chloe quietly closes the door, puts the coffee down by the typewriter, kisses Aron's forehead. "Morning, my love." He stirs. Mumbles in a Midwest-American drawl, "Please let me sleep."

Chloe leans in, starts reading what is on the typewriter. Furls her forehead as she reads.

Awake enough to realize, Aron playfully covers the page with his hand, "No. No. Not until it's done!"

Chloe laughs, shakes her head, "How did a nice Jewish boy like you ever learn to write such scary shit?"

"Not nearly as hard to explain as how he was lucky enough to win the love of such a talented Irish lass." They share a gentle kiss.

RING! RING! The phone. RING! RING! The moment shattered. Both look around. RING! RING! Where is it? RING! RING! Aron grabs and throws back a drop cloth. The phone. RING! RING!

Aron picks it up, is greeted by the voice of Daniel Cooper-Benson, no doubt seated at his massive desk inside his incredibly posh office, the epitome of high-end '70s London décor.

"Hope I'm not waking you, dear boy." Daniel says. "Would you meet me at The Ship, one-ish? I have some rather good news for you. Good. See you then. And big hugs to our darling Mimi and the beautiful Chloe."

WARDOUR STREET, SOHO. The center of the British film industry. Some cynically call Wardour Street the "Home of reverse alchemy. Where gold is turned into shit."

Hammer. Butchers. Amicus. All the horror and exploitation film companies are here, right next to the majors. Paramount. Universal. Fox. MGM. The music industry is here as well. Every important British label and band has an office in these streets. Except the Beatles. They recently abandoned Soho for the fancier surrounds of Mayfair.

London, like the rest of the UK, is all about pubs. Wardour Street's main mecca is The Ship. Pop music and the smell of beer fill every square inch that isn't jammed with bodies. Bell-bottoms. Tie dye. Paisley plaids. Miniskirts. Platform shoes. Beatle boots. Embroidered Afghan vests. Lots and lots of hair. Even a sprinkling of tailored executives. Hard to tell the filmmakers from the pop stars. But no one cares.

Daniel, sitting opposite Aron at a corner table, beams, "I've locked a release date for *The Spell*. This Halloween."

Aron is nearly dumbstruck, "Holy shit! You're joking!"

Daniel gives a slow shake of his head. His face melds into that look that can only belong to a proud father. Not far from the truth. Daniel and his wife, Marion, apparently regretting their decision to be childless, have practically adopted Aron and Chloe. And Mimi is providing them with the joy of a grandchild.

Aron just stares as it sinks in, "Thank you. Thank you. Thank you, Daniel. I can't believe this."

"So, when can we see the final draft?"

Aron slumps, "I'm trying, Daniel. I can't believe how fucking stupid it was to move in the middle of a project. We shoulda stayed in our other flat for an extra couple of months."

"You are a bit too...frugal...sometimes, Aron."

"Jewish. You mean too Jewish."

"I'm not allowed to say that." Laughs.

Aron points at himself, "But I am!"

"Listen. I'm way ahead of you. Marion and I are off to her family's vineyard in Grasse for a few weeks. We need to oversee the winter pruning." He holds out a set of keys, "Keys to the house in Kent...and to the wine cellar. You'll have all the quiet anyone could ask. By now you must know where we keep everything. Yes?"

Aron nods, "Wow! You're unbelievable, Daniel. But I'll have to check with Chloe. She is getting ready for her big show."

"Already did. Said she could use the break. She is gleefully packing. Just come back with that great script even greater!"

IN THE SPRING, summer, and autumn, there are few places anywhere lusher or more beautiful than the rolling hills and country roads of Kent. Houses and churches dating back to the eleventh century are common. It's a mystical journey back in time. But in the winter, especially January, the omnipresent cloud cover and the nearly non-stop rain transform it into a dark and foreboding landscape. Once the sun gives up its few hours of struggle to penetrate the gloom, a pervasive blackness enshrouds everything.

The headlights of the tiny Renault 5 reflect off the sheets of rain rather than illuminate the road.

Bent over the wheel, his face nearly pressed against the windshield, Aron searches for any evidence of the road ahead. In the back seat, Chloe, squeezed in next to Mimi's travel cot, gently strokes the sleeping baby's back, as soothing to the mother as it is to the child.

They had left London in late afternoon in hopes of beating rush-hour on the A21, but having never been here in the winter months, they were unaware how dark the roads would be once they left the highway. Nor had they foreseen the dangerous weather presently engulfing them.

Aron breaks the silence, "Ever hear the phrase, 'Can't see your hand in front of your face'?"

"I think this is payback for all the scary stuff you foist on your audiences."

"Shit!" Aron laughs, "Maybe you're right. Guess I better start writing romance novels."

"Bad idea. You'd starve to death."

"What! You don't think I'm romantic?"

"You're the sweetest man ever." She smiles, "Probably because you purge all the bad stuff in your writing. So don't change anything. I love you."

"I love you, too."

Chloe looks out into the rainy darkness. "Do you think we're close."

Aron squints out at the road. "Minutes away, I think."

She nods, adds, "I'm actually looking forward to meeting Daniel's mother."

Aron's eyes shift to Chloe in the rearview. "Daniel's mother? What are you talking about?"

"Didn't he tell you? His mother is staying in that tiny crofter's cottage attached to the house."

"His mother! I didn't even know he had a mother. Talks about his father all the time, but I don't remember him ever even mentioning his mother."

Chloe jokes, "If he had a father, he had to have had a mother."

"Ha, ha. I just thought she must have died when he was pretty young."

"Apparently not. But he did say they've been estranged for decades. And that she's quite weird."

"Weird? You mean like eccentric?"

"No. He used the word *weird*. He also suggested we do ourselves a favor and not get too friendly with her. Say hello when we get there, goodbye when we leave. Have nothing to do with her in between."

"That *is* weird. Did he say why?"

"Nope. Only thing else he said was…", breaking into her perfect Daniel, "Don't invite her into my house. I don't want her in there."

"Weird."

THE RENAULT 5 comes through ornate gates, flanked on both sides by tall hedges that separate the estate from the road. As if on cue, a blinding flash of lightning illuminates the seventeenth-century Tudor house. Aside from the eerie shadows cast by the bursts of lightning, the distant chorus of thunder, and, of course, the remoteness, very little is actually spooky about this grand home.

Leaving the headlights on, umbrella in hand, Aron leaps out, hurries around to open the passenger-side door for Chloe. She gets out, takes the umbrella. Aron undoes the fasteners holding the travel cot. He covers Mimi before re-emerging into the rain. They rush to the front door.

The heavy door glides open. Aron CLICKS! on the foyer light. Even though neither of them is very tall, they both duck as they enter.

Chloe smiles. "If this was one of your scripts, the door would have creaked, and the light wouldn't have worked."

Aron nods, "Yeah but we're here for me to write a script, not to be in one."

"Considering your current subject matter, I'm very glad about that."

He kisses her, then lifts the shoulder strap of his leather satchel over his head, puts it down, "I'll go get the bags." He disappears out the door.

Mimi let's out a tiny cry that dissipates the moment. Chloe sets down the cot on the entryway table, picks her up, and cuddles her. Mimi in her arms, Chloe steps into the next room.

CLICK! Light fills a sitting room that couldn't be more perfectly decorated for a country home of this vintage. The low, beamed-ceiling, massive floor-to-ceiling fireplace, and crude, steep staircase complete the classic look.

ARON IS ALREADY soaked as he slams the Renault's hatch door, gathers the luggage and groceries, and heads back to the house. He is almost to the door when he stops. Looks to the side of the home. Then eases over. Peeks around the side.

A FLASH of lightning! Aron sees the eerie, overgrown cottage from his script. A CRACK! of thunder. He almost reacts before laughing at himself. The tiny, semi-detached crofter's cottage at the rear is no spookier, no more unkempt, than the house itself. In fact, it's quite charming. And just like the cottage of Aron's imagination, its windows only emit the slightest flickering light. Aron notes the similarity, then heads back to the front door and the main house and disappears inside.

HELD FACE-TO-FACE BY her mom, Mimi beams a huge smile. Aron leans in over Chloe's shoulder. He gently kisses both his 'girls.' "We are so lucky. We have the best and happiest baby in the world." Chloe nods her enthusiastic agreement.

Aron softly sings, "I'll light the fire… You place our flower… in the room… Where we'll sleep… tonight."

"You wouldn't like it if Graham Nash rewrote your work, would you?"

"Jeez! I thought I was being quite clever…and romantic."

Chloe kisses Aron's cheek. "You light the fire… I'll place our flower… in the room… Where we'll sleep… tonight."

NEATLY STACKED LOGS sit inside the fireplace. Aron pokes a flaming piece of fatwood into the kindling.

Success. Flame spreads through the kindling.

"Well done! You have talents of which I was completely unaware."

Aron nods, "Having to learn about all kinds of things you may never have to do is one of my favorite things about being a writer." Stepping close to Aron, Chloe smiles proudly. "And very soon, a director." Aron grins.

Chloe remembers something, "While I fix Mimi's dinner, do you think you might go knock on the cottage door to let Daniel's mother know we've arrived?"

"Took a peek when I was bringing our stuff in. It was pretty dark in there. She's probably asleep."

"It's barely eight."

"Old people sleep a lot."

KNOCK! KNOCK! KNOCK!

Chloe laughs. "Wrong."

As Aron contritely edges toward the front door, it flies open. A swirling, tornado-like cloud of darkness fills the doorway. That spindly, aged hand, with long, unkempt nails shoots out of the black cloud, reaching for Aron.

"You must be Daniel's mother, Mrs. Cooper-Benson," says Chloe. She steps up from behind Aron. Smiles.

No dark swirling cloud. No spindly hand. Only a diminutive eighty-year-old who forces a smile onto her rigidly stern face. Pure white hair, pulled into a perfect bun atop her head, frames her round face and deep-set blue eyes. The smile, an expression she probably rarely uses, seems unfamiliar to her face. She holds a heavy, dark red shawl tightly about her shoulders.

Chloe nudges Aron aside, "Please Mrs. Cooper-Benson, come in out of the rain."

"Alice, dear one. Please call me Alice. I'm not nearly the old fuddy-duddy my son would have you believe." Her smile melts back into the blank, somewhat off-putting glare that appears to be the face she most often wears. "Thank you," she says as she steps inside. An awkward silence hangs for a moment as the three study each other. The old woman's eyes lock on Chloe. Then, with words devoid of all emotion, she says, "I understand you've brought a baby."

"Our daughter. Mimi."

"How old is she?"

Forcing an extra friendly tone to make up for what may have been taken as rudeness, Aron blurts, "Seven months. But she's very quiet. Almost never cries. So, she won't be a bother to you."

"May I see her?"

Chloe's maternal instinct kicks in. "She's asleep. Traveling and all that. You being a mother yourself, I'm sure you understand."

A nod. Although her expression says otherwise, "Please let me know when it's convenient." She turns and goes, leaving the door open behind her.

Aron peeks out to see that she's gone before closing the door. He and Chloe lock eyes. Simultaneously they mouth, "Weird."

THE LAST TINY spoonful is scooped from a baby bowl decorated with drawings by Beatrix Potter. Mimi's face beams as her mom feeds her one final taste. Mother and daughter sit in a wonderfully carved antique rocker. The subdued light creates the illusion of a Vermeer painting.

Aron comes to the upstairs bedroom door. Peers in at the loves of his life in this idyllic setting. He walks over to the pair, takes the bowl, and hands Chloe a prepared baby bottle. "As soon as she's asleep," he whispers, "come downstairs. I've prepared a feast. It awaits you." Chloe blows Aron a kiss as he tip-toes toward the door.

KNOCK! KNOCK! from downstairs.

Instant anger wipes across Aron's face. "This is going to be a problem."

Chloe shrugs, "She's a lonely old woman, Aron. Go let her in. Let's just get this over with."

With an exasperated sigh, he leaves. His footsteps descend the stairs.

Mimi's bright eyes smile up at Chloe as she nurses her bottle. The faint sound of the front door opening and closing. Muted voices accompany ascending footsteps. A light tap! at the bedroom door. Aron opens the door to usher Alice in. Chloe forces a smile as she looks to their unexpected guest.

Alice takes one step into the room. She never sees Chloe's smile. Her eyes lock only onto Mimi. As if magnetized, Mimi's eyes snap to the old woman's face. Nearly wrenching herself out of Chloe's arms, the baby's whole body stiffens. The bottle THUDS! to the floor. Before Chloe or Aron can even react, a deafening, screeching scream, emanating from the infant's very soul. A sound beyond the possibility of coming from a baby. Her mouth, stretched open beyond its limits, trumpets this unearthly cry. Aron and Chloe freeze in terror. Alice, unmoved, holds her unyielding stare.

Chloe breaks from the paralysis of the moment. Frantically wraps her arms around her bellowing child. Pulls her to her breast. Simultaneously smothering the ungodly sound and comforting her child. Aron throws himself around the two, adding comfort and protection. Mimi's outburst subsides into uncontrolled crying. Aron looks toward the doorway.

The jagged nails of the spindly hand lunge at Aron's face, taking a swipe. Aron pulls back out of its way. The hand is sucked back into a swirling black cloud. It instantly dissipates. Alice stands rigid. Her stern expression is a stone mask. Without the slightest hint of emotion, "I'm sorry if I frightened the baby." Taking a step backward before turning, she quickly leaves.

FOR OVER AN hour, Chloe and Aron soothed Mimi. The poor little thing convulsed in tears until she had no strength left to stay awake. Once they have calmed her, Chloe stays until she is certain her little girl is sound asleep and resting easy. Aron goes downstairs to finish preparing dinner.

THE MAIN ROOM flickers from the combination of the roaring fire and the collection of perfectly placed candles. Tonight, Aron has outdone his usual culinary skills as well as his presentation. Chloe comes tiptoeing down the stairs.

Aron whispers, "She asleep?"

Chloe nods her response, "I'm pretty sure we're not going to hear a peep until morning."

"I've never heard a sound like that come out of a baby... Ever. Let alone from Mimi."

"It was rather scary."

"It's that woman who's 'rather scary.'"

Chloe grins, "You write horror, my darling. You can imagine anything to be scary. She may be weird, but she's not scary."

"Mimi wasn't scared? Come on, Chloe. She was terrified."

"Hungry. Over-tired. And startled. She'll be fine."

Aron isn't convinced, "I'll tell you one thing, she's not setting one foot into this house again. I've locked every door and window."

"You are too cute. That's why I love you so much." She looks at the table. A perfectly arranged spread of roast chicken, roasted vegetables, and a beautiful fresh salad. She points, "And that's another reason I love you. Let's eat!"

DARK. DEAFENING SILENCE. A tiny lamp on the dresser serves as a nightlight, the only illumination in the guest bedroom. Mimi, curled up and tucked in, is deeply asleep in her cot. Across the room, near the window, covered by an overstuffed, down-filled duvet, Aron and Chloe lie still and entangled on the large bed.

Chloe, her eyes softly closed, her breaths relaxed and peaceful, is nestled against Aron, her head on his chest. Aron's sleep is not nearly as peaceful.

A sound, barely audible, penetrates the heavy silence, cuts through Aron's fitful sleep. Eyes ease open, slowly search for the source. He remains motionless.

What is it? He strains to listen. Is it real or imagined? It hardly breaks the threshold of audibility, but he *is* hearing it. Or he thinks he is. As the sound starts to define itself to him, he wants to shake it off. Deny its existence. Exactly as he had imagined it coming from the cottage in his script, rhythmic chanting is filling the air around him.

Gently, he eases his arm out from around Chloe, trying not to wake her, not to make a sound of his own. He rolls out from beneath the duvet onto the floor. On all fours, he creeps toward the windows. Gets to the wall. Presses himself against it. Rises up to the windows. Looks out. Nothing but blackness. He puts an ear to the glass.

If he wasn't awake before, he is now. The sound is real. Coming from outside.

Slowly turns to look out. There is only blackness. Like a naughty child in fear of being caught, he keeps as low to the windowsill as he can. Eyes and ears seek the source of the eerie chanting voices. Every clue tells him the same thing. The crofter's cottage.

It is difficult to see the cottage from this window, or from any window in the house, as a matter of fact, but he presses the side of his head firmly against the glass until he's able to look down toward the tiny cottage from this second-floor room. He squints into the darkness. The windows. He can see the tiny windows. Faint, flickering light ekes through the ancient glass. Aron stretches for a better view.

Behind him, the wrinkled, spindly hand grabs his shoulder! He spins!

Chloe presses her fingers to Aron's mouth to keep him from waking Mimi. Whispers, "What are you doing?"

"Can't you hear that?"

Chloe listens. Shakes her head.

"Put your ear against the window."

"What am I supposed to—"

Aron interrupts, "Just put your ear to the window."

She does. Initial curiosity soon melts into a grin. "I think Daniel's mama is into group sex!"

"You think that's an orgy?"

Chloe nods, "What do you think they're doing?"

"I think it's a coven."

"And I think I can't wait for you to write just another good old-fashioned slasher film instead of this occult thing you're working on. You're possessed!"

The chanting stops. Aron throws his look back to the window. Presses up against it. Not with the same fervor, Chloe does the same. Below them, the shuffling footsteps of the elderly. Muted voices. Indistinguishable words. The fluttering light from the open front door of the cottage does little to define any shapes. It's nearly impossible to see anyone clearly, but it appears to be a dozen people, women and men, lumbering towards the gate. Car doors quietly open and shut. Engines start. One by one, four cars move off. The thick hedges only allow momentary glimpses of their headlights. The door of the cottage is heard to shut.

Chloe glances at Aron, "What time is it?"

Checking his glow-in-the-dark *Star Trek* wristwatch, "Like five after three."

"Hmmm! Mrs. Cooper-Benson is quite the party animal, isn't she?"

"Chloe, I can't believe none of this is freaking you out."

She leans into him and kisses him on the cheek, "I love your imagination. I love you. And I love your *Star Trek* watch." She nudges him toward the bed, "Go back to sleep. I'm just quite happy you're not writing about poltergeists, or you'd be seeing ghosts in every shadow... Which I don't believe in either."

They crawl back underneath the cozy duvet and wrap themselves around each other. "I know how to get your mind off all that witchcraft nonsense."

Aron chuckles, "Oh, do you?"

"Uh-huh. As long as you promise to be very quiet and not wake Mimi."

"Not a sound."

THE MORNING LIGHT trickling in through the windows does little to eliminate the gloom. Aron, a floor lamp pulled up behind him, sits at an antique secretary desk, typing away on his portable, his leather satchel nearby. Pages neatly arranged in piles. He's on his third cup of coffee. Well into his work. Chloe, in robe and slippers, Mimi in her arms, comes quietly down the stairs. Without turning, Aron says, "Good morning, my beauties. There's a bottle warming for our little one, fresh coffee and porridge for you. Just want to finish this page and I'll join you." He punctuates his greeting with a kissing sound. Chloe returns the air kiss and heads to the kitchen.

KNOCK! KNOCK! KNOCK! Both stop. Eyes to the front door, then to each other. Aron puts a finger to his lips, gets up, tiptoes to the window, carefully looks out. Rolls his eyes. Turns to Chloe. Mouths, "It's her."

Chloe smiles, whispers, "Who were you expecting? Ruth Gordon?"

With a sarcastic smile, he whispers back, "Funny." Glances out the window then back at Chloe, "But she does have a chocolate mousse."

"You're joking."

"Kinda'. Not a chocolate mousse. Looks like a cake. Go in the kitchen. I'll get rid of her."

Aron swings the door open halfway to reveal Alice.

Trying to force a smile through her always stern mask, she offers the cake, "An apology for scaring your baby yesterday. I baked it this morning."

"Sweet of you. Thank you. But unnecessary. And Chloe and I are both on diets."

She holds it up higher. "No, no, no. I insist. Very low calorie. I'm quite health conscious. I made it for you. Just take it and promise me you'll at least try a bit. Please."

Aron reluctantly takes it, "Thank you. I have to get back to work now." Smiles and starts to shut the door.

MEOW. He jumps back. Looks down. A large tabby is on its way in. "Shoo!" Not kicking it but trying to block its entry and move it back outside, he ends up doing a nervous little dance. "Please Mrs. Cooper-Benson—"

"Alice."

"Um, Alice, it's just I'm very allergic to cats. Please grab it."

She reaches down and scoops up the cat. "Another apology is due. Enjoy the cake." She turns and is gone without another word or glance. SLAM!

Aron rushes into the kitchen and heads right to the trash bin. PLOP! He drops the cake inside and quickly jams the lid back on.

Chloe just looks at him. "I didn't even get a chance to see it. Was it at least pretty?"

"It looks like a fruit cake. Have you ever seen a pretty fruit cake? No. Fruit cakes are all ugly."

"A Christmas pudding from Fortnum & Mason is basically a fruit cake, and they're quite pretty."

Aron looks at her skeptically, "You're joking? Right?"

Chloe cracks a smile, "I hate fruit cake. Even Fortnum & Mason's Christmas pudding. That must've been why Minnie brought Rosemary a chocolate mousse. Rosemary probably hated fruitcakes too."

"I wonder whether Ira Levin invented that mousse thing, or if it came from research?"

"I can understand why you write this stuff, but I can't fathom why you believe it's real."

"I write about what scares me. If my scripts don't scare me, they won't scare audiences."

Chloe grins, starts toward the trash bin, opens it. "Let's be scientific. Why don't we test it?"

Aron slams the lid closed. "I'm not fucking eating it. And neither are you."

Chloe sports an elfish smile, points, "Feed some to her cat."

Aron turns to look. The large tabby, crouched in the dining room doorway, returns his stare. "How in the hell did that thing get back in here?"

Chloe hands Mimi to Aron, "I'll get it out of here." Chloe unlocks and opens the kitchen door, grabs a broom, herds the cat out into the yard. Slamming the door behind it.

"I'm telling you, Chloe. Every door and window is shut and locked. This is too freaky."

"There is certainly a plausible explanation. And if anyone can figure it out..." Chloe plucks Mimi from Aron's arms. "You can." A quick peck on the cheek and Chloe heads upstairs.

FLASH! OF LIGHTNING. CRACK! of thunder. The staccato percussion of the pouring rain reminiscent of the CLACK-CLACK of a typewriter. A pair of hands push aside mangled, twisted branches to clear a path. Aron's eyes stare straight ahead. Rain cascades down his face. His hands continue ripping away the gnarled foliage blocking his way, his unbroken gaze locked on what these wooden tentacles are trying to hide. It's the cottage. Barely lit. Writhing vines engulfing it. Another FLASH! of light washes over the façade. The cottage seems to answer the lightning with an even more intense explosion of light from its windows. The door of the cottage bursts open, emitting a blinding glow. A dark shape jettisons out of the glow. The spindly hand darts toward Aron. A haggard face races to catch up with the hand. The eyes, the mouth, the features of this horrid mask are those of Mrs. Cooper-Benson. The long fingers grasp and tear into Aron's belly.

ARON PUSHES AWAY from his typewriter, jumps to his feet. The cat SCREAMS! as it flies from Aron's lap, hits the ground and scurries away, disappearing from the salon and into the kitchen. There is hardly time to react. RING! RING! The phone. RING! RING! Aron just stands frozen for a moment. RING! RING!

"Are you going to answer that?", Chloe calls from upstairs.

RING! RING! Aron picks up the phone. "Hello."

"How's it going, my dear boy? Settled in? Finding everything?" Daniel's barrage of questions finally gets around to, "Is my mother keeping to herself and out of your hair?"

Aron lets this one sink in before firing back an answer. After all, she is Daniel's mother. Aron forces a smile onto his face and into his voice, "You didn't tell me she was a party animal."

"What are you talking about?"

"Last night. She had a whole bunch of people over."

"After midnight?"

Aron is surprised at Daniel's response, "Not sure what time they got there, but they didn't leave until after three."

"How many people?"

"A dozen, maybe."

"Has she been to see you?"

"She came over yesterday, wanting to meet Mimi, then showed up this morning with a cake she baked for—"

Daniel's voice explodes from the phone, "Pack up and leave!"

Confusion fills Aron's face. "What?"

"Get the fuck out of that house! NOW!"

Aron almost gets a word out before Daniel roars, "NOW!"

MRS. COOPER-BENSON, HER stony face frozen in its usual stern mask, stares out the cottage's tiny window. She watches the Renault 5 disappear out the gate. Anger replaces all emotions.

"THAT'S NOT LIKE Daniel at all." Chloe utters from the back seat, again crammed in next to Mimi's cot. She leans forward, "No explanation?"

"Nothing. Why does the word 'weird' keep popping into my head?"

"Because it is."

A DARK ROOM. The slightest CREAK! of a door. A sliver of light invades the darkness. The light falls upon a baby's cot. Mimi lifts her head, looks toward the source of the light. A shadow creeps across the child's face. An unearthly SCREAM! erupts from deep within the infant's soul. The spindly hand darts out. Grabs Mimi's face.

RING! RING! Abruptly jarred away from his thoughts. RING! RING! Aron leaps from his typewriter to snatch up the phone. "Hello."

"Aron, dear boy, it's Daniel. I owe you an apology and an explanation for my abruptness Tuesday."

"You don't *owe* us anything. But Chloe and I are both pretty curious about why—"

"Are you both free for dinner this evening? Marion and I would love to have you over. And Mimi, of course."

CHIMES! RUMBO, A plump, aging Beagle, lets out a HOWL! His tail wags like a metronome set to prestissimo, takes off down an elegant, Oriental-rug carpeted corridor to the entry hall.

Intercepting his liveried butler, "I'll get it, James.", Daniel opens the massive front floor.

Rumbo excitedly greets Aron, Chloe, and Mimi. The townhouse is a pre-Victorian masterpiece located in Belgravia, London's most prestigious and most expensive neighborhood. It reeks of old money.

The dining room, sporting a table that could easily seat twenty, is elegantly set for four, with a highchair stationed at the head. Daniel leads the Schneider family in. James disappears into the kitchen just as Marion, an apron protecting her modest couturier dress, emerges with a platter of perfectly sliced pork loin.

Marion, whose father was Emilio Thibaut, the world-renowned French chef, has every reason to be a snob, but she is the exact opposite. She's attractive, yet prematurely matronly for someone in their early fifties. She's also warm, open, genuinely sweet, and wonderfully friendly. And thanks to her father, she too is an amazing chef. Her "throw together" meals are other people's haute cuisine.

Once seated, James corks and serves the wine. Daniel begins to explain his behavior and tone of voice the other day, prefacing his disclosure with, "You are probably going to find this a bit hard to believe…"

Marion brings out course after course of delectable dishes as Daniel unravels his story.

"My mother is a witch. Not a just a Wiccan or an Aleister Crowley-type practitioner, but a full-fledged Black Arts, Satan-worshiping, spell-casting occultist." He relived for them the horrible memories from his childhood, of the times he was locked in a closet or a cellar, or tied to a tree while his mother and her coven held their ceremonies.

Daniel's father, one of England's leading film directors of the silent era, who successfully graduated into talkies, had been trying to gain custody of his son from the time he and his wife had separated.

Because he was a prominent show business personality, his father's attorneys were reluctant to use her witchcraft as the primary factor in the case. They thought a judge might find it overly dramatic.

But a charge of abuse, following a severe punishment received by young Daniel at her hands, his father was finally granted custody. That was the last time Daniel had seen his mother until toward the end of the previous September, when he received a letter at his office. She claimed to be quite ill and homeless, living in a shelter near Portsmouth. "So, I drove down to see her."

Both Chloe and Aron listen intently, shocked by these revelations. Neither interrupt with questions nor remarks of their own.

"She swore to me that witchcraft was no longer a part of her life, that she had given it up years ago. I was skeptical, but unfortunately, I chose to believe her." A mix of sadness and anger wash across Daniel's face. "I wasn't surprised when you told me what was going on."

Marion reaches over. Squeezes her husband's arm in reassurance.

Daniel looks to her with love in his eyes, then turns back to Chloe and Aron. "I had hated and feared her most of my life, but never did I want to believe she was truly...evil." He takes a sip of his wine. "I warned her. Told her I wanted none of her Satanism practiced in my home." His eyes drift off to some neutral unoccupied space. "I've since thrown her out, taken her back to Portsmouth, put her into a small furnished flat." He turns back to Chloe and Aron. "I told her I'd pay the rent, as well as provide her with a monthly stipend, as long as I never hear from her again."

Moved by Daniel's emotions, but being a true non-believer, Chloe gently asks, "Do you believe that her...um...practices... er...her spells...are malicious? As in, they're meant to do harm to people?"

Daniel just stares at Chloe for a protracted moment. His face is devoid of any judgment. Finally, he nods. "Yes. She killed my father."

Chloe freezes. So does Aron.

After a long silence, Daniel continues, "First she destroyed his career. Then he deteriorated physically. The best Harley Street doctors, one after the other, could find no cause for what was ailing him. But I knew. I heard her say it. She told him she'd make him suffer. I heard it. I'll never forget her tone and the look in her eyes."

PITCH BLACK.

RING! RING! Aron bolts upright from a sound sleep.

RING! RING! Chloe stirs.

Aron fumbles for the phone. RING! RING! He grabs it, "Hello..."

"Mr. Schneider, this is James, Mr. Cooper-Benson's butler. I am sorry to disturb you, but I didn't know who else to ring."

THE SKY IS showing a faint glimmer of morning. The strobing lights of emergency vehicles bounce off the stark white walls of the Square. The Renault pulls to the curb close to the nearly silent chaos. Aron jumps from the car. Runs to the house. Starts up the front steps but stops dead before reaching the top. Paramedics wheel a gurney out of the front door. Down the steps. A body is strapped to the bed and covered with a sheet. Tears well in Aron's eyes

Once the gurney has passed, Aron wipes the tears from his eye. He dashes inside, but James quickly intercepts him.

"Mr. Schneider. Mr. Cooper-Benson is upstairs. I'll take you to him."

DANIEL, IN PAJAMAS and a robe, sits on the edge of the unmade bed staring blankly at nothing. His whole being is just frozen. Rumbo sits at his feet. Neither Daniel nor the beagle acknowledge Aron's presence.

Aron slowly steps into Daniel's line of sight. Kneels in front of him. After a moment, Daniel finally focuses on his young friend. His lips start to form words. He whispers, "Marion's dead. She took her away from me." He locks eyes with Aron. "My mother killed her."

TEARS COURSE DOWN Chloe's face as she holds Mimi tight, rocking her little girl back and forth in an oversized rocker. "I can't even imagine."

Aron, looking pretty shaken, sits opposite them in their bedroom "Me neither. To just wake up and find the person you love…"

"Do they have any idea what the cause of death is?"

Aron shakes his head, "Nope. But they'll be doing an autopsy."

Chloe cringes, "That's horrible."

Aron agrees.

"But you know something, Aron? Once they find out what the real cause was... that she had some unknown condition or something... I'm sure it will be a great comfort to Daniel."

"It'll be a comfort to me, too. This really has me spooked."

Chloe reaches out a hand to Aron. He takes it. Chloe squeezes his hand.

CAUSE OF DEATH: Undetermined.

On the morning of Marion's funeral, the coroner's office issued a preliminary report on the autopsy. The details included a description of multiple organ failure precipitated "possibly by a heart attack." But there was insufficient evidence to confirm a singular cause.

THE VOICES OF the Anglican choir echo through the magnificent 150-year-old Holy Trinity Church in Sloane Square. It is filled with the elite of both the entertainment and culinary industries. Marion, in an open casket, lies at the foot of the altar. Daniel, looking twenty years older than just a few days ago, sits slumped in a front pew. Flanked by Aron and Chloe, their arms around him, he stares transfixed at his beloved.

At the very back of the church, a diminutive woman enters. Head to toe in black. A veil obscures her face. She takes a seat in a rear pew. Her hands, adorned in black lace gloves, clutch an inverted crucifix hanging from a chain around her neck.

The psalm ends. The choir and organ fall silent. A hollow emptiness fills the vast space. The Rector steps to the altar. He welcomes the immediate family to come forward to say their final goodbyes.

Daniel—broken, feeble, assisted by the Schneiders, rises. Steps to the casket. Trembles as he looks at Marion. Reaches to her. Hand quivering. Gently touches her cheek. His gaze lingers for a moment, then he nudges Aron to help him back to his seat. Chloe stays at the casket, her eyes filled with tears. She touches her fingers to her lips, reaches out, transfers the kiss to Marion's cheek. As she withdraws her hand, she momentarily grasps the edge of the coffin. Without a hint of warning, the heavy lid of the metal coffin slams THUD! crushing Chloe's hand. She SCREAMS!

Shock ripples through the congregation. Vocal reactions reverberate. Many rise to their feet. Aron seats Daniel, rushes to Chloe, followed by several others.

At the rear of the sanctuary, the diminutive woman in black is gone.

"TO BEST ENSURE no permanent injury, it will be at least eight to ten weeks before you will be using that hand again, Mrs. Schneider." The hand specialist, Dr. Menninger, looks from the illuminated X-rays to Chloe.

"Please tell me you're joking. I have a show opening in March." Chloe holds up her right hand, now encased in a large, immobilizing cast, "This is the hand I paint with."

The doctor replies flatly, "Three fractured metacarpals is quite a serious injury. You are rather fortunate surgery is not necessary. The recovery time would have been considerably longer, otherwise."

Chloe turns to Aron, buries her face in his shoulder.

RIP! ARON TEARS a page from the typewriter. Angrily balls it up. Throws it across the room. "Fuck!"

Chloe stands in the doorway, watching him. "Aren't we the pair? I can't paint, and you have writer's block. Guess we'll have to go on the dole."

Aron laughs, "Maybe I will have to try my hand at fucking romance novels after all."

"Seriously though, this is as good a time as any for you to have writer's block. Until Daniel is back to work, there's no one waiting for that script anyway. Right?"

Aron nods agreement, "And that could be a while. I called him earlier. James said he still doesn't want to talk to anyone... Even me. It's been more than a week."

Chloe comes over and hugs him. "Sorry." She has a thought, "Call Jonathan, or one of your other friends. Go have lunch. Talk about anything other than Marion, Daniel, his mother, my hand, or the script. It will be good for you."

IN 1926, ALMOST forty-five years ago to the day, John Logie Baird demonstrated the world's first working television in the room where Aron and his friend Jonathan Demner now sit. The second-floor flat that overlooks Soho's Dean Street, is now Bianchi's, a private restaurant that caters almost exclusively to the entertainment industry. Elena, the petite and motherly (yet still sexy Italian owner/maîtres'd), flits from table to table. Not unlike The Ship, trendy establishments like this are a congenial mingling of Saville Row and King's Road types. Two of the latter, Aron and his friend, Jonathan Demner, another ex-pat American, a New Yorker, chat away at a corner table near the windows.

"Los Angeles? You're kidding?" says Aron, a bit surprised.

"Nope. If an asshole like our old friend Michael can go there and get something going, someone as charming as me." Jonathan pulls a face and laughs at his own words. "...Should be able to rock the world. Don't ya think?"

Aron smiles and nods, "I should try my luck too—someday."

"Shit, you'll have a movie or two under your belt by then. That'll make it a fuck of a lot easier."

Aron shrugs, "Yeah, if I ever get this script done." He pats his ever-present leather satchel.

Elena comes to the table with the bill. "Thanks."

Aron grabs it. "I got it."

Elena touches Aron's shoulder, "Mr. Schneider, when you see Mr. Cooper-Benson, please give him my sincerest condolences."

Aron smiles at Elena, "I will. Thank you."

As they come down the stairs and emerge into Dean Street, Jonathan remembers something. "Hey! Did I tell you about my friend Paul? From New York? The producer?"

Aron nods.

"I pitched him your cannibals in the Underground idea. He loved it!"

"Thanks. But I gotta finish 'Spells' first before I start thinking about something else."

"No, you don't. Chloe's right. Get away from it for a while."

"I'll think about it."

"Just do it!"

"Which way you going?"

Jonathan gestures, "I have a meeting near Soho Square."

"I'm heading the other way." Aron shakes his satchel. "Got to go to the Xerox place. Getting nervous not having a copy of the rewrite."

Jonathan gives Aron a hug, "Love ya, bro."

"Love you, too."

Aron watches Jonathon head up the street. He turns to go the other direction. Stops dead. Daniel, his gaze aimless, comes slowly toward him. Dressed more like himself than he has been lately, he's still not nearly as put-together as usual. Aron waves, but Daniel is oblivious. He walks right past. Gently, Aron takes his arm.

"Daniel…"

Daniel stops, turns. His unfocused eyes find Aron's face. No recognition.

"Daniel, it's Aron."

"Marion's dead, you know." Aron is stunned, but Daniel just repeats, "Marion's dead, you know."

"Where are you headed, Daniel? Are you by yourself?"

"Marion's dead, you know."

Holding on to Daniel's arm, Aron hails a cab. Just as he gets Daniel inside the cab, he hears a woman's voice shouting his name. He steps out of the cab to look for the source.

Elena looks down from an open window on the second floor. "Mr. Schneider!" she shouts. "Mrs. Schneider is looking for you. She is at the doctor with Mimi. She wants you to get there as soon as possible. Knightsbridge Pediatric Clinic."

Aron pales at the news. "Thank you, Elena."

SLAM! He slides into the cab next to Daniel. "Belgrave Square, then on to Knightsbridge Pediatric Clinic on Brompton Road. Fast as you can, please."

Amused, the cabbie replies, "Righto, Double O Seven!" The diesel cab clatters up the street.

CHLOE, FOR ONCE not her usual *'everything's cool'* self, jumps up from her seat in the clinic's waiting room. She runs to Aron, embraces him the moment he appears.

"What happened?"

"She just started vomiting and crying uncontrollably."

"What do they think?"

"They're examining her right now. They asked me to wait out here." She's upset, but also a touch embarrassed. "I think I was making them crazy."

Aron hugs her tightly. "I would have been worse."

A gowned figure, Dr. Bolotin, emerges from the examining room. "Mrs. Schneider..." He sees Aron. "And you must be Mr. Schneider."

Aron nods. "How is she?"

"We've calmed her a bit, but we still have no idea what is causing these symptoms. We suggest she be admitted, at least for tonight, so we can run more tests. One or both of you can stay with her overnight. Quite customary with a child her age. A nurse will be right out to attend to the details." He disappears back into the examining room.

"I'll run home and put somethings together for you and Mimi."

Chloe is surprised. "You're not going to stay, as well?"

Aron tries to fake a smile. "I'd only make you as crazy as you did them."

Chloe doesn't buy it. "What is it?"

He tells her about Daniel, says he wants to go back to the house to check on him.

"And what else, Aron. I know you too well."

"I have to find out what she wants."

Chloe is taken aback, "She?"

"Daniel's mother."

"I know who you meant. I just can't believe I heard that nonsense come out of your mouth."

Aron gets defensive. "Look at everything that's happened! Marion dying. Your hand. Daniel losing his mind. Now Mimi getting sick…"

"Coincidences, Aron. I'm sure you've heard of coincidences. A lot of scripts are built off them."

"Two, maybe three things can be a coincidence. But this is now beyond coincidence!"

"'Beyond' is the right word. As in, what you're suggesting is 'beyond'-fucking-belief."

"I have to do this, Chloe."

DANIEL WAS UNABLE to tell Aron where the new flat was, but James searched Daniel's desk and found the letter with the shelter's address. It's a two-hour drive southeast from London.

THE SUN IS just setting on Portsmouth as Aron pulls up in front of the women's shelter.

At the shelter, he learns that Mrs. Cooper-Benson has been by to visit several times recently. She had actually invited a few friends to tea at her new flat. One of her friends scribbles down the address for Aron.

THE FLAT IS in a very plain building, reminiscent of council housing in London. Aron notices a call box just a few yards down the street.

A NURSE POPS her head into the dimly lit room. Chloe sits near Mimi's crib and stares at her little girl. An IV and sensor wires entangle the sleeping child.

A whispered voice: "Mrs. Schneider?"

Chloe turns.

ARON CLUTCHES THE receiver the second he hears Chloe's voice. "How is she? How are you?"

"No change here. Mimi is sleeping. They're running all kinds of tests. Nothing yet."

"First of all, I love you and Mimi more than I can put into words."

"But you're a writer."

Aron smiles at his wife's wit.

"Aron, we miss you. We're worried about you, and we want you to come home…safely."

"I just want to talk to her. Maybe prove you're right."

"I'm always right. Don't you know that by now, silly boy?"

Aron's smile broadens.

"Be kind and polite. Promise?"

THE FLAT IS on the second floor of an apartment building that looks more like a motel, with each unit's door accessible from the exterior. Aron finds the correct apartment number and knocks.

No answer.

Knocks again. And again.

The next-door neighbor opens their door to reveal a craggy old man, cigarette dangling from his mouth, drunk and slurring. "You trying to wake the dead, mate?"

"Sorry if I disturbed you. I was just looking for—"

"That pompous old biddy what moved in there?"

Aron nods.

"Ain't seen her for days, lucky for me." SLAM!

Defeated, Aaron leaves. Unnoticed by him, a curtain in a window of Mrs. Cooper-Benson's flat is carefully pulled aside. Those unmistakable evil blue eyes watch him go.

A BLINDING FLASH of LIGHTNING! A deafening crack of THUNDER! The headlights of the Renault 5 pierce the pouring rain as they lead the car through the gates of Daniel's Kent estate.

Aron's eyes widen as he pulls to a stop, looks out. He leans forward, disbelieving. Through the rippling torrents of rain that cascade down the windshield, the house looks transformed. Writhing, creeping vines encrust the entire façade. He cautiously opens the car door. Steps out into the rain to confirm what he thinks he is seeing. Strangely, although he seems unaware of it, he remains dry amid the deluge. He steps toward the house. The undulating vines are there, and behind them, the front door flies open. He steps closer, peers through the vines into the dark void beyond the door. Aron fights his way through the tendrils, disappearing as they close behind him. The door SLAMS! shut.

It is other-worldly inside the house. There are no lights, just an eerie grayish glow that makes everything seem dead, emanating from everywhere and nowhere. The sound of the storm outside is gone. Silence.

Aron steps into the sitting room, reaches for the light switch, toggles it up and down. It neither makes a sound, nor does it turn on the lights. He takes a step. Even his footfalls are silent. Rubs his ears. Maybe they are the problem. No. He can hear his fingers in his ears. Stomps his foot. Hard! Echoey. In the distance, he hears it. Shouts, "You're here! Aren't you?"

His words come back thunderously loud. Endlessly echoing. Shock him.

Just as the echoes of his voice fade, the whole house rumbles. BOOM! BOOM! BOOM! BOOM!

His eyes dart up to the ceiling. Footsteps! Each louder than the one before. Suddenly, they go from a slow walk to a sprint. They draw Aron's eyes to the top of the stairs.

It's the tabby. It's huge! The size of a mountain lion. It ROARS! Springs toward Aron. He falls back, his arms stretched out to protect himself. Teeth bared, the tabby flies toward him. Then… vanishes.

Aron looks. Nothing. Then WHOOSH! Behind him, the fireplace explodes into flame. An inferno. The spindly hand shoots out from behind the flames. He skitters back to get away from its grasp. The hand and arm belong to an ancient hag. She steps out of the flames toward him. Her face is haggard, etched with deep lines. Her skin is gray, dead. Her lips are cracked and dry. But her eyes! They are those blue evil eyes of Mrs. Cooper-Benson.

Holding his leather satchel in front of him like a shield, Aron just stares. "What do you want?"

She just glares at him.

"What do you want!" he shouts.

The spindly hand shoots out. Its nails, like talons, sink into the leather satchel, rip it from Aron's hands. He dives to grab it back. She pulls away. Steps back into the flames. Aron again grabs for his satchel but is repelled by the intense heat of the flames. A SCREAM! Emanating from the depths of hell, fills the room. Still clutching the satchel, the hag bursts into flames! The SCREAM! continues as she transforms into ash. The SCREAM! fades. Her ashen form collapses. The satchel drops into the flames. The flames carry the ashes up the chimney. Aron stares in disbelief. The flames dissipate as suddenly as they began. Its light and heat sucked up the chimney with the ashes.

Totally undamaged, not a char from the flames, nor a scar from the talons, the satchel lies on the floor of the fireplace. Aron slowly reaches. Picks it up. Opens it. A rush of ashes, like a geyser, explodes from within. A HOWL! from the chimney draws the cloud of ashes from around him. Like the hag, they vanish up the flue. The satchel is empty.

A silent lightning-like FLASH! The colorless pall vanishes. The house transforms, returns to its cozy self. Everything is as it should be. There is nothing in the fireplace except the ashes and remains of the logs from the fire he had built on their first night there. Then he notices something else. Sunlight. He looks out the window. It's daytime! How could that be? It was pitch black and raining when he got here. His head reels. Have I been here all night? Did I dream all of this? Chloe must be worried sick. Or pissed as hell.

THE NURSE AT the reception desk answers the phone, "Knightbridge Pediatric Center. Mrs. Chloe Schneider? Thank you, let me check for you." She shuffles through the registry in front of her. "She's no longer here, sir. Her child was released this morning."

RING! RING! "HELLO? Aron! Where the hell are you? I've been so worried!"

"I'm so sorry, Chloe. I must have been so tired when I got here. I just crashed."

"Gotten where?"

"Not important. How's Mimi?"

"We're home. She's fine. They said it was just some 24-hour bug."

"That's good news. Haven't had much of that lately."

"Where are you?"

"At the house in Kent."

Chloe starts to ask "why" but changes her mind. "Come home. Please. Come home."

ARON ENTERS THROUGH the front door of the flat, stops dead. A smile spreads across his face. The endless hallway that cuts a swath down the middle of the penthouse is uncluttered and beautiful. The high-gloss, bright white woodwork perfectly complements the satin-finished mustard-colored walls. The gray runner that runs down the middle of the refinished walnut-stained parquet floors—although still mostly protected with butcher's paper, looks even better than imagined. There is still evidence of construction, but most of what is left to do now hides behind closed doors.

"Chloe!"

Chloe, Mimi in her arms, comes out the bedroom door. Hugs and kisses are exchanged. Aron gives lots of love to both. "This looks amazing!" Chloe nods agreement. "We owe Daniel our gratitude. He was right about finishing the common area first. You really feel the progress this way."

"Any word on how he's doing?"

"No."

"If you don't mind, as soon as I take a shower and change, I think I'll pop over there, check on him."

Chloe smiles warmly. "Of course, I don't mind. Mimi and I love Daniel." She nuzzles Mimi. "Don't we?"

THE DOOR OF the Belgrave Square mansion swings open. James, with an expression about as close to surprise as he is capable, looks out. "Well, how coincidental is this? Mr. Cooper-Benson just asked me to ring you. Please, come in." James motions Aron in. The door closes.

Aron eyes James. "He's alright?"

"Much better today, sir."

"Yesterday… at least I think it was yesterday… he didn't seem to recognize me."

"Yes, sir. It was indeed yesterday. But since then, he has received some news that jarred him back to reality."

"Where is he?"

"Upstairs, in his study."

DANIEL SWIVELS HIS chair as Aron enters the room. "My mother is dead," Although this proclamation is so matter of fact, it carries no emotion, neither sadness nor joy, it visibly shocks Aron. "Don't waste a moment's sympathy on that evil crone, dear boy."

"How did she die?"

"Fire. Apropos for a witch. Don't you think?"

"Where? How?"

"Seems some old drunk who'd been known to have set himself on fire several times while falling asleep with a lit cigarette in his hand managed this time to ignite the whole block of flats."

The face of the craggy old man with a cigarette dangling from his mouth invades Aron's very being.

The memory of the cigarette explodes into a fireball. The old man, and everything around him, is devoured by flames. Walls melt and burn. A Bosch-like image of Mrs. Cooper-Benson, lit by the blaze, stares defiantly until agony finally wins. Her flesh blisters, sizzles, and is consumed.

The same SCREAM! that echoed from the hearth again echoes endlessly. Daniel's voice, quoting Shakespeare, becomes an eerie narration behind the old woman's howl and Aron's nightmare vision.

"Eye of newt, and toe of frog, wool of bat, and tongue of dog, adder's fork, and blind-worm's sting, lizard's leg, and owlet's wing. For a charm of powerful trouble, Like a hell-broth boil and bubble. Double, double, toil and trouble; Fire burn, and cauldron bubble…"

Daniel's voice draws Aron from his vision, "It's been over 300 years since the last witch-burning in the UK…" A shrug. A slight laugh. "I'm not sad that my mother was the first to renew the tradition."

A VERY PLAIN headstone marks a freshly dug grave. The inscription reads:

Alice Cooper-Benson
nee Molland
Born September 21, 1896
Died January 26, 1971

"Fire burn, and cauldron bubble…"

Chloe, Aron, and Daniel stand at the foot of the grave in this barren, unsanctified corner of a large public cemetery. All three holding umbrellas to protect them from the light rain. Chloe also holds a simple bouquet of flowers.

The sullen looks on the Schneiders' faces are in sharp contrast to the grin that spreads across Daniel's. "I thought that epitaph was quite fitting, clever even."

Chloe looks at him, miffed, but the expression quickly softens. "You really hated her, didn't you?"

Daniel, his eyes locked on the grave, nods slowly. "She caused me nothing but pain my entire life. She took everyone I ever loved."

"But not Marion," Chloe says. "You told me yourself: the coroner's final conclusion was primary cause of death was a cerebral aneurysm, just like what killed her father."

Aron is surprised by Chloe's rebuttal.

Daniel refuses to take his eyes from the grave. "That proves nothing. It only identifies the weapon, not the killer."

Chloe is ready to respond, but Aron squeezes her hand and gives her a stern yet loving look that tells her to let it go.

Chloe lays the flowers on the grave. Without a further word, the three turn, slowly walk away through the maze of equally simple headstones.

In a tone of voice somewhat inappropriate to the time and place, Daniel reminds Aron, "You still owe me a script, young man."

"Can we please talk about that at another time?"

"Cemeteries spook you, do they?"

Their voices fade into the distance as they disappear into the rain.

Maybe it's just the rain, but the freshly shoveled dirt atop the grave seems to shift. It is more than just the rain. The bouquet of flowers begins to tremble as the ground beneath it shifts. Slowly, those aged spindly fingers reach up from beneath the soil. They grasp the bouquet. The flowers wilt, turn black. Petals fall. Turn to dust before they hit the ground. The hand recedes back into the grave, taking the bouquet with it.

Twelve figures, veiled in black, appear out of the rain. Hardly distinguishable, they surround the grave. A chant—that same familiar chant—softly rises.

ARON DIDN'T HAVE to explain to Daniel why he never finished the rewrite of "Spells." Daniel fell deathly ill within days of burying his mother. He died within three weeks. Like with his father, the doctors were at a loss for a diagnosis.

VOX CANIS

Carl Lucas

"THIS HARNESS BELONGED to your great-great-grandfather, Buckler.
It's more than fifty years old."

The older dog lifted the harness out of the antique wooden box
that kept it hidden from sight on the shelf in his closet. Buckler
watched with focused anticipation, as his father, Peleus, laid the
harness out on the ground in front of him.

"Your uncle wore it for a few years while he finished secondary
school. Before they gave him one of those yellow vinyl ones they
wear at the sanitation department."

Buckler marveled over the intricate designs stamped into the
leather. He leaned forward and breathed it in deeply. He could
still smell his uncle's scent buried deeply in the fibers, and faintly,
another scent he assumed was probably his grandfather's. The
buckles seemed more complicated than the modern -self-fas-
tening- versions he'd seen on other dogs. He placed a paw on
one and looked at his father inquisitively. The old dog smiled.

"Yeah, those are a pain in the ass, but once we get the size
right, they should fit for a while. You've still got some growing
to do, but not much, I reckon."

A flutter from the perch higher in the room indicated that
Peleus's vox, an aging Australian magpie, had fluttered down to
rest on Peleus' bright red harness. The bird winked at Buckler,
a trick Peleus had taught the bird when he was younger. The
bird leaned its head back and made the sound of the old dog's
laugh. "Unless of course you're planning to put on a few pounds
before the ceremony."

Buckler smiled and sneezed at his father in response. He approached the harness carefully and slipped his head through the loop on the back. He'd watched his father and his brother put their harnesses on many times, so he was mostly confident he could do it without his father's help.

He stepped his paws into the front leg hoops and used his nose to guide the brass perch where his vox would eventually sit—over his head and high on his back. Once he felt that the vox was properly lined up, he stood up and let the harness slide into place. The fit was nearly perfect.

Peleus smiled proudly at his son. His vox squawked an approval. "Like you've done it a thousand times."

Buckler squinted and wagged his tail. He romped excitedly into the kitchen to find his mother, a medium-sized, Span-iel-Shepherd mix named Asteria, preparing breakfast. His excited barking drew her attention to the leather harness. She squinted her gray eyes and smiled her approval.

Years ago, Asteria had lost her vox when a strain of histoplas-mosis spread among several species of birds. Doctors were able to administer antibiotics, which saved the vox of many a citizen that year, but Asteria was not so lucky.

After a vox dies, sometimes the owner will revisit the aviary, seeking to bond with a new vox, but Asteria never considered this. Even though her vox was unable to form words or under-stand what was happening to it, Asteria felt its pain. Its fear. And at the moment of its death, she felt its desperate scream to stay alive. Asteria had no interest in experiencing that pain again.

Buckler bounded over to the panel on the floor that contained the different colored buttons that puppies and other mute dogs used to communicate. He quickly punched in the sequence and a small, worn speaker on the wall responded in a monotone female voice.

"Do you like?"

Buckler frowned at the speaker and made an adjustment on the panel. This time, there was a voice with a more appropriate baritone.

"Sorry. Do you like?"

134 · CARL LUCAS

Asteria wagged her tail gently as a response and turned back to making breakfast. Buckler's face fell at his mother's muted response. He quickly pressed a sequence of buttons.

"What's wrong?"

Asteria paused to consider her answer. After a moment, she joined Buckler by the button panel. She changed the voice to "female" and entered her response.

"Very important. Caution. Must be safe."

Buckler wagged his tail.

"Yes. Always caution."

Asteria found his youthful optimism endearing and decided not to push the subject any further. She returned to her preparations just as Peleus's vox swooped through the door and into the room.

"I hope breakfast is as good as it smells from upstairs," the bird said.

Buckler playfully barked at the bird as it fluttered around the kitchen, checking its feeding perch for seed and diving in hungrily.

Asteria tapped a quick message on the panel to inform the room that breakfast was ready and carried a dish by its handle to Buckler's space on the large mat in the center of the kitchen that served as the table.

"I guess after today," the bird chirped between beak-fulls, "we'll need another perch and feeding dish."

Buckler shuffled over to his dish, only to discover his anxiety had returned. *I really hope so*, he thought.

Buckler headed down the street toward his school. These days, the city looked more like a jungle than a thriving metropolis, the plants having reclaimed most of the spaces where humans used to hurry along their busy lives. It had been almost fifty generations since a human being had stepped foot on these roadways, but somehow, the lights never went out.

Buckler's former history teacher had explained it like this:

Dogs throughout history were trained to understand human commands, perform basic tasks, and become more sophisticated with each generation, thanks in part to genetic memory.

By the time the humans disappeared, after the Big Sick, the dogs of this city were handling most of the day-to-day operations—more than anyone in the twenty-first century could have imagined. Canines maintained solar panels, water treatment plants, even basic manufacturing. A new canine social class was formed' but its entire ethos was dictated by their human masters.

The dogs were loyal and hard-working, and mankind benefited from their efforts right up until the end. (Buckler had always wished he could have met one, like a human child dreaming of dinosaurs.)

And after all the humans had disappeared, the dogs just kept working. They kept the machines serviced and running. They formed a complex government based on a caste system of labor. Some dogs worked on the farms, some dogs maintained machines, and other dogs distributed the products created by those machines. Every dog had a job to do.

Buckler looked across the street and saw a few of his old classmates, heading off to perform their daily tasks, their voxes swarming around their heads, chattering excitedly. Buckler barked playfully at his old friends. One of them, a female named Hilary, looked up at Buckler from across the street and smiled. Her vox, an Asian starling with green wing feathers swooped across the street to greet him, landing lightly on his harness.

"That's a lovely harness you have there, Mr. Buckler, sir." Her vox's voice was high and sweet, almost musical. But Buckler was biased. He'd had a crush on Hilary for almost a year and for a moment, it seemed like they might end up a pair. But that ended two seasons ago, when Hilary matched with her vox on her first try, along with most of the class. They all graduated from school and began working in their individual castes. But not every dog matched with a vox that day. Some had to stay in school and keep trying.

Buckler was now on his third and final attempt. If he didn't match today, he would start his adult life as a mute, one of the lesser members of society, charged with the most menial of tasks. The tasks themselves didn't bother Buckler, but the loss in status frightened him. The idea that he might not ever be good enough for Hilary. That she would always see him as just a dog. That she would never hear his voice.

He smiled at Hilary's vox, and shyly woofed a reply.

"Is it today?" the starling asked excitedly.

Buckler snuffed an affirmative and wagged his tail.

"You'll get it this time. I believe in you."

Buckler looked again to Hilary across the street. She smiled again and wagged her tail. Buckler suddenly felt a warm glow through his body. A glow that quickly faded as a large blonde Labrador named Fury stepped in front of Hilary, blocking Buckler's view. Fury was a year older than Hilary and Buckler, and already an established male in the Alpha class.

Everyone had their job to do, and the Alpha class made sure everyone did it. Enforcers of rules and schedules, Alphas served as general managers over the entire society. They usually came from good breeding stock, and a lot of their authority was handed down from their Alpha parents before them. And this particular Alpha had set his sights on Hilary.

Fury sent his vox, a large, jet-black raven, across the street to confront Buckler and Hilary's vox.

"Hilary, you're going to be late for your shift at the health clinic. You should catch up with the others." Fury's vox had a loud, sharp voice, painful to a dog's sensitive ears.

Buckler winced. He wondered if Fury was using the louder voice on purpose, knowing that the other dogs were safely across the street.

Hilary's vox turned to Buckler. "Good luck today."

Buckler smiled and wagged his tail as Hilary's vox flew back across the street and rested on her bright blue harness. Fury's vox lingered, looking at Buckler for an uncomfortable amount of time.

"Shouldn't you be on your way to school?"

Buckler's tail drooped behind him as he turned back down the street.

The school was an old human high school that had been repurposed after their extinction and had since been used for generations to teach dogs the basics of survival. It's here they learned how to read, how to spell, how to form human sentences and understand them. The school would assign dogs to a caste and then help train them to understand and perform the tasks expected of the caste.

Buckler's father was a manufacturer. He worked in the glass factory, making replacement solar panels for homes. Buckler had been learning how to build and install these solar panels and had become quite familiar with the rudimentary electrical system that provided the city with power. He wasn't an Alpha, but like every dog, his job would be an important part of keeping society moving. But still, it was a job he could do a lot better if he had a voice.

Buckler sat on his mat at the back of the class. He was the oldest dog in the school at this point and felt more than a little self-conscious about it. Almost full-grown, Buckler realized he was almost as big as their teacher, a Labradoodle named Xenophon, whose vox, a bright blue mockingbird, swooped around the class.

"I need you all to settle down. Blossom, Fencer, I need you both to place right now, so we can get started," The two dogs ignored Xenophon and continued rough-housing. Xenophon raised his voice. "PLACE! Or I'll put you both in detention. SEPARATE detention. Not fun detention like last time."

Both of the young dogs tucked their tails and sulked away to their mats. Buckler couldn't help but smile at this. When he was younger, he used to wrestle and get in trouble with Hilary like that. Xenophon's rebuke of young love brought back a wistful nostalgia for days not that long ago.

With the students finally in place, Xenophon stepped to the front of the class. "Today is a very special day, one steeped in tradition and vital to our survival as a society. Today is Vox Canis, and it's the very special day when some of you—hopefully all of you—will receive your voice."

Around the room, tails wagged excitedly.

"As always," he continued, "we start today with a video that teaches us the history and the science of Vox Canis. Because it's not only important that you understand why you have this ability, you need to understand why it is special and how it separates dogs from the rest of the animals on the planet."

Buckler stared at Xenophon like he was listening, but his thoughts were miles away. He was starting to feel afraid. Afraid that he might never match with a vox…

"Buckler."

Buckler snapped at his name being called.

"You've done this a few times. Would you mind helping me set up the video?"

Buckler wagged his tail and woofed an affirmative. Buckler was a good dog.

Using his paws and teeth, Buckler pulled down the screen in the front of the classroom and pushed the projector into place. He switched the projector on and bounced across the room to turn off the lights before returning to his mat.

The screen flickered to life with the image of a human scientist, Dr. Kellan Murphy, being interviewed by a tall blonde female reporter, sitting on a stage with her name, Rebecca, emblazoned on the wall in huge letters behind her. They were seated in large comfy chairs as the camera panned around to reveal a studio audience, all clapping dutifully as the applause signs lit up.

Buckler wriggled on his mat excitedly. He'd seen this video a few times now, and it made him happy every time. This was the video that explained his existence. This video was why he was special.

"…and so, we'd like to welcome to the studio today, Dr. Kellan Murphy—linguist, genetic scientist, and dog lover."

Several tails in the class wagged gently at this.

"*Thanks for having me.*" Dr. Murphy spoke with a soft Irish accent that had been flattened by years of university and public speaking. But if you listened, you could still detect it. Sitting next to him on the stage was a Border Collie whose name all dogs knew from the time they were pups. His name was Sparx.

"*Dr. Murphy, you've dedicated your entire career to understanding how dogs communicate and to helping expand their vocabulary. Is that correct?*"

"Yes, the bulk of my research over the last thirty-seven years has been working with these magnificent creatures. The aim was to improve training efficacy and to expand the range of their physical capabilities. In the early years, we started with a series of floor buttons as a way to train the dogs to understand sounds as language. They would memorize which buttons were attached to the words they wished to say. It was very simple, but overall limiting, as we could only provide so many buttons, and it became clear that the more our dogs communicated, the larger their vocabulary was becoming. To give you an idea of how hard programming a series of buttons was becoming, some dogs at the time could understand as many as a thousand words. That's more than twice the vocabulary of Koko the gorilla.

"For many years, I worked with computer scientists while we attempted to build voice boxes that could read brainwaves from the dogs and separate their thoughts into words. But these types of experiments couldn't happen without multiple painful surgeries, and I have to admit, once we had trained our animals to understand our language and to communicate their needs, it became impossible to go forward with such brutality."

"Why is that, doctor?"

"They asked us to stop."

"The dogs asked you to stop?"

"Yes. Once they could communicate their pain, we had no choice but to stop hurting them. The effects of this phenomenon had a profound impact on myself and my staff. We learned we couldn't ethically cut open a healthy brain of a creature that could verbalize their fear and suffering. It fundamentally changed the way we worked in the lab. But also, it changed who we are as people."

"But that wasn't the end of your life's work."

Dr. Murphy chuckled. *"For a few years, it was. We continued to work with the dogs to teach them more words and by doing so, we learned a lot about how they communicate. Which as it turned out, is far more complicated than science previously thought."*

"How so?"

"When we began studying canine brain waves, we discovered that when dogs communicate with humans, they activate a similar

part of their brain that humans do, but when they communicate with other dogs, we observed an increased activity in their pineal gland and the secretion of a hormone that could be sensed by other dogs nearby."

"Through this discovery, we were able to conclude that dogs could communicate their thoughts, emotions, and desires through hormones. And the more vocabulary we taught them, the more active their pineal glands became when communicating with other dogs. However, this seemed to create a level of frustration between the dogs, since they now wanted to communicate the more complicated human sentences to their playmates but had to default back to the button boards in order to do so."

"The dogs wanted to talk to each other the way we talk to them."

"Yes. In hindsight, it was inevitable."

"Amazing. So how did you cope with this issue?"

"For years, we studied the hormonal release from their pineal glands, and we developed genetic supplements to help expand the abilities of the organ in an attempt to make their original form of communication more complex. But this only frustrated the dogs further, and we almost abandoned the project altogether.

"But then one evening, I stumbled across an article about bird songs, and I learned that bird songs form inside a bird's brain in the same place as a human's mind forms words. We already knew that the complicated voice boxes of many birds were able to recreate human words, something we've seen before with parrots and parakeets and magpies, but it turns out that the ability to mimic human sounds is actually present in far more birds than we originally realized. Birds such as ravens and crows, even seagulls, all had voice boxes capable of the range required to mimic the human voice. They just choose not to.

"And, if you know anything about birds, you'll know they also have pineal glands. After our discoveries about how dogs communicate, we began to attribute this same phenomenon to birds, specifically as to how they fly in flocks, with all of complex spontaneous movements—turning and diving simultaneously.

"So, I asked myself, 'If dogs lack the vocal abilities to form words but have this ability to telepathically send their thoughts

and ideas to other dogs, and birds seem to have this same ability, what if dogs could telepathically send their thoughts to birds, who could then translate those thoughts into sounds. Sounds that we as humans could understand."

"I'm sorry, I want to make sure the audience understands. You aimed for birds to function as the voice of dogs, so they could talk to us."

"And each other."

"And how did you go about accomplishing that?"

"Well, we started feeding our test birds versions of the same genetic supplements we fed to the dogs in an effort to not only stimulate their pineal glands but also to create enough genetic similarities in the two species that their instinctive, hormonal communication methods would hopefully connect the same way they connected with their own species. And after a few years of these treatments, we eventually succeeded."

"You telepathically connected a dog to a bird."

"That's a bit of an oversimplification, but yes, essentially. It took years of hormonal genetic therapy to achieve, but we did it."

Rebecca looked down at Sparx, the loyal Border Collie who had been sitting obediently next to Dr. Murphy.

"And is this one of your test subjects?"

"Yes, this is Sparx. He performed the first successful avian bond in our initial subjects and has been communicating with us by proxy of a myna bird." Dr. Murphy motioned to an assistant offstage, and the assistant brought out a birdcage, with a large myna bird perched inside. She set it on the table between Rebecca and the doctor.

"So, this dog—Sparx—can understand me, and not only that, but he can talk back to me by way of this myna bird?"

"That's correct. Perhaps now would be a good time to turn this interview over to Sparx, and you can ask him a few questions instead."

"You want me to interview the dog?"

Dr. Murphy looked puzzled. *"I was told you were willing to do this."*

Rebecca laughed. *"Yeah. I mean sure. But I thought you were going to do the button thing again. I thought this would be just a more advanced animal trick or something. I wasn't expecting... this.*"

"*I apologize. It's hard to prepare someone for what you're about to see. Please, talk to Sparx like you would anyone else who would come on your show.*"

Rebecca chuckled and smiled nervously at the audience—shot a glare at her producer. "*Do I talk to the dog or the bird?*"

"*Either. They can both hear you, but only the dog can understand you.*"

"*Um...okay. Hello, Sparx. I'm Rebecca. Welcome to the show.*"

Sparx stopped panting and stared directly at the reporter. After a brief pause, the myna bird suddenly chirped up, its voice nearly human.

"*Hello, Rebecca. Happy to meet.*"

The audience gasped as Sparx stepped forward and lifted a paw. A gobsmacked Rebecca slowly reached down to shake hands with Sparx. As she did, the audience erupted into cheers and applause. Sparx whimpered slightly at the crowd response.

"*Many people. Bright lights. I am anxious.*"

Rebecca was suddenly filled with concern. "*Don't be anxious sweetie. They just can't believe what they are seeing.*" She turned back to Dr. Murphy, astounded. "*How could you... Why would you do this?*"

"*Excuse me?*"

"*Why would you dedicate your entire life to teaching another animal how to talk?*"

Dr. Murphy looked down at Sparx, who looked back up with the look of love and adoration that only a dog can give. "*I've dedicated my entire life to these noble beasts. I have never known another creature to be this loyal, to love this unconditionally, to put the needs of their pack before their own. These creatures are a special gift.*" He ruffled Sparx behind his ears. "*And I always wondered what a creature like that would have to say about the world and how they viewed our place in it. I believed we could gain wisdom from that. And what is life, if not a pursuit of wisdom?*"

BUCKLER AND THE rest of his class stood outside a large dome nestled in the center of what used to be the city zoo. A large sign with the word "Aviary" hung over the entrance. A few older dogs milled about the outside, pushing hoop brooms and doing other tasks to maintain the building that housed the scores of birds bred with very specific genetic traits.

Xenophon instructed his students to queue up, and Buckler purposefully positioned himself at the back of the line. If he failed again today, he didn't want to do it with the entire class watching.

"Alright, pups, let's get started. I will walk each of you into the aviary airlock, I will give you one last round of instruction, and then you will enter the aviary on your own. If today is your day, you will find your voice. Or more appropriately, your voice will find you. Good luck to you all! Telamon—you seem eager, so I guess that makes you first."

Telamon, a Boxer pup with spindly legs, excitedly followed Xenophon into the airlock. A few minutes later, he reappeared, a bright green parrot resting on his harness. He barked at his classmates and his new vox squawked an impossibly loud "Hello!"

The other dogs barked excitedly, and his friends surrounded him, congratulating him with nuzzles and yips.

This repeated for a few hours, as one by one, the dogs entered the aviary, and one by one, they each emerged triumphant, a bird riding atop their harness, singing song lyrics or reciting poems, or—as was the case with one mischievous Bulldog—shout out every swear word in the book.

A smiling Buckler made a mental note that one of his first words should be equally rebellious.

Xenophon scowled at this but allowed it. It was up to each dog to decide how to use their voice, and Xenophon had taught them the best he could. He smiled with satisfaction as each member of the class found their individual voices, and he secretly delighted in hearing the unique tones that each voice seemed to bring.

Before long, it was Buckler's turn. Xenophon turned to Buckler. "Are you ready, pup?"

Buckler looked nervously back at his classmates, all distracted and shouting over each other. Volume control and decorum would eventually come, but for these students, today was their first Vox Canis, and when you discover your voice for the first time, it's usually hard to keep quiet.

Xenophon took note of Buckler's anxiety and quickly made a decision. "Telamon! I need you to gather up the class and help me walk them all back to school for graduation. Buckler and I will be there shortly."

"Let's go, pups! Line up!" Telamon shouted like a drill sergeant, and a few of the dogs mocked his authoritarian tone ("Someone thinks he's an alpha all of a sudden..."), but the mood was too high to be spoiled. Chattering away, and mostly ignoring Telamon, the dogs filed out of the zoo.

Alone now, Xenophon turned back to Buckler, who stared at the aviary with fear. "I know this isn't your first time. I know you've felt this disappointment before. But I also know that whatever happens in there today, the dog who comes out will still be Buckler. A kind, clever dog whose life will not be dictated by the turn of a single event.

"So, I want you to put your fears aside. I want you to clear your mind of anything but what's happening right now. I don't want you to be worried about what you're going to say once it happens. That will take care of itself. Once inside, I want you to close your eyes and concentrate only on reaching out and finding that heartbeat. The one that beats in a rhythm that complements your own. It'll be faster than yours, but once you hear it in your mind, feel it in your bones, you'll know. It will almost be like you exist in two places at once. And in that moment, I want you to think of only one thing, loudly and clearly: your name. And I want you to place that thought into the new presence. And when you hear your name, I want you to open your eyes and realize that what you heard was your own voice for the first time."

Buckler looked up at Xenophon and smiled. He was ready.

Buckler stepped into the aviary for what would be his third and final attempt. Above his head, hundreds of different birds fluttered around, squawking and nesting. Buckler found a good spot, roughly in the center of the dome, and sat down.

With a deep breath, he closed his eyes and began to concentrate. His ears twitched as he heard birds chattering above him. He folded his ears back and concentrated harder. His own heartbeat filled the silent void in his head, but there were no other heartbeats to hear. Nothing for him to latch onto, to bond with. As the minutes ticked by, Buckler's hope of finding his voice began to fade.

And that's when he heard it. Just a fluttering at first, but something other than his own heartbeat was suddenly making noises inside his head. This new sound excited Buckler.

Slowly but surely, the heartbeat became clearer, and Buckler concentrated harder than ever before. Yes! This was it! His vox was here, and it was time to hear his voice. Smiling, he conjured up a single thought: *Buckler*. He tried to send the thought into the mind of the creature whose heartbeat was pounding in his head, but just as he reached out, he heard something else. A second heartbeat?

Buckler was confused for a moment as this second heartbeat began to fall into a rhythm with the first. And then suddenly he heard a third. And a fourth. Buckler's head began to fill with the frantic heartbeats of dozens of birds. Wait…

Hundreds.

Buckler kept his eyes clamped shut, desperately trying to separate the first heartbeat from the chaos in his head. It was too loud. He couldn't think. He began to feel dizzy. He wasn't sure what was happening, but he knew if it didn't stop, he would pass out. He couldn't let that happen.

Overwhelmed, he began to feel himself slip from reality into darkness, the drumming of the hearts now unbearable. Clinging to consciousness but refusing to open his eyes and break the connection, Buckler screamed out of his brain the only word he could hear in his head.

"PLACE!"

Hundreds of birds all shouted the same word at the same time and simultaneously, every bird in the aviary fell silent, along with the chaos in his head.

That wasn't supposed to happen, Buckler thought, a new fear creeping in.

Buckler opened his eyes and was startled to discover hundreds of eyes perched all around him—all staring, waiting.

Unsure of what to do, Buckler slowly walked forward, nervously looking over every bird nearby. The birds all stared back, silent.

Stepping toward a tree growing in the center of the dome, Buckler noticed one particular scrub jay with blue streaks and black feathers. The feathers on its head were ruffled and formed a crest shaped like a little crown. Inexplicably drawn to it, Buckler closed his eyes and reached out with purpose. He quickly found the bird's heartbeat, matched it to his own. Feeling an almost zen-like control, he formed the words he wanted hear and willed them into this new vessel.

"Buckler," the scrub jay said. "You son of a bitch, you did it. You found your voice."

Once bonded, the rest came easy. He simply willed the bird to go where he wanted. The bird didn't seem to mind, believing each new thought was its own inspiration. Buckler's thoughts began to fill with visions of what the bird could see and hear. He told the bird to soar around the aviary and almost immediately made himself dizzy, even a bit nauseous.

He laughed and willed the bird back to rest on the harness on his back. The scrub jay happily complied, finding a small cup with food waiting for it. This was going to work out perfectly for both of them.

Buckler trotted happily back to the air lock, but was taken aback by a stunned Xenophon, the teacher's face a mixture of awe and fear.

"What's wrong?" Buckler's new vox spoke clearly and at a proper volume. "I found my voice. I did it."

Xenophon's vox stammered in search of words., The dog's hind legs trembled with fear as he slowly backed away. "Don't do that again," he finally managed to get out.

"Do what?"

"Don't…connect with all of them again. It was too much."

Buckler's posture became submissive. He was afraid he might have broken a rule. "Did I do it wrong?"

Xenophon sat down and took a deep breath. "You connected with every bird in the aviary, even mine out here. I felt you touch its thoughts, and for a moment, you seized control. I couldn't speak. You were in charge of my vox. I had no voice."

Xenophon looked at Buckler with severity. 'Listen to me, Buckler. What you did is special, but in a dangerous way. The power to control others' voxes, to literally speak in their voice on their behalf, is a power others would try and abuse. You must promise me you will never use it again."

Buckler was scared. "I... I promise. I don't even know how I did it the first time."

Xenophon continued. "And we must keep this a secret. No one can ever know. Swear you'll never tell another soul what happened here today. As far as anyone knows, your match was made like any other. Without incident."

Buckler swallowed hard. "I swear."

Xenophon's bristled fur relaxed. "Good."

The two dogs started the walk back to the school, Buckler wresting with his thoughts, Xenophon musing quietly to himself.

"Nothing good will come of this, I'm afraid."

HOLOGRAM STORE

Brea Grant

"THERE'S NOTHING UP that way but a hologram store."

The woman in fatigues stared at Crystal, expecting some kind of explanation beyond that. Staring used to make Crystal squirm, but not anymore.

"From the '90s. It never closed down," Crystal added.

The woman didn't respond. She looked exhausted.

Fatigued, Crystal thought. *Fatigued and wearing fatigues… that's kind of funny.*

"You know with the necklaces that have a big eye in the middle of them? In a pendant—"

"I get it," the woman huffed. "You know you're not safe here. This area is full of debris."

Crystal hated it when people talked down to her. She lifted her hands to shrug but the restraints pulled back tightly, clanging against the hard metal of the yellow food court chairs.

There was this day back in Junior High when a guy—some kind of community leader—came to Crystal's classroom to teach the students about advertising. It was supposed to be one of those things where the kids were educated about the dangers of media, but instead, the girls just talked about how the magazines the guy brought in were outdated. This one part stuck with Crystal, about how fast food chains choose yellow and red decor so you leave faster and make room for more customers. Those colors trigger something in humans that makes them want to get up and go.

Crystal tugged at her restraints tied to these stupid yellow and red chairs and thought about how the Heaps o' Pizza she was sitting in front of probably could've used more customers back when they were open.

The other two soldiers hustled around the corner in their makeshift military gear.

"There's nothing that way. Just one of those weird hologram stores. I didn't even know those things were around anymore."

At that moment, Fatigued started to look more like 'Pissed' as she lifted a gun to Crystal's head.

Guns, Crystal thought. She used to have a great amount of respect for them. She once watched a guy accidentally shoot himself at a party. Like, in front of everyone. He was showing off and made a joke about pulling the trigger. Then he did. She could barely even look at them after that. Not even in the movies.

But then all this shit happened and Crystal, along with everyone else, realized there were way scarier things in the world—or the universe, rather.

Crystal always disappeared into her own thoughts when things went to shit. Thinking of how the world went from alright (depending on who you were) to fucking terrible overnight. Everyone was just trucking along and then the world as everyone knew it came to a sudden end. Aliens or whatever came down and they left a bunch of junk behind in the form of swirling black holes that killed a large percentage of the planet. The few who survived could easily be divided into two categories: 1) Leave me alone, I've survived enough (that's Crystal); or 2) Assholes. The people standing in front of her were assholes.

Anyway, she thought, *I'm not really scared of guns anymore.*

"Answer me now. You said it's just you in the mall?"

This lady reminded Crystal of those *Law & Order*-type shows, back when she'd sit on the couch and marathon them. That's the dumb shit she missed. Eating ice cream out of a tub, watching the detectives get the run around until…BAM, they solve the case. *They never fell for the dumb tricks the criminals were trying to pull.*

"ANSWER ME!" Fatigued yelled, jolting Crystal out of her Mariska Hargitay fantasies.

"Just me," Crystal responded. "Just me, living alone, in the mall."

"Look, one of our team members is severely wounded," the weary looking guy who confirmed her intel about the hologram store pleaded. "Please, just help us out."

Their buddy inside the Heaps o' Pizza let out a wet, raspy breath. He got a little too close to one of the giant vortexes that dot the landscape around the mall, and he wasn't doing well. He needed immediate medical attention.

So, these folks aren't sticking around for long, Crystal thought. This place was a chock full of alien debris and even the small ones could sneak up on you. Crystal would be walking around and a new one would be right in front of her. And even the little ones, ones that hide behind a door or a shelf, could do just as much damage as the big ones. Once they have you, they rip you apart, limb from limb. No matter the size.

Fatigued dropped the gun, as if to give up.

This woman has given up a lot. Crystal could tell by the look on her face. She spent the pre-apocalypse dealing with complicated people—soldiers, bureaucrats, kindergartners—and it had made her so damn tired.

Can't feel bad for her though, Crystal thought. *Because she is definitely an asshole.*

"You understand we are trying to help you, right?" Fatigued was gearing up for a rant. "This town is in the middle of a contamination zone and you should have evacuated over a year ago. This would go a lot faster if you would just tell us who else lives here and we can all get the fuck out."

"There's someone else over here!" the random soldier yelled, interrupting what Crystal expected to be a long tirade. And like a bunch of good *Law & Order* characters, they all ran towards him. *Damnit.*

When all this shit went down, Crystal really saw the assholes come out. They came in different versions, sure, but they were all jerks.

It wasn't a great time to be a nice person. It's hard to be nice when you can't trust anyone and the Internet goes away. Remember the Internet? Those were great times. Crystal sure could've used the Internet when aliens showed up because every dumb idiot thought they knew everything since they had seen a science fiction movie or two and there was no Internet to prove them wrong. Who can you trust when the guy from the Jiffy Lube acts like he knows what the hell is going on?

Crystal stayed quiet, trying to hear what they were doing. They were probably all staring in through the gate on the front of Big Ben's Furniture. Because that's where Randy was. Inside, not staying hidden. Even though that's what he was supposed to do. Not that she blamed him. Not like he knew any better.

The noise of the store's heavy security gate being lifted made Crystal sit up straighter.

"There's an old man over there," Fatigued stormed back. "You said no one else was here."

"He doesn't really count."

"It looks like he's living in there," she added. "And he said he was the mayor."

"Maybe he is," Crystal responded. "Look, he's sick. I need to take him to the bathroom, okay? He's been in there for too long by himself. Let me do that and then I'll tell you everything. I promise."

"He doesn't know what we're talking about. He seemed surprised about the alien—"

"*He's sick*," Crystal said again.

Fatigued rolled her eyes as she let Crystal go.

Thankful to be released, Crystal grabbed Randy by the hand and led him to the bathroom down the mall corridor.

INSIDE THE BATHROOM, Crystal heard Randy unzip his fanny pack and pull out his comb. He was supposed to be brushing his teeth but vanity always got the better of him, so he started with his hair. *Hopefully he would use just a little bit of toothpaste this time*, Crystal thought as she listened to Randy hum a Woody Guthrie song to himself. He never could remember *all* the lyrics but he surprisingly remembered some of them. He always said Woody Guthrie was the quintessential American songwriter.

But humming meant he was not brushing his teeth.

"Are you brushing?" Crystal called from outside the bathroom.

"Yep!" Randy responded.

"Did you go to the bathroom already?"

"Mind your own business, Crystal."

"Okay. But did you?"

"Yep."

"You need help brushing?"

"Hell no," Randy responded, a little angry.

Fatigued joined Crystal outside the bathroom. She had come from Big Ben's, said she needed to make sure Crystal wasn't hiding anyone else in there, but Crystal knew that they just wanted to take anything good Crystal had hoarded.

"Dementia?" Fatigued asked.

Crystal nodded.

"My grandmother had dementia," she said plainly.

Crystal used to worry about getting old. There was this one day in particular when she noticed that the skin on her arms was starting to web and become loose, no longer clinging tightly to the muscle and bone. That was the first sign of aging she ever noticed, and she was pretty young at the time. But everyone has their own thing. Lines on their faces. Sagging tits. Or seeing your parents get older. Watching their sharpness start to go. Their hearing get a little worse. The light in their eyes start to disappear as they fade into the past.

But now something different brought everyone together. That realization that everyone is going to die felt different. It felt more realistic because they'd all seen it up close and personal.

Suddenly, Randy started up on the chorus.

"*This land is your land… This land is my land…*"

"You're not brushing if you're singing!" Crystal reminded him.

Fatigued couldn't help but crack a smile. Maybe she wasn't an asshole. "Where were you two before this?"

Crystal was working at a nursing home when it happened. Most of the workers left and never came back. They had families to worry about. Their kids were at school. It all happened so fast. One minute we were all watching the news. *An alien landing. What the fuck?* And then all this "debris" they left behind. Debris that treated human bodies the way fucked-up kids treat grasshoppers.

Pretty soon, the family members started showing up to the nursing home, people Crystal had hardly seen before that. They were grabbing their parents and grandparents. At first, Crystal's boss urged these concerned families to keep their loved ones at the nursing home. Many of the residents had needs that could only be cared for by professionals. But eventually, even that jerk looked around and decided it was time to go.

Crystal didn't have anywhere to go. No family, really. No one to worry about. No one worried about her.

"Just living a normal life," Crystal replied.

"From California...to the New York island..."

"He seems kind of old to be your dad," Fatigued commented. "What's your name?"

"Crystal." She hesitated when giving her name. *Did Fatigued catch that? Hopefully not.*

After it all happened, it just ended up being her and Randy. He was the last patient left. No one had come to get him. Crystal called his family but so many people were killed. Who knew if they were still alive? The folks on the news were quick to call all of East Texas a hot spot. Whoever didn't die, fled. Randy's kids could have been in either camp. And they had kids themselves. Maybe they decided that taking care of a 75-year-old man with Alzheimer's during the apocalypse might bog them down.

On her first day at the nursing home, Randy said Crystal looked like his daughter. The longer they were alone together, the more confused he got. His daughter's name was Crystal, which was a pretty name. So, that's who she became after the world ended. Who was she to correct him? She had kind of let her life go off the rails before the aliens anyway, so why not just become someone new?

At some point, the television finally went to just snow. Randy looked around, and as if noticing for the first time, asked, "Where is everyone?"

"I think we're alone," Crystal responded.

"I don't need anyone else if I have you, Crystal. My daughter is all I need."

And he meant it. Crystal didn't think twice about it. She decided to take care of him, keep the assholes away, and make this hotspot of a town their own.

Starting anew sounded kind of great.

Fatigued spoke again. "You said you'd tell us who else was here."

Crystal sighed. "There's a person in the public library. A former librarian. Two or three teenagers live on Edson Street—over near the gas station. And I think there are some people in tents near the lake outside of town."

"That's it?"

"That's it."

"We'll come back tomorrow and get you. It's not safe here."

Crystal gritted her teeth. She really did hate when people talked down to her. It's not like she couldn't see the hundreds of swirling black holes ready to take her and Randy out at any time. Of course it wasn't safe here. But was it really safe anywhere? And isn't safety relative at this point?

"You're not doing him any favors keeping him here," Fatigued added.

And that's all Crystal could take. She could deal with the gun, she could kind of deal with being talked down to, but this was an asshole move. Crystal was a trained nurse. She knew how to take care of Randy. It was literally one of *the only things* she knew how to do. And now this lady was being questioning that? What happened to respect for the front line? Dammit. Crystal really hated assholes.

"Actually, there's another person," Crystal added quickly. "In the hologram store."

"I didn't see anyone."

"They live in the back. Probably hiding."

"Thanks," Fatigued said as she gathered up her team.

Crystal hurried Randy up, tucking his toothbrush back into his fanny pack, rushing him back towards Big Ben's. Randy complained, but Crystal knew he would forget about it in a few minutes.

She just didn't want to hear it—their screams when they went into the back of the hologram store. That one almost got Crystal a couple of weeks ago. She was looking for a stupid necklace, just something to cheer Randy up. But if she had taken one more step in, she would've been ripped to shreds.

She pulled down the metal gate in front of Big Ben's and locked it from the inside.

"Dinner?" Crystal asked Randy.

"Sounds good to me." He smiled and settled in on the couch. "I love dinner with my daughter."

Crystal smiled back and tried to ignore the screams she could hear in the distance. *Was that a gun shot?* She opened a can of tuna.

"Dad, you wanna sing that song again?"

He did, drowning out the noises from outside the store.

THE WORLD OFTEN ENDS

Justin Benson

ALONE AT THE rocky edges of the Pacific Ocean, it was deathly still among an undulating kelp forest. The light of the late afternoon sun shined atop the murky sea water, but the ghostly refractions beneath the surface failed to reveal the enormous form resting upon the seafloor. Some animals could feel its presence as the thing passed through them, but most could not.

The Insacrient knew the end was always coming no matter in which planet, galaxy, universe, dimension, or otherwise it dwelled. It did not hate, love, or experience any other emotion itself, but it could sense the desires of the creatures all around it. It felt the will of all things, and the destruction or creation used to pursue that will. Entropy guided its annihilating touch, but the mechanisms for how it did so were beyond material comprehension. Here in 1999, in this universe, on this expiring planet, it was aware of everything happening in every universe across all of space and time. To know all of infinity was too much to feel, but this apocalypse would be the exception.

It held the young body with the markings until the convulsions ended. It absorbed the child's destruction the same way stars eat nuclear fusion.

The rising tide lapped against the young man's pallid skin, sending a small cloud of sea flies off his milky eyes, the insect frenzy eclipsing the later afternoon sun. And as a sea anemone closed its tendrils and lunged its barbed nematocyst into a mackerel, the Insacrient sensed a muffled splashing up at the surface.

Sharing that same patch of sparkling saltwater, Leticia felt her arms were nothing more than hollow bones covered in what would someday be dust. Feeling her board under her lifting ribcage, the lactic acid in her shoulders and triceps burned. The sound of her heavy breaths grew louder in her head. The swell picked up speed as it walled up over the abrupt change in depth. Feeling her board accelerating over the ledge just slightly faster than the rapidly forming wave, she felt a sense of satisfaction buried in her nerves. She gripped the fiberglass with her teenage hands, preparing to sweep her feet under her and onto the pimpled surf wax.

But as the swell completed its transformation into a hatch-back-size chamber of water thundering toward shore, a terror shot through Leticia. She instinctively pulled her legs to her twiggy ribs, straddling her surfboard, stopping her just short of the ninety-degree drop down the face of the accelerating wave. The pitching barrel to her right growled.

Northward along the coastline, Leticia was sucked back toward the angry trough left in its wake, briefly flailing like a dog learning to swim.

From her count, this was the seventy-eighth time she had failed to commit to riding the beastly reef break barrel. Tallied on the Kelly Slater calendar her mother bought her for Christmas, she indicated the failures in blue Sharpie so the losses could neither be ignored nor erased. But she also knew that the dangers of not making the drop were very real. Horseshoe was the rare Southern California reef break with real consequences, and it was a spectacle to all who witnessed its power up close. Her shame of letting another barrel go to waste was further softened as another terror took its place: three more waves in the set lined up on the horizon of the Pacific, each bigger than the next. By missing the initial wave, she had paddled herself square into the trio's impact zone.

She frantically paddled for the horizon. As the reef boiled with escaping air from the prior wave, her cupped hands seemed to have stopped exerting any force on the foamy saltwater. And as she pushed down to duck-dive the first wave of the clean-up set, she heard her board's skegs slice through eelgrass, grinding into the rocky reef. Weightless with the biochemistry of survival, she felt the ice-cold water crash down upon the sudden shallowness of the barbed underwater crevices, the rush of water taking her.

The lip of the wave cracked onto the shallow water of the reef, and Leticia's body went from feeling powerless to non-existent in the sudden vastness. She thought this must be how astronauts feel staring back at Earth for the first time, except there was no wonder, just a desperation to not snap her neck and drown. Before she submerged to complete her duck dive, she looked to her left and saw the gaping maw of the barrel.

In the videos she rented from surf shops and dubbed using her mom's two VCRs, the cylindrical tubes of water always looked so beautiful. Often presented in graceful slow motion, they looked almost like a gentle amusement park ride made of something softer than water. In reality, they were things of speed and power, responsible for countless bloody wounds and broken bones. Riding one would be more like BASE jumping than meditating, but she craved the accomplishment all the same.

Underwater, the garibaldi that guarded their rocky dens watched as she was sucked backwards toward the rumble of the passing wave. Air trapped in the barrel blasted out the back of the wave like horses set free in a minefield. The rainbow display of light that sparkled in the mist made Leticia think of her mother and her jesting commentary on the end-of-the-world prophecies said to happen when the clock struck midnight on January 1, 2000. She knew them all by heart: the Y2K computer formatting error; Jerry Fallwell's prediction that God's final judgment would happen on New Year's Day; the Nuwabian Nation's belief that all the planets of the solar system would collapse into the sun. But none of the predictions would get it right, because on New Year's Day 2000, fifteen-year-old Leticia would save the world.

In the turbulence of the passing wave, the bubbles seemed to change the density of the water in a way that felt impossible to swim against—like swimming through thin air. Her lungs burned as she clawed for oxygen. She finally burst to the surface and gasped for air, but amid the turmoil, the urethane leash at her ankle became too taught and snapped the board back at her, straight into her forehead. If not for the adrenaline, it would have felt like the first time she was punched in the face by a girl rollerblading at the basketball courts by her mom's apartment.

In the depths beyond the reef, the Insacrient felt more in tune with Leticia as her blood flowed from the fresh cut on her head. Its ancient instruments of curiosity examined her. It sensed something in her fear, something it did not yet understand. It still desired to end the world—just like it had so many others—but Leticia presented one last curiosity.

Swimming to the surface encompassed by infinity, Leticia did not feel herself pass through the Insacrient's unknowable mass.

Back on shore, she ripped the Velcro leash and rinsed her board in the ankle-deep water. She looked back to the sunset on the horizon. There were only a couple surfers remaining in the lineup, and an evening glass-off was settling in. The paddle out and back to shore from the unusual rock reef formation unsettled Leticia. She often wondered if sharks in the deep observed her with their primordial senses, just barely detecting that she is not their normal food. She had read somewhere that sharks were pretty particular about eating seals, so she always bought colorful wetsuits to make the distinction easier for them. When curious seals popped up in her peripheral, she sometimes mistook them for surfers in black wetsuits, even tried to strike up a conversion with a few. But at the end of the millennium and apocalypses seemingly everywhere, a shark attack seemed like an even bigger personal tragedy in the comparative triviality of it all.

A great white shark was in fact nearby this evening, but its senses were so overwhelmed by the Insacrient that its three hundred serrated teeth barely twitched when a seal swam passed its face.

Ankle-deep in fluffy white sand and the smell of rotting seaweed, Letitia again paused to admire the last waves of the day. Winter west swells were messy, usually attacking the reef as one giant wall of water. But late summer south swells like this one hit the reef at the perfect angle, creating a giant tube that pitched out into a meticulously formed, violent barrel that sounded and felt like a million units of hydraulic energy. The peak formed a perfect A-shape, the left peeling a growling tube that spit the mist of trapped air before tapering shut. The right was a brief roller coaster shot into an opposing wave that sent aerialist surfers up to twenty feet into the air, landing in the deep-water safety beyond the reef. The nature-made ramp was really just a visually interesting parlor trick that took little wave-riding skill. Riding the barrel, however, was something that Letitia respected more than anything else in the natural world.

The expansive kelp beds outside the surfline enhanced the evening glass-off, rendering the water surface into an olive oil-like texture. But Leticia's admiration for the ocean's last gift of the day was interrupted by a drunken yelp—a decayed mouth of teeth and sun-damaged lips yelling angrily at something with a cackle. The locals of this beach were a special kind of human wreckage forged in an island-esque isolation. As Leticia walked toward the crumbling stairs that led away from the beach, some particularly crusty old locals drank their daily dose of malt liquor, drunkenly smiling at the tiny trickle of blood extending from where her surfboard hit her forehead. They were dangerous on the wrong day, when they didn't recognize you, but their violence was reserved for the male surfers from out of town. They didn't know she wasn't from La Jolla, but she was pretty sure they knew she wasn't a boy. She reasoned that this is why she had access to the better waves, which made her feel even worse about her crippling fear of them.

On display in front of the wall where the drunken locals sat, like aqueous carnage meant for their leathery skin amusement, was the break simply known as Marine Street. Massive shore-break sent stoned body-wompers kamikazing through the exploding watery pits, then rolled them onto the white sand like sadomasochist walruses. Leticia heard rumors that once every century or so, Marine Street became one of the best surfing waves on the west coast. At the end of every millennium, they said. Supposedly, it was like a perfect day at Lower Trestles, but only the most faithful would get to ride—the ones who believed and showed up when the time was right. It was just folklore though—like old watermen telling tall tales about whales breaching the surf line-up, or rabid seals attacking tourists.

Down the beach, Leticia noticed several lifeguards urgently pacing between the shoreline and the next street over. It was unusual to see lifeguards this time of year, since the summertime crowds full of tourists were long gone by now. Leticia looked to another beach access street called Dunemere. She had only seen the wave in front of Dunemere break during giant northwest swells, the kind that punctured ear drums due to the sudden and immense change in water pressure. On those freezing-cold winter days, grizzled watermen holding broken boards with bleeding ears was a common sight.

Leticia asked a platinum-blond kid in a Volcom T-shirt what all the fuss was about.

"They think that guy Johnny—the one who rides those old wooden longboards—they think he drowned. They found his board down at Rockpile."

Leticia expressed sympathies and moved on. Her interactions with Johnny were limited to a nod and a grin every so often, but news of his death was still quite a shock. She knew he identified as a skinhead of sorts. He even had a Nazi tattoo on his upper thigh that she could sometimes see when his shorts bunched up at the waist, but he never bothered her despite her skin color.

It was the second death this year, the first being a kid who broke his neck while fighting with a Windansea local at a house party up the street. A freak accident that seemed preordained as 2000 years after Christ loomed down on humanity. It had put a media spotlight on localism, but the violence remained. In her decade of conscious existence—basically since her earliest memory of riding La Jolla Shores whitewater at five years old—Leticia had observed surf culture and noticed it was full of unsavory attitudes that defied its softer public image.

The latter-day hippies with environmentalist stickers on their station wagons were often the same people practicing their own brand of conservative extremism. Caught up in hyper-traditional ideologies masquerading as stewardship, the conflicts were often determined by their chosen wave-riding equipment or geography. The longboarders hated the shortboarders, the shortboarders hated the bodyboarders, everyone hated the kneeboarders, and anyone who lived east of Claremont was a *fucking kook*. It reminded Leticia of the wars she learned about in school, the ones involving the Abrahamic religions. She knew there was a darkness running through all of humanity alongside nobilities of equal measure.

Leticia's mother had finished her run on the beach earlier than usual and was already waiting in the car, with the heater running. The cold-water currents and upwelling had come early this year, and even in her four-millimeter-thick wetsuit, Leticia's toes were numb. She peeled off the wetsuit, exposing her bathing suit top, then wrapped a towel around her waist and pulled the neoprene legs off. There was always the awkward moment of tugging the sand-caked, bunched-up ankles off, but she had learned years ago the balance needed to steady herself and not trip around the parking lot. Near her crumpled wetsuit, extending from her skinny ankles like a mutilated shadow, the sidewalk was stained with old surf-wax graffiti, some proclaiming *kooks go home*. Something else caught her eye in the chipped red paint of the nearby curb—a strange symbol that confused Leticia with its geometry.

The Insacrient floated above her now. If it had a shadow, most of San Diego would have been cast in darkness.

She disliked the feeling of toweling off the sand from her frigid toes before getting in the car, but the discomfort would save her from cleaning the floor mats later. From the CD player, *Pennywise* screamed on low volume, and Leticia was charmed that her mother would always unconsciously drive faster when Leticia played her pre-surf-session amp mix. The melodic skate punk fueled Leticia—it was the perfect score for pulling into a barrel at Horseshoe and smacking a giant 180-air on the way out. The reality, however, was usually hopping around tiny, windblown slop, or like today, failing to conquer her fear of the powerful thing she wished to ride.

The Insacrient followed Leticia home, soaring above them along the 5-South all the way to Barrio Logan. Dwarfing the murals of Chicano Park, it observed Leticia's every emotion, thought, and movement, like a single measurement of the cataclysm.

When Leticia and her mom got home, there was a man standing in front of her apartment, selling tamales to skateboarders. On a nearby porch, some men in cut-off Ben Davis pants, work flannels, and heavily starched short sleeve solids watched over it all with bagged liquor, not unlike the drunks in La Jolla. When Leticia and her mother first moved here to K and 20th Street, fleeing from her mother's last boyfriend, some of these original neighborhood gang members had stopped by. One of them walked with a limp and had a knife-wound on the left side of his shirtless belly, with "619" tattooed across the scar. They regarded Leticia and her mother, then kindly said that if they ever needed anything to let them know. They never spoke again but would often smile and nod from their run-down craftsman porch. The roosters in their backyard would announce the start of every day. She wondered if getting a scar tattooed is painful.

As Leticia rinsed her wetsuit using her apartment building hose, her cat ran from under the heavily modified, robust chrome exhaust of a '94 Honda Civic to a large Victorian home on the street perpendicular to her own. Leticia laid her wetsuit across oil-stained concrete and followed the cat. The massive Victorian home it ran to was highly conspicuous among the otherwise low-income apartments built in the '60s. Its ornate moldings and mysterious old-world stained glass were placed in sharp contrast to the *Día de los Muertos* ornaments and calavera textures of the adjacent duplex.

A silver-haired woman with root-like toenails told Leticia that the home was constructed by a spiritualist from Europe in the 1800s, long before the rest of the neighborhood was built. The owner was said to have died upright at his piano, playing his final song. A sign outside said "Ville Montezuma," and it was sometimes open for tours, though most patrons were afraid to park their cars nearby given the reputation of the neighborhood.

Whenever Leticia looked inside the house, she half-expected to see phantoms, but she never saw anything except a dark room.

The Insacrient sensed Leticia's wonder. A century ago, it had heard music from this dusty place, and despite having little interest in the ape-like animals that inhabited this planet, it had listened.

Pulling up to the beach the next day was a surreal sight. The first storm of the season had taken away the white sand, exposing rock formations patterned like demon fingers beneath the wall where the crusty locals normally gathered. A salty, middle aged, blue-eyed man who referred to himself as a "La Jolla native" sat with his feet dangling above the sea-rock abyss, swigging from a forty-ounce with abandon, his smile broader than his beat-up Rainbow-brand sandals. Among the craggy sandstone and dead kelp, a glint caught Leticia's eye. A strange metal circle was fused into the rock, like an otherworldly drainpipe oxidized for thousands of years.

It was actually much older. So old, in fact, that to those who experience time, the two millennia that followed the more well-known messiahs would be rendered insignificant by comparison.

All of Horseshoe was a mess. Massive close-out upon massive close-out slammed into the exposed rock of the extreme low tide. Leticia looked to the daytime full moon, its tidal force seeming to rattle a nearby rusty stop sign that a stoned driver had hit last year.

What was truly unusual, though, was that right out front at Marine Street, the conditions were more painterly and perfect than Leticia had ever seen in Southern California.

Through her mother's dirty windshield, she could see where the storm had stolen the sand into the ocean. But the soft white tufts of geological grain had not gone far and had created a temporary sandbar over the deep-water reef. Swells from thousands of miles away in the southern hemisphere of the Pacific Ocean were now creating the mythological waves she thought were the fictions of tale-telling surfer bros.

Marine Street looked like a nautical miracle, an idealized painting of the California coast. Perfect six-foot walls of oily smooth glass unfolded so uniformly, they looked man-made. Neither too big nor too small, they peeled along the coast with a tranquil beauty. The autumn Santa Ana winds from the east created a surreal mist atop the peaking waves.

Just then, there was an explosion that shook the dead-end asphalt. Some teenage boys had tossed a seal bomb into the storm drain, their Seaforth Sportfishing T-shirts stained with Taco Bell and Mad Dog 20/20. They ran off in laughter as a drunk local threw a full can of Natural Ice at one of their heads.

Just beyond the break line, several people held hands in a circle. This must have been the memorial for Johnny. Large swells gently lifted their carefully perched torsos sitting atop their boards and rolled them toward that newborn sandbar.

The Insacrient did not understand the ritual but had seen ones like it on this plant for hundreds of thousands of years. According to its infinitely layered observations, a single life of their bipedal kind leaving this world to rejoin the rest of existence was like a shifting breeze that never stopped.

Leticia walked carefully along the sharp stones until she came to the metallic circle in the rock made naked by the storm. If she knew what it actually was, she would have buckled at the immensity of it. This was just a small part of a structure that was bigger than the Grand Canyon, older than the Earth's minerals, and concealed for eternity in a cavern as large as San Diego itself. If some curious UCSD chemistry grad student had chosen to examine it, they would have discovered that though this isotope appeared terrestrial, it was not.

Hovering above Leticia like a dragon made of vapor, the Insacrient knew it as a construction too old to be forgotten, from a world more advanced than the one that now suffocated and burned this place. A world before the giant reptiles, before the giant insects, before the last several mass extinctions. A world that could no longer be detected in the fossil record of the beings who now inhabited it, protected inside an alloy created from the rarest of elements.

Leticia looked upon the glinting material and shrugged her indifference at what was to her some rusty metal. The Insacrient watched her indifference and its desire to restart this world returned, its incomprehensible form pulsing with disdain. If Leticia's senses were not limited to the survival of her species among mere Earthly threats, she may have observed a force so dark that immediate suicide would be the only reasonable response.

The water had gotten even colder overnight from the big surf's upwelling, and massive sheets of seaweed had fractured from the offshore kelp beds creating a dark brown shorebreak at the south end of Marine Street. Leticia had body-surfed in this kelp shorebreak before, and the feeling of being trapped under the heavy seaweed was a claustrophobia that she would not endure again. The kelp that had made it to shore was now covered in those undulating clouds of flies, and it smelled like dead possums rotting in the sun. The crusty locals had gathered once more on the graffiti wall and were now smoking skunk weed and laughing at a tweaker who had fallen off the railing into the exposed rocks below.

The Insacrient could feel the energy of another end approaching, but in this moment, its invisible soup of subatomic particles vibrated mostly for Leticia.

Knee deep in the frothy ocean, Leticia lowered her board onto the water, climbed onto the rash-like pattern of surf wax on the deck, and paddled out.

The waves were precise, almost mechanical, every single one beginning in the same triangle frame to the south, then peeling along an elegantly tapered shoulder. The pattern was so easy to navigate that there was no duck-diving whitewater, and thus no painful rush of cold water into her wetsuit. She paddled onward with her unusually dry hair tickling the sides of her face.

Leticia watched the curling insides of the perfect empty barrels. She observed the crack of the lip hitting the shallows below it, and the rumble of gravity asserting itself upon hundreds of pounds of cold sea water.

The Insacrient knew of the ancient place that was buried in the sand. It knew many others like itself that had dwelled in that place long ago. It knew how these entities used red fluid and soft matter to create doorways. It knew how to manipulate massive bodies of water to create the perfect vessel for getting back to the rest of its kind. But it knew nothing of the beauty that Leticia experienced out there on her board.

The Insacrient did not displace water as it looked up from the eel grass at Leticia's legs dangling from her surfboard. It did not move any Earthly matter at all as it simultaneously communed with what was at one time its home. It examined the top of the Leviathan building encased in the long-forgotten metal and remembered a time when millions like itself worshiped at its base far below—back when they moved in vessels powered by a system of propulsion that no longer existed, perceiving things with senses that no longer operated in this world. It was clear to the Insacrient that death, the universe, and whatever the universe was expanding into, are all the same thing. To the Insacrient, infinity was the same duration as one second. But for as alien as humans were to the Insacrient, there were still certain things about them it could understand—like their desire to destroy.

Leticia, however, desired to live in harmony with what surrounded her.

The Insacrient sensed the waves from a far-away ocean approaching. Having set them in motion, it knew they would soon form the cylindrical geometry needed to travel home. These ripples had voyaged many miles along the darkness of ocean canyons, gliding over the ghastly titans unknowable to the Homo sapien mind.

Despite its fascination with this one particular organism using the strange fiberglass instrument to ride its vessel, the Insacrient began to commune with the protruding apex of the ancient structure. It felt both the immense power of the architecture below—a device with the power to remove every sphere in this solar system—and the amusing distraction that was Leticia's anomalous spirit.

She was approaching the Insacrient's cylinder, one of the few it would use to get back to its world once this one was no more.

Like so many times before, Leticia felt her heart pound in her chest as she paddled as hard as her body would allow. She again felt the surge of cortisol and stomach acid, the sudden realization of how truly insignificant she was in comparison to the ocean, the universe, and the totality of all that is, ever was, and ever will be. As the swell became a watery cliff over Marine Street's mystical sandbar, her palms pressed into the fiberglass of her board with an unusually confident grip.

The water was so clear she could see the contours of the sandbar even as the sea rapidly surged upward over its shallows. She hopped onto her board, her feet landing exactly where she had hoped. Then, before she could catch her breath, her stomach was in her throat. She had dropped in faster than she had anticipated, just barely avoiding a disastrous freefall. Despite the surprise, her rail and skegs gripped the water, and her bottom turn was spot on. Muscle memory took over and she found the perfect line on the face of the wave. Time slowed and distorted, as all of this normally would have taken place over what a human observer experiences as about two seconds.

What Leticia didn't know was that the fabric of spacetime had *actually* evaporated in that moment.

She ducked down as the lip curled above her head and cast her sun-kissed form in shadow. It was quieter inside the barrel than she had expected. The sound of the barrel lip slamming into the sucked-out shallows was like being inside a cave and hearing a waterfall far in the distance. Water continuously sucked out from below her, the fiberglass under foot crackling each time it reconnected to the slope of the barrel. Her legs burned as they stabilized, but increasingly it felt like she wasn't moving at all. The water moved around her, but the relative speed of the barrel to her board made the tube appear frozen in time.

She looked to her left, to where the face of the wave had become a half-pipe of glistening sea water, the psychedelic reflections like the oily rainbow seen in puddles. She gently touched it with her hand, creating a calligraphy-like brush stroke that traveled up, around, and over the aquatic cylinder.

She pulled back her hand and allowed new water to travel up the walls of the emerald room and erase what she had created. She looked at her reflection in the wall of water and saw her past, present, and future, her death and her rebirth. She saw cities she'd never traveled to, people she didn't know, loves she had not yet experienced. Her tears mixed with the waters of the ocean.

In that moment, the awestruck Insacrient's focus abandoned the ancient instrument on the beach, and it felt a shift in the pattern of all it comprehended. It knew the liquid cylinder could send it home, but it did not know where the cylinder would take the beings of this plane who were to be caught in its destructive path.

Leticia looked straight through the emerald wall of water at herself, still crying at what she did not know, oblivious to the gigantic entity mere inches from her face. The exit to the barrel grew wider, and her board fired like an arrow toward the opening. Her head kissed the thinning lip of the barrel as she shot out into the open air right as it closed behind her, a spit cannon of spray cooling her back.

She kicked off the dying wave and sank several feet into the ocean until she came to a stop. Lowering her body to a prone position on the board, the Insacrient knew nothing of her pure smile, but it did not matter.

The Insacrient knew what she was—knew it could not end a world that had yielded such a creation.

Leticia would paddle back out to grab a few more waves before the sun set, her worries about the future left to another day.

That night, Johnny's body calmly bobbed in the shoreline, the dissipating waves gently nudging him to the shore. A blue shark had scavenged his left ribs and a piece of his right leg where the Aryan tattoo used to be, but otherwise, he was intact. On his pallid lips was a smile, and in his stiff fingers a handful of seaweed. The Insacrient considered this sacrificial creature with the strange markings, then thought again of Leticia. Despite the mercy she had unwittingly provided this world, the Insacrient would eventually create another cylinder to travel home among the never-ending cataclysms to come. But for now, it would return to its deep-sea abyss to hibernate among the many beasts reigning beyond the senses of man.

TOP SECRET This document consist of ___10___ pages.

Cy. ___1___ of ___1___ Cys. Series: ___C___

Copy ___ Must 7 copies, each ___
of 10 pages

FUGAZI

TOP SECRET

AUG 2 1975

OFFICE OF
INFORMATION ASSURANCE

446-45
946-72-A
Document No. 13

TOP SECRET
AUTHORIZATION
Name _____
Date 8/5/75

DEPARTMENT OF DEFENSE
MILITARY LIAISON COMMITTEE
P. O. Box 1814
Washington 13, D. C.

EXCLUDED FROM GDS

TOP SECRET

Baker 9

C446

322

ASSISTANT SECRETARY OF DEFENSE
MILITARY LIAISON COMMITTEE
P. O. Box 1814 Washington 13, D. C.

TOP SECRET

Serial: F 0762
2 August 1975

TOP SECRET

TOP SECRET

MEMORANDUM FOR OFFICE OF INFORMATION ASSURANCE

SUBJECT: FUGAZI   C446

PURPOSE:

    1) To advise you of the details concerning a report made by Lt. James Morris to the Chairman of the Military Liaison Committee for the Assistant to the Secretary of Defense. 2) To incorporate pertinent information concerning an attack on US soldiers engaged by unknown entities into the FUGAZI case file. 3) To share the transcript of the detailed account to further a potential investigation.

BACKGROUND:

    On July 12th, 1975, an after action report was received, detailing a failed mission that led to an encounter with unknown entities after a helicopter crash on Nui Ba Den (Black Virgin) Mountain in Vietnam. The report details the entities with which the squad engaged, led by Lt. James Morris and the subsequent KIA's of Pvt. Derek Leemon, Cpl. Jerome Distrito, Ssg. Harrison Grant, Pvt. Lamarr Bridges, Pvt. Jacob Dahl, and Pvt. David Perez. They were not engaged in conventional combat and were killed by these alleged entities. We could not recover their bodies for further confirmation.

OBSERVATION:

    Lt. James Morris is credible and does not seem to be under any sort of psychological distress that would impair his judgement. He remains one of the most respected and decorated soldiers the United States has to offer, serving in every major conflict since WWII, with multiple tours and commendations.

    Even with limited evidence, this corroborates testimonies by other soldiers. This could be a new biological threat on the battlefield, using citizens as weapons; a method we saw the Nazis try to employ, years ago.

RECOMMENDATION:

    A disinformation campaign is recommended among the ranks of soldiers recently deployed to the region detailed in this report and returning soldiers in the US. With our withdrawal from Vietnam imminent we suggest swift and quiet action from your unit.

    We do not suggest actively discrediting Lt. James Morris. We do not foresee security issues arising in his promising military career, as we do with other soldiers who have been deployed in this region.

    If you approve, it is recommended that we cite this report alongside others of tiger attacks, and wildlife sightings, citing fatigue and distress as a determining factor in the misidentification of threats.

Baker 9

- 1 -

322

TOP SECRET

TRANSCRIPT

Interviewee: Lt. James Morris
Interviewers: Dr. Carl Walske, Dr. James R. Cowan, Dr. Steve J. Lukasik
Date: 1 August 1975

WALSKE: For the record this is DR. CARL WALSKE, Chairman of the Military
            Liaison Committee for the Assistant Secretary of Defense, DR. JAMES
            R. COWAN Assistant Secretary of Defense (Health and Environment) and
            DR. STEVE J. LUKASIK, Director of Defense Advanced Research Projects
            Agency. Can you state your name for the record?

MORRIS: Lieutenant James Morris.

WALSKE: Thank you, Lieutenant and for making the time. I know you've already
            been given a debrief, but the initial report made its rounds and
            well...

LUKASIK: We're very interested.

MORRIS: Where do you want me to start? When I saw...

COWAN: Whatever you're comfortable with...

WALSKE: Your character or your credibility isn't under review, Lieutenant.
            You've fought in every major war since World War II. You're an
            exceptional American and a hero.

MORRIS: You believe me.

LUKASIK: You're not the only one who's seen it.

WALSKE: Let's take it from... the crash. We'll give a brief description of the
            mission in the report.

MORRIS: According to our intelligence, there hadn't been patrols on the
            mountain for weeks. Did someone explain to you about the mountain?

WALSKE: Yes , to me. But not Steve and James. The top of the mountain is
            controlled by the United States where we installed a radio tower and
            the rest of the mountain is controlled by the NVA.

MORRIS: Yes, that's right, sir. As soon as we exfilled the radio station we
            were struck by small arms fire and then what I believe was a Dshk
            12.7mm MG that finished the job.

COWAN: How'd you discern that?

- 2 -

MORRIS: I've been shot at a lot sir, this was my first time getting shot down.
            It had to have been a large caliber and you can't mistake the sound.
            It's been around since the thirties, even when I was in WWII. On the
            way down I managed to keep us level and not spin. The trees slowed us
            on our way down and we crashed with no serious injuries.

WALSKE: And can you point to on the map the whereabouts you crashed?

MORRIS: Q27, sir.

WALSKE: And you made contact here?

MORRIS: With a group of female fighters, yes.

LUKASIK: Not the NVA?

MORRIS: No. They were dressed in a uniform I'd never seen.

WALSKE: And their description matches the reports given to you before this
            debrief, correct?

MORRIS: I hadn't heard about this--

LUKASIK: It's not widely known among the ranks.

MORRIS: Soldiers talk a lot, so I hear a lot.

LUKASIK: Not when we want to keep it quiet.

WALSKE: Can you state their description for the report?

MORRIS: They didn't wear any concealment. They dressed like the women in the
            villages we'd seen daily, but they wore a white hood on their heads
            that also concealed their faces. Like if a nun's hood had a mask
            attached to it and holes cut out for the eyes.

WALSKE: Were they armed?

MORRIS: Yes... they had our weapons. M16, .45s, M1 Carbine, and one had a hand
            grenade that went off during the firefight.

WALSKE: How many were there?

MORRIS: Seven. And one child.

WALSKE: A child?

LUKASIK: There's nothing in here about a child.

MORRIS: No, I left her out of my initial report.

WALSKE: Why is that?

COWAN: Lieutenant?

- 3 -   322

TOP SECRET

MORRIS: Sorry – I didn't include her because I didn't think she was important.

WALSKE: But now you do?

MORRIS: Yes sir.

COWAN: Was she killed in the firefight?

MORRIS: No, after the hand grenade went off and the tree fell, it was quiet until we heard her crying. She was next to the fallen tree. Couldn't have been more than ten years old. Stood there shaking with an AK in her hands. Next to her was a fighter whose legs were pinned underneath the tree. We didn't know at the time, but that's when we saw... what would be the things that attacked us later on. The little girl seemed

LUKASIK: Describe what you saw pinned under the tree?

MORRIS: That's in my initial report—

LUKASIK: I didn't read it. If you don't mind repeating yourself, Lieutenant... please.

MORRIS: Ok... The trunk of the tree had crushed the fighter's chest, but the head and the entrails were ejected from the cavity in the neck.

LUKASIK: What did the cavity look like? Was it torn? Was there a lot of blood?

MORRIS: No. It was clean, like that's how it was supposed to function, but the tree falling on it kept it from escaping.

LUKASIK: You're saying the entrails were pinned from the weight of the tree?

MORRIS: Yes, keeping it from escaping.

COWAN: Escaping? The force of the tree didn't do that?

MORRIS: That's what we thought. We were wrong.

WALSKE: So you're saying this was one of the creatures?

MORRIS: Yes sir.

WALSKE: And the child? Is she dead at this point?

MORRIS: No sir, we all decided that we were going to take her with us and keep her safe.

LUKASIK: And your squad was okay with you making that decision? There wasn't any pushback?

MORRIS: I'm the leader, and whatever decision I make is everyone's... That's why this is my fault.

WALSKE: Their lives?

MORRIS: Their deaths.

WALSKE: I'm not exactly following. You didn't choose to get shot down.

TOP SECRET

MORRIS: No sir, I chose to take her with us. That's what got them killed.

COWAN: If we're going to talk about--

WALSKE: Sorry doctor, but I'd like to get back to what you just said after you're done.

COWAN: Of course, as do I... I want to ask about Private Leemon's injuries.

MORRIS: What about them?

COWAN: How did they come about and how did the symptoms manifest?

MORRIS: After the firefight and disarming the girl, we trekked down the mountain without incident for about forty five minutes. But we could tell we were being followed. It was getting dark and there was this vibrating noise, it kinda sounded like a speaker that was on but wasn't playing music. The sound would zip over the top of the trees or alongside us. They were always around us. That's when Leemon got stung. None of us saw it, but he said that it lifted him about five feet off the ground, stung him, dropped him, and took off.

COWAN: Stung?

MORRIS: Yeah, it was a large puncture that had immediately begun to swell and wasn't bleeding. Reminded me of a scorpion sting. I got one in New Mexico during a drill. Looked just like it, but there was a rotten smell to the wound like it was festering, it was already turning black and green.

COWAN: Where did the creature sting him?

MORRIS: Shoulder area near the neck. I'd say about an inch deep.

WALSKE: You didn't see the creature?

MORRIS: Not yet. You want me to--

WALSKE: No no, finish for the doctor.

MORRIS: What else did you want to know, sorry.

COWAN: The symptoms.

MORRIS: Right- just give me a second. It's- Not easy to talk about. He was a kid... eighteen.

COWAN: Take your time. You want a water or coffee?

MORRIS: Is it okay if I smoke?

WALSKE: Go right ahead.

MORRIS: Thank you, just a second... Ok. The Private started to experience a burning sensation.

Baker 9

- 5 -

322

COWAN: Where? Around the wound?

MORRIS: No, he said throughout his body. Down to his bone. I thought it was
            more of him being traumatized than actual pain. Soldiers can
            sometimes invent injuries in their head after a battle or close call
            to try and slow things down. So, I elected to keep moving and about
            twenty minutes later he showed me his arm.

COWAN: Which arm? The same side as the sting?

MORRIS: Yes.

COWAN: And it was swelling?

MORRIS: No, it looked like one big blister and when you moved it, you could
            feel that it was full of fluid. It felt like a water balloon.

COWAN: What did the medic say?

MORRIS: Our medic, Distrito, went to drain it, but as soon as he did he noticed he
            couldn't feel the bone in Leemon's arm... Distrito kept asking him to
            wiggle his fingers but his hand... the best way to describe it is it
            was like a medical glove filled with water. That's when Leemon took a
            turn. This is the part I don't like to talk about.

COWAN: Do the best you can? It might save others if this happens.

MORRIS: I don't think you can save anyone from this.

COWAN: What happened?

MORRIS: The puncture the medic made wouldn't stop leaking fluid, and as he
            kept checking him he started to notice that the bones in Leemon's
            shoulders were missing. We quickly came to the conclusion that he
            was dissolving from the inside. That whatever bit him had some kind
            of venom that could... do this. Leemon died shortly after that. I
            couldn't give you an exact amount of time... it was minutes. It just
            tore through him. I've never seen someone in that much pain. We tried
            to give him morphine but it would just open up another hole in him
            and he'd start leaking everywhere.

COWAN: Was anyone else bitten?

MORRIS: No.

WALSKE: Then you saw it shortly after?

MORRIS: Yes sir, almost immediately.

WALSKE: Can you describe it?

MORRIS: It was getting dark, everyone was shaken up but we were moving at a
            good pace. I kept the child near me on my left so I could protect her
            and raise my rifle. We came across this woman on a walking path we

- 6 -

322

Bakers

had found. We knew it was probably for patrols but at this point, I was fine with shooting at whatever moved. As soon as I put the child behind me... there's this uncorking sound... and her head detached from her body.

WALSKE: The child's?

MORRIS: The woman on the path. Her head detached, and her body dropped to the ground and she was just a floating head with all of her organs exposed. You could smell it... it was metallic vinegar odor. The spinal cord was still attached but it could move independently and it curled up in an attack position. Her teeth were so white... you could see them perfectly in the dark... they looked lit up. That's when I heard the sound that I described in the earlier attack. That speaker sound I was describing... it seemed to be her entrails, vibrating. And that's when I noticed she could also move certain organs independently as well.

LUKASIK: Jesus.

COWAN: What about the body? Was it still intact?

MORRIS: Looked to be. It looked like the skeleton was still intact, but like I said from the firefight before, there wasn't any tearing, it was a clean detachment.

WALSKE: And that's when you were attacked by more?

MORRIS: Yes sir. Again, I heard that uncorking sound about thirty meters away, but it was multiple times. At least a dozen. We tried to shoot them, but they would dive on us from above the trees. They seemed to be able to use their entrails as limbs and their spinal cord as a stinger, exactly like a scorpion... Distrito, our medic, was wrapped up into what I think was intestines. He was taken somewhere else. I heard his screams travel across the treetops southbound, and then kept going until it got quiet... not because he was dead but because of the distance. Then Jacob... well he got... he looked like a shriveled up raisin. I don't know what they did to him. It looked like a bite, or he was gashed or gored by something but if I had to guess? It was a bite. That's when it became clear we couldn't engage them effectively, so I called for my last two soldiers to run.

WALSKE: Where's the little girl during all of this?

MORRIS: In my arms, I had picked her up. I should've realized right then and there.

WALSKE: What?

MORRIS: That's why they weren't attacking me.

WALSKE: Is this when you came upon the village?

Paket 9

322

MORRIS: Yeah, we thought we were saved. They took us in, fed us, and cleaned up the girl. It didn't strike us as weird at the time but... there were no NVA there. It was all women and this strong smell of vinegar.

LUKASIK: This isn't in the report; it says you fled the village after it was attacked.

MORRIS: I know. Because I didn't have time to think about it.

WALSKE: What's the importance of the village?

MORRIS: That's where they worship these things or keep them or where they live... I'm not entirely sure. The only thing I could think of is what I was told when I had R&R in Malaysia... I doubt this would be pertinent to the report because it's a folktale.

COWAN: I'd be interested, if anyone objects?

WALSKE: Go ahead, Lieutenant.

MORRIS: I was playing poker with some marines and the dealer was an older local. He told us this story. Probably a story they tell kids so they don't run off into the jungle, about this monster... The way he told us, well it scared us half to death... He called it a Penanggalan.

WALSKE: Ok. Satisfied Doctor?

COWAN: Yes, but one question, do you think it was a Penanggalan?

MORRIS: As a member of the United States Military? No.

COWAN: Personally?

MORRIS: Yes.

LUKASIK: Why?

MORRIS: Because everything the dealer described matches what I saw... it just didn't fit the tale... But war changes everything. Every deployment, soldiers talk about seeing or hearing or encountering strange things. It's part of being in a place you don't understand, but... I still don't understand what they were.

LUKASIK: Are they a weapon? Do you think?

MORRIS: No, not at all. For a number of reasons.

LUKASIK: What reasons?

MORRIS: Because of what happened in the village.

WALSKE: Can we get back to the village? Agree?

COWAN: Good for me.

- 8 -

322

TOP SECRET

WALSKE: Continue Lieutenant.

MORRIS: After they fed us, they dropped these walls of a thatched building that looked like an exposed church. There was an altar and rows of baths instead of pews. As soon as the walls came down there was an overwhelming smell of vinegar. Before we could realize what was happening, they had me and my soldiers restrained to stakes that were spaced out in front of the church. It was some sort of ritual... and then the uncorking sound again. The women that had taken care of us started to sing and the... whatever they were... entities came in from around the village out of the jungle. They hovered over to the altar and dipped their organs into the baths. They did it in the way birds bathe. It was quick and splashed everywhere. The singing continued throughout. Then I saw the child. She had symbols on her clothes... she was special to them for some reason. Which... thinking about it now... they didn't come for us after the crash... They were escorting her to the village. They ate my men in front of me and dipped their entrails in these baths of vinegar. They were saving me for the end I think. But that's when I got free and killed one with a knife.

LUKASIK: So they're killable.

MORRIS: Sorta.

WALSKE: That's when you got away?

MORRIS: Yeah. I knocked over some kind lantern that started a fire in their church and... grabbed the girl and headed for the base of the mountain. I fought like hell, signaled for the LZ, and that's when I got picked up. I'm sure the pilots and everybody else saw them chasing after me.

WALSKE: The smoke you laid down helps a bit but there's about ten witnesses that saw. Where's the girl? She was with you? Wasn't she?

MORRIS: Yes, sir. I thought I was protecting her. I thought I was giving her a chance at escaping, maybe finding a better life... I don't know. As soon as I stepped onto the chopper and looked back, I could tell... She didn't want to go with me. She didn't want anything to do with me... she wanted to stay with the monsters. I was saving someone who didn't need to be saved.

WALSKE: I want to thank you for your amended statements here today Lieutenant. Let's stop the--

END OF RECORDING.

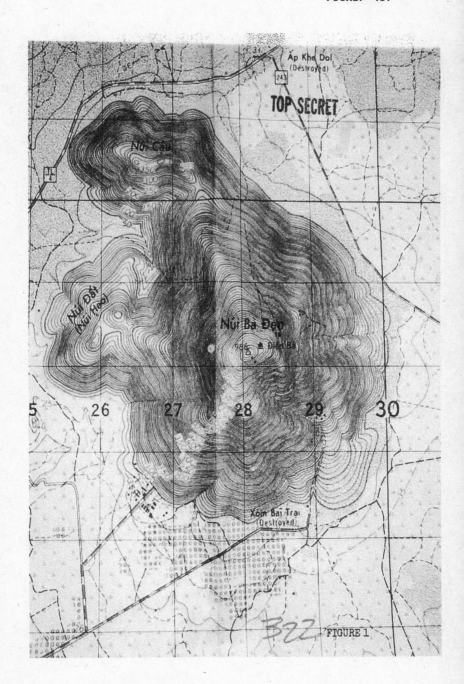

FIGURE 1

BREATHE

Nick Peterson

WHILE IN ORBIT *above Russia, cosmonauts were the first to report the slowly growing yellow circle that was later named the Death Bloom. But the Bloom wasn't a chemical attack by some foreign enemy. It had come from Earth—a final act of self-preservation, a fever to suffocate and destroy mankind with nitrogen.*

As the Death Bloom crept across the globe, people fought over water, oxygen, guns, and shelters. More than a billion people died in the first twenty-four hours. Political leaders and their wealthy donors assured the public that the oxygen would return, but in secret, they built oxygen bunkers for themselves and their families while the middle-class and poor tore each other apart to survive. Conspiracy theorists vilified the leaders, claiming this was an orchestrated attack to control the world, but there was no grand scheme, no political motivation.

Eventually, scientists developed a way for humans to breathe the deadly nitrogen gas, but not everyone's DNA responded positively to the treatment, and the world was separated into two groups: Oxys and Nitros.

YEAR: 2035
DEATH TOLL: 5,000,000,000+
GLOBAL POPULATION: 887.4M Oxys; 13.5M Nitros

Neal exited one of the last oxygen vaults in the nation. His face was covered by a mask that pumped nitrogen from a small backpack and through the metal implants in this jawbone. For the last five years, he had been forced to train as a sniper and charged with the duty to kill anyone on sight who tried to breach the oxygen vault. Neal's job made him sick to his stomach—killing desperate people who just wanted to live—but his time of service was almost up. The Death Bloom was predicted to push over the mountains any day now.

A crowded mixture of Oxys and Nitros filled the streets of the city as two men on motorcycles pulled into an alley behind a local bar near the vault. Neal walked into the same bar and past the large N-symbol.

Air hissed from the sealed doorway as Neal detached the mask from his jaw. In this bar there was no oxygen, only nitrogen. He hung his mask and backpack on a rack near the other nitrogen tanks, then took a seat with a group of friends near the bar. The owner, Oliver, stood behind the bar. He had to wear an oxygen mask in his own establishment.

After a few drinks, the front door hissed open and two bikers in motorcycle helmets entered. Neal and fellow vault-sniper Tony watched the two masked individuals march over to Oliver.

Oliver, trying his best to be congenial, handed one of the bikers a card. "It's hard to drink beer through a helmet, gentlemen. There's an excellent Oxy bar owned by a friend of mine just down the street. That card is worth two drinks over there. On me."

The speaker in one of the motorcycle helmets crackled to life. "I remember when this was a respectable place to drink. Not filled with yellow-blooded vermin."

Tony jumped from his seat, grabbed one of the bikers by the arm, and flipped open a knife. "Outside! Or I slice your red-blooded throat!"

The speaker crackled. "The Nitros will not inherit the Earth."

And then without warning, the second biker pulled something from their belt and threw it at the window. It stuck to the glass with a gooey SPLAT and slowly streaked down the windowpane while a timer on the device counted down.

It was a bomb.

Neal grabbed the bomber's shoulder but only managed to rip a patch that had been sewn to the jacket. He grabbed for the biker's wrist with his other hand to expose a nine-digit number tattooed there. It was a number he knew, and his eyes widened at the sight. "Tracy?"

The biker froze. But before they could answer, the bomb exploded, and oxygen rushed into the room. Warning sirens blared to life and yellow emergency masks deployed from the ceiling.

The bikers drew their guns and began shooting everyone in sight. "No masks today, you fuckin' pissheads!"

The Nitros thrashed as bright yellow blood spewed from their mouths.

The bikers grabbed the nitrogen tanks from the wall near the entrance and threw them out of the window. Tony grabbed a small emergency breather and attached it to his jaw.

Neal's ears rang and his yellowing face boiled. An emergency mask dangled nearby. He lunged and pulled it onto his face. His eyes burst open as nitrogen rushed into his lungs.

The bikers tore down the last of the dangling emergency masks and escaped out the window.

Outside, the bomber ripped off their helmet to reveal the face of a young woman, covered in snake tattoos.

"How the fuck did that guy know your name?" her partner asked. Tracy knew him only as Lion.

Tracy looked to be in shock. "I—I don't know," she lied.

"Hey!" The voice was Neal's. He was masked-up and sprinting toward them.

Lion lifted a shotgun from the bike and aimed.

"No!" Tracy shouted. She pushed the gun away as he blasted it. Lion yelled at her. "The fuck?!"

"There's been enough killing tonight!"

They jumped onto their motorcycles and raced away.

Neal watched the bikers disappear into the night, then looked down at the shoulder patch still in his hand. The patch was embroidered with a number: thirteen.

After Neal had been shipped off to the Nitro Military Academy, he quickly lost track of Tracy. He had heard stories about her father losing his job and having to move them to the less desirable part of town, but he never knew she ended up in Section 13.

From behind him, a piped smacked his head, and everything went black.

NEAL WOKE TO find himself immobilized, with a burlap sack over his masked face. He tried to move but stopped when he realized that the leather strap around his neck was part of a garrote, a torture chair designed to squeeze your neck until it snaps.

A blond man ripped the burlap sack from Neal's head. Neal quickly scanned the room: workbenches, maps, bomb-making materials, three Oxy thugs, and...Tracy, standing in the corner, unnerved by the sight of Neal in the chair.

A man paced the room, and Neal recognized him immediately by his voice. He was Tracy's father, Karl. The last time he saw the man was five years ago during the first Death Blooms. Back then, Karl was an angry, ill-tempered businessman, and Neal was in love with his daughter. But now, this former white-collar father was lean, tattooed, and ready for battle.

"Just so we're clear," he said, "I can rip that mask off of you anytime I want and end you." Karl cranked the garrote. The leather strap tightened around Neal's throat.

Tracy couldn't watch her father kill the only man she ever loved. Ever since Neal had been taken away by the government all those years ago, to be converted into a Nitro soldier, she had tried her best to forget about him. But as soon as she heard his voice and saw him again, all of her old feelings rushed back into her heart. And now her father was going to kill him.

Karl continued to tighten the garrote while questioning Neal about the city's plans with the oxygen vault and the next Death Bloom.

Tracy's eyes darted around the room in search for a way to save Neal. Then she saw it: an unused sticky bomb.

Karl leaned close to Neal's ear. "It's too bad they never gave you an IQ test before they converted you. Maybe you would have been smart enough to stay the fuck away from us." He cranked the garrote for what should have been the final time. It should have crushed Neal's throat and sent yellow blood spouting across the room, but instead...

BOOM! The basement window exploded.

Tracy screamed, "It's the Nitros! They're coming for him!"

"Get out there, get 'em!" Karl yelled.

They all ran out for the fight, but Tracy stayed behind to untie Neal. She leaned in close. "Hit me in the face."

"What?"

"Did the nitro make you stupid? Do it now!"

Neal didn't have time to debate, so he obliged her request. "I'll come back for you," he promised.

Tracy sucked the blood from her lip. "Now take the back exit. That way."

Neal escaped out the back just before Karl returned. The man froze at the sight of his injured daughter.

Tracy fell into a puddle of fake tears. "Daddy! I tried to stop him, but..."

Karl touched his daughter's swollen lip and hugged her tight.

A CROWD OF Oxys had gathered inside the abandoned bar that Tracy and Lion had bombed the night before. Karl was to give a speech, possibly his last. Once the crowd grew too big for the room, Karl climbed onto the bar top and addressed his audience.

"The Nitros have built a Vault," Karl preached. "A sanctuary for their chosen few, their privileged elites and their cronies. But did they invite us? No! Did any of you receive a lottery ticket? Did you? I didn't! They didn't invite us because we're not the compliant sheep they desire for their vision of the future. We're independent thinkers who refuse to deny the truth. They didn't invite us because they built a prison designed for one purpose only: to enrich themselves at our expense. The Nitros see the apocalypse as a reset button, but we're here to show them they're wrong. Our children have been stolen by the Nitros and turned against us. I weep for the loss of our sons and daughters, for the children who have been mutilated by their perverse science experiments. The Nitros are not human! They are soulless creatures, animated by unholy ways. The history of the Earth flows within the red blood of our Oxy veins. We are the children of Aeolus, and from his blood we inherit greatness. Together, we can ensure the existence of our people and preserve the future for our children."

Karl jumped down from the bar top and led the crowd outside and into the streets. His followers were armed with guns and knives. They marched as one to the Oxygen Vault.

Other Oxy gangs had joined Karl's rebellion on its way to the Vault—the Badgers, Tigers, Jackals, and Scorpions—and they were now over two thousand strong. They marched united, ready to unleash years of pain and suffering. Oxy men scaled the towering metallic walls of the Vault and attached magnetic bombs to the cold, unyielding metal. Nitrogen guards wielded a massive water cannon and used it to blast away the climbers, but their aim was poor and most of the planted explosives remained.

In the midst of the chaos, an electric SUV ripped through the streets towards the Vault, maneuvering through the mayhem to avoid fires, shotgun blasts, and other careening vehicles. Behind the wheel, Neal swerved to avoid a masked man who had ran in front of him, but the top-heavy vehicle gave way, fishtailed hard, and then slammed into the man as it rolled twice and landed on its roof.

With a deafening explosion, the bombs set by the rebels detonated, shaking the Vault's foundation and causing its metallic gates to crumble. The mob breached the building. Tracy, however, had been knocked down by the blast and lay motionless on the ground.

Neal, meanwhile, had almost climbed out of his crashed SUV when a knife-wielding Oxy man leapt over a burning car nearby and charged Neal with the intent to kill.

But just as the man lunged at Neal, a powerful gust of Nitro air swept over the street, extinguishing the fires and freezing the knife-wielding assailant's body midair. The once-threatening figure landed lifelessly, mere inches away from Neal. Death had claimed him and everyone around him—silenced by the unbreathable air.

As Neal surveyed the desolate wasteland, his worst fears were confirmed. The world had become an inhospitable shell, stripped of its former glory. The magnitude of the devastation hit him with a force he could hardly comprehend. The planet, once vibrant and teeming with life, now lay barren and lifeless, its very essence extinguished.

With trembling hands, he unclipped his own mask, his eyes brimming with tears. Reluctantly, he took a deep breath outside without a mask, the first one since five years ago, steeling himself for what lay before him. And that's when he saw Tracy.

Neal ripped an oxygen mask from the belt of his frozen attacker and rushed to Tracy's side. He attached the mask to her face and tenderly caressed her hair.

Suddenly, a fit of coughing racked Neal's body. The oxygen that had been released from the Vault had invaded his lungs. He fumbled for his emergency breather, but before he could secure it to his face, Karl emerged from a nearby wreckage and struck Neal from behind, sending the man stumbling forward and his mask pinwheeling far from his reach. Karl then delivered a brutal blow, crushing at least three of Neal's ribs.

Gasping for air, Neal grabbed a piece of exploded debris and smashed it across Karl's jaw, the force of the blow causing the man's eyes to roll back as he crumpled to the ground.

Neal looked back at Tracy, who was now waking up.

But it was then that a desperate Oxy man ripped the mask from her face, secured it to his own, and then fled into the night.

Neal watched as the poisonous nitrogen assaulted Tracy's lungs. He tried to get up to help her, but was met with a boot to the face.

The last thing he heard before his world faded to black was the terrifying sound of Tracy's blood-soaked screams.

THE MAN WHO SAVED THE WORLD

Jared Moshe

THE PARING KNIFE easily sliced the fruit. Juice dripped onto Seth's fingertips. For a moment, he considered licking it, but he knew better. The punishment would be death.

He opened the kitchen cabinet and removed four gold-and-white China plates. He laid them on a tray beside the cutting board and a stack of blue silk napkins. Traditionally, the ceremony had been held in the sunken garden, a pretentious marble pit at the northern edge of the villa. However, Seth found hosting in his home to be more conducive to camaraderie. So, he changed it. This was a perk of Guild leadership.

He walked down the hallway to his private study, pausing by the window to look down at the stone courtyard. A tree stood in the center. Gnarled, twisted, and still blooming thousands of years later.

Everyone knew the story: Adam and Eve ate from the Tree of Knowledge and were exiled from the Garden of Eden. They had Cain and Abel, and from them humanity was born. Hundreds of years later, they die.

Only the Guild knew what came next. Adam and Eve were reborn, with no knowledge of who they were or what they had done. It was a chance for redemption. If they could find each other and consummate their love, they would return to Eden.

Before that could happen, the guild would kill them. Someone had to save the world.

SETH ENTERED HIS study and set the tray on a coffee table. He closed the heavy door that separated the room from the rest of the house. The ceremony was private. His family wouldn't eavesdrop, but Seth was habitually cautious. He rolled his Eames chair from behind his desk and positioned it between the couch and two recliners. His muscles ached. He stretched slowly, feeling the tension in his legs. For the first time in his sixty-five years, he felt old.

He wondered if this would be his last ceremony. He was nineteen at his first—the youngest acolyte in modern history. The fruit tasted surprisingly sweet back then, and his vision was clear. In it, he saw Adam reincarnated as a young veteran; Eve, a waitress. He tracked them to a bar in San Diego. He was almost too late. The two had briefly met, but lucky for Seth, Adam was still waiting for Eve's shift to finish. Seth shot him five times in the chest and stole his wallet to make it look like a mugging. For preventing the return of Eden, Seth was made leader of the Guild.

"You're doing your breathing thing again," said Imani. It was just like her to enter through the house instead of the study's private entrance.

"You're early," said Seth.

"Am I?" She removed her emerald-green coat and fell into her favorite chair—the sheepskin recliner that Seth purchased for himself as a wedding present.

"Why so stressed?" she asked.

"You know why."

Imani shook her head. "Mmmm. No. It's more than that." She had been seeing through him since they were children.

"I like being the boss," said Seth.

Imani laughed. "Yeah, but you hate the paperwork."

Adam and Eve only reincarnated once every generation. In the time between, the guild sold its skills to the highest bidder. The most lucrative contracts were with countries that needed to train a private army. Lucrative, but also bureaucratic.

"You remember when I succeeded Lucious?" Seth said. "As soon as he lost power, no one wanted anything to do with him. He was always barging into conversations, hoping someone would listen for longer than two minutes." He shook his head.

She waved the thought away. "Lucious was a shitty leader. When I take over, I'll make you my consiglieri."

"If you take over," he said.

"Do you honestly believe one of the others could kill the next reincarnate before me?" she said.

"I could."

"Lucky for me, we have a retirement age," Imani said, smiling.

Imani was Seth's oldest friend, and although he was not allowed to play favorites, there was no one who he'd rather have succeed him.

A polite knock came at the side door. Seth unlocked it and Hyun sauntered in.

"Well, here we are. Another go at the rodeo," Hyun said, bringing two fingers to the brim of his white Stetson.

Mocking the gesture, Imani brought two fingers to her braids.

Seth had always found Hyun's cowboy-shtick impressive. It made people feel at ease and forget that the man had single-handedly killed 312 people.

"I was thinkin'," said Hyun. "How 'bout we make ourselves a little wager this year?"

"I'm not much of a gambler," said Seth.

"Sure, ya are. 'Sides, this one's simple. It's been nine years since any of us have had a clear vision. A thousand dollars says this year'll make it a clean decade."

"I'm not betting on the fate of the world," Seth said. "Ever."

Undeterred, Hyun plopped on the recliner next to Imani and removed his hat. "How 'bout you? You up for a little game?"

Before Imani could answer, Rachel barged in. She eyed Imani and Hyun seated close together. "What are you two conspiring about?"

"Well if you knew, it wouldn't be a conspiracy, would it?" Imani said.

Rachel clenched her jaw. It made her face look spiteful. As cousins, Seth and Rachel shared the same angular features, and he couldn't help but wonder if he looked just as off-putting when he became annoyed.

"It's nothing. A bet," Seth said.

Rachel scoffed. She adjusted her long skirt and took her place on the couch.

"Where's Jules?" asked Seth.

"He's coming," said Rachel.

A moment later, her son Jules arrived. At eighteen, Jules was now the youngest acolyte in modern history. He slipped off his coat, revealing a jet-black tactical knife strapped to his leg.

"No weapons at the ceremony."

"It's my statement piece."

"Leave it in the closet," said Seth.

Jules gestured to the paring knife. "Isn't that a knife?" Then he pointed at the gold-handled Saif above Seth's desk. "And that's a sword. Those are weapons."

Seth simmered.

Jules continued, "There's also two lamps, four visible chords, and your collection of historic stoneware. We're assassins, everything is a weapon."

"The kid's got himself a point," said Hyun.

Rachel beamed. "He's a clever one, my boy."

Even Imani smirked with enjoyment.

Seth relented and motioned Jules to the couch. He closed and locked the doors, then placed one piece of fruit on each plate, and one plate in front of each person.

"Is that it?" asked Jules. "Shouldn't there be more razzle-dazzle?"

Seth didn't understand how such an impetuous boy survived being buried alive for forty-eight hours when he can't even survive being quiet for forty-eight seconds.

He would make a terrible leader.

Rachel leaned back. The thick fibers of her gray blouse scrape the leather couch. "You never should have moved us out of the sunken garden. It was sacrilege."

So would his mother.

"Since some of us are new here," Seth said, "I'll do a quick walk-through."

"Walk-through..." Rachel shook her head.

Seth ignored her. "Everyone eats at the same time. You might see something. You might not. Each vision is unique so remember everything you can. Faces. Background details. Words are especially helpful with identifying who and where they are."

Jules raised his hand.

"Yes?"

"No Adam or Eve were identified at the last nine ceremonies. Does that mean no one had a vision? Or were the visions inconclusive?"

"There were limited visions. Dead ends," Seth said.

"But you've had them," Jules said.

"Some of us did."

"I saw the back of a boy fly fishin' in Montana," said Hyun. "Searched the state from head-to-rump, but never found him."

"And I could've sworn I saw a brunette woman jogging," said Imani with a shrug. "Who knows where."

Jules crossed his arms, petulant. "That's unfair. You guys all have more intelligence to work with."

"Which they have just shared with you," said Seth. "They didn't have to do that. But as you alluded to, we have not been able to identify a reincarnate for a while. That's bad. Adam and Eve are out there. They could be finding each other right now. When the fate of the world is on the line, it's not about who wins and who loses."

"Is it though? Is the fate of the world really on the line?" Jules said.

A hush descended on the room. Seth clenched his jaw. Hyun straightened. Even Rachel mouthed, "Jules…"

"I'm only saying, nobody but God knows what bringing about Eden will mean. It could mean the end of the world, or it could mean a lifetime free buffet at Caesar's palace."

Seth gripped the edge of his chair with hands that had become white-knuckled knots.

Imani touched his arm. "Let it go. He's trying to provoke you."

Seth wasn't sure. He stepped towards Jules. "The only other law is this: should you find yourself at odds with another person in this room, you are not to hurt or interfere with each other. If you do, you will be exiled from the Guild—then hunted and killed."

"Even if you succeed in riddin' us of an Adam or an Eve,"

Hyun added.

"Damn. Who do you guys think I am, huh?" said Jules, offended.

"I would never..."

His words were left unanswered.

"Seth's right," Imani said. "Stopping Eden is more important than who our next leader is. I vow right here and right now that I will share whatever I see." She spoke firmly, her voice calm and potent.

To Seth, she sounded the epitome of a leader.

"Ditto," said Hyun.

"I will too," said Rachel a moment later.

All eyes turned to Jules. He rattled the ice in his glass. "Yeah, of course."

Seth nodded, feeling a little less worried about the future of the guild for the first time in a while. "Well, if that's that," he said, "bon appetit." He popped the fruit into his mouth. The juice was as sweet as he remembered. He chewed slowly, savoring the rare flavor.

Rachel whispered a silent prayer before eating.

Hyun took small, delicate bites.

Imani used a fork and knife.

Jules reacted like a starter pistol had been fired. He crammed the fruit down his throat in a single half-chewed gulp.

Seth worked to clear his mind: to forget about his impending retirement; to forget about the possibility of another failed ceremony; to forget about Jules's words. He had only felt doubt once before. It was when he shot his first Adam. As the life faded from the dying man's face, Seth could see all of Adam's memories reflected in his eyes. A thousand lifetimes experienced in the second before death. Seth felt as though he had killed a child who had just learned how to walk. And that's when the question popped into his head. "Did I really just save the world?"

He shook off the memory. Doubt only makes one's faith stronger, he reminded himself.

He looked around the room to find the others seated in silence. He wondered when the fruit would take effect when, without warning the light began to shift. The hue from the outside had turned blue. Seth looked out the window.

Instead of Renaissance brick, he saw the ocean.

His muscles tensed. He inhaled slowly and let the vision flow around him. The ocean became a river. The river was broken by a rock. On top of the rock was a woman.

Seth watched her leap into the air. He saw the flash of a rope swing against a sunburnt sky, but her face was lost in the glare.

The shadows widened.

A yellow, Italianate house came into view. Seth picked up his brush and painted it blue. He noticed his clothes had changed into white coveralls, and he was perched atop an unsteady ladder.

Below him, stood the woman. He still cannot see her face. Only her brown hair, bobbing as she passed.

Seth screamed, "Look up!"

She didn't.

He jumped off the ladder and landed in a swimming pool. He wiped water from his face and raised his eyes. He saw part of a carved sign. Blue letters on a green background.

Laughter behind him. Then a voice: "OMG. You look like a drowned rat."

He wheeled around.

It was the woman. He saw her face. Her blue-green eyes. The freckle in her iris.

Seth's heart nearly stopped pumping. His stomach twisted into knots. He leapt up and found himself back in his living room. Sweat rolled down his forehead. He looked at the others.

Imani's eyes were closed, head at rest. Hyun sat straight-backed, pupils dilated. Rachel was sprawled across the couch, Jules squeezed into the corner.

Without hesitation, Seth snatched Jules's knife from its holster and sliced open Hyun's throat.

Hyun's eyes snapped back to reality. His hands flew to his split jugular. But he was dead before they got there.

Seth clocked Rachel in motion behind him. She drove her palm upwards towards Seth's nose. He dodged and caught the blow on his shoulder, then brought the knife down on her exposed Brachial artery. Blood blasted like water from a firehouse. Rachel dropped.

Seth wheeled towards a still-dreaming Jules, but before he could attack, Imani slashed him across the chest with the paring knife. His right arm went limp. The tactical knife slipped from Seth's fingers.

Seth dodged the next swipe of the blade. He had trained Imani. He knew how she fought. He ducked and drove his left hand into Imani's windpipe, shattering it.

Imani gasped for air and gurgled blood. She died looking at her best friend with pity.

Jules came to with a jolt. He blinked. His eyes came into focus. He found Seth towering over him, his hands red with blood.

Fear flashed across Jules's face. "Please! I wouldn't…"

Seth smashed Jules in the head with a lamp, and Jules fell. Two more blows assured the kill.

Seth's chest heaved. He surveyed the scene, mind churning. He took the paring knife from Imani, wiped the blade clean with a napkin, and placed it back on the coffee table. He then pressed the napkin to the wound on his chest. He slipped Jules's knife back into his hand, then adjusted the angle of the body slightly, so it more directly faced Rachel and Hyun.

Satisfied, he unbolted the door leading into the house and hurried down the stone hallway.

"Priya!" he called. When there was no answer, he tried again, louder this time. "PRI!"

A moment later he heard footsteps pounding down the stairs. His wife appeared. She gasped at his wounds. "What happened?"

"Jules went wild! He killed the others!"

"Oh my God!"

"It's a goddamned nightmare. Call a Guild meeting. Everyone. ASAP!"

"I'm on it," Priya said, already heading back upstairs to retrieve her phone. But then another thought stopped her. "Was it a success? Did you see them?"

"No," Seth said.

He went to the kitchen and looked outside to the tree bathed in moonlight. He'd have to kill it. They kept pesticides in the shed. There had to be something that could cause a natural-looking death.

"Dad?" said a voice.

Seth turned. His daughter Dia stood in the doorway, half-asleep in her blue and purple cat pajamas. "Go back to sleep," he said. "It's late."

She squinted, her eyes slowly adjusting to the light. She noticed the blood. "Dad! OMG!? What happened?" She was wide awake now.

"Don't worry. I'll be okay," he said.

Dia hurried to the cabinet beneath the sink and dug inside. She reached past a box of diatomaceous earth and grabbed the first-aid kit they kept there. "We have to sterilize it."

She cleaned and debrided the wound, careful to remove any fabric or hair. Her hands were remarkably steady for a girl not even ten. "What happened? Who did this to you?" she asked.

"I took care of it. There's nothing to worry about," he said.

She hesitated.

Seth clocked the sweat on her arms, the troubled expression on her face. "What's wrong?" Seth asked.

She stubbed her heel into the marble flood. "I had a bad dream."

"Want to talk about it?"

Dia licked her lips. "I was in a forest... I think. There were lots of pine trees, I know that. And I was chasing this woman."

Seth's stomach dropped.

Dia continued. "It was Eve. I knew I had to catch her. It'd been forever since you killed Adam."

His heart cracked.

"I ran fast—faster than ever. I even jumped off this insane cliff that totally should have killed me. And I grabbed her. I was going to become a leader just like you."

He had taught her too well.

"What happened?" he asked.

"I messed up." She stared at the ground. "Everyone was so mad at me."

Seth stepped towards her. She was crying. He wiped away the tears with his thumb. "It's okay."

She refused look at him. "You were so mad at me…"

"I'm not mad. It was just a dream," he said.

Dia said nothing for a moment. Then she raised her head. Her blue-green eyes glimmered. The freckle in her iris was clear.

"You're right," she said. "I'm going to kill her for real."

SPROUT

Jordan Goldstein

I WASN'T ALWAYS the town witch.

I grew up here, on this plot of land, outside the small town of Daybreak, Kansas. My parents, whom I loved very much, both died when I was sixteen. After that, I guess my self-imposed reclusion rubbed people the wrong way.

The chatter was innocent at first, but the growing talk of me eating stray cats, worshiping the devil, and murdering my folks started to feel crass. I have no issue with being alone, so I don't see why others do.

IT WAS PRETTY late, around 11:15 or so, when I bore witness to a summer meteor shower. My folks loved this type of stuff. They'd spend most nights outside, just sitting quietly next to one another. To them, there was no purpose in talking too much on nights like tonight because they felt it would spoil the fun.

But when they did speak, they spoke plainly and somewhat sensitively about the hues and mixtures of light in the sky. I can't articulate as well as they did about what transpired above me on this night. I just thought it looked pretty.

At some point during meteor shower, a small meteorite fell from the sky and landed in my corn field. Its bright blue glow made it easy to find even amid the tall rows of corn. I walked over to it, knelt down, and noticed it seemed to be pulsating. Then, it flamed out.

CHESTER, MY SMALL Jack Russell Terrier, slept beside me on the couch while an old Arthur Kennedy western was playing on the television. This was my time of quiet comfort. Being able to linger in the silence of the night while having it blend with faint gun battles and lover's quarrels from the tube. It's what I cherish most.

But my solace was cut short by a steady rumble which started to shake the foundation of my house. I shot up and rushed to the kitchen, where I saw the dishes clatter about. I turned back towards the living room and saw through the front room's curtained window a repeating flash of light. The light streaked across the curtains, went dark, then seconds later, streaked across the curtains again. Chester started barking at the sight, and I went to the window and peeked through the curtains to inspect.

Outside was a large pickup truck, driving circles all over my crops, the bucking headlights streaking across my face with each bumpy, cornstalk-crushing revolution.

I immediately recognized the truck as belonging to Sam Miller, a local teenage burn-out, and I knew that his friends Billy Young and Eddie Palmer were most likely in the car with him, all stoned out of their minds and cracking up like red-eyed maniacs. I ran out onto the porch and hollered at the truck, "What the fuck are you boys doing?!" I had closed the door on Chester before he could follow me outside, and he was now barking loudly from the window.

The truck did another full spin, then fishtailed to a skidding stop until its headlights were locked on me Sam gunned the engine, and the truck exploded from the cornfield in a flurry of dirt. I froze in fear as the truck sped up my lawn and hooked a hard right at my porch. It was then that Eddie, who was sitting in the pickup's flatbed, hucked an empty beer bottle from thirty yards out that just barely missed my head and shattered against the front door behind me.

Oh, fuck this, I thought.

I ran back inside while the three assholes continued to tear up my field, and pushed a barking Chester back before he could dart outside after them. I went to the bedroom and from the top shelf in the closet, grabbed my father's old hunting rifle. I rushed to load the rifle, but the combination of haste and nerves only caused me to drop a number of rounds onto the floor. I loaded what I could and thundered back down the stairs to the front door.

But this time, I forgot about Chester.

That crazy dog bolted out of the house faster than I could react and galloped straight for the pickup truck, no doubt out for blood. I tried calling him back, but it was no use. So, I did the only thing that came to mind. I raised the rifle and fired a warning shot into the air.

At the sound of the shot, the truck slammed on its brakes, shifted gears, and accelerated towards the main road as a means to escape. But a last-second pull-turn resulted in the truck's tire crushing Chester, which caused the vehicle to hop up and then slam back down so violently that Eddie Palmer was ejected from his seat in the back. The boy's head hit the ground with such force that a piece of his upper vertebrae literally shot straight out of his skin.

The truck didn't stop, though. Just skidded onto the main road and sped off into the night.

EDDIE PALMER WAS an athlete. He played right field for the Daybreak High Thunder. He wasn't very good, but scrappy enough to always be along for the ride. He had a wide smile, with bright blue eyes. Sure, he could be an asshole to me sometimes, but he was still just a kid.

I later came to learn that Eddie didn't want to be on the truck that night, or to throw that beer bottle. He was an underclassman on the team and underclassmen did what they were told.

EDDIE'S FACE WAS pressed against the dirt, his head now a ninety-degree angle to his neck. His body was stiff, mouth agape, eyes drained of life.

Sheriff Robert Wall told me over the phone that he and the local ambulance were on their way, so I just sat and waited on the porch, looking out at the mangled corpses of Eddie and Chester and the broken stalks of corn that litter the field beyond.

The meteor shower continued to light the sky. That blue glow caused by the meteorite from before began to shine again. Then, it started slowly spreading to more parts of the field.

I was a little confused, but as my mind started to wander, the sheriff's patrol car pulled up.

SHERIFF WALL AND I sat in my kitchen, waiting for the ambulance to arrive. He got a radio call that said the van was caught in a mud-pit a few miles away.

After a long period of quiet, he broke the silence and said, "I don't know if I'm going to be able to help you here."

"Yeah." I said.

"It's just—"

"I get it."

We sat for another moment, listening to the sound of distant cicadas.

Then, slowly…a moaning sound came from outside the house.

Sheriff Wall went to the front porch to investigate.

"Sophia," he called back to me. "Come here, please."

I went to the porch and was shocked by what I saw. It was…Eddie.

His bones were still broken, his body still contorted, his face still bruised and bloody and covered in dirt, but now…alive. His bones cracked with each breath he took. The dirt on his face had crept into his eyes and it was glowing now, pulsating.

My heart started to beat fast. In the distance, the bright red lights of an ambulance appeared. The glowing blue field undulated purple as the lights passed.

As if needing something trivial to ponder in this moment of cosmic uncertainty, Sheriff Wall looked at me and asked, "What are you growing here, Sophia?"

"Corn," I said.

TWO DAYS AFTER the incident, a convoy of high-ranking government types took over Daybreak. They locked down the town, rounded up everyone against their will, and subjected them to all sorts of tests and medical examinations. I assume they were trying to see if what had happened to Eddie could happen to anyone else.

Since I was directly exposed to the land where Eddie got a second chance at life, I was asked to quarantine at the farmhouse. I told them about the meteorite and the dirt moving by itself along Eddie's face, trying to connect any logical reason for how something like this could happen. They noted the information, but I never felt like they took it seriously.

They left a few weeks later and the town of Daybreak tried to go back to what it was, but that was easier said than done. There was still a great sense of confusion, particularly among the faithful who did their best to reconcile the event with their long-held beliefs. The mood was tense, and a lot of that pent up anger was directed towards me. I was the sinner responsible for the plague. No one seemed to care much about Eddie, though. Which was weird because the boy went on to survive.

People call him a miracle, but he's a miracle that requires 24-hour care and assistance. His mind is fine—no brain damage. Not even a slight cognitive impairment. But his body is a different story—it ain't ever going to fully recover. He still has no heartbeat, not since his resurrection at least, and I'm not quite sure his body still has blood—what good would it do without something to pump it? His bones have healed as much as they can, but everything is still mostly mangled and unusable.

Eddie was a foster kid, though. His mother had died of complications from pneumonia when he was twelve, and his daddy walked out on him shortly thereafter. His foster parents wanted nothing to do with the lifetime of expensive care they were now facing, so after visiting Eddie once at the hospital, they left and never came back. Eddie's eighteen now, so he lives alone in a house the town helped purchase for him.

I visited him once, but I don't quite know why. Was it guilt that drove me there? Compassion? I've never gone back though. Don't need to. Eddie Palmer is dead. All that remains is a disfigured corpse slumped in a wheelchair, drooling from the side of its mouth, the blue glow behind his eyes fixated on an old television set that plays nothing but old reruns at a volume too loud for most ears. The place smells awful, like rot and raw sewage, and there's garbage everywhere. I'm not quite sure how he eats, sleeps, or uses the toilet, or if he even needs to do any of those things, but it gives me the chills to think about it for too long, so I don't.

Not sure I'd call what happened to Eddie a miracle. But what do I know. I'm just the town witch.

THE DECEPTION OF YOUTH

Sarah Bolger

I DON'T USUALLY linger after a find, but the unrelenting news coverage piqued my morbid curiosity. After all, this was one of my more nuanced undertakings, and I suppose it warranted their attention. What I found truly remarkable was the misplaced faith so many journalists and the Garda had in the innocence of youth. They all uniformly believed this simplistic, polarized narrative: wholesome children, and irredeemable adults. That angels are taken, and monsters take.

The media sobriquets—"Monster", "Sick Culprit'—didn't bother me, since I certainly don't capture or torture, I found their misguided profiling amusing. Perhaps the girl would have enjoyed knowing how many gullible townsfolk bought into the 'sinless' and 'virtuous' narrative. She would have loved hearing such platitudes as 'missing darling' and been chuffed by how many fawning neighbors searched and worried for the wool-gussied wolf. How she just "lit up a room…"

I sat in the coffee shop where I first saw her, neatly braiding two teabag strings together in a knot Brother Thomas would be proud of. I looked out at the one major intersection between this town and the main city road (and by major, I mean the only one with two lanes; one, if you've got a horse box.) I watched a tasked father tightly grip his two boys outside, grabbing his eldest by the collar and pushing his youngest through the crossing and back into the family van. He wore a green corduroy jacket and a belt that even John Wayne would find tacky.

Belts, a fascination of mine. I like to count their unevenly added holes as a way of identifying the maturity of my finds. Growth lines of unwanted change, their stretched leather containing valleys of condensed fat. Bulging between their protruding gut and their even thicker trunk. I always take the belt. I like to leave my finds in their most natural form.

I took a sip of tea and positioned the six-day-old front page so it was clearly visible to the occupants of the coffee shop, blanketing my table with a layer of hearsay. *"Nine-year-old St. Augustine school girl missing...mass search underway...cobalt-blue bicycle found... Distraught father speaks out."* I didn't care to know her name, but with her smudged face splashed across the front of every newspaper and street corner, it became hard to remain ignorant.

Before she was found, children stopped wearing their school crested duffel coats, stopped riding their brightly colored bicycles, and were now steadily shadowed by a watchful guardian at all times. It was as if she single-handedly robbed their roads of color and plunged the locals back into some Doris Day-wholesome black and white picture. The one where the shiftless parents were forced to wake, feed and actually care for their young.

Outside, a damaged road sign clattered in the wind, creating a rhythm that matched my erratic heartbeat while I waited for the day's search party to arrive, to get my daily dose of the do-gooders army, desperate to be the ones to find the missing girl.

I sat in the exact position where I first spotted her. Perhaps parting ways with a neighbor, or an older sister. I remember her gently nibbling the edges from around a bagel with obsessive devotion. She seemed—to the untrained eye—simply focused on creating smaller and smaller circles. A child-like facade. But I knew what to look for. Her head steadied and her eyes gradually wandered upwards. As casual as a handshake, she swiped a Toblerone and tucked it into the waistband of her unevenly hemmed skirt as she wandered towards the exit. She hovered with a poised elegance in the doorway. No facial change, no burdened exhale. No appearance of guilt whatsoever. I stared, fascinated by this young girl. She looked round once and our eyes met for just a moment. Then she unashamedly walked right out of that cafe.

I followed her home, watching her snake slowly down the pathway on that blue bike. Her legs stiff and straight as her wheels obediently rotated, flowing like a wave over a paved concrete ocean.

I knelt beside a nearby car, searching the ground aimlessly for keys I hadn't dropped. I watched from a distance as she sat on the stairs outside her house, removing muck-caked loafers and revealing mismatched polka and dot-free socks.

I turned away as a middle-aged couple walked towards me on the street, trying to be less conspicuous. I desperately tried to catch sight of the girl through the grime-smeared side-view mirrors of the car. Through a thin film of dust, I watched her reflection calmly eat the stolen chocolate. I thought I'd see the child shine, proudly gleaming with deception, savoring every bite of her delicious duplicity. Instead, I saw a girl whose pale, plump face was devoid of any joy or satisfaction.

The wind blew harder, but she didn't seem to feel it.

She reached into the wicker basket on the front of her bicycle and pulled out a thin, dark object. I squinted into the car mirror. My neck whipped violently back around when I saw what had replaced the sweet in her smudged hands. A cracked and stained gray leather belt with a steel turquoise buckle. *My find. My belt.*

No longer was I admiring the little thief. Now, I acknowledged a more troubling truth. My mind spun and I fled.

I FELT AN ache; a sickening bulge of bile as I hopped the enclosure and looked around the withered, abandoned farm. How did she find this place? Flashes of memory as I retraced my footsteps with percussion-like precision. The reliving of my actions always created an air-sucking awareness within me. As if falling in the dreamworld, uncontrollable images bolted me into the past. I know the dead can't hurt me, but their last moments burrow into me like worms. I guess I'm a kind of empath; a collector and curator of grief and trauma, tightly clinging onto all that is harmful and ugly. I too bleed out with every puncture and feel deserving of every peaceful moment that is contaminated with hateful self-realization. Those feelings never pass, I just distract myself with new noise, or new hunts.

The church's distant bells chimed for noon. I shouldn't have been there, not in broad daylight. Damn that little brat for forcing me back there.

The crumbling remnants of stone stables rested amidst the disorder, littered with cigarette butts and trampled black cans. I skirted the perimeter, overgrown hedges veiling me in a welcome shadow. I looked around carefully, memory twisting.

I quickened my pace, forcing my way through razor-edged bramble and thick web, finally spotting my hidden cubbyhole.

The hideaway wide open, the thin metal handle clattering in the breeze, risen from the bog and uncovered for the world to see. My mementos, my tools, my secrets, all excavated. The unearthed yellow bucket of treasures glaring right at me.

Why would a child ever come through here? Why would a mere kid dig through this grime?

With a sodden spirit I inspected my trove, comforted by the possessions that remained, and moved to rage by what had been looted. I knelt among the refuse, encircled by uncoiled wire and stained browned rags. I found an infestation of half-eaten candy wraps and a timeworn watch sun bleached; too large and heavy to sit on her pickpocketing wrists. Was she creating her own loot, or contributing to mine?

The sheath of my carving knife was empty. She had my fucking knife.

THE WAITRESS CAME over to clear my table. I smiled and took a perfunctory sip of tea, removing my arms from the table and gifting a full view of the headline staring up at her.

She smiled dimly back, gathering my teapot and spoon onto a tray, missing my intention entirely. Smiling through me, but never *seeing* me.

Observation is a skill I pride myself on. Like a trench coat-wearing detective from the old films, I too can recognize minor flickers of lust, barely audible giggles of cruelty, and sideways glances of greed. I clock it all. That's why I spotted the little bitch that day; spied her poisoned thought bubble from across the room. The corrupted will of a dulled life force, making little eye contact and moving with the restraint of the shackled. I know all too well that weight, of being unique, with acute abilities and a diseased disrespect for all that surround you. To see yourself, you need to see others.

I scanned the article for the thousandth time. *Bundruddy girl missing, last seen in St. Augustine area on cobalt-blue bicycle. Police said "Autumn Heck, 9, was wearing a school crested overcoat and pink woolen cap with a rainbow-colored bobble."*

I can assure the gullible *Sunday Bulletin* that she was wearing no such hat. The child wore something that resembled stretch leggings with a simple old shirt and was freezing cold to the touch with no hat, scarf, or overcoat.

The father had lied.

Did he have any idea where his daughter had been escaping to every day? Did he not know his baby left this earth the night before he announced her missing? In the middle of winter, his emaciated daughter cycled a half mile down a dark country lane in a napkin-thin shirt, with pocketed provisions to keep her hunger at bay, in search of more of my trophies.

He lied. He lied to the journalists and to the police, because the truth sounded neglectful.

Made him look like a bad father.

Two women in high-vis jackets entered the coffee shop and I stiffened. Marked their every movement. Conscious of my demeanor, I put my teacup down and loosened my shoulders. Slouched, relaxed, ready for their eyes to glaze right over me.

"Brutally cold out there", one of them said to the waitress, obnoxiously loud for such a small space. They took a seat by the bathroom and shook their heads at the questioning glances from the surrounding tables. "No luck."

These people were useless.

Even so, there would be no shame in being found at this point. I'd thought about giving myself over to the police even before the girl. The thrill of convincing strangers of my remorse set my nerves on fire. Practicing the look of penance. Absorbing their awe at me being the killer. Explaining my reasoning, my understanding of who this girl was, and why she needed to be gone. Its premise felt too complicated for a profession that possesses no medical qualifications or expertise in the human psyche. I would be foolish to trust a man or woman who needed a badge to feel important, and sirens to announce their presence, with such a delicate parable.

"Her poor Da," someone said. I suppressed a sneer.

There's no excuse for bad parenting. My folks were lunatics, unqualified for the task of raising a child. In the wee hours of their debauched gatherings, when the music started scratching, I'd sieve through the snoring partygoers like a moonlit road sweep, grabbing their illicit possessions. I'd bag their misplaced and forgotten toys: the decorative lighters, ornate penknives and neat curls of cash all in a beach bucket that had never even glimpsed the ocean. I'd keep them as punishment, creating a black hole of matter in the garden, hidden under an unkempt rosebush. Unloved and wild, the bright and yellowed flowers sprouted from weeds, its thorny languid arms closely protecting my loot.

In the early hours of a moonlit morning, I caught a pungent stranger pissing all over my back garden playground. It was that very night I felt the first tear of rage wet my puffy cheeks. The stench of her fermented urine and stale sweat was overpowering. A snake of dark liquid leaked towards me as I hid in the shrubbery. She lost her footing and toppled onto her side with a drunken giggle. She shimmied on the ground like a worm, messily trying to smooth her bunched skirt from her waist.

I crawled from the shrubbery like a wraith.

"Sweetie, give me a lift up!" The lady belched and raised her hands up into the air like she was the star in the finale of a dance number. I deliberately tucked myself close behind her head, gripping her temples between the bones of my kneecaps.

Her pearlescent earrings twinkled as she continued to shimmy, more pathetically now, like an upturned turtle.

Holding it like the sharpened pencil I'd held in art class just that morning, I stuck my claimed penknife into the soft of her neck.

It took her too long to realize what I'd done. The freedom I had bestowed upon her.

I remained still and mute as my small hands held the knife in place. She squinted at me in confusion, before her eyes rolled back in her head as she desperately tried to stem the flow of blood from the wound in her neck. Her eyes refocused and we looked at each other in silence, her ragged, rancid breath clouding the crisp air between us. Her evaporating soul's last form of communication. You have to be quick to catch all the emotions that surface in someone's last moments. I've gotten better at it with time. I've learned their last seconds are the prize in all of this. The most honest emotion I've seen to date is defeat. The highlight reel mainly consists of pain and desperation, but with skill, you start to recognize guilt, and that's where the beauty resides.

Watching someone realize where their body will be found, and the state it will be found in, is captivating. The how, where, and why is their own doing. All I do is freeze time.

She spilled out all over me that morning, leaving me alone in my garden once again. Blood and urine fertilizing the land. I buried the stained knife, one of her pearl earrings and—without realizing it—my childhood, deep beneath that dense soil in that twilight hour.

People are fools to underestimate the young. When the trauma of life exceeds the pain from the birth canal, you didn't create a child, you created an animal. God clearly picked favorites, and I wasn't it.

THE FISHING LINE was tightly connected to either end of the spindling lane, stretched taught precisely two feet off the ground, and the girl went nose over tail in a blur of cobalt blue. The bones of her elbows crunched as she rolled back and forth across the asphalt, hugging her torso with muffled moans. The moonlight highlighted the bruising on the bridge of her nose. The human body houses us, nourishes us, fights constantly for our well-being, battles disease and relegates our pain. And, all we do is abuse it. Taking for granted our overworked anatomy until the moment we're hemorrhaging. The dying plead with their bodies, expecting a miracle dial tone from rat-chewed circuitry. After years of disrespect and negligence they arrogantly expect internal magic.

No magic, no miracle and no skill would save the girl. Just like nothing would save me.

The contents of her wicker basket lay strewn across the path and I took her line of sight hostage as I calmly gathered the stolen goods: The turquoise belt buckle, one of the female's watches, and the knife.

Feeling seen is an aphrodisiac, a potently addictive drug. When you go through life compelling no second glances, you start to crave something beyond normal recognition. Holding the gaze of the dying as they tumbled into the void made me feel examined and revered.

Ghosts don't exist. If they did, I would be the most deserving of their haunting.

She lay still. Calm. Our breathing created a rhythmic hum that filled that moonlit lane. I sat cross-legged beside her splayed body. It took me years of cold bodies and self-analyzation to come to terms with who I was: I'm not a predator. I didn't seek out my victims, but they always found their way to me.

The girl had no idea what illness we shared. She didn't realize the insidious rabbit hole she'd fallen into, or had any idea of the contaminated possessions she held close. Probably couldn't fathom her compulsion to isolate and to steal. The confusing pull towards my hideout. This illness takes effect on a cellular level, leaving only a sickening contempt for those who regard you with beauty, or who treat you as a child, when you've never experienced love, nor the cradle. This kid was as deserving of my actions as any other of my finds. The only difference between this girl and anyone else who felt my blade was that she was infected before I found her.

It could have been fascinating to see the poison take hold. To watch it fester and churn in another. Perhaps I could have informed her, managed her, or become an enlightened guide through her inescapable fate.

But I'm not her fucking mother.

DEAD NO LONGER

Owen Egerton

ARE YOU MORE alive than me?

You once quipped over beers that I live small while you walk tall. You, with your vagabond swagger and month-long drinking bouts. Me, with a wife, child, and a mortgage.

Teddy came with me to the bus depot to pick you up. It had been nearly two years since we'd seen you, and he had only been four then. Now he was a rambunctious six-year-old, eager for his traveling uncle's stories and don't-tell-your-mother jokes.

"How come Uncle Len doesn't live here?"

"He likes to travel."

"Does he have a job?"

"Sure," I said. "Sometimes."

When you stepped off the bus, you gave me a funny closed-mouth smile. You kneeled before Teddy, pulled your ears and pointed at your nose. Teddy grinned and squeezed your nose. Your mouth sprung open and out came a shiny, wet quarter. Teddy erupted in laughter.

"You put that in your mouth?" I laughed.

"I bet you've put worse things in yours, you damn pickle sniffer."

I let the off-color joke slide, hoping Teddy didn't get it, and went in for a hug. You smelled of beer and bus-hours.

You'd always been the free one, the funny one, with a natural charm that I could never match. While I slogged through an MFA and banged out draft after draft of a novel, you worked construction—swing crane till sundown, drinking till to dawn, and never staying anywhere long enough to get bored.

Then on a job in Oregon, in what you called your worst and best day, a steel I-beam swung free and smashed your left hand against a concrete block. For your mangled hand and two lost fingers, the company paid out enough for you to live on for years. So, you traveled. Beach towns and ski resorts. You'd call me when you were drinking, lecture me that security is the enemy of art, urge me to abandon Texas and join you in Aspen, Santa Cruz, Key Largo. "Bring your laptop, if you want."

But it was clear when you stepped off the bus at the Austin Greyhound that the money was gone. You looked worn, tired. A decade of drink and bar food had taken a toll on your skin and weight. There was a sour air around you that had me wondering how long it had been since you'd had a shower.

I was the older brother. The got-it-together brother. Only, I didn't have it together. I had sold that first novel and not sold the next. Kath and I bought a pool with the advance of that first book and promised ourselves a hot tub with the royalties. There is no hot tub.

It was fun having you at first. You were a drinking buddy, a late-night horror movie companion. Kath always liked you. She didn't have siblings herself, so she relished the brother our marriage awarded her. Kath's doula work was taking off, and it was good to have your help with Teddy when she was called to a birth. To Teddy, you were a hero. For him, you were adventure, humor, and mischief.

But a week became two weeks became a month became a house guest who didn't clean, cook, or work. You'd hole up in the guest room and sleep or play '90s rock—*Black Crows, Alice in Chains, Sublime*—or sometimes just mumble to yourself. You offered to varnish and build out our back porch, but the supplies I bought lay untouched in the garage and all the beer I had was gone. You lied about job interviews and future plans, and asked for cash to hold you over—five bucks, ten bucks. And if I balked, I was the uptight bastard who wouldn't help a brother through a rough day. I'd give you twenty, and you'd come home drunk. You had a painkiller prescription for your hand that you'd kept filled through the years. You never seemed out of control, not to me at least. But you were sinking deeper than I realized.

I am to blame for what happened as much as you.

When you called from jail, I was only a little surprised. You'd been picked up drunk at a neighborhood park. Bail was set at $2,500.

"Jesus." I tapped my forehead. "For public intoxication?"

"Yeah, yeah, I know," you murmured. "The judge is a total dick."

Someone was mumbling orders in the background, and I heard you yes *ma'aming* and then back to me. "Get me out here, would you? I'm good for it."

You knew and I knew you were not good for it.

"Len…" There was a sick silence. A moment where I could pull back. You felt it, too.

"Listen, I fucked up. I know. I need to get my life back on—" The phone clicked dead.

We didn't have $2,500. Could we put that much on a credit card? Could we afford to do that? Did it matter?

"You can't keep enabling him. It's not helping," Kath said. "And there's Teddy to think about."

"Teddy?"

She sighed and met my eyes. "Yesterday, he was standing out by the pool. Just watching the house. Teddy wanted to go swimming, but I wouldn't let him. I couldn't even let him go outside. It wasn't a thought-out thing. Just a gut reaction. Something about him is off."

I nodded to all this, but I'm not sure I heard. I already knew I would be driving to the police station and paying my brother's bail.

THE BAIL WAS for more than Public Intoxication. Above that, typed on the bail sheet the clerk handed across the counter, was another charge: Exposure to a Minor. I paused. I thought of Teddy. I thought of Kath's words. I paid anyway.

By the time we were driving home, you were half sober, your face blotched red. The acidic smell of alcohol and sweat filled the car. You tried floating a joke, but it fell flat, and we sat in silence until I exited the highway.

"Are you going to tell me about the kid?"

"What kid?"

"You exposed yourself to a kid."

"Who said that?"

"It's what you were charged with, Len."

"Ah shit. No." You shook your head side to side like I'd failed to grasp a simple concept. "I had a beer, okay? One beer."

"One beer."

"Mr. Lemon gave me one because I ran some crackheads out of his store."

"He gave you a beer?"

"Dude, these crackheads were trying to steal a six-pack of Bud Ice and I caught them, roughed them up a little. He couldn't sell the six-pack because it'd been taken out of the store, so he gave it to me."

"You said one beer." How the hell did we get here? What does this have to do with anything? I'm not your dad. You're not sixteen.

"I drank one and handed out the rest. You know, a couple to the yard work Chicanos, a few for the guys in the park."

"What about the kid?"

"I had to take a piss. That's it. I was taking a piss in the park and there was some school field trip or whatever. I was out of sight, but some kid comes running by before I can zip up and starts crying. I try and calm him down, tell him it's okay. Show him a magic trick."

"Jesus."

"And he goes off screaming to the teacher. The end. Total bullshit."

We were now parked in our driveway, the engine clicking cool.

"If your life were a novel I was writing, I could only imagine a few possible endings," I said, almost more to myself than to you. "I don't like any of them."

You looked at me, your eyes red and small. Then you climbed from the car and walked inside. By the time I followed, you were already disappearing into your room.

You put on *Sublime.*

I don't practice Santeria, I ain't got no crystal ball...

I stood outside your door, hand raised to knock. To say what? Quiet down? Time for bed, it's a school night?

The song ended and began again. I lowered my hand and headed to bed.

Kath was awake but said nothing, and I offered no explanations.

THE NEXT MORNING, Kath left early for a consultation, and I wrangled a sleepy Teddy into school clothes and through a messy breakfast. Upstairs, music was still playing. In the rush of the morning, I didn't catch it, but while herding Teddy out the door, it clicked—it was the same song playing.

…I ain't got no crystal ball…

A single song had been playing on loop all morning, possibly all night.

"Dad, we're late." Teddy pulled me out the door.

THOSE DAYS, I was spending hours at IHOP, answering emails, googling my name, and occasionally tapping out sentences.

When my first novel, my only novel, was being readied for publication, I told my agent I was afraid I'd be a one-hit-wonder. The hubris. My book came and went, milquetoast reviews and dismal sales. I was a no-hit-wonder.

Writing had been adventure and liberation, then a career, then a career that no longer paid. Now I sat in the back booth of an IHOP, growing soft on pancakes and cheap coffee.

That afternoon, after taking hours to type half a bad page, I returned home. I walked through the front door and stopped. Upstairs, muffled but undeniable, was that same damn song: "Santeria" by *Sublime*. I didn't move. I listened until the song ended. Then it started again. How many hours was that?

I walked up the stairs and knocked on your door.

"Len?"

…All I really want to say…

"Len? You in there?"

...*It's love that I need*...

Maybe you'd skipped town and left us holding the bail. I hoped to God you'd left. I tried the door, but it was locked.

"Len. Open the door."

...*Daddy's gonna love one and all*...

I slammed my shoulder against the door. I did it again, harder, panic in my throat.

"Open the fucking door, Len!"

"Daddy?"

I turned to find Teddy standing small behind me, his eyes frightened.

"Hey T-Rex," I said, rubbing my shoulder. "Everything is okay. Just talking to Uncle Len."

"Something smells."

He was right. Something did smell. I had been smelling it for the last several minutes and not acknowledging it.

"Is Uncle Len okay?"

"I'm sure he is," I said, not sounding sure at all. "Now go help your mother."

"With what?"

"With whatever she needs help with."

He frowned but headed downstairs. I waited until he was gone and then threw my whole weight against the door. It gave with a snap. And there you stood. Naked, dried filth down the back of your thighs, your skin yellow. You didn't seem to notice me. You faced the window, chattering a stammered moan.

"Daddy?"

I turned to see Teddy had come back.

"Go to your mom, Ted."

"Daddy? Uncle Len—"

"Go!"

You took two steps toward me, a pair of soiled pajamas bunched around your ankles. Your skin was bruised blue and purple, and your eyes... you didn't seem to know me. I had to fight the urge to run from the room and slam the door. I was nearly sick with something like pity, or maybe disgust.

"We're going to help you, Len," I said, covering my mouth and nose. "We're going to get you help."

KATH WAS A natural at caretaking, a gifted doula. Her voice instinctively grew calmer to counter stress or panic.

"Okay, Len, I'm just going to towel you off, okay? There you go. Now let's get you into these sweatpants."

I tried to steady you, tried to get you to look at me, but your eyes wouldn't focus.

"He's lucky to be alive," Kath whispered. She handed me a nearly empty pill bottle from the bedside table.

YOU AND I sat in the St. David's ER waiting room. A woman sat with a blathering, pale old man, and a young father held a towel against his child's head. He checked the wound, and I saw it was an open, red gash, but not bleeding. The child didn't yell or cry. He only gazed out as his father rocked him on his lap.

We were brought back to a curtained-off room. You rolled back and forth on the bed, knocking against the metal railings. I handed the tall nurse the pill bottle. The nurse pressed his lips together in what could have been described as a smirk or a frown. My face flushed with guilt—why? Why my guilt?

A blue-eyed doctor checked your vitals with stoic efficiency. You tried to touch her hair, and I slapped your hand.

"It's alright," she said, abandoning your pulse and pushing a stethoscope to your chest. She looked to the tall nurse. "What's the wait on an EEG?"

"They're backed up till tomorrow." He took a step back. "Is he like the others?"

The doctor shot him a look, but he didn't shut up.

"Jesus, he is, isn't he? Jesus. That's twelve today. That's a full dozen."

"Matt, do you need to take a break?" she said, her voice firm, nearly threatening.

The nurse, Matt, turned to me. "He's not sick. He's not high. He's dead."

"Matt!"

"They've been coming in all day. No pulse. No brain waves. Dead, but moving."

"Matt, get the hell out of here."

"Look at him!" He screamed at me, high and frantic. "You see his chest moving? You don't, 'cause he's not breathing. Have you seen him blink? I mean, even once?" Matt clapped hard an inch from your face. You didn't flinch. "No breath. No brain function. That's dead."

"Sir," the doctor said to me in the same threatening tone she used on the nurse. "He is not qualified to make any kind of diagnosis. I assure you—"

An aged, naked woman fell through the curtains into the room, her arms raised, her body splotched white and blue. She had a jagged cut below her ribcage.

"Oh Jesus," Matt squealed. "I saw her die. I saw her dead. She died in that bed this morning!"

The doctor jumped to the woman. Putting her hands to her chest, she guided the woman out. Something fell off the woman, something red-brown and gelatinous. Not falling *off* her. Falling *from* her. It landed on the floor with a wet splat. It was clotted blood, thick and purple, shining moist in the white hospital light. It had fallen from her open body.

Matt looked at me, his body shivering. "It's *Revelation*. It's the fucking end times."

I tossed your arm around my neck and dragged you out of that place.

IT WAS EVENING when we arrived home. We sat in the car, parked in the driveway, just as we had the night before. I could see the warm light of the kitchen and Teddy sitting at the table scribbling with crayons. Kath stood at the counter, chopping vegetables, a glass of red wine beside her.

"Bud Ice," you said. The first thing you'd said that day. "Bud Ice. Bud Ice."

"I don't think we can do—"

You grabbed my face and pushed my head into the car window. Just hard enough to hurt.

"Jesus, Len."

You weren't looking at me. You stared out the passenger window, dragging your remaining fingers down the glass in a stuttered squeak. "Rice-A-Roni."

I guided you through the front door, you weaving and popping your lips like a toddler.

"Honey?" Kath called from the kitchen.

"Be right there," I called back. "Dinner smells great."

"It's salad. It smells like lettuce," Kath said. "Pizza's on the way."

I lifted your legs one by one up the stairs. It was like maneuvering a thick, fleshy mannequin. Kath had changed the sheets in your room and, it seemed, emptied a full can of potpourri air freshener.

You wouldn't lay down, and each time I moved to leave, you followed me to the door. Holding your shoulders, I steered you back to the bed, but you fell, pinning me down. I could smell you then, and the smell was wrong.

I crawled out from under you and left you mumbling into the pillows. I closed your door. Then locked it.

KATH AND TEDDY were already at the table, serving up the freshly arrived pizza. I must have looked a mess. I could see that worried look on Kath's face.

"Long day," I said and sipped—gulped—my wine.

"Is he here?"

I nodded. But it felt less than true.

Teddy dove into a story from school, something about glue poured into the electric pencil sharpener. Kath laughed, her eyes shining. I took a second slice of pizza.

I did not tell them what had happened. The high-squealing nurse. The red-brown glob falling from the naked woman's abdomen. Len's yellowing eyes and sour smell. How could I mention all this to Teddy? Half of parenting is hiding the truth of things, from mass shootings to sex. And I was already doubting what I'd seen. Look at us, happy at the table. The world couldn't be so mad. You were sick. You were resting upstairs. We'd care for you as we had cared for my mother in her last two years.

"Did you see the news?" Kath said, pouring me another glass. "They thought that Senator Romans died."

"He died?"

"No! It was a misdiagnosis," she laughed. "They were wheeling him to the morgue and his eyes popped open. I swear, some lawyer is going get very rich on that one."

THAT WAS HOW it began.

No mass-panic. No societal collapse. Only the realization that dead doesn't mean what it once did. A person dies—a full, clinical death—and an hour or so later they come back as something not quite dead. Reality leaned into uncanny those first weeks. A kind of communal what-the-fuck. We kept Teddy home from school. Kath let him daze in front of Disney+ while we scoured the internet for news. Talking heads quick to provide explanations—viral outbreak, hypnotically induced comas, wrath of God. Each theory having the tenacity of a soap bubble.

Though we had imagined the scenario in countless films, comics, and games, we were not prepared. They don't bite or hunt the living, they don't thirst for brains. As one commentator put it, "The worst that can be said about them is they loiter."

We couldn't even agree what to call them: Creepers, Moaners, Slow-Beats, Rotters. The only general consensus is that no one calls them Zombies. I call them Dead.

We can't even agree if the Dead are dead.

The Dead have heartbeats, despite original reports. Closer examination detected about one beat every two minutes. The Dead have brain waves. Nothing compared to a living, active brain, even a comatose brain. Instead there is a steady, low hum, like the static astronomers observe resounding from the birth of the cosmos.

Matt the nurse was correct about two things. The Dead do not breath; their lungs shrivel like bad fruit. And the Dead do not blink.

The morning after that first day, you were in the guest room, digging one of your scarred fingers into your cheek and chanting, "Anthill. Anthill. Anthill."

The Dead speak. They blurt words and phrases. They laugh, scream, sing snippets of songs. We've been assured it's meaningless. The Dead call out for coffee or a taxi or their child. But bring them coffee or a taxi or even their child and there is no discernible reaction. In all the studies, no Dead has been recorded saying anything it did not say while alive. Nothing but cracked echoes.

Anthill was the Irish Setter you and I had as kids.

Eventually the Dead's vocal cords exsiccate and fray. Their words become incomprehensible, scratched growls that deteriorate into mute gasps.

We learned all this later.

I KEPT YOU locked in your room. I'd visit in the mornings, when you were most alert. I brought you food and books, all untouched. Once a week, I changed your sheets, though I never saw you sleep. I tried spoon feeding. You took the food, even chewed, but swallowing seemed beyond you, and the food fell from your mouth in mashed clumps.

After a week or so, Teddy went back to school. Kath attended a birth. The world inexplicably continued. I suppose that's what worlds do.

I returned to my booth at IHOP and burned through a short story about babies born with the fully formed minds and memories of famous historical figures. Baby Napoleon, Baby Cleopatra, Baby Nietzsche. It wasn't an awful story, but it wasn't good. What was notable, what made me giddy as I dug into my pancakes, was the fact that it was complete.

I was humming as I walked up the front steps to the house, but before I opened the door, I caught sight of the guest room's off-white curtains billowing out through the broken pane of glass. I stopped humming and heard the scraping just around the side of the house. That's where I found you, moaning and lurching on the glass-coated cement. Your left leg bent wrong to the side and white bone jutting out from your calf, ripping through the sweats, yellow fat glistening on the jagged tip. You were trying to stand, scrambling like a newborn calf. Each time you put weight on your leg, the bone pushed out further.

I was careful taking you in. Though the Dead don't feed on the Living, a scratch or a cut from one would kill you within a day. Kath had heard of a father letting his baby breastfeed from the Dead mother's breast. The baby was dead—and then not-dead—by morning. Some sick bastard in San Francisco discovered that sexual contact would kill you even faster.

I boarded up the guest room window with planks I had purchased for the porch extension. Then I tied you to the bed. I used four of our father's ties—tacky things we'd given him for Christmas and Father's Day. I bound your wrists and ankles to the bed posts. You didn't resist. But there was something pitiful and panicked in your high-pitched groan.

We weren't the only family dealing with a Dead. An entire industry sprung up. Sitters promised in home care for "the departed" (a term that seemed particularly inaccurate). Dead Homes popped up all over the country, and like nursing homes or mental institutions, they varied in quality. The most expensive were former five-star hotels, with suite rooms and 24-hour attendants. Others were dog pounds, the Dead kept in cages and hosed down daily.

Some hired Takers, crews who'd collect your Dead and not tell you where they were taken. In Baltimore, a block-wide fire led investigators to discover that a warehouse had been filled nearly to the ceiling with Dead stacked upon Dead. It was never determined if the fire was accidental or intentional.

Plenty of people simply pulled up beneath an underpass, opened the car door, and let their Dead lumber away.

There were, of course, mercy killings. Attempts to dismember, dissolve, or in some other way destroy whatever the Dead are. Most failed. At first, most of us believed decapitation or a massive brain injury would do the trick, just like the movies. But that myth was quickly dispelled by the videos of headless Dead flooding the internet.

There's a case, one of many making its way through the courts, of a woman who fed her Dead husband to their Rottweiler, piece by piece. Was it murder? He had legally been declared dead. Did the hum of his brain and that heartbeat every 120 seconds amount to life? Arguments and protests abound. "A heartbeat means life!" and "God decides what's dead." Countered by, "Help them die," and "THEY are not THEM!" The Rottweiler case is expected to reach the Supreme Court, but until then, it is technically illegal to cause harm or forcibly restrain the Dead.

I'd find Teddy staring down the hall to your locked room, listening to you slur out radio jingles behind the door.

"Is Uncle Len sick?" he'd ask. "Sick like the people on the news."

"He just needs some rest, Teddy."

Some, not many, believe we are witnessing the next evolutionary step of humanity, a massive leap toward eventual immortality. That the Dead are a new kind of life, with slow beats and steady hums, like trees with century-long lives. And we, the Living, are nothing more than fish gaping at the first of our kind to slither onto shore.

The concept of achieving a "Good Death" is gaining popularity. A Good Death, it's said, ensures no return. Many, very many, feel it's better to plan a Good Death than risk dying by chance and returning as a ghoul. Some maintain starving to death works. Others say drowning. Cruise lines offer all-inclusive escapades into the North Atlantic and turn a blind eye as half their passengers jump overboard.

Most assume only an end that obliterates the body guarantees a lasting death. Burning is most common. The city is rampant with botched-burn Deads—people, sometimes whole families, who'd set themselves ablaze but had fizzled out or been doused by well-meaning first responders before the job was done. These Deads, the almost-all-Deads, cry the loudest, as if in constant world-bending pain. The scientists swear it's not a current pain, only the remnants of their last moments, their nerves remembering the pain. They fail to explain what the hell the difference is.

Kath and I didn't mention you. We discussed the situation as a whole on a global scale, a local scale, even a philosophical scale. But we avoided the facts of our particular predicament as resolutely as we avoided your door.

You were rotting in that room. I no longer attempted talking with you. Stopped trying to feed you. I left you tied to that bed, day in and day out. At first, I ached with guilt, but as your body rotted soft, I hardened. Eventually, you'd rot away. Eventually, there'd be nothing but a stain. This was our unspoken hope. So, the sound I woke to that night made my skin popple.

...I don't practice Santeria, I ain't got no crystal ball...

I leapt from our bed and out to the hallway.

...I had a million dollars...

Your door was cracked open. I stepped closer and under the music, I made out whispering and laughing.

...But I'd... I'd spend it all...

I pushed the door open and there was Teddy with his back to me, standing by your bed.

"Teddy," I said in a croaked whisper.

"I put on the song he likes." Teddy turned to me, revealing his small hand with two fingers in your rancid mouth. "I'm looking for quarters."

I leapt forward, slapping Teddy's fingers from your mouth. Teddy pulled back, cradling his hand. I looked at your changed face—your black and yellow skull-tight skin flaking like sun-bleached roadkill, your receded lips giving you a garish grin. You were not my brother. You were no longer you.

"Dad," Teddy said. "I'm bleeding."

I turned and saw the dripping red.

"Did he bite you?"

"No, Dad," he said, holding his hand to his chest. "When you pulled my fingers out, one caught a little on his teeth. It's just a scratch. I'm okay."

I took him in my arms and squeezed him until he gasped.

I woke Kath. I told her about waking to the music, seeing Teddy in your room. I intended to tell her what I had done, but as she sat up in bed, all sleep gone, almost guessing the oncoming horror, I couldn't. I could not.

"He bit him," I said. "He bit our boy."

She slapped and screamed and pushed me away, taking Teddy and curling around him in our bed.

Len, I am sorry.

It was still dark when I hauled you down the stairs and to the car, dragging you by your good leg. As we drove, I watched your face, the marble-like remains of eyes catching the rain-bent light of streetlamps. Nothing there. No one there.

The underpass near the water treatment center was crowded with Dead. It was a frequently used drop. For reasons unknown, the Dead remained in the vicinity. Other Dead joined them.

People left clothes, sleeping bags, food—all untouched and molding. The Dead stood in the shadows, out of the rain. Some crawled, some twitched, all motiveless movement. It was nearly dawn. The Dead are more restless at dawn. Maybe each night they've forgotten the world is anything but black, and the first light of day terrifies.

I left the car running, climbed out, and opened the passenger door. I had to yank you out. I sat you down on an unused sleeping bag and wrapped a blanket around your shoulders. You called out something wordless as I turned back to the car. I took a last look. You raised yourself, standing for a moment, trying to step but collapsing forward on to the wet ground, half your face splashing in a puddle of muddy water. Your black tongue lapped at the mud in a parody of drinking.

I did not help you. I did not say goodbye. I climbed into the car and drove home to my wife and child.

TEDDY SWEAT ICE that day and into the night. Sometimes he woke and gazed up at us, confused.

"We could take him to the hospital," I said.

"You know what they do," she said, touching his damp brow. "They keep them. Study them."

"We have to do something."

"There's nothing."

We sat wordless, watching him twist and sweat through his sheets all through the night and the next day. He woke in the mid-day heat, his eyes polished glass. He put three fingers to his chin, signing for water as we'd taught him as a baby. I put the glass to his lips, but the water only dribbled from his mouth.

On the second night, Kath finally slept, dozing fitfully in the same rocking chair she had breastfed a baby Teddy to sleep so many years before. I stayed by Teddy, holding his hot, tiny hands. His breath went strange. His sweat soured. He opened his eyes and seemed surprised to see me.

"Dad," he said. "I was calling for you."

"I'm right here, T-Rex."

"I was calling for you and you didn't come."

"I was right here the whole time."

He shook his head now, frustrated with me. "You can't hear me, but that doesn't mean I'm not talking."

He closed his eyes and breathed in shallow hiccups.

I took him in my arms, feeling that life still in him. I cradled him from the room, careful not to rouse Kath. I carried him down the stairs and into our garage.

"Keep breathing, Teddy. Keep breathing."

The plastic lawn bags were jungle green and industrial strength. I placed him in the bag, delicately curling him in on himself. He blinked up at me, and I had to wait until he shut his eyes again before I could tie the bag closed.

I held him to my chest, hushing him through the plastic.

The pool rippled blue and shadow, and I held my son in the bag above the deep end. I said his name. I said I'm sorry. I let go of the bag.

It sank down, bubbles escaping up. The bag landed gently on the bottom, rolling a little to one side. I watched it. A minute passed. Then ten. Then an hour. The waters never moved. I had murdered him. I had saved him. A Good Death.

"Where's Teddy?"

She stood in the sliding door.

"He's gone, baby," I said. "He's all gone."

She fell to her knees, heaving. I was going to go to her, to weep with her, to begin to mourn. But the water shifted.

I turned and stared back at the bag. Nothing seemed different. It was just as it had been for an hour. That's how it should be. Dead and nothing. I begged it not to move. But just as I was about to breathe again, the bag twitched. Through the soundless water, I saw my child's hand press against the plastic, stretching it till the green thinned yellow.

I dove in. I dug my nails into the bag and ripped until my son's face emerged, mouth open in a mute cry. I tugged him to the surface, the bag caught on his foot and limply dragging behind him like discarded skin.

WE DIDN'T END.

That's perhaps the hardest truth.

We did not end.

We kept him with us in our bed, but he didn't sleep. We kept him close, but his smell was not the smell of our son. I took the varnish intended for the porch and coated his skin to keep back the change. It only trapped in the rot, then cracked like old paint.

We surrounded him with games and stuffed animals he never touched. He wandered through the house, mewling. More and more, we'd find him bumping against the sliding glass doors or fumbling with the front doorknob. We kept every door locked.

Eventually, we put him in his room and locked that door, too. We checked on him constantly. Then less so. Then hardly at all. Occasionally, I catch Kath slipping Pop-Tarts under his door. I want to believe there is nothing we can do, because I do nothing.

It's been eleven months since the onset. Elections happen. Television shows air. People get married. Babies are born, though significantly fewer. More and more Dead wander the streets, the empty places. They stare at us. Even the ones whose eyes are gone stare.

Kath no longer works as a doula. She went back into advertising and now earns three times as much. I'm working on a new novel. Kath says it's my best writing yet, but she said that last time.

Less than a year, but it's hard to remember a time before the Dead. Children are now born that will never know a world without them. They are as ubiquitous as smart phones and soft drinks. Death is the landscape of the now, and the world smells of decomposition in the way nineteenth century London must have smelled of horse manure and coal. Cemeteries and war monuments are strange reminders of the time when death was buried. Nothing is buried now. The Dead are a constant, present promise. What we are, they once were. What they are, we soon shall be.

The Dead rot spectacularly. The wet change, the bruise-autumn colors turning to green, mold growing, insects nesting, the fuzz of new life. This morning, I found a Dead in our driveway. It looked like a meadow on two feet. Grass and weeds covered its body, flowers sprouting from what had been eyes, moths fluttering close, and small birds buzzing near and feeding from seeds. Its body was more soil than flesh, more life than death. It was beautiful. And as it limped on down our road, I could see through the growth the three remaining fingers of your left hand.

KATH AND I have talked. Kath and I have cried. Tonight, we will open Teddy's room. We will bathe him one last time, sponging his body with warm water, milky with soap. We will dry him in the oversized towels he adored. We will leave all the doors open.

THIS IS NOT MY FACE

Gigi Saul Guerrero

Inspired by true events, 1995 Mexico City

KIDS SAY THE darndest things, don't they? Sometimes kids even say the funniest things, the grossest, and yes, even the spookiest things. It's not uncommon to hear a new parent say their child said something unusual or creepy.

My mother, Romina, always says I, at an early age, acted *differently*. Very differently! I guess you could say I saw the world through an 'unlikely' lens. I would point to buildings and say, "that wasn't there before" or, "this used to be a..." I would utilize vocabulary which was far more advanced. I would question everything. In short, I would see, or rather criticize, things kids my age shouldn't have been aware of.

One day everything changed. It was a Saturday in the afternoon in Mexico City. Romina was at the nearby *Tianguis* picking out the groceries for the week. "Yum," she smiled at the perfectly shaped Mamey fruit shining on the stand. As she picked one up, she smelled it–almost took a bite at that instant–when a mother's instinct told her to go home, *now*. She opened her eyes and saw a disgusting rotten fruit too close to her mouth. The strong stench of waste invaded her nostrils. She dropped the Mamey immediately,

One thing for sure is that Mexicans are very good at listening to their inner voice. Some say it's your guardian angel, others say it's your ancestors watching over you. Another reason why *familia* is so important.

Feeling a pain in her chest, my mom rushed home, dropping the produce she had. A perfect watermelon rolled down the hill and had it not been for it my mother wouldn't have made it home. Who knows what would have happened to me. It rolled onto the street causing traffic to stop, smashing to smithereens and painting the cobblestones red, startling the cars just long enough for my mom to run across.

As she entered our home, she found my sister huddled in a corner of the kitchen covering her ears, pleading.

"Make it stop! Make HER stop!"

My mom remembers the fear in her eyes. My sister was only nine years old–she couldn't understand what was wrong with me. My mom brushed her cheek, kissed her forehead and said "Sí, mi amor."

Romina's heart dropped as she heard the painful sobs which turned into screams of anger, like shattering crystal against a chalkboard, all coming from the bathroom. As Romina let go of her hand, my sister softly whimpered, "don't leave me, mom, please."

With a reassuring smile Romina let go as she winked.

My mom walked towards the bathroom with all the courage she could muster, yet driven by a need to save her baby. She opened the bathroom door slowly to reveal her youngest child yelling at the top of her lungs into the mirror.

"NOOOO! THIS–THISSS IS NOT MY FAAAAACE!" My tiny fingernails were digging into my face, my cheeks bleeding from the despair.

I turned and yelled at my Mother.

"THIS IS NOT MY FACE!"

Tears streamed like rivers from my eyes.

Shock overtook my mom for a second. She recalls feeling my great-grandmother touching her shoulder, giving her the strength she needed. My great grandmother died two months after I was born.

With a firm grip she held onto my hands as I screamed and kicked back with all the strength I had. Finally, after what seemed an eternity, I asked, "WHAT NUMBER MOM ARE YOU?"

My chest heaved as I panted, my gaze strong, menacing, defiant. Speechless, she looked past my rage and gently smiled.

"ANSWER ME! WHAT. NUMBER. MOM. ARE. YOU!?"

Complete silence.

She stared at me, with fear in her heart coupled with steadfastness.

"I am the last one you're going to have."

Those words rang loud in my core, like a bell had been tolled.

"The last one?" I asked as my voice changed in pitch.

"Yes, mi vida, the last one. I love you and will love you more than any other mother you ever had."

At that precise second, I passed out in her arms. Like falling into a heavenly cloud. Finally at peace.

Twelve and a half hours later it had turned into Sunday. I woke up. I woke up as a different person. I woke up as *me*. The real me.

ROLL THE BONES

Ariel Vida

1.

DEAD BRANCHES CRACKED in whipping winds. Somewhere in the distance, a boulder groaned and split off a mountain ledge. The unforgiving gale kicked rusty sand—nearly ethereal in the moonlight—up into strange, otherworldly shapes.

Under the din, barely audible…wheezing, ragged breathing.

A young boy pulled himself on hands and knees to crest a craggy, jutting slate of crystalline rock. Weather-beaten and shaking, hardly able to get to his feet. Almost lost in the wind, a distant voice called back across the vast expanse to him.

"Nico?"

Nico whirled around desperately amidst the swirling dust, before spying a hunched form far in front of him. *"Mat!"*

Surging forward, he rubbed uselessly at the sand caking his eyes as he stumbled up the dune and fell beside the other boy. The same age, no more than ten winters old, clothes much too thin for the freezing desert night. "Mat? Mat, get up…"

Mat tipped back to sit on his heels, offering a weak, wry smile to his friend who hovered anxiously. "I hear ya, shush." He swatted away Nico's shivering hands, forcing them back towards his pockets and out of the biting wind. "It's gonna be fine…quit your worryin.'"

For several minutes, they both trembled in the howling storm, exhausted and terribly small among the never-ending peaks and valleys that spread out into an endless, moonlit horizon. Mat gritted his teeth together, mustering some new depth of determination, and hauled himself to his feet. Lurching once, he glared up at the sky as if to challenge its force.

"C'mon." He gave the collar of Nico's shirt a tug, and they continued on.

TIME SEEMED TO bend and stretch hazily, until even the wind could no longer be heard, falling away like an echo. In what felt at once like years and the blink of an eye, Nico stumbled again, crashing against cold sand and struggling unsuccessfully to keep his eyes open.

Using all of his energy to roll over, the boy stared up at towering crests of contorted, rocky spires. They bent and twisted into the inky black and melted into the stars, the outline burning itself into his mind.

"...Mat?"

No answer. Only the eerie stillness of a barren desert. The utter silence reignited the fading embers within Nico, and he whimpered, pushing to his elbows. A few paces away, Mat lay crumpled. Unmoving. Sand had already collected on his clothes, beginning to bury him under its grasp.

Nico let out a strangled sound, and as he forced himself to his knees, his eyes fell upon something in the distance. A figure. A dark silhouette, moving slowly towards the mountains.

"Help! Help, please!" His voice was swallowed by the desert, but the tall form paused. Nico could barely make anything out through the dim moonlight and his own exhaustion, but the man appeared to consider for a long moment...before walking towards the boys.

Nico dragged himself over to Mat, fumbling as he shook the limp body, clutching at an upturned hand already half-buried in dust. "Mat, *Mat*..."

Long-dried foliage crunched underneath boots and rusted spurs as the stranger knelt next to the panicking boy. No concern or haste seemed to register.

"Your friend is gone."

Nico recoiled as if struck, but couldn't get out any words. He clung to Mat, falling apart at the seams, yet nearly dry of tears.

"Few could have lasted out here." The man's voice was flat and detached. With a breathless sob, Nico turned bloodshot eyes up to the shadowed face as the stranger moved to stand.

"No. No, you have to help him!"

The man did not spare a single look back to the boy. "Few can reach someone passing through that veil. It's a very thin border. One you are stepping into as we speak."

A broken sound of fear and denial escaped the boy, but there was a heavy truth in the man's words. Nico's arms were no longer holding him up well at all, and the world seemed to gray and waver.

"In fact..." The man looked over—or past—Mat's body, as if watching something Nico could not. Calculating.

Nico turned to match his gaze and saw nothing. But there were sounds on the wind that weren't there before. Ebbing in and out, far-off echoes as if coming from down a long tunnel, or deep underwater.

"It is a rare moment to both be in-between..." The man tilted his head slightly, the moonlight catching his eyes under the brim of his hat.

"Please, *please* just help us."

The man ignored the boy. He was still staring across Mat's body, where the distant echoes spilled out from some unseen void.

There was nothing left in Nico, final embers going cold. "I'll do anything. *Please.*" He beseeched the stranger one last time, with all the breath he had left. The man finally turned to look back at the dying boy, and something shifted on his face.

Something knowing.

2.

IT WAS THE last Nico recalled of the night... unless his thoughts twisted too far down into the tar pit of memory, a suffocating abyss he was ill-equipped to escape from. Twenty years gone by and each morning ever grateful for the first signs of the gold sun rising, searing away that night's cold chill where its claws still hooked themselves in his chest.

The brilliant light crept slowly over staggering red vistas as Nico rode across the desert. Pausing briefly near a lone scraggy tree, he unfolded a piece of parchment and studied it intently, his other hand carding through his horse's mane. A kind gesture, but one that also helped quell some brimming anxiety caused by the document.

After a few moments and a resigned sigh, Nico tucked the paper safely within his jacket and whistled softly to the horse, riding onward.

Coiled spires of petrified trees painted the desert horizon like an endless maze, yet one Nico navigated with ease. There was no other soul in sight, just distended shadows of distant birds circling the beryl-colored sky.

Reaching a short ledge that plateaued against a copper mountainside, his horse perked up in anticipation of their destination as she trotted up the steep, recessed path.

Sun-bleached swaths of fabric stretched across the camp, a temporary spot that one could leave in a hurry. The otherwise hidden nook overlooked the entire expanse of wide dunes, and the tattered canvas cast much-needed shadows.

Mat, reclined against an outcropped rock, was the very picture of careless comfort in the shade. He tilted his hat up an inch as Nico dismounted, smirking, then dropping it back down as if returning to doze.

"Mornin."

Tying his horse next to Mat's, Nico topped off their water and unclipped a canteen and cartridge belt from a post while grinding out the last coals of a fire. Mat finally groaned, making a bit of a production out of the process of standing up and stretching. He squinted into the rising sun as if it might have been personally out to inconvenience him, producing a flask from somewhere within his jacket. Pouring it into two cups, he nudged one across a makeshift table.

"New assignment?" Mat leaned against the creaking board and pushed the cup farther over to Nico, who didn't move to sit, but broke into a long-suffering smile. He took a pointed look towards the sky as if to double-check that it was, in fact, still rather early for whiskey.

Feigning innocent surprise, Mat motioned 'cheers' to the untouched cup and downed both himself, standing and dusting off his jacket with a shit-eating grin.

"You're the life of the party, pal." He began to pack up the camp, unhurried, intentionally swatting Nico with a saddle blanket on its way to the horse. "Boring as hell round here till you come by!"

Nico sighed, shaking off sand from his own hat as Mat continued on.

"So how ya been? Longest stretch since a job, or close to it? Started to think maybe ol' Calloway kicked the bucket and we were scot-free."

Nico snorted incredulously. "Pretty sure Calloway would tell death itself to fuck off, and it would listen."

Mat's grin widened as he hefted the saddle onto his horse, looking theatrically wistful. "Hmm, and I bet I'd miss it. Was beginning to worry I'd have to start riding into towns of my own choosin' and swindle the locals, just to remind myself of the good old days…"

Nico played along, but his smile didn't reach his eyes, disquiet under the surface. "I've actually heard there's other ways to get by."

Mat scoffed. "Bullshit. Rumors and lies! Who ya been talkin' to?" He poured Nico coffee from a beat-up pot before tossing it in a saddlebag, leaning in as he handed over the cup. Gaze deadly serious, one hand gripped Nico's shoulder firmly. "Stay away from people who say things like that. They sound like bad news."

Nico rolled his eyes as Mat swung up onto the saddle and assessed his friend's lack of enthusiasm. "You don't like doing these jobs, but you don't like *not* doing 'em either. You're a real piece of work, pal."

Nico silently stared down at the tin cup.

"When was the last time you just enjoyed a day? Not a gig for Calloway, or any other job, or whatever the hell you're always busy with. Just let yourself have a swell ol' time?"

Nico's eyes darted across the horizon, voice thin. "Cut it out. I don't tell you how to live your life."

Mat broke into laughter like it was the funniest goddamn thing he'd ever heard, nearly tipping off of the horse. "Yes you do! *All the time!*"

Nico pressed his face against the saddle, sagging in exhaustion. "I get it. It's fucking annoying. Point made."

Still laughing uncontrollably, Mat took off as Nico groaned and pulled himself up to follow suit, riding into the reddening sun.

THE PAIR RODE across increasingly strange vistas, colored streams and buried bones emerging from the sand as if a vast sea once receded and never came back. Rocks twisted in jagged ridges and glinted with salt and copper. Shadows of spindly-legged animals retreated into cracks and fissures in the mountains, while the horses' hooves broke up imprinted waves carved by the wind.

At each shantytown they passed came a ruse the men could do in their sleep. They both showed what appeared to be a bounty document around: Nico overtly guileless and helpful, tinkering on some broken wagon wheel while gently imploring for information, poking at what crimes the mark seemed to have committed, while Mat slid into games at bars with rakish charm and flourishes of cards.

A lead—the man likely headed to the next town over in search of desperately-needed coin, a fresh slash of a scar across his face—and they were off to the next tangle of battered buildings. Sparse, sunken, and warped, as though it had all been shaken up in a bottle and dumped back out upon the desert to bake in the sun.

Heading separate directions from the livery stable, Mat grinned. "Gonna scope out townsfolk, exits, critters…everything you need to feel swell before Cal locks this fella up?"

Nico nodded distractedly, focused on the last lazy tendrils of scarlet and gold sinking below the horizon .

Mat continued pondering. "Sure would be nice to see some of the coin from these bounties, I bet Cal brings 'em into those fancy big cities…"

Stopping sharply in his tracks, Nico looked over his shoulder. "This is all he asks of us. He gets the reward."

"Yeah, yeah!" Mat waved behind his back without turning around. "We just do the dirty work *and* hafta pay for our own drinks!"

THE WALLS OF the makeshift bar were constructed with textured, deeply saturated fabric that billowed with the desert night winds as colorful lamplight danced across the floor. A withered man dealt Mat into a game as he rolled a die experimentally between his fingers. "Anyone new come by these parts lately? Disturbin' the peace?"

The dealer grunted. "Just you."

"Aww. Y'all are too kind." Mat practically preened. "I heard about someone that mighta been headin' here to hide out for a spell…"

"An' where'd ya hear that?"

Mat downed another drink. "Oh, you know how people talk."

"A lotta them shouldn't." A cold-eyed woman gave him a pointed glance and Mat flipped one of the dice, almost aggressively cheerful. "Alright, alright. I'm just looking for a new partner on my next adventure, quick an' easy grab of some silver—" He checked his hand, pushing the last coin into the center of the table…and a wiry man with a deep scar across his nose glanced up at the mention of the job.

"That ain't enough of a wager." The dealer ground out, and Mat shrugged with a sigh. "So sorry, that's all I got on me."

"Doesn't have to be just coin here, pal. We put it all on the table."

Nico leaned against another player's chair, tone conspicuously barbed. "You sure look like you've had fine luck in the past."

Mat took a long moment to assess a revolver on his belt in a finely detailed holster. Bronze pocket watch on a sturdy chain. Torn but intricately embroidered bandanna. "Fine. All-in. Everything that's mine to give."

A murmur of approval emerged from the small crowd. The dealer nodded as the others rolled dice and drew cards. All laid down their hands.

Rude jeering spread across the table. Mat had lost.

Cavalier, he tossed a loose coin pouch onto the table alongside shit from his pockets: crumpled rolling papers and a sugar cube for the horse. One tipsy player pawed at the pistol on Mat's belt.

"Naw bud, *these* aren't mine to give. All belongs to an ol' friend. I'm just watching it for him while he's locked up. I gave y'all everythin' I promised...*but* I got that tip on more silver if you're—"

Nico cut in. "Scum like you always got tall tales of big money." His path to grabbing for Mat cut conveniently in front of the man with the scar, roughly jostling his chair as he snagged hold of Mat's jacket. "I'd bet anything you *stole* all these goods."

Growling, the older man heaved himself to his feet and shoved the pair apart. "Unless you're the goddamn sheriff, how 'bout ya bite that smart tongue?" Hunched low, he yanked Mat aside to the bar.

Mat's eyes widened in foolish, dawning recognition. "...Grafton Birch?"

"Just tell me about this fuckin' venture."

The final step: When and where to meet Mat the following night. A fifty-fifty split. Just a quick drop on a kid that looked little more than a blacksmith's apprentice, but carried an *incredibly* large purse to settle his father's hefty debt.

Greedy eyes glinted with anticipation, and Mat smiled. "Looks like we have a deal!"

LESS THAN A week's work. Another night and another saloon. Spirits were high as a large stained-glass window hung overhead, cracks spidering throughout as it illuminated the smoky room below with streaks of emerald and yellow. A neglected stage took up a far wall where Mat played an old guitar, gathering a modestly-sized and immodestly-drunken crowd that clapped and hollered along. Nico remained at a table in the corner, thoughts elsewhere, but he smiled softly as other patrons joined the ruckus and the room was immersed in a lively, carefree din.

3.

OUTSIDE, THE MUSIC barely filtered across the barren landscape to a gnarled meeting post on the outskirts of town. A crumbling wooden platform was flanked by several lifeless, bowed trees.

Grafton approached. The man's hand hovered by the revolver at his hip as his frown deepened. His eyes narrowed at the distinct lack of Mat. Or anyone else. No incoming riders on the horizon, and no promised silver to be stolen.

He checked his pocket watch and huffed in annoyance. Expecting a trick perhaps, but not nothing at all. Mumbling obscenities under his breath, the man lit a cigar to wait a moment or two longer for the promised fortune.

Behind him, a shadowed figure moved soundlessly through the trees.

The festivities of the bar reached a crescendo in the distance, but as it did, the far-off sounds seemed to be sucked away in the wind. The desert fell strangely still as Grafton, noting the odd hush, turned to see the stranger approaching.

Unhurried. Unarmed.

But Grafton registered a threat when he saw one, quickly lifting his revolver—

Before it could even be leveled to aim, Calloway was in front of him. Grafton's arm shattered like brittle ice, bent backwards as the entire gun slammed upwards with little resistance, iron plunging into the man's throat and up through his skull.

Snapping off a crooked branch from the closest tree, in less time than a breath, Calloway flipped it down and *through* the man's ribs with a wet crunch. Then out and back into one knee, twisting him up like a dried beetle.

What was left of Grafton's jaw still contorted impossibly in a gurgling scream, only going quiet when his neck itself was split in two...splintered spine lodged up through his throat.

Backlit by the moon, Calloway glanced down at what was left of the man strewn across the platform.

Satisfied.

4.

RILED UP FROM the revelry of the bustling saloon, Mat slid back into the table, one arm cradling three more glasses. The other fished dice and cards from a pocket, glancing eagerly around the room for the next enterprise.

Nico gave an appreciative, quiet nod as one of the drinks slid across to him, but it stood in stark contrast to his friend's energy.

"C'mon. Another one down! Who shit in your soup, pal?" Mat leaned forward, lowering his voice conspiratorially. "I'll shoot 'em, if you need."

Nico half-shrugged, eyes on the glass as he nudged it back and forth across the grimy table. "Like you said...it'd been awhile this time. Thought maybe he wasn't coming back. And we'd just be...done."

"I'm hurt. Didn't want to see this mug anymore?"

Nico rolled his eyes, heartened by the familiar bullshitting, but not fully distracted.

"Nico. You're the one that confirms what pieces of shit they are. So what's all that bad about tracking down some awful sons-of-bitches and bringing 'em to justice?" Solemn and noble, Mat sold the look of a serious politician: "It's for a good cause."

"But haven't we..." Nico's voice cut out at the sound of slow footsteps—boots and old spurs—striding across the porch outside.

The curled, battered doors eased open, and a tall silhouette cut into the colorful light on the floor. Patrons didn't fully hush, but there was an immediate tensing throughout the room.

Calloway's very presence parted the milling crowd as he strode up to the pair's table.

Donning a heavy jacket that glinted dark crimson in certain light, he bore no visible weapons...yet was immediately registered as someone to give a wide berth to. Coolly collected, he sat down without greeting either man, taking a long drink off the third glass.

Unlike Nico, Calloway's arrival didn't seem to dampen Mat's spirits in the slightest.

He tilted his own drink like a festive salute.

"So. Convinced another one to go straight?"

Calloway smirked slightly. "More or less." Reaching into his weather-worn coat as he spoke, he produced an old envelope— similar to the bounty Nico carried before—and slid it to the center of the table.

Nico shifted restlessly, eyes darting between the document and Calloway. "Another?"

Calloway's dark gaze bore into Nico, an unamused standoff. Whatever entertained him about Mat did not appear to extend to Nico.

The younger man wilted. "I mean...that's fine. I just—what's going on?"

Calloway made the smallest motion of a shoulder, too digni- fied to be called a shrug, but conveying the same indifference. "I have been searching for this mark for quite a while. This is the first I have known of the whereabouts. It may well be the last one that I am in need of service for."

Nico's eyes widened, urgently searching Calloway's face for some hidden truth while reaching for the envelope, but his expression was impenetrable. Mat took another generous swig of his drink—seeming only half-interested—but behind the glass, his eyes intently focused on the conversation.

Calloway's gaze raked across both men. "You will meet me at the end of the narrows outside town in three days. Sunset."

His eyes brokered no further questions as he stood, leaving the half-finished drink and disappearing into the night.

The bar teetered as patrons' nerves settled, hushed voices rushing to discuss the stranger.

Mat tipped his chair back casually, finishing off his own glass, an easy grin splitting across his face. "He's always got so much pep."

But Nico still stared down at the envelope, and Mat faltered in stunned astonishment.

"*Hey*, finally—the last job!"

Nico's fingers ghosted across the folds, but seemed incapable of opening it. "Why does he want to meet us there? He doesn't join us till we find the mark, and it's *never* been back to back assignments…"

"Maybe he already knows exactly where the fella is and when he's gonna be there, and just wants us to back him up." Mat shrugged, unconcerned, while an extremely skeptical look twisted Nico's face.

"Calloway needing backup."

Mat hummed in consideration. "Alright, so he wants us to run point or create a diversion. Somethin' different." He flicked the dice into the side of Nico's glass with a loud *clink*, drawing attention to its untouched state. "Didn't ya hear the news? This'll be the last one, you should be celebrating!"

Nico's lips twitched in spite of himself but as he finally opened the envelope, the hesitant smile died as quickly as it had emerged. Mat leaned in curiously as Nico smoothed the single page across the table, going even more tense.

Just a map, with one small town indicated towards the northwestern corner.

"Huh. No mark?"

Nico shook his head. "I've never heard of this place before. Never." Mat cocked his head, interest piqued but not alarmed, as Nico pulled a few more papers from his jacket and laid them out. Different maps covered in handwritten marks and notes. On the new assignment, he indicated the narrows by the town.

"This…shouldn't be there. You can't just go through these mountains. This route? It doesn't exist—*there isn't anything there.*"

Mat squinted at the page, readying the faceted whiskey glass like a magnifying tool in a hunt for something distressing. "Well, the thing is, people do *make* paths sometimes, so…"

But Nico's gaze had gone somewhere far away, and Mat frowned, setting down the glass at once. His friend seemed to shrink into himself, eyes fixed on the distinctly twisted mountain range. An echo seemed to engulf the room.

Mat's voice turned uncharacteristically soft. "Nico, hey—" Nico felt his throat sealing up, claws of panic tightening around his lungs. "*Nico.*"

Mat jostled his arm, and Nico looked up sharply.

Under the thundering rush of a heartbeat in his ears, the commotion of the saloon slowly filtered back in. He swallowed, throat dry, and could swear he tasted sand as he glanced where Mat had tugged at his sleeve. Anguish flashed across Nico's face before he could mask it, sitting upright and forcing composure, lest Mat ask something he wouldn't be able to answer.

With his best attempt at a steadying breath, Nico pointed to the map again. "You can't go past those mountains. There's nothing there."

Something discerning flitted in Mat's reaction, but he played along with an encouraging smile. "So…it's new, just been found! Isn't that what you spend all your damn time doing—checking out every corner of the desert? Ain't this somethin' you'd be doing for fun, anyway?" He dug a fist into Nico's arm at a rapt staccato. "Come on, now. You love all that research and readin' you travel so far for, right?"

Nico hesitated even longer. "…I don't know."

Mat paused, a bit startled. "You…then why're you doing it?"

No answer.

Mat scrubbed a hand across his face. "You're just spendin' your entire life grinding yourself into the sand… *Why?*"

Nico winced slightly and Mat quickly switched tactics, pitching his voice low. "Nico. Pal." Picking up the map, he studied it with genuine focus. "I get it. I do. It's strange. Calloway's a real strange guy. Dunno how he even found us that night, but it was real kind of him to bring us back home, and we'd be damn rude to ask too many questions. But we're almost done with everything he's asked of us. You can't tell me you're not excited."

Nico took a moment too long to answer. "Yeah—no, no I am."

Even attempted sentiment couldn't suppress the escape of a gleeful laugh. "Fuckin' hell, and that's why *I* run the cards, you can't lie your way out of a burlap sack!"

Nico slid out of arm's reach as Mat clapped a hand against his back, sighing so hard it physically dropped his shoulders. "...And if it's *not* the last one?"

"Mmm." Mat didn't seem the least bit concerned. "I could always do 'em on my own. I happen to think they're a real good time! But half the time *you* look like Calloway's making you eat horse shit." He caught his friend's eyes. "...you know, I'm not actually gonna get myself killed the second you're not supervisin'."

Nico seemed to choke on his next breath, looking down at the envelope. "I wanted to do them, too. It's all Calloway asked of us." His voice was stilted, the words rote. "It's the right thing, stoppin' these people."

Mat snorted. "Yeeaah, you think I'd get myself killed!" He shook his head and chuckled, fondly amused. "Asshole. Reckon you'll have any fun tonight, or just collect dust?"

Nico slid farther down in his chair as if to shrink away from the questions, or possibly to become one with the floor. Mat drummed his knuckles against the tabletop, gesturing to an abused piano abandoned near the stage. "Just look. That there is a damn shame!" He stood up, *'cheers'*-ing a glass at Nico, who still didn't meet his eyes.

"C'mon, pal—to the last gig!"

As Mat bounded off, Nico moved stiffly to pocket the map, utterly crumpled in his shaking hands.

5.

AT THE OUTSKIRTS of town, the desert felt palpably restless under a bronze moon—as though the sand itself was settling on an unseen, broken foundation. Otherworldly scarlet dunes bent themselves into warped slopes and twisting slot canyons. The wind kicked up dust in weak, fleeting bursts, like the last sporadic fits of a moth too close to a fire.

For the first time in many moons, the canyons seemed to shift. Disorienting angles arced in every direction. Never-ending rock walls pressed in as if breathing. Peculiar spikes of nearly translucent, blood-red stone jutted out from the sand, and a foreboding echo emanated from deep within the mountains.

Unearthly and almost…in pain.

Followed by another, and another, overlapping at different pitches, as if strangled or wailing, before being swallowed up by the howling gale.

Beneath the meeting post, what was left of Grafton's body had stained a large swath of sand an even deeper crimson, chips of bone and muscle scattered across the wooden platform. Someone stepped across the creaking boards, a faint jangle of spurs, and the mutilated pieces were slowly dragged off into the darkness.

Sliding through the sand, trailing bloody red mud, it was perhaps a trick of the dimming starlight or a particular gust of wind…

…but the mangled limbs still seemed to stir.

6.

THE SAME MOON *loomed lower and larger twenty years ago. Stars sank away into an inky oblivion, but the moonlight alone silhouetted the unmistakable outline of the mountains' gnarled spires.*

"It is not often that one steps across that border, just as another is moving on into the next realm. Sharing the plane, in-between… even for a moment."

Nico stared up at Calloway, barely able to follow his words. With every short, hitching breath, the world seemed to pull farther and farther away, flickering out of existence. Nico's fingers twisted in Mat's sleeve as if it was the only thing still holding them both there.

His voice was small and wrecked, shredded with misery. "But can you help?"

Calloway looked over Nico like one might regard a crushed insect, broken beyond repair and going still at his feet. "Death is not something to fear, if you have done nothing wrong. Some say it is...open. Infinite. And yet—" He spoke as though relaying facts he had no investment in, but after a beat, the tone shifted colder.

"To defy nature, to ask that of the desert..."

Nico couldn't get enough air to speak, but tried nonetheless. "Please. It was my idea to come out here." Sobbing on dust, every word excruciating. "I, this—this is all my fault. Please."

"It is said that to ask such things of the desert is unforgivable."

Nico weakly pulled his knees up to his chest, trying futilely to keep his head upright to take in Calloway's decision.

"But, if you agree to the judgment...certain requests may be granted."

The rest of the world had gone utterly silent. The only sounds left were those distant, tortured echoes and Nico's own stuttering heart. The hand clutching Mat's arm trembled, and he couldn't hold on any longer. Numb fingers slid down into the cold sand.

"Are you willing?" Calloway knelt in front of him. He leveled Nico's haunted gaze with his own, while the light in them went dim. "Whatever the cost?"

As his eyes fell shut, the boy managed to nod.

WEAVERS

Gille Klabin

ZOE STEPPED THROUGH the dream door into a dark, echoing cavern. It slammed shut behind her with the audible suction of a walk-in freezer, or a space shuttle being sealed for launch.

"I can't believe how long it took you to find me," an irate, high-pitched voice echoed across the vast room. Zoe's eyes could not penetrate the inky darkness.

"I—I'm sorry," she said uncertainly. It's the first time I've ever taken direction from my dreams."

She stepped further into the chamber. How could such a cavernous room exist behind such a small door? She'd seen it at the end of every dream she'd had for months, a small, round door at the back of the men's changing rooms at her local YMCA. It was the pedestrian specificity that had stuck in her mind like a splinter, that had made her feel like she'd lose it if she didn't investigate.

As she ventured further in, she saw the shimmering of a colossal concave wall made of glass. Glimmers of light flickered from beyond, and Zoe marveled at its beauty.

"What is this place?" She whispered to herself, awestruck.

"I apologize about the size of the door," the voice answered. Like a bipedal ball of cotton candy, a figure emerged from a shadowy corner of the room. A small and perfectly rotund being, he commanded a curious energy; he looked both dejected and desperate at the same time. Zoe stared at him in disbelief, this cartoonish little man in his bright coat looked like a red bell.

"You're the little man from my dreams," she said.

He smiled as he approached her, pulling on a pair of ornate diamond-patterned gloves.

"Size is relative, but yes, you would recognize me from your dreams. After all, I'm the one who made them."

When Zoe's dreams began, they were formless and cryptic, lacking direction or purpose, but they had gradually solidified so that, by the end, the little man often gave quite specific instructions, and he was a real dick about it.

"OK what's happening? Is this another dream? Am I dreaming right now?" Zoe said.

"I assure you this is no dream. I've been trying to meet you for some time now Zoe. I'm Arlo," he said, and stuck out his little gloved hand. Zoe raised her hand to shake in a daze, but Arlo seemed to have a change of heart and immediately retracted his own.

"Ah, I don't mean to be rude. I wish I could perform a familiar gesture for you, but I can't realistically have you touch my hands."

"Oh. Of course," Zoe answered, attempting to mask her confusion.

Arlo turned away from her to face the towering glass wall. He raised his hands, and it lit up with a cloud of orange light, its amorphous glow flickering and dancing as Arlo motioned and waved his hands through the air.

"You don't mind if I create while we chat, do you?" He asked.

"Buddy, I am so many steps behind, just tell me what's going on and you can do whatever you want."

"As it happens, this is the first time in history one such as myself has had to explain themselves to a human, so I find myself unsure about how best to approach it."

"Maybe you could start with what this place is and why you brought me here," Zoe said.

"No, that's a terrible idea," Arlo snapped. "OK, let me start here; this beautiful light you see in front of us, it's called 'Thread'. It contains every imaginable emotion, thought, concept, and purpose. Every facet of feeling exists in Thread."

Zoe turned to face the glass wall. She could see different contours rippling across the surface of the Thread, like vines snaking up a tree.

"With Thread, a Weaver can create anything a mind could conceivably experience." Arlo turned to her. "And can you guess what I am?"

"Um…a Weaver?" Zoe said.

"Exactly. I, and the many other souls with whom I share this realm, are the Weavers who create dreams."

"Whose dreams?" Zoe asked.

"All of them, my dear. The dreams of all humanity." Arlo reached to his side and, seemingly from nowhere, plucked a stool from thin air and slid it behind Zoe.

"Please, sit, sit."

She lowered herself onto the stool and stared at the swirling cloud of Thread illuminating the room with a rich, golden shade of orange. Curiously, she felt this glow as though it was originating within her, its infinite warmth and complexity swelled like a flurry of indecisive emotions deep in her chest.

"Weavers and the Thread have existed in a beautiful symbiotic dance for time unfathomable to a human. In that vast epoch we have explored the beauty and tragedy of all existence. Together we have guided the subconscious of mankind's story."

"This is fucking wild, man. "The scope of what Arlo was saying was so impossibly profound, yet he delivered it like a waiter rushing through the day's specials. "Did you guys create humans too?"

"No, you came to be just as all things came to be, we just steered you into exploring existence in as indirect a way as possible".

"So, every dream anyone has ever had was created by the Weavers?" Zoe asked, awestruck. "Are you…are you angels?"

"Don't be absurd. All those ideas are things we weaved into your minds' millennia ago. Angels, as it happens, were placed in a dream by the same Weaver responsible for baptism, the *Men In Black* franchise, and those wooden clogs the Dutch wear."

Zoe stared blankly at Arlo. His impatience was starting to show.

"We simply operate at a higher level of existence than you, understand?"

Arlo lowered his hands and shifted his attention away from the Thread. The lights dimmed and he stared intently at Zoe, as though trying to gauge her state of mind. She lifted her face to look at him with a purposeful expression.

"When I was a teenager, I had all these dreams that I was pursuing architecture, but whenever I pitched my designs I would raise my hands and all my fingers were-"

"Made of penises, I know," Arlo interrupted, an impatient edge to his voice.

"Those dreams gave me crippling anxiety," Zoe said. "I dropped out of school. Why the hell would you do that?"

"Be quiet girl! I simply do not have time to debate the philosophy of our purpose with you." Arlo erupted at her. He spun away and began pacing the room, hand on his chin like he was considering how best to continue his explanation.

"I might not understand what a Weaver is, but I definitely recognize an asshole when I see one. I think it's about time I got out of here." Zoe got up to leave.

"No, please, wait." Arlo stopped pacing. "You humans, you like movies, yes?"

"Yeah, I guess." She sat back down.

"Well, imagine all of existence is one big movie. Weavers are like the producers, writers, and directors of the movie."

"Then what are we?" Zoe asked, not sure she wanted to know the answer.

"Think of yourselves as the background extras." Arlo smiled, but Zoe's frown betrayed her offense. "That's not to say you don't matter of course. After all, you need extras to make a movie; you're just not...*that important*."

"For someone who calls himself a writer, you sure have a shitty way with words," Zoe said. "And if I'm so insignificant, then why the hell have you been trying so hard to manipulate me into coming here?"

Arlo's patronizing expression dropped. "Yes, well...that's a touch more complicated."

"Well everything so far has been a fucking breeze, so lay it on me, pal," Zoe poked at him, enjoying a momentary slip in the power dynamic.

Arlo paused, gathering his thoughts.

"When Weavers rest, we do not sleep like you simplistic humans."

"Dude." Zoe warned. Arlo ignored her.

"When we rest, we recharge ourselves from the Thread. We are nourished by the infinitude of the cosmos, the sheer immensity of existence. It doesn't leave much room for frivolities like *dreams*. And yet…and yet…"

"And yet what? Spit it out, pal."

"And yet I had a dream!" Arlo blurted out, and immediately covered his mouth with his hands.

"Okay… Good for you?" Zoe said.

"Yes, I had a dream. For the first time in millennia of existence. And you were in it Zoe, *you* appeared in *my* dream." Arlo looked away, embarrassed by the confession.

"So? What does that mean?" Zoe asked.

"It could mean many things. I can't be certain, this situation is unprecedented."

"Well, I promise you I'm not infiltrating your dreams on purpose, man." Zoe felt little compassion for this ill-mannered orb of a man.

"There must be a *reason* Zoe, you have to help me figure out *why*."

"Well, you've made it pretty clear you think I'm a moron, so it looks like you're on your own." Zoe stood up and headed for the exit.

In a fit of panic Arlo ran past her and spread his round body and tiny arms across the doorframe.

"Please, Zoe, I apologize. I'm not used to the formalities humans employ to protect each other's feelings. We Weavers are a curt and pragmatic type. I beg you, please, help me solve this."

Zoe stalled for a beat, watching Arlo squirm. He looked so panicked. She sighed and turned away from the door, walking back into the grand chamber. Arlo scurried to her side and walked beside her, looking up at her with a pleading hope.

"OK, so Weavers can't weave into each other's sleep, right?" Zoe asked.

"Correct. We can only affect lesser creatures." Arlo said.

Zoe raised her eyebrows. Arlo seemed not to notice.

"Well, maybe you're being demoted," Zoe said. "Maybe you're becoming a *lesser creature*."

"No, not possible. All Weavers would have to band together to pull off something like that, and I can't imagine what I could have done to warrant such a heartless attack," Arlo said.

"Yeah, because you're such a charmer." Zoe said. "What about someone above you Weavers?"

Arlo stopped dead in his tracks.

"Someone above the Weavers? What do you mean?"

"Well, if you arrogant little bastards are playing around with our human experience, then who's pulling *your* puppet strings? Who's seeding thoughts in *your* mind and watching *you* spin out like some demented peep show?"

Zoe felt energized by this line of thought and paced back and forth with more purpose.

"There's got to be a hierarchy here, right? Maybe the even-higher realm of entities are goofing around with *your* subconscious and making *you* reevaluate everything. I mean, it would serve you right."

Zoe turned to gauge Arlo's response to her theory. The sight of him immediately softened her approach. He sat on the stool he had earlier offered to Zoe, his face draining of color as he loosened the top clasp of his red coat.

"No, that can't be it, it can't. There's nothing above us. We're the Weavers, we create it all. Why would there be someone above us? We're brilliant, we're utterly brilliant. Who would make something like that? No one could! We are the makers, *we're* in charge," Arlo gushed forth in uninhibited bursts.

Zoe knelt down to Arlo's height and tried to comfort this irascible little man she had no particular fondness for. "Come on buddy, surely you've asked yourself if there's someone or something else above *you*?"

Arlo's wide eyes and pallid complexion betrayed that he had not.

"In all the millennia of manipulating the subconscious of an entire species, you've never asked how and why you do what you do?" Zoe waited for the epiphanic light in his eyes, but Arlo's expression was more like the unsuccessful scramblings of a dial-up modem.

Zoe took a deep breath.

"I say this with undeniable irony, my friend: welcome to the real world."

YEAST

Lola Blanc

I STARED AT Jasper in silence, measuring my next response. His back was to me, facing the breathtaking view of the city beyond the sliding glass doors as he typed furiously at the dining table. Clacking away. Drowning out my presence.

Clack clack clack.

I always do this. I always say the wrong thing. Idiot.

I know what you're thinking, but don't worry. Of course, I know I'm not an idiot. Growing up, adults heaped praise upon me for my excellent grades and my voracious appetite for reading. Some girls were good at soccer or cheerleading or wearing cute outfits; I was smart. That was what everyone would say about me. Especially once I got pretty. "Wow," they'd muse, "you're pretty *and* you're smart."

It's just that Jasper really *did* know more than me. He was always referencing authors I had never read. Philosophies I didn't understand. Meanwhile, I'd replaced my reading habit with reality TV, and began filling my free time with various forms of highly digestible entertainment. I regret that now.

I shifted uncomfortably in the cream-colored sofa behind his cream-colored chair, pretending I didn't see him stiffen when I mispronounced the name.

"Immanuel *Can't*," I had said, like a fool.

"It's *Kahnt*," he'd replied evenly, trying very hard to keep his voice neutral, which was sweet of him. He couldn't stop the disdain from slipping through—and I understand. I do. I'd giggled nervously, said oops, and finished the paragraph I was reading aloud before he went back to his computer.

And there we were. In silence. *Can't, can't, can't.* I can't believe I didn't know that. I didn't have enough friends who talked about Kant. I'd never read any Kant. *Why haven't I read Kant?*

"I'd really like to read some *Kant,*" I ventured, careful to pronounce it correctly.

He glanced back at me. "Well. Maybe we could do a book club," he replied, "I can give you a little lesson."

I smiled. "I'd like that."

Got him.

I CAREFULLY FOLDED my clothes and set them into the drawers he had designated for me, just the way he'd demonstrated, and slipped on the off-white silk nightgown hanging in the enormous, meticulously organized walk-in closet. The nightgown wasn't as comfortable as the ratty old band t-shirts I used to wear, but I felt pretty in it. *It's important to not let yourself go as soon as you're comfortable in a relationship,* I thought. Of course, I'd only been living with Jasper for four days, so I wasn't exactly comfortable yet, but I knew it would happen eventually.

Jasper's house—I mean *our* house—was beautiful and minimalist and impressive; everything was white or beige or cream. From the moment I visited, I knew I wanted to live there. I was still new to the city, and I'd never been with anyone as articulate, as logical, as knowledgeable about philosophy and science and politics as Jasper. I felt like I was *growing* when I was with him.

I returned to the bedroom, dimmed the vintage Danish lamp on my side of the bed, grabbed a book of essays by David Foster Wallace, and lay on top of the bed, arranging my legs seductively for when he came back in. I heard him turn off the bathroom sink. He came into the room smelling of peppermint and cedar. I loved how he smelled. I stretched out my arms toward him.

"Come to me," I said adorably. He stopped and surveyed my body, the nightgown riding up my leg and revealing my bare hip.

"You look very pretty," he said.

I smiled. "Why thank you."

He lay down on the bed, took my book out of my hand, and pulled me on top of him. We kissed; I removed the obstructions between us and rode him, slowly at first, how he liked it, then moving faster. I leaned down and he cradled me tightly.

These were the moments I felt closest to him.

The pressure rose in me as I rocked, my moans growing louder, and then louder. I was nearly there–

And then he was finished. I gave him a moment and leaned down to kiss him before delicately disentangling myself.

"Everything okay?" he asked.

"Everything's great! Just going to run to the bathroom," I said.

I went into the bathroom, closed the door, and peed. I did all the requisite wiping and sat there for a moment, reassuring myself that there was no reason to be upset. *It's no big deal. He's made me cum plenty of times.*

And then I thought, *what difference would it make if I took care of myself? He'd never know.*

I put my hand up my nightgown and got myself off.

THE SUN PEEKED in through the windows. As I opened my eyes, two distinctly incongruous sensations entered my consciousness. The first, Tchaikovsky floating out from the kitchen, was a pleasant one. The second filled me with dread: itching, burning, moisture, heat. *Down there.* Unpleasant. Highly unpleasant. I put my hand down my pants and pulled it back out to reveal a light, creamy material on my finger. Damn it. *Damn it.*

I'd had infections in the past, but I'd done everything I could to avoid them since I began seeing Jasper. I took all the appropriate supplements; I used the suppositories once a week; I ate a lot of yogurt. I'd been so careful. A hundred terrors screamed through my head. *What if it lasts for weeks? What if I can't meet his needs? Will he realize he doesn't love me once I can't give him sex?*

I inhaled deeply three times. I knew I wasn't being rational.

I showered in his custom beige two-person shower, wincing as I cleaned up as best I could, and brushed my teeth. I tried not to scratch when I dried off. I got dressed and made my exit into the living room, putting on a cheery face.

"Morning," he said from the dining room, where he did the crossword every morning.

"Good morning," I said cheerily. "That toast smells good."

"There's more bread if you want some," he said without looking up.

"Oh, thank you. I…don't think I should have any for a few days, actually," I said. Yeast feeds on sugar, so eating carbohydrate-heavy foods helps infections to proliferate. This is a thing women know but don't like to talk about.

"Oh? Are you going keto?"

"No—I mean I probably should anyway, but I think I'm having some *female trouble*," I said, maintaining my lightest and most casual vocal cadence. "And it's best not to have a lot of carbs."

He studied me. "I'm sorry to hear that, babe. Do you need to make a doctor's appointment?"

"I can just call in a prescription."

"The wonders of modernity. Let me know if you need anything," he said, smiling before returning to his screen.

"Thanks, baby," I smiled back. He didn't see.

STANDING AT THE white marble kitchen counter, I frantically opened the packaging I'd retrieved from the pharmacy and swallowed the single pill inside. It was bitter and dry and it never went down easily, no matter how much water I drank, but it always worked. I bent over awkwardly, trying to will the burning sensation in my pants away. *It's okay. It's going to help.* From down the hall, Jasper's laughter rang out from his office; he made a joke about late-stage capitalism.

I slowly walked down the pristine white hallway, resisting the impulse to clutch my crotch, just in case he opened the door. I couldn't risk him developing an unattractive image of me in his mind.

I stepped into the living room. The wall opposite the glass doors was lined with books from floor to ceiling; it made me feel like Belle in her library, if her library was white and modern. When I was alone, I fantasized about sliding back and forth along the books on a very tall ladder. Of course, I never shared that with Jasper. He thought Disney was indoctrinating the masses into the cult of consumerism. Obviously, I agreed.

My own single box of books that I'd packed from my apartment sat lonely on the floor. I plopped down next to it. My book collection wasn't anything like Jasper's book collection. He had Franzen, Dostoyevsky, Spinoza, and Derrida; I had self-help books, mystery novels, and photography books. I fished out my copy of *The 5 Love Languages* and squeezed it next to Thomas Hobbes's *Leviathan*.

"Nailed it!" Jasper appeared in the hallway, a look of glee on his face.

"NPR??"

"*The Times*. I think he really got it. He's coming to the launch party to interview me more." Jasper was promoting his new book, a biography of Mikhail Bulgakov. He'd recommended that I read *The Master and Margarita* as a primer, and I'd enjoyed it. As a *Sabrina the Teenage Witch* enthusiast, I'd read anything with a talking cat. But I mean of course that wasn't *why* I liked it. It was the commentary on Soviet atheist propaganda that appealed to me, once he explained it to me.

"That's incredible! I'm so proud of you!" I beamed at him.

"No. You know what's incredible?" He came over and bent down to my level.

"What's incredible?" I asked coyly.

"That my favorite person in the world lives with me now." He leaned in and kissed me deeply.

I swooned. It was briefly perfect.

"Your favorite person started putting her books away," I volunteered cheerily, expecting him to be relieved. I knew clutter made the vein in his forehead bulge, which meant he was stressed, and I hated to be a source of his stress. He squinted at where I'd squeezed in my book, immediately identifying the disruption of his organization system. He broke apart from me and pulled out the book, dangling it from his thumb and forefinger like there was something rank smeared on it. I couldn't see my own face, but I imagine that it turned beet red.

"Charlotte. A self-help book?"

"Should I not have put it there? I was just going by title. I didn't know if there was another system."

"You know I'm particular about my books." He was. I did know that. I wasn't thinking. "We'll find another place to put them, okay? Maybe in the basement. You can have your own area. How's that sound?"

I mustered a smile. "That sounds good. Thank you."

"That's my girl." He smiled and ruffled my head and left the room.

His office door closed. I tried willing myself not to cry, but a tear forced its way out of my eye anyway. It dripped onto the stupid book in front of me. *Stupid book. Stupid book for a stupid girl.* I pushed the book across the floor and climbed to my feet, but as I went, I felt my knee brush against a wet spot on the polished hardwood floor.

I squinted at the spot, leaning down to see better. There was a small pile of a thick, whitish substance, not unlike cottage cheese. I lifted my flirty circle skirt and examined my underwear; the yeast was oozing through the cotton triangle covering my crotch. *Oh my god. Did he notice?* I ran to the kitchen, tore off four paper towels, and began gathering up the discharge, pushing it onto the paper towel and trying not to gag. As I cleaned, I felt a new wet clump soak my pants. A searing itch struck. *Don't scratch. Don't scratch.* I stuffed my underwear with the last paper towel, and used it to scratch myself just a little, just enough to feel some momentary relief.

I threw away the paper towels in the kitchen, covering them with a fresh one so he wouldn't see what was underneath. I went into the bedroom, closed the door, got into bed, and scratched myself as I secretly, quietly, watched a reality TV show.

I WAS FEELING a little better the next afternoon, so after changing my pantyliner I went downstairs to the basement to dance. The room boasted a few pieces of sculptural white furniture that cost more than my car, but otherwise it was empty, so it seemed like the most appropriate part of the house to explore some movement. It had been months since I'd gone to class, but now that I lived with Jasper I was going to start going again. Probably next week. I told the Bluetooth speaker to play Beyoncé. Jasper hated Beyoncé. He said she embodied the hypocrisy of shallow neoliberalism, but her songs made me feel like I belonged to some ancient lineage of women. To me, Beyoncé sounded like freedom and wisdom and femininity. I pulled off my turtleneck and began to move my body, flowing with the sounds. My nether regions were instantly angry at the addition of sweat, a war raged inside me as moisture gathered in my underwear, but I ignored the stinging and focused on the music. It felt good to move. I swirled and swayed and bent and shimmied, spinning around. I was lost in the moment.

And suddenly, there was silence.

The music had stopped, and Jasper was standing there, watching, with an expression that I thought looked something like hatred.

"Sorry, babe," he said, "I know you're not feeling well…but would you mind turning the music down? I'm just having a difficult time concentrating. You know how much pop grates on my ears."

"Oh, sure. Of course. I'm sorry, I know you're working. I don't need to dance right now."

"No, no. No need to apologize. It's nice to see you dancing again. Maybe if it were John Cage I'd feel differently," he laughed.

I relaxed. That wasn't hatred on his face, it was stress from the pressure of his book coming out. *Of course* the music was too loud. He needed the house to be quiet in order to concentrate. I don't know why I forgot about that. He looked at my sweating body, shirtless and shiny.

"So, if you're dancing…does that mean you're feeling better?"

"Um…well, not *totally* better."

"But a little better? The pill is working?"

"I think so. I mean it always works."

"Yeast infections aren't contagious, right?"

"Well, they're not an STD. They're just an imbalance. But I mean…you'd have to…shower after."

"I can do that." He sidled up to me and grabbed me by the waist. "You know I love seeing you sweat," he said, lifting my skirt. He caressed me for a moment and then abruptly bent me over the chair that looked like it belonged in a museum. I didn't stop him. I couldn't resist him, even when I knew it would hurt. Even when I knew how much worse he'd make it. Burning pain scorched through my body. I pretended to like it.

"You're *creamy* today," he said as he thrusted.

It hurt too badly to form words, so I moaned in feigned pleasure. He finished with a loud grunt and extricated himself. I lingered there, trying to let the sensations settle. I knew if I got up, I might fall over.

"You okay?" he asked as he zipped up his pants.

"Yep, just gonna stay downstairs a while."

"Okay. Well, I have to get back to work. Let me know if you need anything."

"Okay. Thank you, babe."

"Love you."

I smiled. "Love you."

I heard the sound of his footsteps going up the stairs and then him closing the door. I gingerly pushed myself back onto my feet, hobbled into the enormous basement bathroom, and cleaned up with toilet paper. It hurt. Badly. I eyed the whirlpool bathtub with high-pressure jets; it seemed soothing. I removed the rest of my clothes, started the water, and stepped in, the warmth tingly on my feet. The water stung as it reached my groin, making me wince.

I wouldn't be able to have sex again for a while, that was for certain. I'd have to turn him down the next time he tried. I grew anxious at the thought. I took three deep breaths, trying to calm my nervous system. *What if it lasts forever? What if he discovers all the worst things about me once I can't give him sex? What if he goes back to Melody?*

Calm down. Calm down.

The stinging was getting worse. I clutched my crotch, trying to breathe through the sensation. Panic tore through my body. *What if he never loved me in the first place?*

I needed to make it stop. I stepped out of the tub and searched the cabinet under the sink for something, anything, that would soothe the pain. Spray cleaners, soap, lotion, roach poison.

Roach poison.

I grabbed it and read the label on the back. 100% boric acid. *Perfect.*

Don't be alarmed! It's a little women's secret. If you swallow it you could die, but when inserted vaginally, it balances the pH so yeast and bacteria can't grow. I wouldn't just stuff *poison* in my vagina.

I opened the bag, grabbed a handful of the powder, and stuffed the poison in my vagina. Dizzying pain. I remember screaming.

I OPENED MY eyes and took in my surroundings. I was in the spare bedroom. Don't worry—it was my idea to sleep there. It had been three days since the first sign of infection, with no improvement, and I didn't want to disrupt Jasper's sleep with my unappetizing secretions. He seemed grateful but refused to say it out loud. Bless him. He'd never want to hurt my feelings.

Everything burned. I sat up slowly, soggy wet noises coming from my underwear despite my ultra-thick maxi pad and examined myself in the mirror next to the bed. My eyes were sunken and hollow, and my hair was stringy. My stomach looked flat from my diet of leafy greens and meat, though. That was something. When I could finally have sex, at least I'd be more attractive. If Jasper could ever even think of me like that again.

Knock knock knock.

"One second!" I squeaked out pathetically.

I sat up straight, quickly smoothed my hair, grabbed the concealer in my purse, and dabbed it under my eyes. "Okay, come in!"

He opened the door and walked in, holding soup on a tray. "One soup delivery."

"For me?" I melted. My eyes misted up.

"Special ordered."

"Thank you, babe. That's so sweet." I took the tray from him and slurped up a spoonful of a clear warm broth I identified as pho.

"Of course. How are you feeling today?"

"Not so good. But I'm sure it's getting better."

"The doctor said it should start to improve within three days or so, right?" He kneeled next to me and began caressing my leg gently, slowly. I closed my eyes as his hand moved further up my thigh. I stopped his hand.

"He did, but…I'm not there yet. I can't."

He sighed. "I figured. Do you think you'll be better in time for the launch?"

"I'd never miss it."

"I'm so glad," he said. "My agent's really looking forward to meeting you. So is Melody."

My spoon, halfway to my mouth, stopped mid-air. "Melody's going to be there?" I tried to keep my tone even. *Don't sound jealous. Jealousy isn't rational. Irrationality is unappealing.*

"Didn't I tell you?"

"I'm sure you did," I said, though he didn't. "I must not have been listening."

"She's at the New Yorker now. Harvard was over a decade ago, and I need all the coverage we can get for this. It's actually *good* that we have a history. She gets me like no other member of the press would. This is the best thing for us."

Be agreeable. Be agreeable.

"No, right. That makes sense."

I smiled and took another sip of the soup. I tried to swallow, but the back of my throat was expelling something. I tried again. No use. Jasper looked at me, concerned.

"Sweetie? Are you okay?"

I covered my hand with my mouth and turned away, but I couldn't stop it. A white, curdled-looking goop forced its way out of my mouth. It poured out of my lips, through my fingers, and into my soup bowl.

No. No-no-no-no-no.

I got up, ran to the bathroom, and locked myself inside before Jasper could react.

I bent over the sink and frantically scraped my tongue with my tongue scraper, but it just kept forming. Yeast, everywhere, from unknown corners of my throat. I caught a glimpse of my eyes; there was a kind of thin white film over them. I splashed water onto them, blinking maniacally.

Through the door, Jasper was saying something.

"Honey? I have your medication. Do you want to take some more?"

"Just leave it outside!"

"Are you okay? Did you throw up?"

"I'm fine!"

"Okay. I'm here if you need me."

As soon as I heard his footsteps disappear into another room, I cracked the door, snatched the medicine bottle, and downed every pill inside.

I WOKE UP scratching myself so hard that the discharge on my finger was tinged with bright red blood. It was dark in the bathroom now. I'd fallen asleep on the floor, and everything hurt. My stomach was rumbling. I hadn't eaten all day.

I slowly got to my feet, trying to avoid looking at myself in the mirror, but I managed to catch a glimpse of my face anyway. It looked pale and swollen and oddly shiny.

I opened the door a little and peeked down the hall to make sure Jasper wasn't out there. I tiptoed out, passing his office on the way. He was speaking to someone on the phone in hushed tones. I could hear snippets of his conversation. I know I shouldn't have snooped, but I couldn't stop myself.

"Thank you. I'm trying… She's beautiful, but…well, we can't exactly have lengthy discussions about Wittgenstein. Know what I mean?" He chuckled. "You were always the rational one," he said to the person on the other end.

Pain. Searing pain.

I stumbled into the living room and scanned the bookshelves, which looked enormous to me now. I reached clumsily and pulled a few books at random. I knocked something over but didn't stop to see what it was.

I brought the books into the spare room and began to read. I had to learn. I had to be *smarter*. That was all that mattered.

I was squinting at the word "schematicism" when I realized Jasper was hovering in the doorway, watching me. Despite my discomfort, I felt a surge of pleasure that he'd found me like that and I hadn't noticed.

"Hey. How are you feeling?" he asked, looking at the book in front of me. "*A Critique of Pure Reason*, huh?"

I tried to smile, but my face was so puffy it was too painful to get my cheeks to move in the appropriate direction, so all I managed was opening my mouth a little. "I thought it would be nice to share some of what's important to you." My mouth formed a bubble on the word "you." I quickly sucked it back in. Act *normal*.

"That's so sweet, honey," Jasper said. "It's a dense one."

"Do you think it's too dense for me?" I asked, a little too sharply. I should have monitored my tone more closely. Stupid mistake.

"No…no. Of course not."

He sat down next to me on the bed.

"Listen, love… I think you should probably skip the opening. I can FaceTime you. It's okay. There will be other events."

"No!" I looked at him with an expression that I can only assume was wild-eyed. "I'm going."

"You're very sick. You need to get better."

"*I'm getting better.*"

"You're not," he said softly.

His eyes were completely blank.

I tried so hard to hold in my sobs, but I lost control and began to cry. He put his hand on my shoulder stiffly, and when he pulled it away it stuck to my skin a little. *Repulsive.*

"FOUCAULT'S EMPHASIS WAS on the division between reason and madness; Derrida articulated a more complex interplay of their relationality," the man's voice was saying on the computer. I mimicked him, memorizing each bit of information.

I steamed my sophisticated, cream-colored Yves Saint Laurent dress that Jasper had gotten me for my birthday. It was the same shade as my slick pale skin. I thought it looked nice against my arms. I shimmied into it, listening intently to a lecture about postmodernism. I felt light and malleable. I felt beautiful.

"Foucault's emphasis was on the division…" I said softly as I brushed my hair.

Looking over my accessory options, I felt nauseous observing the gaudiness of my old jewelry collection. Rhinestones and oversized earrings, gold chains and brightly colored bangles… *tacky.* I selected the thin, tasteful silver necklace I had picked out with Jasper. I had grown so much.

"A more complex interplay of their relationality," I whispered.

WALKING, BUT IT felt more like sliding.

I think I saw a trail of goo following me as I went, but I'm not certain now. My whole body was moist, making my dress cling to my limbs. I hadn't slept in forty-eight hours. I'd been reading, watching lectures, learning. I had so much to share with Jasper.

He wasn't expecting me at the party, of course. He'd been leaving meals for me at the top of the stairs. I hadn't let him see me in days. He thought I'd be waiting for him at home, still sick in the basement, but I was really feeling much better now. He was going to be so surprised.

A car slowed as it passed me, and a man's voice rang out. "Lady, are you okay?"

"I'm wonderful!" I said, or at least I think I did.

I was almost to the bookstore entrance. There were so many people inside. That was great. I was so proud of him.

I stepped inside and heard his voice reading a passage, his audience rapt. I squirmed my way through the crowd, desperate to get a glimpse of him in his shining moment.

A woman recoiled after I gently pushed her aside.

"What the fuck," someone whispered as they looked at me, but it didn't bother me. I was almost to the front.

"And that, perhaps, is the central theme of Bulgakov's life," Jasper's voice was saying authoritatively, "the struggle to maintain his integrity even under the control of an oppressive regime who wished to strip him of his voice, his autonomy, his life."

I can't remember what he read after that, because that's when I saw Melody. I'd never seen her in person before. Her platinum blonde hair looked chic. She held a notebook and pen, and she was luminous. White-hot jealousy surged through my body. She watched Jasper, a look in her eyes that I recognized.

He finished reading, and the crowd began to applaud. I joined them, clapping, though my hands only seemed to be able to make a sickly wet sucking sound. Jasper thanked the audience and stepped out from behind the podium. Melody intercepted, neither of them seeing me. I stayed put, ignoring the reactions of the people around me. I knew *things* now. I belonged here.

As I watched Jasper hug Melody, his hand lingering on her the small of her back, I felt my insides shift. I made my way over to them; it took an unusually long time to move across the room. Everything was heavy.

Melody was whispering something into his ear, her fingers lightly touching his arm, when she saw me. She screamed.

He noticed me just as my legs gave out. His face contorted in horror. "Charlotte?"

"You were brilliant," I tried to say, but my mouth wouldn't form the words.

Speak! You know things now! Foucault's emphasis was on the division between reason and madness. Foucault's emphasis was on the division between reason and madness!

"Fuhcuh's emphuh," I managed to get out.

My lips exploded into goop.

"Don't look! Don't look at her!" I heard Jasper saying before my hearing went. Melody was vomiting.

The last thing I remember is catching a glimpse of my reflection in a mirror on the wall opposite me.

Where my body should have been, there was only a pile of yeast.

DETROIT

Michael Dunker

Story by Michael Dunker, Jess Carfield, and Alex Ruiz

"IT CAME BACK," the doctor said.

Alex sat motionless, trying to absorb this new information, while the phrases *recurring cancer* and *what the fuck* drifted through his head. He stared at a model skeleton's chest cage in the doctor's office, which mirrored his entire existence. He knew the exact direction he wanted to go.

"Now, we have some treatment options, but it's going to be—"

"No," Alex replied. "I want the Kifo Pill."

The doctor paused. The Kifo Pill had been around for nearly a decade, created by the Thanatos Corporation, reserved for hospice patients who had chosen painless euthanasia. Once taken, a patient would feel no side effects and when they drifted to sleep, they simply would not wake up again. Being all of thirty-nine years of age, Alex didn't exactly qualify for this option, but this being his third cancerous stint, he was granted a prescription by the hesitant doctor.

ON THE BANKS of the Detroit River sits Belle Isle, which at one time boasted a beautiful view of the Motor City's grand skyline. Decades ago, the city was shaped by the pillars of the automotive industry and echoed with Motown music, but today the music has faded and the cars remain dormant. Though the locals still cheer on the depressing Detroit Lions and wash down their sorrows with an Atwater beer, Belle Isle is one of the last remaining crown jewels of the 313.

It's there, on a random park bench on Belle Isle, that Alex takes the Kifo Pill, thus starting a ticking clock to the end of his life.

He began calling friends. "Hey bud, it's Alex. I know it's been awhile, but I'm getting all the boys together at the London Chop House tonight. 7:30. Be there. It's important."

Though he called more than a dozen people that afternoon, his neglect of relationships over the years would be the thorn in his plans. He got a fresh haircut, tailored a new suit, and leased a 1969 Pontiac GTO because why not? *If you're going out, go out in style.* Upon cashing out his bank account, he ran into someone from his past, someone he hadn't seen in twenty-seven years.

"Kristen?"

"Oh my God, Alex? Alex Foster?"

"Wow. How are you? I haven't seen you since—"

"Eighth grade."

"Yeah, eighth grade."

Kristen was engaging in a Katherine Hepburn-type way, with her quirky smile and an adorable laugh. The world had been unkind to her, but she always persisted.

Alex hadn't seen her since he moved schools that year, but running into her that afternoon immediately reignited his affection. She was the one that got away and while the pair made small talk like you do with familiar strangers, he eventually saw an opening.

"I actually work at my son's school part-time. Oh, I have a little boy. Well, he's not so little. He's ten. But I work there and then at the Coney in Royal Oak to make some extra cash."

"I love Coney's," said Alex. "Are you working tonight?"

"I am, but not until late. And it's probably out of your way, so don't worry about it…"

"…But I'd love to see you," he said.

Kristen beamed. "Okay then. Maybe I'll see you," she replied.

THAT NIGHT AT the London Chop House, Alex was greeted by an extravagant spread of steak, lobster, and eighteen-year-old scotch. No expense was spared. He was the first to arrive and while waiting for his friends, a series of texts started rolling in.

Sorry, bro. Can't make it tonight.

Hey Alex, I got a family thing. Sorry.

Can't tonight, but let's get drinks next week.

One after another, they all canceled. Crushed and embarrassed, Alex made peace with it, finished his last drink, and thanked the staff for their hospitality. When he was about to leave, Vince, his oldest friend, finally showed.

"Hey buddy, sorry I'm late," Vince said as he looked around at the empty table. "Where is everyone?"

Alex didn't need to say anything, and Vince immediately knew. "Assholes."

"It's fine, they're busy."

"It's bullshit. When you say it's important, it's important."

The pair retired to a bar down the street and after venting frustrations about work & life, Alex eventually confessed his sins. Vince sat in shock as his friend explained he didn't want to fight anymore. He had lived the American dream. Well-educated, well-traveled, well-moneyed; everything capitalism tells you is important, and he was fine with it. Vince wanted to protest but could only listen with empathy. They ordered another drink and Vince asked the eternal question, "what would you do on your last day on Earth?"

"When was the last time you had a Coney Dog?"

THEY TRAVELED NORTH on Woodward Avenue to the Coney Island restaurant where Kristen worked. Most would agree Coney Islands were hole-in-the-wall diners that kept a loyal customer base in part to their comfort food menu, especially after a night of binge drinking because *nothing tastes better than a hani after midnight.*

As they entered, they laughed about their sleepovers in middle school where they pounded Jolt Cola and played video games all night. Vince was curious as to why they traveled to the suburbs for chili dogs when the Lafayette Coney was just around the corner, but he got the answer the moment Kristen walked in the door.

"Well, well, well…"

"Told you I'd come."

"That you did," she replied.

In a booth near the back, Alex downloaded the backstory to Vince who was surprised given Alex never opened up to anyone, let alone a woman, and was privileged to witness such a serendipitous reunion. Alex explained this was his first crush but was forced to leave her when his parents died. He lost two things that day, but now one had returned that sparked an emotional resurrection he couldn't ignore. On the other hand, Kristen's intrusive thoughts began to spiral. *Why is he here? God, he's cute. Is he here because he likes me? Is that a stain on my shirt? But seriously, what the hell is he doing here?*

ALEX ORDERED EVERYTHING on the menu for his last supper. Mozzarella sticks. Wing dings. Four Coney dogs. Two cheesy bacon dogs. One rice pudding. Three cream puffs. A patty melt. Two hanis, one gyro, two cheeseburgers, one tuna wrap, and three orders of pancakes. Within the hour, the food was gone, while Kristen waited in the wings. She quickly cleared the table and delivered the check, hoping that would be it and Alex would be gone. She liked him, but a string of broken hearts couldn't risk herself opening up again.

"So, what time do you get off?" he asked.

"Why?"

It turned out her shift was already over, and Alex convinced her to stay for a cup of coffee. *It's just coffee, it doesn't mean anything.* But it did.

Vince had left and the former lovers picked up the three-decades old conversation like nothing changed. Same energy, same flirtation, same feelings. Kristen opened up about her past of jobs, apartments, and raising a man in a childish world. Alex spoke about his success in real estate, his short-lived marriage, and beating Kristen in basketball in seventh grade, which she adamantly denied.

Though he never mentions the Kifo pill, their reconnection was enchanting until the sun began to rise on a new day.

"I better go. I got a whole family waiting for me at home."

"Do you need a ride?" he asked.

"Like you want to drive me in the opposite direction, no way. You probably got a million things to do."

He didn't and gladly offered a ride. They pulled down a street of low-rent apartments off Eight Mile Road, the same that Eminem rapped about years prior, where they both grew up. Embarrassed, Kristen explained that she was still living at home with her mom and brother, sometimes Aunt Carol if she was fighting with her husband, and her son, Billy. She hadn't gotten back on her feet after her last relationship but was trying.

Alex didn't care. He loved her family from years ago and asked if he could come inside much to her surprise. *Maybe this guy really does like me.*

Kristen's mother, Gloria, was born and raised in Detroit. She was married to a lovely, Italian man named Jim who worked at General Motors until his untimely death nearly decade ago. She was proud of her children, even when they disappointed her. She was an active parent and knew all the neighborhood kids, so when Alex walked through the door, it was like the prodigal son returning home.

"Alex!" she exclaimed, reaching out with a big hug.

"Where have you been? Come here, let me see your face. Oh my God, you haven't changed a bit. It's good to see you."

As the family huddled around their small kitchen table to hear about Alex, breakfast was served with crispy bacon and plenty of laughter. They loved having such a guest and soon,

Alex began to realize this was what was missing in his life. *A family. Parents that give you big hugs. Food made with real butter. Siblings that drive you nuts. And a romantic partner smiling at you from across the room.* This was everything he wanted, though never had until that day—the day of death.

The lingering question of "what would you do on your last day on Earth?" fell upon Kristen and she immediately knew her answer. *A hot air balloon ride.* She had been fascinated with flight from an early age and always yearned to travel, but those plans were long derailed. Alex made some calls, offered to pay in cash, and invited Kristen and Billy to an open airfield for a ride over the city of Detroit. One problem: Alex was afraid of heights. He white knuckled his fear in the interest of checking off a bucket list item for Kristen and as they lifted off the edge of the Earth and soared over the colored treetops, the city looked hopeful and promising. It was a new world for Kristen and Alex gave it to her. Even Billy called it *one of the best days of his life.*

When they returned home, she kissed him.

"Thank you for one of the best days in a long time. Thank you, thank you, thank you."

"It doesn't have to be over."

"Oh, I think it does for me. I'm exhausted, but I'd love to see you this week. Are you free on Thursday?"

"I'm free now," he said.

Given this was his last day, Alex pressed, but this only turned off Kirsten. She had seen aggressive behavior in previous partners and wasn't about to put up with it now, thus she kissed him goodbye, and their night-turned-t0-day ended there.

Alex waited outside for a bit, but eventually left, having nowhere to go. On the drive home, he got lost and navigation directed him towards Vince's.

"I need a favor," Alex said to Vince with a knock on the door.

Alex held considerable assets. A house in Bloomfield Hills. A cabin in Traverse City. A boat on Torch Lake. Two vintage cars. Two new cars. Two million in stocks and no will. He had the American Dream with no one to give it to. Until now.

"Are you sure?" Vince questioned.

Alex was sure. Kristen, who could barely rub two nickels together, would be beneficiary to a four-million-dollar trust and she'd never know it until he was gone. He didn't care as long as she was happy. With that, Alex said his goodbyes to Vince's kindhearted family, then left for the night.

ALEX'S HOUSE WAS massive though filled with nothing important. He walked through his empty castle that included multiple bedrooms, bathrooms, living rooms, day rooms, sunrooms, game rooms, and a pool. A very large pool that Alex, still in his tailored suit, walked into. This was it. He wanted it over, quickly. He submerged himself and stayed under as long as he could, but it's nearly impossible to drown yourself. The gasp for air was frustrating, and once on the surface, he started ripping off his clothes in anger. *Why? Why did I take it? Why am I that stupid?*

As he floated naked, the answers never came.

TEN MILES AWAY, Kristen was suffering equal frustration in a different way, via a mother's will to destroy her children's outdated belief systems.

"Why would you let him go?" Gloria uttered. "He's so kind and thoughtful and wonderful, then you turn around and accept absolute garbage from Tommy?"

Tommy was Billy's dad who was coming to pick up their son for the night, but Gloria was never a fan.

"Alex is a good man and you're throwing him away."

Tommy was handsome with a crooked jaw line. He had met Kristen at Michigan State where they dated off-and-on until he got her pregnant junior year. She lost the baby, which solidified their relationship in an odd way, and they stayed together. Eventually, they graduated, and she got pregnant again, but sometime during the second trimester, she found out he was cheating on her. She forgave him and a short time later, she found out he was addicted to prescription drugs.

She forgave him again and a short time later, she found out it was heroin. She forgave him again and a short time later, she finally got the courage to leave him.

She moved into her mother's apartment as a single parent where his knock on the door always triggered her anxiety.

"Is he ready?" asked Tommy.

"Billy! Your dad's here!"

"You look good. How are you?"

"He'll be out soon," was always her reply.

Tommy had cleaned himself up and became a good father. He took Billy on weekends, sometimes picking him up on Wednesday afternoons to get ice cream at Dairy Mat and had tickets to the *White Stripes* concert that night. He was trying, but the damage was done.

"If he wants to come home, let him. You know how he gets," Kristen said as Billy walked out the door.

With the father and son gone, she reflected on the last twenty-four hours with Alex. *Was her mother right? Was she pushing away another good man?* Kristen wouldn't sit on it for long and without further hesitation, she was out the door.

WITH HIS HAIR still wet from the pool, Alex put on a pair of sweats and a Bad Boys T-shirt. He filled a large bowl of Cinnamon Toast Crunch and cued up *Star Wars: Episode V*, then got into bed. He'd been awake for nearly twenty-seven hours at this point and exhaustion was beginning to take hold.

He closed his eyes to John Williams's ironic score when the doorbell rang. It was Kristen.

"What are you doing here," Alex asked and then she kissed him. They paused, then she kissed him again.

The pair fell onto the bed, and they made love for the next two hours, maybe more. It was an authentic connection, one where the world fades away and for a brief moment, everything is at peace. Afterwards, Kristen fell asleep, while Alex struggled to stay awake. He hadn't told her and couldn't bear her waking up to his corpse, so he started with jumping jacks. Then coffee. A slap to the face. More jumping jacks. One Red Bull. Meditation. Deep breaths. Espresso. More jumping jacks, then another slap to the face until Kristen finally woke.

"What are you doing?"

"I have to stay awake."

"Why?" she asked.

It was time to come clean, though he knew what would come with it. "I took the Kifo Pill yesterday"

A series of *what the fuck, who the fuck, how the fuck* came next. She didn't understand.

"I have cancer," he explained.

It didn't matter and she questioned why he didn't fight it. "I did."

She struggled with the basic idea of it all, but the reality that this man would be gone by tomorrow quickly set in.

"But I introduced you to my kid!" Kristen exclaimed. "I know and I loved him. I'm sorry."

It was no excuse. Alex had lied—like so many others before him—and Kristen couldn't process the betrayal. She got into her car and left immediately. Alex followed and when they reached her apartment, he pleaded with her, apologized over and over, but she didn't want to hear it.

"It's never been like this before, Kris. Not with anyone. And how do you tell the love of your life you're going to die when you just started to live?"

It was all too much. He apologized again, but she said nothing else. She went inside and closed the door behind her asking him to leave, but he instead planted a flag. He walked to his car and waited. He had nowhere else to go.

A SHORT TIME later, Gloria came outside. She said nothing but offered a warm hug and a nod of understanding, which meant the world to him. Aunt Carol, who was fighting with her husband that night, had no faith in Alex and her stance that *all men are assholes* didn't help.

Tommy soon arrived. Billy had gotten homesick after the concert, so he brought him back like Kristen asked. He questioned who the guy was waiting outside her apartment, but she brushed it off. It wasn't his concern, but seeing how upset she was, Tommy offered some perspective.

"I don't need your advice," she clapped back.

"I know, but don't ruin it like I did," he replied. "I know you're pissed, but if he's out there waiting, he knows how special you are and that doesn't come around very often. Wish I would have realized it sooner."

Kristen stood in disbelief. Tommy, who had been an emotional nightmare her entire life, had come back around to be a decent guy. She watched Tommy leave, but her eyes quickly fell upon Alex, who was now lying on the hood of his car, pounding energy drinks and waiting for his one true love on the last day of his life. She sighed, put on a coat, and walked out to him. Alex apologized again and they hugged for what felt like weeks like, then raised the question *what do you want to do?*

They went grocery shopping, which seems odd given the situation, but it's that ritualistic normalcy, that level of intimacy which is lost when you're alone, that he always wanted. So, with the few remaining hours, the two lovers decided to make dinner for each other. They pushed the cart together down the aisle, decided on what to make, then argued about what to make. They bantered about sides, then picked out several different ones, and grabbed an entire birthday cake because why not. They returned home as a couple and cooked their last and only meal together. There was laughter and candlelight. There were talks of regrets and pain. They kissed a lot and danced. They embraced the moment—a moment which could be described as the most romantic of their lives—and it was that simplicity which defines true love.

Going on thirty-three hours awake, Alex had to lay down and Kristen laid with him.

"Thank you for being in my life...if only for a day," Alex whispered as his eyes grew heavy.

"Thank you for coming back...if only for a day," she replied with a kiss.

Within minutes, they drifted asleep. Her hand rested on his face. His legs locked within hers. Then silence.

Until Kristen shot up. "Alex? Alex!"

He didn't respond.

"ALEX!!!"

Nothing.

She waited a beat, then cuddled up next to him. She cried one sad tear and held his body for as long as she could. Eventually, she got up and called 911.

WEEKS HAD PASSED when Kristen ventured out to Belle Isle to watch the sunset over the crown jewel of the Motor City. She found peace in Alex's death, but couldn't shake the unnerving feeling that she'd never find that type of love again. The money didn't matter, neither did the houses, cars, or property. Nothing matters in the end except for being with the ones you love. She knew that most never experience meeting their soulmate, but she did for one day.

While upset, there was one thought that always made her smile. She would think of it often, and she held onto it for the rest of her life. Like the memory of her true love, it never faded.

At least we had Detroit.

MUZZLE

Brett Pierce & Drew Pierce

1.

RILEY SHOT UP in her La-Z-Boy at the loud clatter outside.

Goddammit! Not again.

Annoyed, she jabbed the play/pause button of her remote, freezing *I Married a Murderer* on the TV.

It was just getting good!

It was an unsaid rule for Riley; when she came home after work and her butt hit the chair, it didn't leave for the night. That was her reward for putting up with her shit job, working the deli at the grocery store.

As she threw open the front door, a gust of snow blasted inside, followed by a sharp evening chill. She was reminded of the brutal early winter that had arrived. She pulled her heavy parka over her shoulders.

Goddamn bear making me miss my goddamn show again, she lied to herself. She wasn't missing anything. She had it DVR'd but she wanted to be angry right now.

Leaning out her door, Riley peered down the length of her rusted trailer back to where she parked the garbage cans. Old food and unpaid credit card bills littered the snow. A trashcan spilled past the butt of the trailer, and a mammoth paw clawed at the plastic bag inside.

This wasn't the same black bear from last week. This was a grizzly. Riley didn't care. *I Married a Murderer* was waiting, and it was a good one.

She grabbed the two metal pots off her kitchen stove and leaned out the door again.

CLANG, CLANG, CLANG! She smacked the pots into each other. "Go! Get out of here, you big bastard! Go!"

CLANG, CLANG, CLANG!

"*Vamonos!* Get! Go!"

The bear grew agitated with her noise and swung a claw threateningly in Riley's direction, followed by a growl.

Now I got your attention, ya big dumb bastard.

"Yeah, that's right! I'm talking to you! Go! Get out of here, you smelly piece of shit! Go!" she yelled, slamming the pots harder.

CLANG, CLANG, CLANG!

The grizzly howled louder and more ferociously. Riley didn't care. Now the bear knew how she felt.

CLANG, CLANG, CLANG!

Another roar, and this time Riley roared back.

Then *it* howled, and the trees shook. Riley froze.

What the hell was that?

BAM!

The trailer lurched violently. Something had slammed against the rear of her trailer. Riley tumbled to the floor, landing on her bad knee.

The trailer rocked violently again, followed by a monstrous roar and then a painful moan that sounded like the grizzly. The attack grew louder. Unbearably loud. Riley covered her ears and screamed in an attempt to drown out the horror happening outside. And then it stopped. Silence.

Slowly getting to her feet, she surveyed the trailer. Dishes littered the floor in the kitchen. Her flat-screen lay face-down on the floor in front of the Lay-Z-Boy. Somehow Riley's gin and tonic had not fallen from its spot atop the end table. Shaking, she downed it.

Cold wind gusted, and she shivered. She looked to the rear of the trailer where the bedroom was and saw snow drifting in through the now-shattered window above her dresser. Terrified, she inched closer.

Peering past the shards of glass left in the window frame, she saw it. All the true crime shows in the world couldn't have prepared her for something like this. Blood poured from one half of what remained of the grizzly's decapitated head, the heat from it steaming in the chill winter air. Innards were scattered, and a trail of bloody snow led out into the dark woods, where it disappeared.

2.

THE SHOVEL SCRAPED loudly against the concrete as he slid the tip underneath her foam-crusted muzzle. The sunken cheeks made her fangs stick out like knives. It was possible the cold killed her, but Egg knew it was probably disease by the look of her eyes and coat.

Poor pooch. Didn't stand a chance.

Winter had come early this year, and it was meaner than all of the predators out there in the woods.

He struggled to lift the wolf's corpse onto the truck bed, but with enough effort succeeded, then shoved it in with the other roadkill. *A good haul today,* he thought. Not that it mattered. He got paid the same by the sheriff no matter how many dead wolves or deer he hauled off the county roads. He'd make forty bucks, enough to cover his gas and maybe a beer and a hot fish sandwich at Gill's later.

Fried perch smothered in tartar sauce and a side of coleslaw. Heaven on bread.

Egg pulled the handkerchief down from his nose and took a deep breath of brittle air. He opened the driver-side door, and something fell into the slush at his feet. He picked it up. *"X-Treme Outdoors International—We put you in the Crosshairs! Hunting Guidance and Instruction"* read the magnetic sign. A relic of his failed dream.

His cousin Chauncy had made fun of the tagline Egg had come up with. *"We put you in the crosshairs?* Are we shooting the people who hire us?"

They had started the company together a few years back and had a few clients, but his cousin's people skills left a lot to be desired. Chauncy, however, chalked up their lack of business to "a shit-ass website." Egg agreed, as he did with everything Chauncy said. After all, he was older and the only family he had left after Mom succumbed to her cancer.

"Don't worry if plan-A fails, there are plenty of letters left in the alphabet." Egg could still hear Mom in his head. Her sayings were silly, but with each passing year they felt more like wisdom. Sometimes he pictured her like one of those blue ghosts in *Star Wars* smiling back at him, encouraging him. It made him feel better.

Egg slapped the magnet back onto his truck, and then he heard it—a low hum like a motor. His eyes caught hold of something a good twenty yards off the road. A flash of blue in a sea of white, and it was vibrating.

His feet sunk into the icy crust of the snow as he stepped off the plowed road and approached the thing. By the time he reached it he was out of breath. Snow shifted off the top of a blue tarp that covered a running Putt-Putt generator. Egg's eyes followed two snaking orange extension cords that led away from generator down an old fire trail.

What's going on here?

Egg followed the cords all the way to a white van, parked deep in the woods. The cords led to the rear of the van and were pinched between the shut double doors.

A white van. Hard to spot. Someone living out of this thing?

He looked back down the trail. No tire tracks.

Must have been out here overnight or longer for those to fill in.

A couple winters back, little Brittany Wicks had gotten sick of her dad's drunken threats and decided to get back at him by taking his truck one night when the temperature was well below zero. But she ended up running off the road and into a snow-filled ditch—got stuck, then snowed-in. The police said she had little frozen tears on her face when they found her off Route 15 the next morning.

I'll have a quick look. Take just a minute. Just to make sure everyone is okay. Then Gill's and a hot fish sandwich.

As he trudged closer, Egg realized that it wasn't just a van, but a cargo van like the one's you'd rent at a Home Depot for hauling—no side windows to see inside.

"Hello?" Egg approached the rear doors, keeping a safe distance. "Anyone in there?"

Only the wind answered back.

"A big storm is rolling in. It's not safe to stay out here. You don't want to get stuck out here for a week, you know." Egg bent down and clumped a snowball, then chucked it at the rear window.

Something felt off—dangerous—like when he was hunting, and he could tell a grizzly was near. The hairs on the back of his neck still refused to go down.

He trudged to the front cab and tried to peer inside, but condensation fogged the windows. "Hello?"

He thumped his gloved fist on the window. "I just want to make sure you're okay in there."

Silence.

Egg looked up to the sky. The full moon was barely visible through the dense clouds rolling in. Egg thought of little Brittany.

"Look, I'm gonna give the cops a call just in case!" He hung there for a moment before giving a shrug and stepping away.

BAM! The deafening crunch of metal sent Egg staggering to his left before clumsily dropping to the ground. The van settled, and it grew quiet again. Then came a low rumble, like a growl, hardly audible, but it was there. Guttural. Animalistic.

The vehicle rocked again, this time with such force that the wheels nearly lifted from the ground. Egg gave out a yelp.

SLAM! The van shook with monstrous force. *BAM!* Another hit, the van nearly tipping over as it lurched toward Egg.

Something inside wanted at him! Egg's mind shut down. Fight or flight took over. He shuffled back on all fours, plowing through the snow. Pure adrenaline coursed through his veins as he stumbled to his feet and sprinted for his truck.

He jumped inside and hit the gas. The wheels spun before catching, and he peeled away from the fire trail. Egg switched off the heater and ripped off his knit cap. He was sweating like a pig. After putting enough distance between himself and the van, he started to settle. *What the hell was that?* He wanted to call Chauncy and tell him what had happened. But what would Egg say? That a van attacked him? He could already hear Chauncy calling him an idiot.

Egg hated being called an idiot. Egg was smart. He knew he knew stuff, like the rumble he heard from inside the van. He'd been hunting these mountains his whole life. He knew that sound. *But why would someone keep a wolf as a pet?*

3.

CHAUNCY HAD BEEN waiting inside the gun shop for two hours now, just staring out at the heavy snowfall. *I'll be shoveling out of here if she doesn't goddamn get here soon.*

She had called earlier that morning, and he knew right away what she was calling for. He knew by the way she was breathing into the phone. She was rattled. Women stepped in his shop for one of three reasons: 1) they wanted the authentic sportsman look, so they could blend in better with the guys; 2) they were a recent divorcee looking for protection; or 3) something real bad had happened. He knew this would be one of the latter two, and he was glad.

He picked up his coffee but put it right back down after discovering it had gone cold. *Where is the fuck is this lady? Hopefully she's a looker.* Chauncy liked the lookers, especially the lonely divorcees. Every once in a while, he would get one to go back into the stock room with him for some "Chauncy TLC."

Thunk, thunk! He snapped out of his daydream and looked up to the door.

Finally!

He rounded the counter and used his set of keys to unlock the dead bolts. The woman came in, followed by howling wind and whipping snow.

There was something strange about the way she held herself.

Bundled up in a green parka, hood pulled over her head, she kept his view of her to a profile, as if not to give him a good look. He shut the door behind her.

"Chauncy?" she asked in a gravelly voice, as if she'd been yelling at a rock concert all night.

"The one and only. Getting a little crazy out there," he said with a smile. She brushed melting snow off her sleeves.

"Thanks for staying late for me. Appreciate it."

"I appreciate the business." He led her to the counter and began opening various cases. "I've got a lot of options here for you. Maybe pick a few up and see how they feel. Get a sense of the heft." He gestured to a spread of pistols: a .38 special, a Sig Sauer P239, and a variety of small Lugers, all appropriate choices for a woman with no intention of ever firing her gun.

Out of the corner of his eye, Chauncy got his first good look at her.

Brown hair and a pair of oversized aviators concealed most of her face, but still, he could tell she didn't look healthy. Her skin was pallid and yellow. There was also a scar just below her right eye, covered a bit by her glasses, that ran down the side of her cheek.

Sick! Won't be getting my dicky sticky on this one, he thought.

She caught him staring.

"Can I help you?" she said, her tone icy.

Where was the scared little girl he talked to on the phone? Where was his easy mark?

"Any of these pretty ladies calling to you?"

"I don't need a gun. I have guns. I need a guide, someone who knows these mountains. Someone capable. Are you someone capable?"

You're goddamn right I'm capable. Best goddamn hunter within a hundred miles, he thought, but kept his cool.

"You want a hunting lesson? I can teach you some things," he said with a sleazy grin.

She stood there for a moment, sizing him up and judging him on every detail: the dirty overalls, the raggedy trucker hat, even the small gap in his front teeth.

Chauncey could feel her judgment, like he was the last pick in the schoolyard, and she still didn't want him.

"I don't think this is the right fit," she said matter-of-factly. "Thank you for your time," and then moved for the exit. She reached the door and tugged at the handle. Locked.

"Unlock this, please."

FUCK YOU! he thought. Make me wait here all fucking afternoon!

...Slow down. Keep calm. Keep her on the hook, Chauncy. Show her who's dictating this fucking negotiation. He grabbed the keys off the counter and marched toward her.

"I'm the most experienced son-of-a-bitch in this town. If it's just a guide you need, I'm your man. There's none better." He tried to muster a confident smile, but his anger showed through.

"Unlock this please?" she repeated.

Chauncy fumed and slid a key into the first deadbolt. *Who does this cunt think she is?!* But then he hesitated. *Last chance to twist the knife,* he thought.

"So, what's up with the face?" He pointed to her scar.

Caught off guard for the first time, cornered, she shrunk against the door.

"Someone get a little too rough with ya?" He twisted the knife in deeper. "Other half of you looks pretty, though. Real shame."

"Open the door!" she demanded, but there was fear in her voice now.

There you are! There's the scaredy cat I heard on the phone!

"No!" He mocked, whining like a defiant toddler. She had made him feel weak, powerless. He hated her for that. She needed to be taught a lesson. "Let's see the damage. Then I'll let you go."

She huddled against the door, trembling. "Open it. Now!"

Chauncy took the initiative and reached for her sunglasses...

CRACK!

Chauncy's two fingers stood up at an impossible right angle. He screamed and tumbled to the floor in agony.

She fucking broke them! She broke my fucking fingers!

"You fucking bitch!"

She leered down at him, then with one hand on the handle, ripped the door open, locks and all, then marched into the storm.

Chauncy whimpered in pain as he crawled to what was left of the busted doorframe. It was a mess of broken locks and splinters.

How?

He watched as the red taillights of her white cargo van faded into the night.

4.

ELVIS'S "BLUE CHRISTMAS" played quietly on the car radio. The headlights fought through the heavy snowfall and rested on the carcass in the road. It was hard to tell what it was, with the snow building up around it. *Is it a deer? A bear?* Heather wondered.

This was certain to be the straw that broke the camel's back. She wanted to spend Christmas in Hawaii, but her husband, Ellis, wanted snow, so here she was. The log cabin was her present to him, her apology. Her affair had been brief, and things were still complicated, but she still loved her husband, and she had decided to go back to him.

Ellis reached from the driver's seat into the glove compartment and produced a flashlight.

"What are you doing?" she asked.

He slipped on a stocking hat. "Gonna check things out, make sure everything's okay."

"Why? We can just drive around it."

"What if it's still alive?"

"We'll call the police."

"What's that?" a groggy voice whispered from the backseat.

Heather looked over her shoulder to see Remy, her daughter, rubbing the sleep from her eyes.

The carcass shifted in the snow, and the hint of an animal's muzzle lifted into the light.

Definitely not a person.

"What is that?" Remy asked.

"Probably a deer," Ellis replied quickly.

"Like Bambi?" Remy asked, with the heartbreaking concern only a child could muster.

"Not like Bambi," Heather jumped in. She then whispered her annoyance to her husband. "You let her watch *Bambi*?"

"Not the part where…you know. Do I look crazy to you?"

But before Heather could answer, Ellis exited the vehicle and shut the door behind him.

"I want to come up front," said Remy. She climbed over the seat, tiny blue blanket in hand, and cuddled into her mother's lap. Heather's mother had knitted the blanket for Remy before the girl was born, and it had never lost its comfort magic.

"Your Daddy drives me nuts sometimes. You know that?" They both watched as Ellis approached the carcass in the snow. *Come on Ellis. Let's just go.*

The radio switched to Bing Crosby, and Heather tried to distract herself. "Let's sing this one together, okay?"

Remy started to sing, and Heather leaned in and sang softly into her ear. The smell of her child brought comfort.

Heather sang on, "I'm dreaming of a white Christmas". Remy tensed in her lap.

"It's hurting Daddy," she whimpered.

Heather looked to the road but saw only red snow and teeth. Then…cold blue eyes.

HEATHER WOKE WITH a start, feeling a rush of fearful adrenaline. She was freezing but drenched in sweat. She scanned her surroundings, and quickly remembered where she was.

That's right, the cage.

The nausea hit, and she vomited. It was mostly bile, though, since her appetite had been nonexistent these past three months. She reached through the bars for a towel and wiped the sweat from her naked body. The cage was still intact, albeit a little worse for wear. It wasn't safe for her to be around others when she slept.

The cage she had welded into the back of the van was a necessity. She turned off the electric heater and noticed the IV needle on the floor. It must have fallen from her arm while she slept.

Of course, it didn't stay in.

The bag of chemo to which the IV was attached dangled on its hook just outside the cage, still a third full. She should finish it off, not let it go to waste.

She picked the IV needle up off the floor and reached through the cage for an iodine swab, the smell of which nearly made her puke again. She wiped her arm, then the needle, then reinserted the IV.

After she finished the remainder of the drip, she called the gun store.

Chauncy answered the phone as "The Chauncinator."

Heather kept the conversation short.

It took an hour to pack the generator and then shovel the van out. After she was done, she threw up once more into the snow. This time there was blood. The red on white reminded her of that horrible night on the road.

There was something else. The hair on her spine and neck stood up.

I feel you.

She looked north.

Yes, always to the north.

She could sense his presence.

5.

EGG DRAGGED THE last of his fish sandwich through the mound of coleslaw and shoved it into his mouth. He wiped his chin and looked up to the old grizzly head hanging over the bar.

Hi, Chester.

Chester and Egg were old friends. They shared many beers over many an NHL game here at Gill's. Egg liked to think that before Chester had been shot, the old bear was a Maple Leaf's fan.

"$17.50, Egg," Christine said as she dropped the bill at his plate and continued on into the kitchen. He reached into his pockets and pulled out his cash. Twelve dollars. The rest had gone into his gas tank.

Shit.

Egg looked around guiltily. Could he ditch? No, Christine was a friend, and he'd been coming to Gill's with his Mom since he was a kid. He felt guilty just thinking it.

SLAP!

His magnetic sign hit the bar right beside his plate. He looked over and a woman in a green parka slid into the seat beside him.

"This you? Extreme Outdoors?" she asked. She leered at him from behind a pair of aviators. Her hair seemed too shiny, and she had a scar under her eye.

Egg tried not to look at it. His mother's voice echoed inside his mind: "Ladies don't like men who stare."

Still chewing his food, he said "I'm Egg... I mean, Edgar. My cousin is the only one who calls me Egg."

"Hi, Edgar, I'm Heather. I'd like to hire you."

God must have been listening, Egg thought. *Alright, be professional.*

His mind raced as he tried to remember the pitch he and Chauncy had rehearsed. He found it and switched to his professional voice.

"Extreme Outdoors International can cover anything you require to make your outdoor adventure an authentic experience. We provide all the gear, and we take you through all the basics—starting with small game and working all the way up to the big leagues. We offer a slew of packages, from our Tenderfoot beginner's package to the Warrior of the Wild package. Extreme Outdoors International is here to give you everything you need to become the ultimate outdoorsman,"—he paused, then corrected himself—"outdoors*woman*. We put you in the crosshairs!"

As soon as he finished, he shrunk into his coat. He knew he sounded like a cheap salesman, and he felt stupid. It wasn't him.

The woman studied him through her dark glasses.

"Great. Can you help me kill one of those?" She pointed to Chester.

Egg looked to the grizzly and back to the small woman beside him. "You serious?"

"Yes. And I'd like to start tomorrow?"

Egg didn't know what to say, so he just blathered. "But it's winter, and grizzlies hibernate. Plus, it's dangerous as all hell out there, even for a really good hunter. Have you ever hunted before."

"No, but I'm eager to learn." She slapped a wad of cash onto the bar. "Five thousand. And five thousand more when the job's done."

Egg stared at the cash. The solution to all his problems was right there, wadded up and wrapped in a rubber band.

"I…uh… It's illegal to hunt a grizzly without a permit."

She slammed another wad of cash onto the bar. "Fifteen K."

Egg swallowed hard at the sight. Then he heard Chauncy's voice in his head. *Never look desperate! Let her know who has the bigger pair.* Fifteen grand was fifteen grand, though, and Egg liked her. Even though she looked sick, she was strong like his mom.

"I'm going to level with you, Edgar. I don't have long, and this is on my bucket list."

Egg heard his mom in his head. "The moment you start to wonder if you deserve better, you do."

"Twenty. My cousin and I work together, so ten thousand each."

That's my Egg! Chauncy's voice cheered.

Heather nodded an affirmative and offered him her hand. They shook.

"We at Extreme Outdoors International are happy to make your greatest wilderness dreams come true."

6.

"LET IT SNOW" played softly from somewhere. *The radio is still on,* she thought, as the world filled in. Gentle snowflakes drifted down onto her face. She touched her cheek and felt the broken flesh beneath her eye. She rolled onto side, which caused her chest and stomach to explode with pain. Her clothes were blood-soaked and shredded. It was hard for her to tell what was fabric and what was skin.

Ellis!

Her husband lay dead in the snow, his lower legs missing. She wanted to weep, but coughed blood instead. Her stomach wounds were serious.

Then it hit her.

"Remy?!" she screamed. Panicked, she snaked her wounded body through snow in search of her daughter.

Then she noticed it. Stuck to her bloody wound were the shredded remains of Remy's blue blanket. Heather wailed alone in the snow. The pain was unbearable. She wished for nothing more than to succumb to her own wounds as quickly as possible.

Bright light flared as headlights crawled up her face.

A plow truck.

No! She was going to be rescued! But she had nothing left to live for.

SHE WOKE.

Still here.

A dirty gas station bathroom, she remembered.

Very classy, Heather.

After leaving Egg at the bar, she took refuge here, locking herself inside so no one would come across her.

Heather snatched her sunglasses off the piss-stained floor and looked into the dingy mirror, studying the sick woman before her. This story would end soon, one way or another, and it wouldn't be a happy one. She pulled the wig from her head, revealing her patchy scalp and the stringy remnants of her red hair. Remy had always played with her red curls when they watched movies on the couch. She fought back the tears that now welled in her eyes.

She could feel the changes inside, but something else was different now, too. She leaned in close to the mirror.

It was her eye. It glowed amber, with a dilated pupil. Anger burned inside of her, and like the vomit coming up her throat, she couldn't stop it. The hair along her back stood up and suddenly she could hear everything for miles. She could feel him out there, out past the woods, deep into the mountains.

North.

Her senses were sharp, but her emotions even sharper. I do have a reason to live, she thought. One reason. It's all I have.

I'm coming for you, whatever the fuck you are. This story ends with you and me, both dead in the snow.

MIDNIGHT: A SERIES OF LETTERS

A. T. White

MARCH 11TH(?)

I PACKED MY bags, filled-up with gas, and that was it—I was gone, out, out the door, into the horizon and gone, and I didn't think twice about it.

A single note left on the kitchen table in case anyone should come look for me. Probably never to be opened and soon layered in dust.

You told me once that dust was mostly dead skin. I'm not sure if that's true. I hope I never find out. I like the idea of it too much—a world covered with the people we used to be.

Please don't ask me to justify what I'm doing. Or what I've done by the time you read this. I could tell you it's because I miss you so much that my bones won't settle.

I could tell you how everything that's left here, in California, has become a faded version of itself.

I could tell you about the food shortages, the choke-hold police-state that has tightened around the last groups of us, the gradual encroach of apathy.

I could tell you that it's a chance to breathe some new life into *this* life. Before I sleepwalk it all away.

But the truth is...there wasn't any other choice. I was simply compelled to—

I had a dream last night and I can't shake it. If I hadn't left that house, that street, that city behind today, then I don't think I ever would have.

And while I can't find you in the hills and mountains, the deserts and canyons, forests and coastlines of this cavernous country…I can share them all with you.

So, this will be the first. The first of many letters I will send you. I'll try to document everything as honestly as I can. And I'll try to share as many glimpses into the world that's left as our remaining postal system will let me.

Who knows when each will get to you. I know you can't reply. I just hope that they bring you a tiny window into the World.

I would say, 'With Love,' but that feels obvious.

Please look after yourself. Listen to what the doctors say. They're there for a reason.

Oh, and the dream, (I hear your voice ask in my head); *"tell me about the dream."* Maybe next time. For now, it's just for me.

—Ashley x

MARCH 19TH OR 20TH

IT'S INCREDIBLE TO me that I didn't do this sooner.

It's only been a week and my head is already so much clearer. I can feel my eyes widening. My lungs filling. Even within hours of leaving, the landscape had shrugged my old life off behind me.

Before the 'Visitors', before the War, it would have been easy to drive an hour out here without seeing another soul.

Now it's days.

Only to you can I say that a tiny part of me enjoys that.

I'm enclosing in this envelope some of the sand from where I slept last night. It's so soft it feels like rabbit's fur.

And no. I'm not quite ready yet. But I'll share the dream soon.

—Ashe x

END OF MARCH

IT'S BEEN A few days since I wrote the last letter. Something happened.

I was moving through a small, abandoned town, barely a few streets thrown together, when I heard a helicopter come down about a mile away.

I'm ashamed to say that for at least a minute I considered ignoring it. Just moving on. But you enter my brain so often these days, and I wanted to make you proud.

So, I drove out to where it's carcass lay: Torn, erratic blades like broken fingers grasping from the dirt.

There were two dead bodies. And one that was, incredibly, alive. A woman in her early twenties. Her name is Alex. Another 'A,' like us.

She's a courier for the army and while she won't tell me what—I think she's carrying something important.

She needs to get North.

For now, our direction is the same. And she came with food. So, we've decided to travel together.

I can't say that I'm happy about the decision. She has a handgun. It makes me nervous. And she talks about the 'Visitors' with a vitriol that doesn't sit right with me. One of them brought down her chopper. As if that speaks volumes. She doesn't see them like I do. Despite all that they've done…I can't believe they're all one thing.

Anyways, we're heading up into the canyons now. I'll write more.

I struggled with whether to tell you this, but I think one of the Visitors is following me. I don't say this to alarm you. It's actually strangely comforting.

I felt it before I even left home. But increasingly since then. 'Home.' That's not the right word anymore.

And yes, I know what you'll say, what anyone would say… did it start after? After I lost them? The correlation can't be coincidence, can it? Well, perhaps it is. I don't feel the two are connected. But even if they are, I'm fine with it.

I wish I hadn't written that last part. I know you'll worry. But I promise—you don't need to. We've both always had a sense about these things.

And if I'm right, and it is following…I don't believe it means any harm.

—Ashe x

?

WE TRIED TO move through the valley today. It would have kept us away from the deserts where groups have fled to, and it would have helped us avoid the straightest route—through the mountains—where the 'Visitors' have taken up residence. Or so Alex tells me.

She has a map that was updated two weeks ago. It's all we have to go on.

But only an hour into the hills and we spotted a group of scavengers with prisoners. Alex wanted to help.

There was a clawing in my belly that wanted to do the same, but I'm both ashamed and happy to say that I'm not ready for death. Not yet.

So, I stopped her. I pretended to care about keeping her package safe and getting it to the base. It's important to her. She thinks it can change the tide of war against the Visitors.

All she wants is to make a difference. It's inspiring in a way. But in another—it just makes me feel nauseous to hear her speak.

That much naivety. That much hope. It's too much for my stomach.

If I could, I would dissolve into the ground and move through its soil, like nutrients in the roots—unseen. The slightest of tremors. Nothing more.

There's not a night that I don't think about quietly packing my bag and disappearing into the darkness. Leaving her behind.

I can't quite tell you why I haven't yet. She's less than a decade younger than me, but she feels more alien to me than the Visitors.

I'm certain now that one is following me. Sometimes I wake at night and think I see its tall, willowy figure, standing quietly in the corner of the room. Billowing. Like a match that's been blown out.

But it truly doesn't feel threatening. It feels like looking through a mirror. At a different version of myself. From somewhere far away but right next to me.

Anyways. Tomorrow we will try a different route through the valley. It's just time. The world isn't so scary when you have no reason to be anywhere else than where you already are.

Alex would disagree.

—X

(I'M NOT SURE WHICH DAY IT IS ANYMORE. I'VE BEEN TOLD—APRIL)

I RAN AND my feet almost slipped as skin-to-rubber-to-tarmac slid effortlessly to wet grass.

My arms ratcheted back-and-forth-and-back-and-forth violently. But my mind was burnt with the imagery of the dead body I'd just seen. The heavy eyes and matted hair.

I could hear the footsteps, a dozen yards behind me. More? It sounded like more. But their soles were heavier. Their breathing louder. I can outrun them. I can. It's not debatable. It's science. And time. That's all. I'm thankful I had the presence of mind to take those afternoon runs when the sun was dipping, and she wasn't quite home from work yet.

I'm thankful that I'm fast.

But then I saw Alex ahead of me, turning, her eyes suddenly wide, her arms raising, gun pointing past my shoulder at those pursuing.

Lightning from the back of my skull to the roots of my teeth and up my nose like a wire through my eye sockets.

And black.

I woke to the realization that I wasn't dead. And that I was wrong. I couldn't outrun them. Hadn't.

It took me a full day to comprehend the space that was now missing, in between that blow and the worried faces that now keep appearing above my bed.

We were pursued by Scavengers, that much I remember. They caught up with me, Ashley tried to shoot, but then something happened... Visitor's appeared... A fight... Ashley pulled me to safety, and we hid below a dusty rock... I might as well have not existed... These are all paintings someone else put in my mind... I was an apparition. Bleeding out into the dry, sandy grass.

A scout from a nearby group found us.

They have taken over an abandoned Motel out in the desert. A couple dozen of them. Men. Women. Children. Different races. All of them have lost people. Family. Loved ones.

But there's a strange peace here. Everyone is working together. It's odd to see some things improving. That doesn't mean they're all happy to have us. Some of them don't trust us. Some feel we bring unwanted attention. Some are excited just for a new face. Most are indifferent.

I had another letter for you. But I lost my bag in the struggle. The scavengers must have taken it. How ridiculous. They have a tiny slice of me now.

Sorry. I've been told I have concussion. I know you know what that's like. One blow can change the fabric of your entire life—The movies lied to us. A fucking shameful lie and we all went along with it.

It's been a few days here, already. But sometimes my thoughts feel like catching spaghetti. Alex. Alex. I was relieved, when I woke, that she was here. That she made it. That she hadn't left. I've decided my inescapable fondness for her is because she reminds me of myself. Or of who I once wanted to be.

Before I knew better.

Her package, her oh so important package—it's gone.

But somehow, she doesn't seem phased. Still determined. Focused. She's immediately tried to connect with the people here.

Sometimes I sit on the porch and watch her walking amongst them, and I see myself there: Smiling. Talking. Comfortable.

But the truth is my feet are like weights on the corners of my desire.

Fuck I miss you. I'm sorry. Why can't you reply. It seems so unfair. Sometimes I forget that this isn't just a journal because I can't fathom not knowing if you're getting to read these.

Do you wait, eagerly, to hear some news from me? Do these stories bring you any escape? Any joy?

Please stay strong. Please stay strong. You are the catalyst to my strength and the moment from when we last stood in the same room, to when we do again, is just a dreams length. I promise.

Stay with me in everything I do. I'll try to be braver. I'll try to make you proud. I'm enclosing a photo. The cook here has a Polaroid. So here I am, with Alex.

My friend, the Visitor, seems to have been with me more often these days. Sometimes, when I can't sleep at night, I think I feel its hands gently take my palm, and an immense calm flows through my veins and the back of my eyes roll over with sleep.

Do you remember me saying something similar? When I was a child? It's awakening memories inside me. Something… Or maybe that's the concussion speaking.

I'm not sure what comes next.

—Ashe

APRIL

I'M GOING TO tell you my dream now. The one that made it so I had to leave. The one that led to all of this.

I feel far enough away from home now that it's safe to share it…

I'm in the desert. The ground is cracked. Flat. The sound of distant thunder. But no rain. Not yet, at least. An abandoned water park. Simple and faded. Decades old.

There's a metal stool with turquoise upholstery. A small girl sits on it. Maybe 10 years old. She looks like me. Could be me.

At her feet is a large blood stain.

For a moment, it is quiet. Still for the briefest of moments, but in a way in which doubt is already waking in my chest that perhaps there's never been sound. Not once, not ever in the history of the world.

She opens her mouth:

"I'm going to start by telling you when you're going to die." I just stand and listen.

"So, you can stop worrying. There's no reason to be sad. Or scared... You were always going to die."

She takes her time. Dust blows along the desert floor and past her ankles like starlings swarming in unison at dusk.

"Then I'm going to tell you when you'll be forgotten. So, you can stop trying to be remembered. There's no reason to feel lost... You were always going to be forgotten."

The hollow echo of thunder in the distance, but it might have been inside me. I can't tell.

"Lastly. Lastly, I'm going to tell you that you don't need to be happy. There's nothing wrong with how you feel... You are enough."

I feel her words sink into my marrow as if they are the very center of the Universe. She holds my hands in hers and leans in and whispers to me. Whispers everything she's promised. And while I cannot hear the words—I feel them rename the cover of my life. And I know they are the truth.

"Can you feel that?" She leans back in the chair. "It's like an ocean lifting... Lifting from your chest."

And then... Then I woke.

I woke in the night and reached out for you, but you weren't here. And so, the next day I left.

I can feel you, as I write this, not satisfied. Staring me down and wanting to know what she said. What this little girl that looks like me whispered into my ear.

I told you—I cannot hear the words. But sometimes, sometimes they come back to me in splinters when I dream.

I wonder if I remember the details of your face correctly. Increasingly, day-by-day, I just see a light in my mind where the corners of you once existed.

—Ashe x

TODAY WE GOT to meet the 'Leader' of this Motel Group. Her name is Maria.

She used to be a part of the army when the war broke out. But when she lost her entire family while away on duty; she escaped and fled with her cousins to the valley and eventually the deserts.

I think Alex struggled a little. On the one hand she respects someone who has the passion and strength to create a place like this and to hold it together. To keep it safe.

But she can't understand leaving the fight. There's a war going on. And she won't give up hope that we can still win it.

As if anything is ever really 'won'.

We told her we were heading North. To the base near the Lost Coast.

Maria gave us an updated map of the local areas. There's no safe route that isn't long and arduous. And, of course, time is imperative to Alex.

She also noticed the veins on Alex's arm are turning black. Thin gray tentacles reaching from her right wrist up to her elbow.

I can't believe I hadn't noticed it before.

Alex assured us it was hereditary. And that she's lived with it her whole life.

Is my concussion really that bad? That I wouldn't have noticed or can't remember?

The package Alex was carrying was taken. Alongside a few other minor items. But she's relieved to still have her gun.

I'm eager to get back on the road. To keep moving. Everything moves so fast—if I can just keep moving alongside it—then everything stands still for a moment.

But I will admit there's something comforting about this place. These people.

I've started writing. A novel. Or a novella. What's the different between a short story and a novella? I'm not sure. Not that it matters anymore. Is there a point to making art anymore if no- one will ever see it? That's what Alex would say. But for me? That only makes it even more powerful.

I've been trying to remember the poem you would read to me every night before I slept as a kid. The 'IF' poem.

It eludes me, but it helps me feel safe enough to sleep.

—Ashe x

INSTEAD OF A letter, today I will send you an excerpt from the beginning of the novel I'm working on.

Alex has told me now that all the letters I've been sending will be funneled via the base she is heading to. So, she can ensure they find their way to you.

I don't even think she's just lying to keep us moving.

CHAPTER ONE

BY THE TIME Jonathan realized he was dead—he was already dead, and it was too late.

To be fair, very little had changed, so you could forgive someone for not noticing. The sun still beat down on the arid ground, clouds burnt out of existence as quickly as they formed, the din of a school just getting out in the distance. The mechanical pulse of the train line that skirted the edge of town humming with anticipation.

The World didn't skip a beat or miss a step or even take the briefest inhales of breath. It just continued. In fact, the only hint that Jonathan was, in fact, now deceased, was the sudden smell of burning rubber splintering crudely into the air, and the overturned carcass of his once proud red 60's Chevrolet. Still two years from being paid off. Now limp and crumpled like cardboard.

He stood about ten feet from the now inverted hood of his car and looked down at it. Quickly reasoning that his chances of surviving such an impact were smaller than any hope that he might have survived it. And that wasn't a fact that gave him much comfort.

No, he adhered fairly quickly to the notion that he was dead. And this was the cause of it. And the most shocking thing about the situation was how he didn't feel shocked at all.

What took a little longer to recognize was the creeping electricity that crawled up his spine and dragged itself through the neurons in his brain to tell him that he had, indeed, been dead before. This wasn't the first time. In fact, perhaps it wasn't even the second...or third. There was an unsettling sensation that calcified as a strange flavor on his tongue, which suggested to him that he had spent more time dead than alive.

But perhaps that was just his paranoia speaking.

Jonathan knelt down and peered through the compacted upside-down window of the shotgun seat. Its glass was mostly blown out, but some shards remained, obscuring the mangle of suddenly impacted metal, plastic, and fake leather. But he could still make out the shape of a head... an alarmingly familiar face, contorted, but undeniably human...motionless in the driver's side.

"Fuck."

He said in his head. For some reason out loud didn't feel resonant enough. In his head the word echoed out with the full impact it deserved.

He stood again, and looked out into the desert: Flat, cracked land with sporadic small shrubs and rocks of almost sarcastically random sizes. The nearby town was just close enough to add context but not close enough to feel anyone had noticed.

Jonathan turned his feet and looked around himself, 360 degrees, until he was facing his upside-down resting place once more.

It occurred to him how long it might be before anyone noticed at all. How long before someone came across the wreck and the dead body within before someone called the ambulance that was already too late and the cops who would act as just care takers to ensure things were tidied away so no-one had to think about what had happened.

And then how long until they found out who he was. And took the time to contact someone. Next of kin and such. And had made that awkward conversation that would eventually lead to an emotional reaction suitable for such a tragedy.

How long would it be? Could it take minutes? An hour? Longer? Maybe it would be a day before anyone would even know. Know that he was no longer out in the World, driving his red '60s Chevrolet that still had two years of payments to go. Was he insured? Would someone have to pay those payments off? Would his estate be depleted until it was resolved and his next of kin could receive any monetary value that his life might be worth?

Was he really called Jonathan? He reached inside his jacket pocket and pulled out a small brown leather slip wallet. Inside were surprisingly few bank cards, a couple of worn paper contacts, a number of twenties (he distinctly remembered hating to carry singles) a plectrum, and…his ID.

He peered at it under the baking sun that somehow didn't feel uncomfortable anymore.

Yes. Jonathan. He was right. His name was Jonathan Fowles. Thirty-eight years old. From California. Six foot two.

He felt weirdly proud of himself for knowing who he was and was about to count the twenties, when a glint of light caught his eye.

He looked up and saw a small cloud of dust heading in his direction. A red car was approaching…and fast.

MID-APRIL

I WRITE TO you now in a flurry of emotions. So, I apologize if this is incoherent. But there's a demon inside me and I need to get it out.

And it had started as such a beautiful night.

After a long debate, Alex agreed that I needed a few more days of rest before we could leave. She showed a side of her that keeps surfacing in small bubbles of air, and I inhale them like an addict.

It seems strange to say, but it's brave of her to slow down. And so I decided I would be brave too.

Once a month, they throw an event here at the Motel's bar. There's live music, dancing, double rations of food and alcohol, even sporadic stand-up comedy. Which is something I never thought I'd see again.

Maria holds these nights so the people get some release. And have a focus.

I ventured beyond my normal quiet walking routes and food runs, and I decided to embrace the moment. Otherwise, why did I leave all those weeks ago? And so, I went.

Alex and I had never seen each other like that before. Not as the roles we have become because of the world around us—but just as people.

The fingers of our lives unclenched for a moment, and we were free.

And that's when Alex convinced me, somehow, to get on stage.

I'd like to believe I didn't get up there because I was trying to impress her. I'd like to believe it was just for myself. Because it had been so long and this was a window that might never open again.

But as my gut twists in my stomach right now and my chest burns with anger, confusion, and betrayal—I guess I can't kid myself.

I picked up the guitar and played a song by a band I once loved when those were sentences that were normal..

I played it hesitantly at first. But as others fell in around me and the sound filled my body in a way I haven't allowed myself to trust in years.

Joy. There's no other word for it. I felt unabashed joy.

And for a handful of minutes, there on stage, everything dissolved, and I lost myself.

Until I looked for her. To see her face, joining me, a part of this moment.

Instead, I watched as she was led out of the crowded bar… One of the young women from the group. I didn't even know her face.

I've been that oblivious.

And what did I do? Well, I'm drunk and stupid, and stupidly drunk, so I followed them out. The sound of thunder in the distance as the first spats of rain woke the skin on my face. The confident recoil of liquor at the back of my throat.

I found them. I stood outside, about fifty feet from the motel room, as I watched them inside, the dim lights of the lamps illuminated against the darkness. They kissed. Embraced. And undressed as the thin curtains drew and the spats of rain turned to a welcome downpour.

I stood there for a moment.

Feeling tricked. No-one had tricked me. But I felt, I feel—tricked.

Stupid. I'm so fucking stupid.

I sit now, wet through, scrawling this like a child in my room. Someone is knocking on my door…

SOMETIME IN APRIL

IT'S BEEN THREE nights since we left the Motel.

I'm sorry for how I wrote last. I'm calmer now. My head is clearer. But that night feels like quicksand in my brain.

It wasn't Ashley at the door. As maybe you have presumed (or perhaps I had hoped). No, she hadn't noticed me at all.

Instead, it was a man who had watched me play on stage and saw me come back to my room. I guess he was hoping for some intimacy.

Although as I write this, I realize that perhaps he ended that night feeling how I was feeling when he came to my room and found me wet through and sobbing. And I closed the door on him.

Love is a snake eating its own tail.

I'd be lying if I could tell you what happened next. I remember the door closing and the sound of the rain getting dimmer. Stifled. I remember the fabric sticking to my skin as I pulled my clothes off. And how that angered me.

The fire. There was a fire. And the window was still open.

Alex tells me that the curtain must have blown into the fire.

They broke down my door and I was found, naked, amidst the flames, being held by my Visitor.

I don't remember any of those parts. I just remember feeling calm. And then being thrown to the ground outside. People standing over me and shouting.

Alex appeared and threw a coat onto me and helped me to my feet.

Maria tried to reason with the crowd. But they had seen me with the Visitor.

We couldn't be trusted anymore.

We fled from the Motel that night. Before things turned violent.

It's been three nights. And we've barely spoken to each other. There's a level of distrust that sits in the air now like an acrid fog between us.

Those veins. Those veins on her arm. How could I not have seen them before? And I swear they're growing.

I don't know why I write these anymore. This isn't what I had intended. What I wanted to share with you. But it's become my journey. And perhaps now this journey will end.

We have decided to take the quickest and most direct route to the coastal base. Tomorrow, we enter the forest and push through the mountains.

It should be a day's journey. But we aren't sure what we will find. The Visitors are meant to be hiding there. But that seems less and less frightening to me these days.

I don't even know what date to pretend to write at the top of these anymore.

IT'S BEEN JUST thirty-six hours since I wrote the last letter, and yet I feel like it may have been a lifetime.

We are alive. That much is obvious. We entered the forest, and the tall trees were calming at first. Stretching up above and around us like thin teeth from the ground. Indeed, perhaps there was a moment where we thought it would stay that way. That people were wrong, and the forests weren't to be feared.

But as we moved deeper, we knew we were being watched.

First, they were just shapes in the branches. Shadows. Then from within the foliage; reflections of dim light in the darkest corners. We didn't know what else to do but to keep walking. To move forward and to hope we were wrong.

We didn't say a word. We didn't dare.

It was maybe an hour before it was impossible to ignore them.

They took Alex and there was nothing I could do to stop them. I was powerless. Impotent. She screamed as they dragged her off into the dark foliage and I watched her disappear as I ran uselessly behind.

Perhaps she was right. Perhaps if I'd had a weapon. Something. I could have helped.

I wandered for an hour. Or perhaps minutes. Time moves differently in that Forest. I believed I was alone. That it was over. I allowed myself to give in to the reality that everything had finally come to a close, and I was just a ghost myself, drifting through the trees. Waiting to move on to somewhere else.

But then, as suddenly as she was gone—Alex appeared again. Out of the leaves, clothes torn, face and arms bruised and bleeding, out of breath. Somehow—she had escaped them. There was no time to ask how. They followed—so we ran.

We ran until our lungs were on fire and our limbs could barely stand. Through thick wet green, branches jutting like arms, up, up, up as the ground below us inclined and then fractured into a rock face. Too tall to climb.

Alex, undeterred, noticed an entrance between the roots of a large tree, and she pulled at them for us to climb through and hide. We couldn't see them yet, but we could *feel* the Visitors approaching. Spiders under the skin.

The roots dislocated and the dank smell of bark flooded our senses as we hastily pulled ourselves into the base of the tree.

The Visitors emerged. One by one. I'd never noticed how varied in shape they are. Some tall and willowy. Others shorter, some on all fours. They seemed to sniff the air, but without smelling, and then centered in on our tree like it was gravity, pulling them in.

And after this...what occurred just moments after, and for how long I cannot say...I'm not certain I can describe or feel right to put into words. I would place the blame upon my concussive head and the hazy interpretation of many events over the past week.

But later, when asked, Alex couldn't explain it either.

I remember the ground below us softening and giving way. I remember us falling a few clumsy feet down a dirt hole into the darkness. Alex's face near my face as my arm twisted on impact.

A sudden feeling of panic as we realized we couldn't go back. And a flicker of light as Alex's lighter sparked.

Crawling. On hands and knees. Through what at first seemed like a natural fault in the ground but soon became obvious was in fact a series of intricate tunnels. A way of moving, unseen, from place-to-place through this sprawling forest. A buried labyrinth built by the Visitors.

And we were lost in it. Our only guide being the desire to continue to follow the incline—up-up-up to the top of the mountain.

I remember scrambling in the dark as if we were trapped in the coffin of the forest's veins.

The rest... The small details I can recall... I would have laughed at if someone told me. But if time moved differently in the forest above—down there—in the tunnels—it seemed to move in infinite directions all at the same time.

I saw things. In the darkness. Glimpses of moments from my past. With you. With Sara back in the city. An afternoon rock pool fishing, trying not to slip. An argument late at night that felt at the time as if it would change my life, but that I'd forgotten all about. Biting a girl's lips I liked during a drunken teenage kiss.

I saw myself as an old lady, still driving, through a wide slate expanse that's how I imagine Iceland.

I saw myself with a child in my arms. The sunlight from a nearby window warming the back of my neck.

I saw myself alone. In an empty hotel room. With the curtains drawn so I could still just see the world outside.

All moments. Some I've lived. Some yet to come. Many that won't ever be. At least not here. Not in this version. A glimpse into whatever spectrum of reality the Visitors have lived in for all of these centuries, millennia?

The rest... it disappears from my mind like music in air. The notes ring out of order, sometimes faint, sometimes loud, but the melody eludes me and blurs into abstract the further I drift.

And my dream...the one that started this journey...it comes back to me now in waves that loosen my muscles and tighten my heart. I will die. I will be forgotten. And I am enough.

...And then...then a gentle hand. Unseen. Guiding us out... to the top of the mountain.

It might seem strange, but after we emerged into the crisp night air and looked down the craggy rocks and trees to see the distant blinking lights of the Army base—our final stop—we didn't think to keep moving. Or to speak of what had just happened.

No. Instead we set up for the night and didn't say a word about what we each saw. Down in the Tunnels.

It felt too sincere. Too private. It felt like we'd touched the corner of the Universe and that in itself was enough.

I need a moment.

I'D LIKE TO say that, knowing it was our final night together; we had some beautiful, poignant moment that bridged our complicated relationship and left us closer than ever.

But no. That didn't happen.

Instead, I learned that Alex had been lying to me. For weeks now, ever since I first found her in the carcass of that downed helicopter.

I was so stupid. I kept wondering why she didn't seem phased once the package (her oh so precious package) was gone. Why she was still so determined to reach the base. To finish her mission that she'd clearly failed.

The veins. The growing black veins in her arm that had now spread up her bicep, past the elbow and to her right shoulder.

She wasn't concerned about losing the 'weapon' because *she was the weapon.* The package was just a distraction. The real weapon was chemical. She'd been injected with it to transport it safely to the base for extraction.

That's why she was in such a hurry. She only had so long before it couldn't be extracted anymore. Once it reaches her heart—it would be too late. Both for the 'weapon'…and for her.

I can't believe I didn't see it. I can't believe she wouldn't tell me. We have our differences, but I thought we were walking side-by-side on this journey. The truth is—we were both alone.

Part of me wants to be angry. But the truth is…the truth is…

(DAYBREAK)

WE SAID GOODBYE this morning and parted ways.

There's a relief. In all honesty. Seeing her go. Knowing that is the end of it and I won't see her face again.

But then why does the ghost of panic reach up from my stomach to the back of my throat and make it hard to swallow?

Part of me looked down at the base below and envied the structure. The regime and purpose.

And so, it was strange to see some disillusionment in her. Some uncertainty. As if there was a tiny part of her that wanted to turn away and stay by my side and keep moving. Moving forward. Somewhere, who knows, next.

But she is young. And full of hope. And maybe she's right.

She gave me her gun. She insisted. Her crutch is my albatross. I guess I've changed a little, but I see more options now when I hold it.

I'm heading up the mountain line. And then down to the desert valley. Can you guess where I'll end up?

Yes. Your geography is right. I should be there by sundown with any luck. I'll take a photo for your next letter with the Polaroid the cook gave us.

I don't know where I'll head next. Or what the future is anymore.

HAVE YOU EVER thought about how the greatest curse of humanity is that we have just enough thought and reason to feel that we must be significant. But every piece of evidence of time, space and physics compounds the direct opposite?

I'm here, lying in the skeleton of the place we used to come to. All those years ago. Part of me is happy you can't see it now. It's like being inside a faded photograph. All the details have worn off.

But the impression is the same. And, as I said so many letters ago—only to you can I suggest that there's a part of me that likes it better this way.

Devoid of people. Clutter. Just the suggestion of a world that I never could fit into anyways.

As I look around the worn remnants of this once colorful water park, I just see us. I've climbed to the top of the hill, the slides are broken but still here. Like unearthed bones in the dirt.

And no, I haven't forgotten that this was the place from my dream.

I MISS YOU. More than any of these letters can say. I am alone again and completely free. Why is it that those two things are always hand in hand?

I think I may sleep out here tonight. On the desert floor. Under the stars. They're always up there. Even when the sky is blue and oppressive—they're still there.

We spend so much time looking forward and down. But at any point, on any single day, all we need to do is look up... And there's a sprawl of such incomprehensible immensity that we can't even begin to fathom it.

I think that's one of the reasons that despite everything—I am glad the Visitors came. Or made themselves known.

It was confirmation that we can't even begin to pretend we know anything at all. And now Alex is going to try to help to kill them all.

I'll just lie here for a little bit. And see what happens.

I woke at midnight to explosions. Explosions in the sky.

It took me a few moments to realize what has happening and for those moments I just stood and watched as these colorful bursts of light ignited above me and I wondered if all of it had just been a dream. Perhaps none of it had been real and I was just here with you, watching one of the old park's firework displays.

Perhaps I was still eight years old. And you were here next to me. As another rocket streaked silently into the air, impregnating it for a moment before the blossom of colorful smoke exploded in a loud CLAP.

Green. Then red. Blue. Yellow. Dotting the sky in streaks of heavy colors.

But then I looked around for you and for the briefest of moments—you were there. About fifty feet away from me. Standing like I was. Staring up at the starry sky, watching it become marred with vibrant smudges.

Then my brain shifted, and I realized it wasn't you at all. It was one of them. A Visitor. Standing there. Looking knowingly at the sky.

It turned and saw me, and I immediately knew it was *my* Visitor. In its expressionless face I knew that it had always been with me. From my childhood when it would hold my hand to help me sleep at night. To when Sara died, and I was left with an empty house. To when I found the courage to leave. To when the Motel group found me surrounded in flames and it held me. To when we somehow escaped the tunnels. To now.

It quietly turned back and looked at the sky once more. I felt a sadness in my stomach that I'll never shake.

And then I saw movement. Around me. Sadness was complimented by fear as I found them—dozens of them, one by one—Visitors, emerging into the night. Some from rocks. Some from the derelict walls. Some from the ground itself.

I tried not to make a sound. I felt immobilized with the surreality of the moment. But then I realized they were all looking. All of them—staring up at these opaque clouds that were now falling, heavy with smoke, down, down, down to the ground.

And I just watched. Frozen. As it fell.

There was a brief moment when I realized this was it. This was the weapon. This was Alex falling from the sky in beautiful, mesmerizing trails, hitting the ground and amassing immediately into a building fog that surrounded me and the dozens of other figures that had now emerged.

This was the signature that Alex was probably dead.

Despite the long moment of held-breath—As quickly as I had woke, I heard the screaming begin.

The gas became a thick haze around me as the Visitors wailed. A sound that felt as if we were at the very bottom of the ocean. A soft sound that somehow dug its nails into the back of my skull. I looked for *my* Visitor, but they had gone.

Others now emerged, panicked from the thickening fog—rushing past me, oblivious to my presence.

I'm not sure if it was in empathy for their pain. Or because a thick layer of smoke tore through my nostrils and filled my lungs—But I suddenly ran too.

Direction was lost. Fog consumed everything and what little it left was overwhelmed with the sound of the screams and the panicked fleeing shapes emerging out of the gas and then quickly disappearing again.

I held my shirt over my mouth and ran in one direction. Hoping to find shelter. Somewhere to hide.

The graffitied walls of the old ticketing office emerged like a church and I pushed inside, pulling the weathered door as closed as it would go.

Scrabbling to a back room, I held my backpack to me and waited. Listening as the screams echoed outside.

And that's the sound I could still hear as the seconds turned to minutes to an hour and the exhaustion of fear overwhelmed me eventually into sleep, my knees pulled tightly into my chest, my sweating palms gripping Alex's handgun.

I WOKE A few minutes ago. I wrote some of this while I tried to stay awake. But the rest just now. After sitting here, legs stiff, for almost an hour—I eventually summoned the courage to move.

The screams have gone. The World is ominously quiet.

From a broken boarded up window, I can see shafts of light where the sun has come up.

The smoke still hangs. Thinner now; a dreamy landscape of fog. Now colorless and white. Black marks punctuate the slices of ground I can see.

The fingerprint left when a VISITOR dies.

Did they all die? Was that a test? Did people die too? Did it matter? What about Alex? I should go outside. I should go outside and check. I will.

Just in a moment. Give me a moment and I will.

Dear Mr. Fowles,

I put great thought into whether to include this letter. I've written it almost ten times now. But I decided that you deserve to make that decision yourself and so I have included it separately. Marked as a clear distinction at the end of Ashley's letters that I'm sending you.

My name is Sergeant Alex Linkous. I'm a part of the resistance based on Southern West Coast America. But you know all of this by now.

It is with more sincere regret than I can say that I must inform you of your daughter's death.

She was killed in a misfire on the morning of April 8th, around 7:46 a.m. Probably just minutes after writing to you for the last time. From the account of what happened she exited the building she was taking shelter in during the Army's initial test of the weapon that is leading our front against the Visitors.

Although the weaponized fog had dissipated somewhat, there was still a dense perimeter of thick smoke covering the water park and its surrounding area. Our team, of which I was a part of as Corporal at the time, was sweeping the kill box for results. We were equipped with standard gas masks and assault rifles in case of remaining toxins and Visitor groups. Picking off any that had survived.

Upon nearing the building that Ashley had taken shelter in, fellow Corporal Sean Wilson came across an unidentified obscured figure in the fog.

As they neared, the figure raised a handgun, in Corporal Wilson's mind—with intent to use.

Believing he was under attack, he emptied three rounds in quick succession which killed the subject immediately.

I apologize for the cold phrasing of this description. I was there and arrived at the scene only moments later to find Ashley already dead, on the ground, gripping my gun.

When I returned to base with her body, it was identified that all of her letters had been held up over the past few weeks in transition. So, you hadn't even read her journey. The least I could do was to collect as many as were salvaged and to get them to you as quickly as possible.

I hope they find you and I truly hope your health is improving.

Ashley didn't speak much about her past. I got hints along the way. Filled in gaps from reactions, accidental sentences, tone.

I know she lost someone incredibly important to her, back in Los Angeles. And I know that it tore her apart to not be able to get back home, to you.

I've spent so much of my life fighting for a future. Looking to the horizon and feeling filled with a rage and a determination for how we have to come together.

But now I wonder if perhaps all I'm really doing is holding on to things that have to change. That always would change.

Ashley was able to let that go. She lived in the now. Which often infuriated me. But it is also what I love about her. Loved.

I appreciate we don't know each other, but I find it safe to say that you would have been proud to see how she lived her life.

I'm not sure which direction my own will go now. I feel I have lost the stomach for so many things. And I can't help but carry this blame.

But as I put these words down on a page, I can see why she couldn't stop herself from writing. I feel like I could say anything here, to you. And you would understand.

Perhaps that is stupid. I don't know. Perhaps I'll write to you again. There's so much uncertainty now.

The only thing I know is that sometimes, now, when I can't sleep at night and the pain feels too much—I feel a hand. Holding mine. And my chest settles a little.

With the deepest sincerity,

Sergeant Alexandra Linkous

THE FIANCÉE COMES TO TOWN

Cezil Reed

JUANITA RIGAUD ALWAYS wanted to fit in. Beyond being the only black girl in class, she was picked on a lot throughout grade school because her mother never kept her in one spot—her work required they move quite frequently. Her mother worked with tarot cards and was a self-ordained psychic. Most considered her to be a charlatan, but some believed. Juanita never cared much what others thought about her mother, because she loved her no matter what. In fact, she would come to her mother's defense even when she knew her mom was wrong. Loyalty was Juanita's biggest motivator to do good in the world. Betrayal was unforgivable.

Juanita grew up to become a high-school teacher who taught twelfth-grade government and civics in the small town of Manassas Park, Virginia. She found those subjects to be an excellent way to combine her love of history with politics and the ethics of managing a civil society. She settled in northern Virginia after moving from southern Florida. A better life and higher wages were perks that drew her up north. For a southern gal of Haitian-American roots, she felt the Northern Virginia area would be a nice middle ground. Not too fast, not too slow, and also near the ocean. Juanita was eager to take root in the suburban town and spread her passion for learning.

Her teachings had become a bit controversial as she mentioned frequently "the indelible original sins of this country," which, from her view, were slavery and the racism that caused it. Her teaching philosophy centered the idea that to know the true goals of government, you first needed to study the historical prejudices upon which that government was founded. Her teachings didn't sit well with many of the affluent suburban soccer moms, some of whom personally attacked her. Some teachers praised her efforts, others were indifferent, and some advised her to just toe the school district line, take the paycheck, and be glad to have summers off.

There was one man who especially admired her fervor: Mr. Scott. He was a tall, blue-eyed Caucasian man with the curliest locks of blond hair. He was the Freshman chemistry teacher, but he looked better suited to teach surfing.

Mr. Scott was best friends with the school principal and cousin to the school's superintendent. He felt it his duty to go right into their offices and go to bat for Juanita. He figuratively knocked it out of the park, every time. For her birthday on February 3rd, he put together a surprise party at the school for teachers and students. The birthday party doubled as celebration of Juanita's fearless teaching career, and the passion she brought to the job.

Then on Valentine's Day, he asked Juanita out on a date. They fell in love instantly, and Mr. Scott, having become totally smitten, soon proposed to her a few months later. Her intuition was quite formidable, and it had never failed her before, so when she peered deep into his eyes and saw a pure heart, Juanita said yes.

To celebrate the engagement, Mr. Scott asked Juanita to join him on holiday at his family's home in Montana. The invitation elated Juanita, but also caused emotions of dread. She never truly considered how Mr. Scott's family would feel about him dating a Black woman. But of course, she agreed to go.

IT WAS WINTERTIME now. The perfect time to travel time. They would arrive in the deep woods of rural Montana a few days before Christmas. A few miles out from his family's hometown, Mr. Scott stops at a gas station. As he pumps the gas, Juanita goes inside the station. He suggests that she stay in the car because of the cold. Juanita fires back, "I can get used to the cold." She offers up a warm smile and enters the convenience store.

She chooses a pack of skittles and the Attendant, a woman, stares at her the entire time. Not anything of disgust, but of a look of fear and caution. Juanita pushes the money to her. The Attendant nods her head and quietly whispers, "Thank you." While Juanita exits the store, the Attendant throws the money into the trash. She ties the bag up as if the money reeked of defecation. A panic attack strikes her. She calms herself with a deep exhale and follows that with a grand breath in, with a four count: 1...2...3...and 4. She reaches into her shirt and pulls out a small necklace with a wooden cross hanging from it. She holds it tight. Prays.

While in the car ride with Juanita, Mr. Scott listens to her encounter with the gas station attendant and shrugs. He responds with, "They're a little weird here. Not racist, just weird." She accepts his answer and remains quiet, enjoying the winter wonderland of the Great Northern Plains.

When Juanita arrives, she observes a collection of small homes creating a commune. Some folks come to the window upon hearing the approach of the car. Others remain inside, stare, or turn back to their wooden cabins upon lying eyes on the dark-skinned passenger. Mr. Scott's car stops at a small home that has a number of gifts laid before the doorstep. Juanita gets out and observes the gifted items. She sees crosses, incense, herbs, spices, and a slaughtered goat head. Jaunita is taken aback by the butchered animal. She looks to her fiancé, and he grabs the goat's head and proclaims, "For us, a severed goat's head is an offering of protection from evil spirits." He shoots her a grin and opens the door to the cabin home.

The small cabin is rustic; quaint, but still spacious as Juanita watches a warm fire burn. A knock at the door startles her as she turns and sees two old folks: The Man is referred to as Poppa and the Woman is known as The Mother. They are very, very old. More great-grand parents than what Mr. Scott would describe them as when he turns to Juanita, "These are my parents."

The parents stay at the door and do not cross over. Juanita notices this and finds the courage to reply.

"Would you like to come in? I'm excited for us to have a proper chat."

Poppa responds, with a shake of the head. "We're a bit ill and recovering from Covid. We don't wish to spread any germs." The Mother holds tight to her wooden cross that hangs from her neck while she stares at Juanita and whispers to herself. Poppa responds to Juanita, "Don't mind her. She's just old."

A light chuckle erupts from the two men, only. Juanita forces a smile. A small chit-chat about the drive fills the lull. Juanita watches the two, trying her best to not look at the old woman, who evades Juanita's gaze. The parents leave. The door shuts.

Juanita presses Mr. Scott. "Why is everyone here so bizarre? It's as if they have never seen a black person." He responds, "Honey, they're just old and don't get out much. They're loving church-folk. Safest people you can be around." Juanita mulls over this in silence.

A light snow, quiet and calm, taps against Juanita's tongue late afternoon. The snowflakes melt away as she closes her mouth and dances in the wilderness. She hums and sings. The wildlife notices her movements. Owls and small critters suspend their movements; her presence places them in a subdued trance as they watch this graceful woman prance among them in the snowy forest. Her movements are slow, methodical, frantic, almost tribal with the grace of Tango. Her eyes are closed. She stops, sways about, opens her eyes and sees a trail of black footsteps that have scorched the white earth. Her trail is dark, filled with a black, thin ash that melts into the ground. Juanita looks around and sees Scott's mother in the distance. She scurries away. Juanita gives chase. The Mother shields herself behind a gargantuan, crooked, and grotesque tree. Juanita makes it to the tree and circles around it, searching for The Mother. She looks to the ground. The footsteps end. Baffled, Juanita knows not what to make of this. She looks in all directions—nothing but snowfall and the small village in the distance. *Splat, splat.* Something hits Juanita smack on the mouth. It's black ash. Her gaze tilts up and she sees a body hanging from a tree, engulfed in flames. Blazing char drops on Juanita's forehead. She runs, hollering with rage and unabated fear.

Juanita makes it to her cabin. She sees Mr. Scott speaking to a relative. She interrupts. "Baby, there's someone hanging in a tree on fire." Mr. Scott urges her to speak slowly. She explains herself now, very slowly. Mr. Scott elucidates that they are at seven thousand feet above sea level. He attributes her encounter to a mere hallucination due to the altitude. She doesn't believe him.

Mr. Scott escorts her out to the deformed tree. They look up as they approach the tree. There is no one present. No footprints but her own. Mr. Scott requests that they go to the family dinner now. "Some home cooking will help you settle from the altitude. Mom's making hot stew. It's delicious." he replies with a grin.

It's dinner time. A long table with an impressive spread of soups and stews, breads, biscuits, and steaming jugs of tea are set at the table. A whole hog comes out, head and all. Roughly forty people sit at various tables. One long table sits in the center. Juanita and Mr. Scott are seated at this table with the rest of his immediate family. Poppa and The Mother walk in. Everyone stands up and goes silent. Poppa carries a wooden staff as he hobbles to his chair. The Mother sits at the head of the long table, Poppa to her right.

Poppa announces, "Let us pray." Everyone bows their head. Juanita scans the room and watches this. The Mother stares right after her, almost as cue to mean, "Everyone." Juanita bows her head but squints her eyes. She keeps a subtle watchful eye on The Mother.

Poppa continues...

"Heavenly father....Protect us from evil."

A family member shouts,

"Yes lord!"

Poppa continues...

"There is evil that tempts us. Wishes to destroy our pure and sanctified Eden on Earth. We ask for protection. We ask for the power of God. We ask for the blood. The Sacrifice. We ask for the power of God, O' Lord."

Juanita begins to sweat; her breathing becomes faint and shallow.

"Please identify the wicked and cast it from us, O' Lord. Take us away from the wretched, the pestilence, disease, the pollutants of your great vision."

Juanita's hands grip the seat. She can't keep her eyes closed. She looks dead into the eyes of The Mother who stares back at her with a haunting gaze. The Mother opens her mouth and points at Juanita.

Poppa finishes his prayer with, "Amen."

Juanita's head lands face first into the dark stew. She passes out. The others open their eyes. The people of the village say in unison, "Amen." They all open their eyes and see Juanita passed out. Mr. Scott, stricken with concern, pulls her face up from the bowl of soup. He attempts to revive her.

Later in the evening, a prayer brings in the night as there is a full congregation. They all prey together and touch Mr. Scott as he wallows in grief and weeps. Juanita is not present.

We follow a group of women who huddle to the kitchen area and watch The Mother places a fire to the cauldron. She pours in various herbs, spices, goat lungs, bull testicles, deer blood. Green and orange goo flows into this concoction along with sticks, twigs, and dried roots.

Later in the night, at the cabin, Juanita coughs and hacks up a black phlegm that she spits into a bucket. She has many of Mr. Scott's relatives all around her praying. Her nose drips a dark, green mucus. A cold washcloth is placed on her by The Mother. The group prays over her. Some yell biblical epithets for Jesus Christ, intermittently. Each time they shout, Juanita gags and, ultimately, vomits on herself.

Poppa enters the small cabin, "Cast out this sickness from our home, polluter of our congregation and hegemony. We cast you out, Satan. Your pestilence on our children is not welcomed. We command thee back to the fires of hell." Juanita's eyes close as she falls into a daze. At random moments, with half-lidded eyes, she observes her hands bound to the bed. She looks below and sees her feet bound as well.

She's lifted off the ground. She feels weightless as her and her bed depart the cabin. She looks to either side of the bed and sees the men who carry her.

It's dawn, overcast and very cold. Juanita awakens at the smell of smoke. She looks down at her feet and sees one of the people of the commune place a torch to a pile of sticks at her feet. Juanita's tied two feet high from the base of a tree. She bellows, shaking the snow off the tops of trees. A few catch notice of this and back away.

Poppa reads from the Holy Bible. Juanita begs, "Please stop this!"

He continues reading...

"I have the authority of God, King of Kings, Lord of Lords, and his son, Christ, Prince of Principalities and I name you so, Daughter of Darkness."

Poppa points to Juanita, "incarnate of darkness, void of light, manipulator of the unnatural." A wooden cross points at Juanita. He holds it aloft. Juanita spits at him. She screams, "Liar!" Poppa looks back to his congregation. They all nod in agreement. Poppa proclaims, "*The dark witch* will come forward in the face of the light." He turns back to Juanita as the flames rise to her toes. He continues his declarations.

"Name yourself witch before the children of God. Give testimony of your foul deceits on our son."

Juanita shouts, "I did nothing wrong!"

Poppa responds, "Deceiver!" He looks back to the congregation and yells, "Bring my son."

Mr. Scott, ushered by his brothers, moves to the front. He's without sleep, pale, and weak. His eyes rim with tears as he gazes up at Juanita. The Mother stands on the tips of her toes to whisper a few words into his ear. Mr. Scott's blue eyes turn frigid, the veins in his neck bulge.

Juanita, with all passion boiling in her eyes, "Save me, baby." Mr. Scott's eyes shoot away from hers and then look back at her to utter, "Burn, you bitch." The fire rises up faster, burning her feet.

The sky becomes dark, much like an eclipse but there is no sun. A shadow crawls along the ground, casting the congregation into shadow. A red light glows around Juanita as she vomits out a hearty roar of laughter. Black bile drips from her mouth.

Juanita, in a voice that's deeper and perverse. "You have damned yourself and your children with your betrayal. It is sealed."

She breaks free of her bonds. The ropes unravel as they burn away from her feet, turning to flakes of ash.

Poppa raises his hands and shouts while wielding the holy bible aloft.

"Do not look into the witch's eyes or you will be enchanted forever. Only God can stop her!" trumpets Poppa.

Poppa yells at her in tongues while his congregation falls to the ground, shielding their eyes.

Juanita looks down upon them as she floats. "I came only to share but you have stolen. You invited me to your land, yet I am a stranger. I ate your food, but you made me sick. I dreamed in your bed, but you offered a sleepless night. I fucked and loved your son, and yet I am a whore."

As the snow she hovers above turns to ash, Juanita delivers her final message.

"Yes, the bride of Satan comes disguised in her black skin, only to bring revenge, suffering, and torment for your lack of decency. Now *burn*."

IT COMES BACK

Elise Finnerty & Estellle Girard-Parks

I.

IT WAS 3:30 a.m. and Eva was jogging down Sixth Avenue. The nightmares were back, and she couldn't sleep. A couple were kissing on the corner of Sixth and Broadway, clearly caught in a moment of passion during a sluggish walk home from the bar. The woman's skirt was twisted to the side and the man drunkenly groped her thigh. There was something unsettling about the woman's facial expression. Her smile. It lingered too long. Was too wide. Uncomfortable, Eva turned away to check the road for traffic. A figure stared at her from across the street. A familiar figure with long black hair. A bus passed between them, and the figure disappeared.

IT WAS EVA'S birthday—marking ten years since she had moved to the East Village. When she was twenty, she had come to New York from a small upstate town with dreams of becoming a journalist or a writer. She knew it was a long shot; everyone in New York had the same dream. But Eva thought she stood out, especially with the prestigious scholarship she attained despite spending most of her childhood in foster care. Now she worked for an established newspaper and the novel-writing dream didn't seem so far-fetched. That morning however, her focus was on James, her foster brother. Her thirtieth birthday was also the date he was being released from prison after fifteen years. The novel could wait.

SHE PRESSED THE button on her answering machine.

"Hello, Ms. Hill, this is Ben from Lakeside Cottages. We got your message, yes, the place is available for this weekend. Please call us to confirm."

THE REUNION WITH James was relatively smooth, considering their past demons and what they had to overcome together as children.

"I can't believe I haven't hugged you since we were kids," he said.

Eva pulled away, but forced a smile and led him to the car. She wished she could be happier about reuniting with the one person she considered family, but something nagged at her. The long-haired figure in the street. A sense of heaviness filled her stomach and crawled through her skin like a thick sludge. She wanted to run away. *It's my chance,* she thought. *I could go away just for one last time. Be alone. Clear my mind one more time.*

When they got back to Eva's house, she went straight to her bedroom. James knocked on the open door.

"So, I cleared my busy schedule for you today," he joked.

"Look, I feel guilty about this, but I'm actually leaving for the weekend."

"Oh. Okay," he said. "Well, why don't I come with you?"

Eva avoided eye contact as she continued to pack her belongings. "It's out of state," she said, hinting at the reality that his 'freedom' wasn't entirely free just yet. She gave him a hug and left.

2.

EVA DROVE THROUGH the town strip, taking in her new surroundings. It was clean, beautiful, and quiet. Has she made the right decision?

The streets were empty, except for a street cleaner and one or two locals. A sign hung in the window of a nearby hotel that said, "Closed for the Season".

She stopped at the agency to collect the keys to her cottage.

"Lucky you, you have the whole place for yourself," the girl behind the counter popped her gum and smiled. A wide smile.

EVA FELT A pang of guilt about abandoning James so soon. There was no signal, but she spotted a phone booth and dialed his number.

"Hello?" James' voice answered and Eva immediately slammed the phone down.

What is wrong with me?

She leaned her forehead against the cool glass of the phone booth. From across the street, she saw the young agent leave the office and approach a young man standing in the parking lot. They exchanged a few words and he handed her a small baggie containing what looked like brown scraps of some plant-like material.

EVA'S MIND WANDERED as she drove along the winding road through the thick, oppressive forest brush flanking her on either side. She remembered driving down a similar road, sat in the backseat as a child, on the way to her first foster home. She was terrified when she arrived, but James had immediately set her at ease. He'd always been there for her, right from the beginning. James found a little sister he vowed to protect, and Eva found a big brother she could lean on. She felt another pang of guilt.

The map with directions to the cottage lay on the passenger seat and she picked it up to distract herself. She glanced down at it and didn't recognize the area. Had she missed a turnoff? She looked in the rearview mirror and caught sight of her reflection.

A wide, off-putting smile plastered her face and her eyes were devoid of life.

"What the—"

The car swerved and hit a deep pothole gouged into the road. Eva slammed the brakes and the car skidded to a halt. Shaken, breathing deeply, she took a moment to gather herself and looked back at the mirror, her face normal again.

She got out of the car to inspect the damage. As she circled round the back, a deer emerged from the outskirts of the forest. *How long has it been since I left the city?* It stared at her, but far from being calmed, Eva found the stillness of the deer unsettling.

Then *CRACK!*

Eva screamed and ducked behind the car. A gunshot. The buck dropped dead and only the awful ringing of that sound resonated in Eva's ears. Suddenly everything shut down in her head. It took her a few minutes before going back to reality. That was when she heard his voice.

"Hello?" The hunter stood over her, still holding his rifle. "Sorry if I spooked ya!" He smiled.

"Hi. Yeah, it's okay. I'm fine," Eva replied. She stood up and quickly got back in the car.

"You're staying at the Lakeside Cottage?" the hunter said, spotting the open map on the passenger side. "That's a popular spot."

"Yeah, I can see why." Eva smiled and pulled away. Looking once more in the rearview mirror, she saw the hunter staring after her, gun in hand.

SHE PULLED UP to the cottage as the sun was going down. It was small, rustic, cozy, and hidden away deep in the forest. The front porch opened onto a short path leading to a nearby lake, and an old rocking chair creaked in the wind. A cigarette butt lay on the ground in front of the entrance. Eva frowned. It was still smoking.

WHEN SHE GOT inside, she threw her bags down and took in her space. She opened her suitcase and slipped off her stiff city clothes with grateful relief and began to unpack. She had the conviction that the best way to soothe a troubled mind was to put on comfortable clothes. The hostel-style décor was exactly what she had envisioned; fun little knick knacks left by previous visitors and a "TAKE ONE LEAVE ONE" bookcase in the corner. Eva spotted a guest book and flipped through the pages. A few thank you notes and several pictures of young people having fun on the lake. On the final page she found a note: "Look for the bark." It was accompanied by something that looked like a recipe.

UPSTAIRS, EVA OPENED her suitcase, slipped off her stiff city clothes and began to unpack, when a noise caught her attention downstairs.

"Hello?" she called out as she descended the stairs. Rounding the corner, she noticed the back door was open and her blood ran cold.

Silence now. She closed the door and screamed when she saw the figure of a dark-haired woman standing behind her in the reflection of the door window. She spun around.

"Surprise!" said the stranger.

"Ellie? What are you—" Eva replied breathlessly. "You scared the shit out of me! What are you doing here?"

Ellie stepped forward and flung her arms around Eva. Eva spotted a new tattoo, still red and tender from the needle. A fawn.

THE TWO WOMEN settled in to celebrate Eva's birthday. Ellie searched the cupboards for something to drink and found the remains of a dusty old whiskey bottle. She took a swig and handed it to Eva.

"Hey, look what I found with the whiskey," Ellie smiled and held up a small baggie holding some brown, plant-like material.

Look for the bark.

Eva retrieved the guest book and flipped to the recipe on the back page.

"Let's make it," she said, and began pulling pans and utensils from the cupboards and drawers.

"Are you serious?" Ellie responded, chuckling. "You don't know what that stuff is, or what it does. You don't just experiment with some shit you found in a zip lock."

3.

OUTSIDE, THE FIRE pit shimmered and crackled. Crickets debated with frogs and the cool night air caressed the faces of the two women sitting in silence. Eva sipped from a steaming mug while the lake slept watchfully and small eddies of air stirred, waiting and whispering.

"Do you feel anything?" Ellie asked.

"Nope," Eva said.

They sat silently for a while.

"I was blowing off some steam at a bar once and this guy was with his friends and we got to talking," Ellie said. "We ended up making out and things got turned up a bit."

Eva felt like she had heard this story before.

Ellie kept on going. "He had no condoms. Trying, you know, obviously like guys do, trying to sweet talk me yada yada yada. And then this fuckin' guy just starts kinda fucking me anyway!"

As Ellie told the story her voice started to echo. Eva's breath shorted and she started rocking back and forth. Her abnormally dilated pupils makes it clear that the drugs had kicked in. She felt her chest constrict and her breathing begin to quicken. Her eyes rolled back in her head and her mouth drooped down.

"Eva!" Ellie screamed.

EVA WAS IN front of the lake. The muffled sound of laughter emanated from a long tunnel that grew steadily darker in front of her. The lake seemed awake now, a watchful hush radiating forth from the stillness of its surface. Eva walked closer and saw a figure standing at the water's edge. A child? A little girl with long, black hair, its face twisted into a broken rictus. Its jaw hung open, bent in an unnatural contortion. It released a terrifying, moaning scream. Visions of Ellie's story came crashing into her brain like a lightning bolt, a sudden symbol of illumination and the destruction of ignorance. The bark had caught her with an atavistic turn in the pit of the stomach. She shivered and turned around to see that the child was no more, replaced by a terrifying broken face with mouth ajar in an unnatural position, letting out a terrifying gutted scream.

Eva screamed with it, and her nightmare played out. Her mouth opened and a dark liquid poured out, spilling to the ground and splashing her feet.

A black puddle of semi-solid, gelatinous mass formed at the lake's edge. It shifted and vibrated, taking on a familiar shape. It thickened and curdled, bones snapped into place and the black drained away to reveal clammy pale skin. The creature crawled toward the lake. As it reached the edge it paused, and Eva's breath quickened. Shooting up tall and twisting like a snake uncoiling itself to strike, the creature then dropped to the ground, its bony fingers dragging itself into the depths of the lake.

It was gone and Eva stood alone in the darkness.

STRANGE TO ME

Kyra Gardner

NOTHING EVER HAPPENS in Edmon Ridge. Like most small mountain towns, the biggest news of the week is a bear spotted on someone's porch, or when the occasional drunk falls in Prospector Lake. But this autumn week was different. Becca Williams had been missing for three days.

What was planned to be a late night out for the high school senior had quickly become town gossip. The gossip turned into anxious debates. Did she skip town? Or something worse? It was like a bad game of telephone. Ugly words started to echo through the tall pines about the most maidenly and well-known student at Edmon High. You couldn't fill up at the local service station or shop at the only grocery store without hearing the girl's name.

What happened to Becca?

Jennifer Baker pondered the same thing as she stared blankly out her bedroom window at the last of the amber leaves clinging to the trees.

On her desk sat an unfinished article on a ginger snap recipe. Mr. Wear had stuck her with the baking column, *again*. Other previous *Edmon High Herald* articles were strewn across the small desk. Jennifer sighed and tried to focus on writing. But… Becca. Jennifer's eyes went to the framed photo atop her dresser. It was a picture of herself, Becca, and the third in their best friend trio, Catherine. Becca in her long cheerleading skirt, along with Cat, who appeared to be scratching her legs from the coarse wool, and Jennifer, giggling at whoever was taking the picture.

What if this was our last photograph together? Jennifer thought. *What if she never comes home?*

HONK, HONK!

Jennifer's pencil flew out of her hand as she almost toppled over in her chair. She peeked out the window to see a 1952 blue Chevy pickup truck in her driveway.

"Right!" Jennifer said aloud. She got up, grabbed her book bag, and swiped the belongings on her desk into her purse in one fell swoop. In a skip-and-hop combo, she put on her shoes while throwing on a yellow cardigan. On her way out of the room, she caught a glimpse of herself in her body mirror. *Blegh.*

She paused to quickly brush her fingers through her hair and re-tuck her cream blouse into her green tartan skirt. *Maybe he doesn't even remember*, she tried to convince herself. She could feel her heartbeat in her eardrums as she raced down the stairs.

"Bye, mom!" she yelled as she exited the house through the front door.

The hurried farewell was returned with her mother's anxious warning, "Be back in two hours! You know the new curfew!"

Jennifer jaunted up to the truck, shading her eyes from the sunset glare off the windshield. Out of breath from the run, she flung open the passenger side door. "So sorry Mark, I—"

But instead of Mark's face she was greeted with Catherine's between the two of them.

"Oh, here," Catherine said as she exited the car and motioned for Jennifer to get in between her and Mark. She was dressed in the same purple wool skirt as the photograph, on her way home from cheer practice.

"Are you sure?" Jennifer responded.

"Mark's going to hit my house first before you two get to Becca's. It'll be easier." She motioned with her head for Jennifer to get in the middle seat.

Jennifer cautiously peered into the vehicle. Mark was throwing his letterman into the back seat to make room for her. She blushed and quickly looked down at her feet. *Are they always this far away from my body?* she thought. Her body grew a bit tense.

"There's room for ya now, Jen!" Mark chimed. He gave her a lighthearted smile.

Jennifer held her breath as she climbed into the truck. Her foot awkwardly caught on the running board, and she clumsily fell into the seat. *Of course*, she thought, as she blew the hair out of her face and adjusted herself.

Mark laughed.

Catherine hopped back into the truck and shut the door.

Jennifer sat still—a product of overthinking every move and gesture—and stared out the window at the houses that lined the winding, mountain road. They were all eerily far apart from one another, separated by thickets of trees. Each home was decorated for Halloween to its own taste and style, with the occasional house that refused to participate in the "Satanic" holiday.

Jennifer eventually worked up the courage to say something. She cleared her throat.

"Thanks again for the ride," she said, now looking at Mark.

"No problem," he responded. "It's a rite of passage to be the chauffeur of the group."

Jennifer grinned, then looked back to her feet. She recalled the last time Mark gave her a ride. *Oof.* She shook her head as if it would shake away the embarrassing memory.

A Zippo lighter sparked. Jennifer turned to see Catherine lighting a cigarette.

"Cat, you *know* my old man will kill me if he smells that in here," Mark said sternly.

"Okay, okay, officer!" Cat quipped back. She held up her hands as if she were getting arrested. She held the cigarette between her teeth as she rolled down the window. The fall breeze carried the smoke outside the car.

"I didn't know you smoked, Cat." Jennifer remarked.

"It's…a more recent hobby," Mark said, responding on Cat's behalf.

Cat shot Mark a look. "You would too if your best friend just disappeared into thin air."

Mark shrugged.

You couldn't argue with that, Jennifer thought. *Actually, you couldn't argue with Cat on anything.*

"I'm happy you're going to be talking to her grandparents," Cat said as she flicked the ashes from her cigarette out the window. She turned her body more towards Jennifer. "I haven't seen Mr. or Mrs. Williams come outside since the sheriff stopped by their house."

"The sheriff came?" Jennifer asked.

"I saw Officer Grissom's car in their driveway the other day, with the lights on. He had a dog with him, too." She paused. "I think he was asking for clothing," she said grimly.

Jennifer searched Cat's face for an answer as to why.

"Sniffer dogs," Mark chimed in, while pointing to his nose.

We have sniffer dogs in Edmon Ridge? she thought. Jennifer had never actually been to the sheriff's office. There'd never been a reason to. Nothing ever happened on the mountain.

She looked at Cat. "Is it illegal for me to talk to them?"

"I'm sure it's fine. You're asking for the scoop for your little school story. It's not like you're the FBI." Cat tossed her finished cigarette out the window.

Jennifer felt like Cat's remark was dismissive of her work at the school newspaper, one that helped her earn a full-ride scholarship to Berkeley. *I'm the only one in the group going to university. How dare she?*

Mark up to a beige house that was brimming with festive Halloween décor and parked. He stepped out of the truck and walked over to the passenger side to open the door for Catherine. She grabbed her brown cheer bag and purposely hopped out, throwing her arms over him.

"Thank you, baby," she said as she kissed him on the cheek. Jennifer tried not to look.

Cat walked up the driveway toward her house, waving back to Mark who was now climbing back into the truck. Her eyes then met Jennifer's, and Cat shot her an icy smirk. Jennifer immediately moved from the middle to the passenger seat. The tension was interrupted by Mark slamming his door closed. Jennifer smiled stiffly at him, and the two drove away from the house.

They rode in silence for what felt like an eternity. *Say something, anything, you ditz.*

But it was Mark who broke the stillness.

"Hey, so about the other night—"

"Please," Jennifer interrupted. "It was so silly. We don't have to talk about it."

Mark looked at her and sighed, a little disappointed. Jennifer returned the glance with a half-hearted smile, reassuring him not to go there.

The truck moved on to more rural pathways.

"I really appreciate you doing this." Mark admitted. "Becca *probably* came home from cheer practice the night she disappeared, but that was the last time Cat saw her." He chewed on that thought for a moment. "I think Cat blames herself for Becca's disappearance, since she's the one who sent Becca home early from practice. If we can find out that Becca actually made it home, I'm sure Cat will stop blaming herself so much."

Mark was clearly upset, and Jennifer had never seen him get worked up over anything before. *Well, unless it was his dad,* she thought. But this was different.

"Does Cat think something bad may have happened?"

Mark didn't respond.

Jennifer sat in her thoughts for a moment. She wanted to help, to reassure him.

"I'll get answers," she said firmly.

"It shouldn't be hard. You do have a way with getting people to talk,"

Jennifer turned to look out the window so as to hide her blushing face.

The truck pulled up to the end of a short access road. Up ahead was a faded purple house. The top two windows almost looked like eyes if one of them were scratched out. It had a long crack running down the thick pane. *Must have been a tree,* Jennifer thought. The big brown door served as what would be the mouth to the overall facade. The front lawn desperately needed a good raking, and the trash bins were overflowing.

Mark reached into his pocket and pulled out a box of cigarettes. "Here. I swiped 'em from Cat. Becca's grandpa is a heavy smoker. Maybe you can bribe him if he doesn't wanna talk."

Jennifer's finger brushed against his when taking the pack. The two locked eyes for a moment before Jennifer pulled away. "Um, thank you," she coughed up. "I appreciate it." She gave Mark a meaningful smile, which was returned.

Mark watched her closely as she grabbed her book bag. Jennifer opened the door and slid off the seat. She managed not to trip over the footboard this time. She closed the passenger door and walked towards the access road. As she walked, she offered a clumsy wave back to Mark, who returned it as he drove out of sight.

Jennifer clutched her book bag tighter as she neared the house. *I've never been to Becca's house before*, she realized. She sometimes felt as if she were an outsider looking in on her own friend group. She walked up the squeaky porch steps and to the door. She raised her hand to knock, but stopped. Her heartbeat fluttered while she contemplated going forward with her plan. She inhaled deeply and then knocked three times on the door.

There was no response.

She turned back to look at the driveway. Mark's car was long gone. *Great*, she thought. *I'm stranded*. She pressed her ear to the oak door and listened for any movement inside. To her surprise, she heard a hushed voice and some sort of scuffling.

"Hello?" she said to the door. "It's Jennifer, Becca's friend."

The door creaked open just before she could knock again. A set of pale gray eyes appeared in the small gap in the doorway. "What do you want?" Mr. Williams demanded. His voice was gruff and slightly hoarse.

"I'm Jennifer Baker. I, uh, am a friend of Becca's. I work on the school newspaper, and I was wondering if you'd be willing to sit down for an interview, regarding her disappearance?"

Mr. Williams grunted, "I already said what I have to say to the sheriff. Ask him." He moved to shut the door, but without thinking Jennifer pushed her foot inside the crack before it could close.

OW!

"What are you on about?" Mr. Williams hissed.

"I'm sure you've been hearing the wild theories about your granddaughter going around town. Some of which I know are completely untrue."

Mr. Williams paused, then moved the door open a smidge more to release Jennifer's foot from the trap. She let out a sigh of relief.

"I want to put an end to the gossip. Our Homecoming Queen— and my dear friend—shouldn't have her or her family's name soiled because people are dying for any drop of drama."

Mr. Williams opened the door fully. He eyed her from head to toe. "Five minutes," he said. Jennifer entered and he closed the door behind her. He locked it, then locked it again.

No one ever locks their doors up here. This guy has two?

The house had a rustic feel. The walls were decorated with family pictures, many that included Becca, and delicate cross-stitched artwork, which Jennifer assumed was the work of Mrs. Williams. The old man muttered under his breath and walked into the next room, signaling with his hand for Jennifer to follow him.

They entered a quaint little kitchen that felt rather cozy. Jennifer smiled as she eyed the nearby china cabinet, which seemed to take up most of the room. *Someone clearly has a teacup addiction.* A maroon GE portable radio sat on the tiled countertop, and next to it upon the stove, a tea kettle was heating up. Swing music played through the speaker. The old man adjusted the knob of the stove to a higher temperature and then moved to pull out two teacups from the cabinet.

"Clock is ticking, you know," Mr. Williams said gruffly.

"Right," Jennifer said. She took a seat at the kitchen table and opened her purse. She took out a sharpened pencil and a yellow notepad. She looked up to him, his back still facing her. "So how long have you and Mrs. Williams been taking care of Becca?" she asked.

"Hmph." he responded. "Everyone knows we've been looking over Becky since she was a baby."

"Right, just a warm-up question," Jennifer responded meekly.

"No time," he said, pouring milk into the empty cups.

Jennifer clenched the pencil in her hands. *Just rip the band aid off*, she thought.

"Did Becca come home from cheer practice three nights ago?" she asked.

"No," he said curtly. He fiddled with the cups again.

Jennifer thought back on Mark's words. *Cat was the last person to see her?*

"So, Becca went to school that morning and never came home?" she questioned.

"That's what I said, didn't I?" he retorted. His words seemed almost hollow, like they had no emotion behind them.

"She must have mentioned something about going somewhere, or visiting someone that night? A boy, maybe?".

Mr. Williams whirled around. "She isn't allowed to be dating boys," he snapped. "Not 'til she's eighteen. She's a proper young girl!"

Becca had dated half the school. Everyone knew that. Everyone except her grandfather, apparently.

The tea kettle started to whistle, and suddenly, the radio on the counter started blasting swing music almost as loud as the kettle's growing screams. Jennifer put her hands over her ears. The combined sounds were almost unbearable.

Mr. Williams removed the kettle from the burner, but the radio remained on the fritz. It was now switching randomly between AM stations. Jennifer tried plunging her fingers deeper into her ear canals to block out the noise.

Mr. Williams turned the knob this way and that, but there was no change in the volume. The box then settled on a station playing Sheb Wooley's "Flying Purple People Eater." The old man lurched back as if expecting something demonic to jump from the radio, but just as quickly as it went on the fritz, it shut off. He stood there frozen, staring at the box.

"I'm sorry Mr. Williams," Jennifer whispered, "I didn't mean to—"

Her sentence was cut off by a new voice. "Who is this?" it asked quietly.

Mrs. Williams stood in the doorway to the kitchen. She was dressed in an off-white nightgown. Her long, gray hair was disheveled and ratty. One of her thin hands clung to the door frame.

"No one, dear," Mr. Williams said calmly. "Go back to bed. I'll bring you your tea." His hand shook as he poured water into the teacups. He wore an exaggerated smile. Jennifer looked back to Mrs. Williams, who didn't move from the doorway and continued to stare at her.

Does she ever blink?

"I'm a friend of Becca's," Jennifer finally offered.

"You are?" She walked to Jennifer took the girl's hands in her own. The old woman's hands were cold. Her hazel eyes studied Jennifer. She moved one of her pale hands to Jennifer' face, and the girl recoiled from the cold. Mrs. Williams smiled. "You wear your hair like she did," she said.

Jennifer smiled, and then thought about what was just said. *"Did?"*

A look of sadness appeared on Mrs. William's face as she continued to look at Jennifer. The old man wedged himself between the women and handed his wife a bright pink teacup with a hummingbird on it. The old woman looked down at the colorful china and smiled.

"That's right honey. Now back to bed," her husband said, punctuated by an exaggerated grin.

Jennifer looked at him, confused. *Where was this chipper man two minutes ago?* He gently put his arm across her back and steered her towards the hallway she had come from. The elderly woman turned back to Jennifer for a moment.

"It was nice to meet you, Jennifer," she said.

"You as well," Jennifer replied.

Mr. Williams also turned back to Jennifer, the smile on his face even more extreme now, looking very much like a twitching mask. *It's odd*, Jennifer thought. *His mouth is smiling, yes, but his eyes are sad and tired.* She shivered. *This is far more unpleasant than his short temper.*

"Well, Miss Baker, it was so lovely to speak with you, but I do believe our five minutes are up. I am going to make sure I get my sick wife back in bed to rest. Please see yourself out."

"But I still have—" Jennifer began to dispute.

"Please," the old man cut her off. His face was frozen in a stiff smile.

She respectfully nodded, and slowly began collecting her things from the table. She picked up her bag and slung it over her shoulder. *Something is off*, she thought. She crept to the doorway and watched the couple slowly make their way up the stairs to the bedroom. The old man was still smiling. Mrs. Williams looked down from the landing and briefly locked eyes with Jennifer. The woman's expression turned sour upon seeing Jennifer again. The couple then disappeared into the bedroom, the door slamming behind them.

Jennifer could hear footsteps overhead and vague conversation before the squeaking of springs, as if a mattress were being sat on. Mrs. Williams was back in bed. Jennifer was about to leave when she glanced at the broken radio on the counter, and then to the stove. The stove top was still on. Jennifer went to the counter and turned it off.

There was a sudden clatter from above and she could hear the old man's raised voice. It sounded as if the bed itself had been shoved across the entire floor. A sudden THUD directly above her made her jump. It was followed by the sound of glass breaking.

The radio on the counter screeched to life, blasting the same song at full volume. Only this time, instead of changing stations, it changed the speed of the Halloween tune. "It was a one-eyed, one-horned, flying purple people eater." It sounded like someone was changing the speed on a record player—high pitched squeals to low, guttural groans to squeals once again.

Jennifer covered her ears. Another loud bang came from the room above. Scared for the old woman's well-being, Jennifer dropped her bag and ran up the stairs as the song continued behind her. She tripped halfway up and fell loudly to the landing. She looked anxiously to the bedroom door. Her presence had been announced.

The bedroom door flung open, and Mr. Williams stepped out. He closed the door behind him, located Jennifer on the stairs, and rushed wildly towards her.

Jennifer rose to her feet and attempted to dodge her attacker, but it was too late. Mr. Williams caught her in his arms and shoved her back to the landing.

"What did you do to her?!" Jennifer tried to claw past him, but he was surprisingly strong for a seventy-year-old.

The old man held her at arm's length. His eyes were clearly wet, but a smile remained frozen on his face. *Who is this psycho?!* His mouth quivered at the ends of his impossibly wide grin. He began to shake Jennifer.

"We tried! We didn't go anywhere. We stayed here!" He exclaimed with the same crazy smile still plastered on his face. He paused, noticing the song playing downstairs.

"I told you to go. GO NOW!" He released his grip on the girl, and Jennifer slid away. But instead of leaving, she bolted for the bedroom door. She threw it open, and her jaw dropped at the sight.

The room looked like a child's playroom, hastily thrown together by a mental patient. Lavender paint had been hurriedly splattered on the walls. Crudely drawn inspirational posters were taped or stapled to the walls, as were childish depictions of rainbows and suns, drawn in crayon. Sun catchers hung in the cracked window, reflecting pockets of shimmery sunlight across the disturbing scene. The bed had been flipped over, and the sheet was thrown across the floor. Next to the bed, lay the old woman in a pool of her own blood. Her limbs were distorted, as if her body had been thrown to the ground with extreme force, or from an impossible height. Each limb was twisted in a different direction and her chest cavity was cracked open. Her heart was missing. Jennifer gagged at the horrific sight. Before she could scream, a pair of icy hands wrapped themselves around her face.

"Shhhh," the old man whispered. He turned Jennifer away from his wife's corpse. "It's okay. I can fix this." His face somehow managed to smile even as his eyes were screaming for help.

He pushed Jennifer out of the room and into the hallway. He knelt down beside his mangled wife on the floor. Taking her hand in his, he began to laugh. The laugh turned into a strangled cry.

Jennifer looked on in horror.

The old man's sobs grew louder. He looked back at Jennifer. Tears streamed down his face as he tried to cover his cries with laughter.

"GO!" he shouted.

Jennifer fled down the staircase and into the kitchen for her bag. Like before, the radio had turned itself off. She sprinted to the front door, where her trembling fingers fumbled with the two locks. After a panicked moment, she managed to get them free. She vaulted down the porch steps and out onto the lawn. A loud CRASH of glass sounded behind her. She turned to witness the old man's body falling through the air towards her. His body collided with the lawn right at her feet and splattered Jennifer's cream blouse with fresh arterial blood. The breath left her body, entirely.

Did—did he just?! Jennifer could barely think over her racing heartbeat. The was a deep and jagged cut along the old man's collarbone and his face was horribly contorted, his jaw unhinged from his skull. A sound like a harsh breeze came from up above the house. Jennifer looked up to see *something* in the distance flying away from the house, disappearing into the dusky mountain mist.

Jennifer lurched forward as she gagged at the gory mess. She backed slowly away from the corpse, fearful that breaking eye contact with it would lead to more madness. As soon as she hit the edge of the driveway she turned around and bolted for Catherine's house.

It wasn't someone that took Becca. It was *something*.

TOWARDS THE LIGHT

David Lawson Jr.

HIS EYES DESPERATELY tried to peel open—an all too familiar feeling piercing through them. Trying to clear the sand from his sleep-ridden sockets has become part of the daily routine. The tiny granules scratching the delicate lens as his lids slowly separate from one another.

All his memories of home are gone. The only thing racing through his brain now is: *What am I going to eat today?* The desert is unforgiving when it comes to providing things needed to sustain life, and Charlie has constantly needed to find new ways to make sure he doesn't end up like the rest of his team.

As he finishes clearing the intruders from all the crevices they've lodged themselves in, another thought invades his still drowsy mind.

Charlie digs through his pack until his hand stops rummaging and his eyes light up. "Well, I'll be damned," he mutters to himself. He pulls a small travel-size bottle of whiskey from the pack—the kind people refuse to pay for at hotel minibars back home. He grins sardonically at the memory. *Remember minibars? Remember home?*

"Happy birthday to me," he says aloud. He has no idea what the actual date is, but he's alive and has a bottle of travel-size whiskey to enjoy, so he's calling it: Today is his birthday. "Time to celebrate—legally this time." He twists and rips the cap off, then slams the tiny bottle down like it's nothing, which it basically is. The alcohol burns his cracked throat as it goes down, causing him to wince with pleasure.

He turns the empty bottle upside down to prove to himself there is nothing left.

Not even the least bit buzzed, he grabs a pair of beat-up old boots—military issue—and slips them on. The boots are always at the ready, laces loose, footbed waiting, just in case he needs to make a quick escape in the middle of the "night." *Hit the ground running,* as they say. He laces the boots tight at the ankles and then exits his tent into the bright blue light of Deneb.

"Another day in paradise," he says to no one. He pops a hydration tablet from the pill canister in the pocket of his uniform, which would best be defined as a cross between a space suit and military BDUs. The latter of which does nothing to camouflage him against a completely foreign backdrop.

As is the next step in Charlie's routine, he goes over his supplies. It's become equal parts pragmatic and cathartic at this point. Pragmatic for obvious survival reasons. Cathartic because it serves as a constant reminder of everyone he has lost. He looks out over the collection of uniforms and gear. He has neatly stockpiled and organized the serviceable items that can be of use to him.

He slowly reaches over and picks up a set of boots with "McAndrews" scribbled onto the inside and outside portion of the tongue. The boots are too small for Charlie, making them an outlier within the collection. As he runs his fingers over the marker-laden material he can almost hear her words.

400 DAYS PRIOR

"ALRIGHT, FINAL BRIEF time! Settle in folks, today we go over everything," Col. McAndrews announces, standing in front of a white board full of schematics, mathematical formulas, and a list of Rules of Engagement. She commands the room in a way that seems more forceful than her years or her eyes would indicate upon first meeting her. Charlie looks around the room, it is filled with a diverse group of people, some of which are obviously there more for their brawn than their brains, and others undeniably there for their intellect. There is a nervous energy in the room in a way that none of them have felt before, which is strange given that some of the team members are long in the tooth. "Rabbit, what is our mission objective?"

Rabbit, the most physically impressive, stands up, his uniform doing its best to confine his muscles, "Not to die, ma'am."

McAndrews picks up an eraser off the ledge of the white board and throws it at him playfully, but it hits hard enough for him to know she also meant it. "Wrong. Snoopy?"

Charlie stands up. In a manner making it apparent that this is not the first time, or even the hundredth time, they have gone through this exercise. "We are to travel to the newly discovered planet of Ajaxion in an attempt to understand it's erratic rotational pattern while orbiting Deneb and report back." He pauses long enough for a smile to crest over McAndrews's face. "And also, not to die."

DING. McAndrews hits an old schoolhouse style desk bell placed beside her.

PRESENT DAY

CHARLIE SNAPS OUT of his daydream unsure of if the noise he heard was just in his head or something in his current situation. He places McAndrews's boot back onto the platform, with the rest of his supplies, and covers them with a brown tarp that has a camouflage underside—a reversible tarp meant to be utilized in whatever situation the crew found themselves in.

He looks around, intently scanning the horizon for any indication of danger. His gaze lingers longer while looking over the edge of the cliff that his base camp is perched on. Below, something terrible happened. The ground is charred and littered with twisted metal parts of a spaceship, something you'd never know if this was the first time seeing it.

The hairs on the back of his neck slowly fall back into their dormant state as his breathing becomes controlled again. He sits down next to his gear, a two-person all-terrain vehicle—looking more like a tank than a 4-wheeler—and his makeshift tent, with two lines carved into the post closest to him. He pulls a protein bar out of his pocket and slowly unwraps it.

It's crazy that they spent two years planning for this mission, and almost another year getting here, and now they are all just gone in the blink of an eye. Questions begin racing through his head.

Why were he and Rabbit chosen to do the deep perimeter check that day? What if Rabbit had woken him up earlier? Why had Deneb shifted position in the sky that day? And why so suddenly? What was that thing he and Rabbit saw ripping through their ship when they got back? If they were there, could they have stopped it? Did they see it coming? Were they scared? Did they feel it?

Why did Rabbit leave him?

Is anyone coming to save him?

The progression of questions continues until he reaches the final one: Is this where I die, too? After that, his mind loops back around and begins the series again. This daily meditation used to just take up a couple minutes every morning—now it takes hours.

Today however, his trance is broken early. Above him, something that had only happened once before happens again. The bright blue dot of Deneb, which normally fluctuates from around 8° up to 12°, is slowly moving directly above him.

In the two months the team had studied the erratic fluctuations from the surface, Deneb had never moved more than half a degree in any one 24-hour cycle. The plan had been to expand the search area both towards and away from the terminator line in an attempt to learn the cause of the anomaly.

For some reason, Charlie had always felt more comfortable moving towards the darkness, as counterintuitive as that would seem. So that "Day Start"—the term they utilized to begin a new 24-hour cycle—when he and Rabbit were scheduled to take the Argive 6 to the twilight zone and report back, he was excited.

40 DAYS PRIOR

"GET YOUR BAG *fucker," Rabbit chirps. Charlie, with his bag already over his shoulder, makes his way over to the vehicle. He understands the value of having a person like Rabbit on the team, even if he doesn't particularly enjoy his company. Rabbit is a true philistine through and through, and while Charlie doesn't consider himself sophisticated in the arts, he has always felt that mathematics have a certain beauty to them that can't be described.*

They hop into their transport and Rabbit pushes a series of buttons that starts the engine with a quiet hum of an intense electrically powered motor. Slowly, the craft begins to push off the ground, and its tracks and sprockets recede into the body.

Charlie always feels a bit like Marty McFly when going for a ride. He can't help but wonder if they made the Argive 6 this way because of Back to the Future, or if it truly was the most efficient design.

Off they go towards the darkness. They have roughly a three-hour trip to reach the edge of the light. They aren't scheduled to stay there long this time, only two cycles. Charlie settles in for the ride and drifts off to sleep.

He is awoken by Rabbit shaking him.

"Charlie, get up, turd goblin," Charlie isn't sure what he did to earn that nickname, but then again, it's difficult to figure out why Rabbit does or says any of the things he does. "We should be approaching the light line by now, but Deneb is rising and sitting at around 25°."

Charlie looks up at the star, which is actually closer to 16°, but he isn't going to correct him. Rabbit slows the Argive 6 down, and it settles to a stop. It is only then that they notice Deneb rapidly rising above the horizon.

"We've got to get back to the team," Charlie says in a barely audible volume.

PRESENT DAY

CHARLIE LOOKS TOWARDS the sky as the bright blue star creeps up the sky. A strong feeling of deja vu washes over him. A knot forms in his stomach. The time he has spent dwelling on how he would feel if this occurrence ever happened again has not prepared him like he had hoped.

He instead finds himself unable to move. Deneb, which was positioned squarely between the makeshift markers on the tent pole, now sits several inches above the top-most carving, and it's slowly, but noticeably, rising.

After some quick calculations, he estimates that Deneb is at approximately 26° and rising 4° every fifteen minutes.

"Four hours," Charlie mutters to himself. "I suppose today is as good as any to find out if all those nuns from Catholic school were right."

Charlie slouches down. From his seat, he reassesses his current situation, now colored by the eerie dread lurking in the sky. Silently watching Deneb's position march up the tent pole, Charlie exhales loudly.

His fingers instinctively reach down to a sheath on the side of his belt. They linger there, running gently over the copper snap. Click. The sheath being unfastened echoes down into the valley below Charlie's perch.

The sound the knife makes sliding from its home is somehow both inaudible and deafening. The blade is in immaculate condition, a byproduct of someone with too much time on their hands. The leather wrap of the hilt is stained red, a byproduct of someone with too much blood on their hands.

Charlie holds the knife up to his eyes. His face is devoid of emotion. He can't count the number of times since Rabbit's departure that he thought about running it up his wrists. Thank God he only has that tiny bottle of booze with him. Any more than that and he surely would have completed that task long ago.

He retrieves a small stone from the left cargo pocket of his pants. In another well-practiced act of mediation, Charlie drags the blade in a circular motion across the stone. The grating sound of steel against stone had made Charlie cringe the first couple times he heard it, but now it calms him. He flips the knife over and begins sharpening the other side. "RABBIT" is expertly etched into the side of the blade, now facing up. Charlie runs his fingers along the intricate lettering, still as tacky as the day he first saw it.

Charlie flips the knife over again and continues to sharpen the other side. Small circles, always in the same direction. Small circles. In the back of his mind, he knows this will likely be a futile task. The blade is plenty sharp. He hasn't had to use the knife since the night Rabbit attacked him. And even if it was the sharpest blade that has ever existed, whatever was coming for him wiped out his entire crew, and they had been packing serious firepower.

He looks back over to his markers. Deneb is now at approximately 50°. Has he zoned out, or is it moving faster? Charlie tries to get up but finds himself feeling noticeably heavier.

Unable to move from his chair, Charlie looks back at his marker: 55°. Whatever is causing this shift is definitely moving faster than it was when he first noticed the anomaly. He wills himself out of his perch, every movement a struggle.

As he creeps towards the edge of the ridge, Charlie notices something in the distance. To be more specific, he notices a lack of something. Where's all the detail that should be there? It's not every day that an entire landscape just disappears.

Charlie can't stop himself from staring. Every few moments, he catches a glimpse of something amid what can only be described as nothingness. He is transfixed, rooted to the spot he is standing in, and yet, simultaneously, he is pulled towards the edge of the cliff overlooking the valley.

His post markers are obsolete. Deneb has now crept higher than the pole. It is clear that whatever is causing this rotational fluctuation is headed right towards him. But how?

As quickly as it came into view and moved from the horizon towards Charlie, the Nothingness stops. Charlie estimates that whatever is moving towards him is now only nine or ten kilometers away.

There was part of him that originally thought: Maybe whatever it was that took everything was some sort of weather phenomenon, something natural? But looking down now, he realizes it was most certainly wishful thinking.

Charlie steals a quick glance above him and sees that Deneb is now directly above him. This darkness—no, this nothingness—in front of him is most certainly the cause.

Why did it stop? Why is it just sitting there, taunting him? What is this?

Charlie is conflicted on how to feel by this new set of questions. Suddenly his old set doesn't seem so dire.

He keeps his eyes fixed on the landscape around the void. It doesn't seem to be changing, but Charlie is having a hard time focusing on something so far in the distance. He sees a small hill slowly being engulfed by the Nothingness. Charlie isn't sure he would have even noticed this, except for the fact that he has stared at every inch of this landscape for months now.

Whatever this is, is creeping towards him, almost stalking him, it seems. Charlie stands there, staring directly into it, daring it to come forward.

Charlie reaches down and once again retrieves his knife from its sheath. With it firmly in his hand, he screams, "If you want me, come and get me!"

Then silence. And not just the silence of Charlie's words being finished, but a complete lack of any sound, as if it had all been sucked up into a vacuum. The Nothingness hastens its pace towards Charlie. With every passing second, he feels as if he's being pulled closer to the ledge.

All at once, Charlie feels himself pulled off the cliff. Confusion sets in when he realizes that he is not heading down, as one would assume, but instead being pulled towards the ever-closer abyss.

Charlie closes his eyes.

When Charlie opens his eyes, he can't see anything until he looks up and finds the blue light of Deneb, shining directly above him. The darkness closes in around the star, bringing a new and total blindness. His eyes are wide open but there is nothing to see. Nothing.

Surrounded by the Nothingness, Charlie drops his knife and closes his eyes again.

ABOUT THE AUTHORS

Jay Baruchel continues to cement his leading-man-status with many exciting projects. He recently starred in the FOX series *The Moodys* and the critically acclaimed FXX comedy series *Man Seeking Woman,* based on Simon Rich's book, *The Last Girlfriend on Earth,* and executive produced by Lorne Michaels. Jay co-wrote the hockey cult feature film *Goon* with Evan Goldberg, and was nominated for two 2013 Canadian Screen Awards for Best Supporting Actor and for Adapted Screenplay. He reprised his role in *Goon: Last of the Enforcers,* which he also co-wrote, and for which he made his directorial debut. Other selected film credits include *This Is The End, Knocked Up, She's Out of My League, Tropic Thunder, The Trotsky, The Sorcerer's Apprentice,* and the Academy Award-winner for Best Picture, *Million Dollar Baby.* He also voiced the lead role of 'Hiccup' in the DreamWorks Animation *How to Train Your Dragon* franchise, in which all three films grossed over $1.6 billion worldwide. Most recently, he co-wrote, directed, and starred in the horror thriller *Random Acts of Violence,* starring Jesse Williams and Jordana Brewster. He also stars in the Netflix spy thriller series, *FUBAR,* opposite Arnold Schwarzenegger.

Justin Benson wrote and co-directed the indie feature films *The Endless, Spring, Sychronic, Resolution,* and *Something in the Dirt.* Along with his producing partners Aaron Moorhead and David Lawson, they run the boutique indie production company Rustic Films. Born and raised in San Diego, he has resided in Los Angeles since 2003, currently in a Hollywood residence near his romantic partner. They hope to have a dog someday, as well as a yard suitable for large Halloween parties.

Lola Blanc is a filmmaker and musician whose films have been showcased by festivals like Fantastic Fest, Nantucket Film Festival, and Hollyshorts, as well as outlets like *Omeleto, Billboard,* and *Fangoria.* Blanc is a founder of Fatale Collective, an all-female horror filmmaking collective. Their debut anthology short *Bleed* screened at a number of prominent genre festivals. Much of her work is inspired by her childhood experience believing in a self-proclaimed prophet, including her podcast *Trust Me* on the PodcastOne network, in which she and her co-host interview survivors of groups like NXIVM, the Manson Family, Heaven's Gate, and QAnon. As an artist, Blanc's songs and dark videos have garnered tens of millions of streams. She has appeared as an actress in *Under the Silver Lake* and *American Horror Story.*

Sarah Bolger hails from Ireland and started her career when she was just six years old. Bolger can be seen in a season of the FX Original Series *MAYANS M.C.* In 2021, she starred in *We Broke Up,* opposite William Jackson Harper and Aya Cash. Previously, Bolger starred in Abner Pastoll's festival success *A Good Woman Is Hard to Find.* This followed her leading performances in the independent feature *Emelie,* which made its debut at the 2015 Tribeca Film Festival, and Relativity's thriller *The Lazarus Effect,* alongside Olivia Wilde, Evan Peters, and Mark Duplass. Bolger first made her memorable and award-winning debut at the age of eleven in Jim Sheridan's *In America* for Fox Searchlight. Since then, Bolger has top-lined Mark Water and Paramount's *The Spiderwick Chronicles,* Mary Harron and IFC's *The Moth Diaries,* and Max Mayer's *As Cool As I Am,* opposite James Marsden and Claire Danes. In television, Bolger played pivotal roles such as 'Bloody Mary' in Showtime's Golden Globe-nominated and IFTA-winning *The Tudors.*

C. Robert Cargill is a co-founder of Crooked Highway. He is the Clarke Award-shortlisted author of *Sea of Rust,* and the books *Day Zero, Dreams and Shadows,* and *We Are Where the Nightmares Go.* He is the co-writer of films *Sinister,* Marvel's *Doctor Strange,* and *The Black Phone.*

B. J. Colangelo is an award-winning filmmaker known for her shorts *Labrys, Margaret,* her feature film *Powerbomb,* and her contribution to the anthology film *Deathcember.* Additionally, B. J. has spent the last twelve years of her life analyzing entertainment, with bylines in *Film, Fangoria Magazine, Playboy.com, Vulture, The Daily Dot, Autostraddle, HorrorHound Magazine, Blumhouse.com, Shudder,* and *What To Watch.* She also co-hosts the popular podcast, *This Ends at Prom,* with her wife, Harmony, analyzing movies marketed to teen girl audiences from the cis and transgender lens.

Michael Dunker was born outside Chicago, Illinois, and graduated from Sycamore High School in 1999. He enlisted in the United States Air Force as a radio communicator and deployed three times to the Middle East and South America. After receiving an honorable discharge in 2003, Michael graduated from Michigan State University, with a degree in psycholog. In 2007, he started writing screenplays and directing short films. His work has been accepted by multiple screenplay competitions, including the Academy Nicholls Fellowship, Austin Film Festival, Scriptapalooza, and the Final Draft Big Break Screenplay Contest. This past summer, Michael attended the Nostos Screenwriting Fellowship in Tuscany and recently completed his third short film.

Owen Egerton is an award-winning novelist and filmmaker. He is the writer/director of several films, including *Mercy Black* (Blumhouse, Universal) and *Blood Fest* (Rooster Teeth/Warner Media). He is also the author of a number of books, including *The Book of Harold the Illegitimate Son of God, How Best to Avoid Dying,* and the PEN Southwest Book Award-winner *Hollow,* which was named one of NPR's Best Books of 2017. He also created the acclaimed reading series *One Page Salon,* and is one of the talents behind the award-winning comedy show *Master Pancake Theater.* Egerton has been voted Austin's Best Author six times by readers of *The Austin Chronicle.*

Elise Finnerty recently finalized her directorial feature, which she wrote, produced, directed, and acted in during the height of the lockdown phase of the Covid-19 pandemic. After being chosen as the opening-night After Hours film for CFF, her film received the award for Best Feature by a First Time Director. Its international premiere will be at Fright Fest in London, and it will continue its festival run from there. Her production company, Red Booth Productions, co-founded with her business partner Estelle Girard-Parks, is home to award-winning short films and theater. Their last short film, *The Hunt*, which Elise wrote and directed, was the recipient of the Remi Award at Houston's International Film festival. Elise is currently working on a comedy-horror series titled *Headshot*.

Kyra Gardner grew up with a dad in special effects makeup, so blood and guts became normal for her at a young age. Combat nursing was her first goal, but she soon discovered that real blood is way grosser than the fake stuff. She's been pursuing a career in directing since attending Florida State's film program, and she plans on creating quirky fantastical films from the lore of her unconventional childhood.

Janina Gavankar is one half of a writing and directing duo with Russo Schelling. Their first offering, *Stucco,* earned a Special Jury Award at SXSW 2020, an Academy Award Qualification, and has been seen more than forty million times online. Amongst their many projects are the feature *Rakshasi,* based on a Hindu myth, and a partnership with Soledad O'Brien on the docuseries *Screw City.* They recently announced their first podcast with HBOmax.

Estelle Girard-Parks created Red Booth Productions alongside her business partner Elise Finnerty. Her producing credits include an international commercial for a luxury handbag brand, a television pilot, multiple short films, a few off-Broadway plays, and a feature film. Estelle and Elise have been recognized with a Remy Award for best short film, and most recently, an award for Best Feature for First Time Director at Chattanooga Film Festival for their feature debut *The Ones You Didn't Burn*. The film premiered at FrightFest in 2022. Estelle recently joined the team of Augusta Films, created by Peabody and Emmy award-winner, Nancy Buirski. Their newest feature documentary *Desperate Souls, Dark City and the Legend of Midnight Cowboy* will be premiering at the 79th Venice International Film Festival, followed by Telluride International Film Festival and the Hamptons International Film Festival.

Jordan Goldstein is a writer/director whose work, both past and present, hopes to touch upon genre film in the most humanistic way possible, while also maintaining an entertaining and pulpy core. Over the years, Jordan has directed, written, and edited various short films that have touched upon different genres. With each story, Jordan's hope is to explore intimate human themes while also consistently providing a visceral experience.

Brea Grant is an award-winning writer/director. She wrote and directed *12 Hour Shift* (Tribeca 2020, winner of Best Screenplay at Fantasia 2020), starring Angela Bettis and David Arquette. The same year, she wrote and starred in the film *Lucky* (SXSW 2020). She recently wrapped on directing the film *Torn Hearts* (2022) for Blumhouse/Paramount, starring Katey Sagal. She has written and directed for Netflix and the CW, and recently wrote and directed on the upcoming series *Unconventional*. She has written four comic series, including the recent, *Mary*. She co-hosts a book podcast called *Reading Glasses*.

Gigi Saul Guerrero is a Mexican genre director/filmmaker and actress now living in Vancouver, Canada. She's been described by *Variety, L'Attitude Latinxt* as part of the new wave of Latino talent; scored a First Look Deal with Jason Blum's Blumhouse Productions; and has been praised as one of the top, emerging directors in the horror genre by *Empire, Dread Central, Fangoria,* and *Bloody Disgusting*. Guerrero is co-founder of Luchagore Productions in Vancouver, Canada. She has directed an action-packed episode for *The Purge,* season two, and the feature film *Culture Shock* for Blumhouse Productions Television, winner of Best Primetime movie at Imagen Awards, She is also an actress and most commonly known for her voice-over work such for *Super Monsters* (Vida), *Marvel Superhero Adventures* (Spider-Girl), fan favorite character, Varzia, on the video game, *Warfare,* and Mischa Lebron in Peacock's animated series *Supernatural Academy.*

Gille Klabin grew up in a combination of USA, Israel, and Austria, eventually ending up in England, where he began making videos at the age of eleven. With stop-motion toy films in his past, Gille graduated from Westminster University's Film School and worked as a production assistant and location scout while directing music videos for unsigned bands. Gille's colorful, energetic work eventually led to him directing videos for several major record labels and making commercials and shorts in London. In 2009, he moved to Los Angeles, where his documentary, commercial, and music video work have all flourished. He created a host of videos for several electronic music artists and a handful of national spots for tech, food, and alcohol brands. Gille strives to tell stories that are striking, and that create vivid and engulfing worlds. In 2020, he released his first feature film *The Wave,* starring Justin Long, which was selected for Fantastic fest and is available on all VOD platforms.

David Lawson Jr. developed a love for film at an early age while living in Baltimore, Maryland. After graduating high school, he enlisted in the U.S. Air Force. He served for over four years as an Airborne Radio Operator aboard the AWACS E-3 Sentry, deploying for both Operation Iraqi Freedom (Iraq) and Operation Enduring Freedom (Afghanistan). There he not only met many people with the same affinity for cinema, but also took to heart their core values: integrity first, service before self, and excellence in all you do. He has since brought those values to Los Angeles, where since 2005, he has been working his way up the commercial and feature film ranks. After years of working as an independent producer, David joined Snowfort Pictures from 2015 until 2017. Then, along with long-time collaborators Justin Benson and Aaron Moorhead, he formed Rustic Films. His features include *Synchronic, The Endless, She Dies Tomorrow, Afer Midnight, Something in the Dirt, Trash Fire, 68 Kill, 24x36: A Movie About Movie Posters, Spring,* and *Resolution.*

Izzy Lee is a writer/director, abstract painter, and former film festival programmer and genre journalist. Her award-winning tales have screened at major international genre festivals such as Fantasia, Overlook, Morbido, FrightFest, Fantaspoa, Brooklyn Horror, Boston Sci-Fi, Boston Underground, Chattanooga, and more. In 2022, Lee earned Certificates of Completion from Sundance Collab's Directing Television, Directing Actors, and Visual Storytelling courses. Additionally, Lee has directed nearly two dozen shorts, and she shadowed director Adam Egypt Mortimer on the SpectreVision feature *Archenemy.* She's currently developing a long-awaited feature that's a middle finger to the church and the patriarchy. See what she's up to at nihilnoctem.com.

Carl Lucas is U.S. Army veteran and has produced several independent features, including *The Rambler* (Anchor Bay), which was accepted in the Midnight Section of the 2013 Sundance Film Festival. He recently produced the independent horror films *Fender Bender* (Chiller/ NBC Universal), *The Field Guide to Evil* (Neon), Slamdance award-winner *My Name Is Myeisha* (Shout Factory), the 2019 Fantastic Fest selection *The Wave* (Epic Pictures; also written by Carl), and the *The Old Way,* starring Nicolas Cage.

Malachi Moore is an award-winning writer/director. He received his MFA in Writing for the Screen from Loyola Marymount University, where he refined his own voice by drawing from the distinct perspective of his past. Born in Atlanta, Georgia, his calling to self discernment has led him to live throughout the country, exposing him to an array of creative professions and candid experiences. His work aims to exhibit the internal effects of cultural paradigms on the Black male's psyche, incorporating humor and romance within to make themes of existential dread and identity more palatable—you know, some real "Feel-Good, Family-Friendly" kind of stuff.

Aaron Moorhead is half of the co-directing duo behind independent films *The Endless, Synchronic, Spring, Resolution,* and their most recent, *Something in the Dirt.* With his friend Justin Benson, they have directed episodes of Jordan Peele's *The Twilight Zone,* the Netflix series *Archive 81,* and *Moon Knight* for Marvel Studios. He is a founding member of boutique production company Rustic Films, which the two run with their producing partner David Lawson. He is an Eagle Scout and almost got his black belt in Tae Kwon Do, but gave up before he got there for some reason.

Jared Moshe is an award-winning writer/director who marked his transition from accomplished producer to the director's chair with the indie feature *Dead Man's Burden,* one of *Paste Magazine's* "100 Best Westerns of All Time." His most recent film *The Ballad of Lefty Brown,* released by A24, premiered to rave reviews at SXSW. The film starred Bill Pullman, Kathy Baker, Jim Caviezel, Tommy Flanagan, and Peter Fonda in one of his final roles. Jared previously developed *Aporia,* with Neda Armian (*Rachel Getting Married*)—with Paramount, J. J. Abrams, and Bad Robot producing. Most recently, he set up his Hawaiian noir *The Big Island,* with Divide/Conquer and the white-knuckled action thriller *The Father,* with Record Player Films and Automatik. He is currently executive producing a TV show on the Colombo crime family, with David Permut (*Hacksaw Ridge*).

Wanjiru Njendu is an award-winning, Kenyan-American filmmaker. Her creative imagination earned her the nickname "Magic" at a young age. Wanjiru is a member of the Academy of Motion Picture Arts and Sciences (Oscars), and her films have played in over one hundred festivals. Her award-winning short film *Boxed,* which has played over one hundred film festival selections, was selected for the 2021 Nuits en Or, Académie des César, and won Best Short Film at the Hague Global Film Festival, and the African Movie Academy Awards. In 2021, *Boxed* was also honored with the Abraham Lincoln Award for Best film on Liberty and Equality by the Chicago International Indie Film Festival, organized by the American Film Society. Wanjiru was honored by the Roxbury International Film Festival with the 2021 Rox Vision Award. She recently directed a horror short *Stray,* which was acquired by 20th Digital Studios, with a feature option. She was the shadowing director on the Netflix series *Daybreak,* under Mark Tonderai. Wanjiru has worked for Disney Studios and Universal Pictures' Creative Marketing. She is currently filming a docs-series *Built for Good,* on Green buildings in Africa, and a documentary about a children's S.T.E.M. (Science, technology, engineering, and mathematics) organization in Kenya.

Nick Peterson grew up watching MTV, sci-fi films, anime from Blockbuster Video, and playing video games. He graduated from the Experimental Animation program at Cal Arts. Nick's films have been screened at festivals such as Sundance and SXSW. His award-winning music videos have garnered over five hundred million views, and his Chrysler commercial played during the Super Bowl. He currently lives in Los Angeles.

Brett Pierce & Drew Pierce are the writing/directing team behind 2020's #1 horror hit *The Wretched,* and the renowned zombie cult film *Deadheads.* They have been obsessed with the horror genre, having grown up amid the production of Sam Raimi's cult classic *The Evil Dead,* for which their father served as the photographic effects artist. Currently they are in development on multiple horror projects.

Cezil Reed is a WGA writer/director based in LA who prides himself on learning about character and plot via extreme, physical conditioning: weightlifting, yoga, running, and Brazilian Jiu Jitsu. He's directed two feature films within the horror sphere: *The Taking* and *Not Alone.* His next creative ventures will use the horrors of living in America as a backdrop, coupled with characters with supernatural abilities and challenges. He's currently partnered with Neo Noir: a boutique production company focused on genre.

Russo Schelling is one half of a writing and directing duo with Janina Gavankar. Their first offering, *Stucco,* earned a Special Jury Award at SXSW 2020, an Academy Award Qualification, and has been seen more than forty million times online. Amongst their many projects are the feature *Rakshasi,* based on a Hindu myth, and a partnership with Soledad O'Brien on the docuseries *Screw City.* They recently announced their first podcast with HBOmax.

Gary Sherman is a director, producer, and screenwriter. He has more than a dozen feature length films, nearly three dozen dramatic television series, documentary, industrial, and music films on his résumé. His career began in Chicago with a documentary about rock and roll legend, Bo Diddly. His feature film credits include *Death Line,* named by the British Film Institute among the Ten Great British Films by American Directors; *Dead and Buried,* considered by many one of the foremost iconic zombie films of the '80s; and *Vice Squad,* a critical and box office hit. TV credits include ABC-TV's *Missing Persons,* starring Daniel J. Travant; A&E's *The First 48: Missing Persons,* co-creator/ Executive Producer; ABC-TV's *Sable* creator/Executive Producer; and Showtime's *Poltergeist: TheLegacy.* He is currently co-writing and Executive Producing a original dramatic pilot for Halcyon Studios.

Graham Skipper is an actor/writer/director/producer of genre films, best known for his work in Stuart Gordon's *Re-Animator the Musical,* the films *Almost Human, Beyond The Gates, The Mind's Eye, Bliss, Dementia I & II,* and his feature directorial debut *Sequence Break.* He is published in Simon & Schuster's *Video Palace: In Search of the Eyeless Man, My Favorite Horror Movie, volume one.* He lives in Austin, Texas, with his circus performer wife and their dogs, Mufasa and Dax.

A. T. White is a filmmaker and musician from the UK, who lives in LA. He likes wide-open spaces, empathy, watermelon juice, and driving across the entire width of America, two-to-six times a year. His favorite movies are *Se7en, You Were Never Really Here, Buffalo '66, Nine Days, In the Mood for Love, Lost in Translation, Princess Mononoke,* and *Swingers.* His debut feature *Starfish* had its world premiere at Fantastic Fest, and a theatrical run in North America in 2019. He made the film for his friend who passed away. He runs international boutique production house Dive Dark, takes 35mm photos for his alternative arthouse journal *Neon Wolves,* and he hosts the movie podcast *We Are Geeks.* He is also the lead singer/songwriter of UK band *Ghostlight,* who put out their new album *Dive Dark* in 2020.

Ariel Vida is a filmmaker of the strange and surreal. She is the director of the features *Vide Noir* and *Trim Season,* as well as several music videos, including Lord Huron's "The World Ender." She has also production designed and art directed over one hundred shorts, music videos, commercials, and feature films, including *The Endless, She Dies Tomorrow, Synchronic, Archenemy, Shadow Kingdom,* and *Something in the Dirt.* She lives in Los Angeles with her cat Sniffy, and it's likely that while you're reading this, she's watching *RRR* again.

ABOUT THE CURATOR

DAVID LAWSON JR. developed a love for film at an early age while living in Baltimore, Maryland. After graduating high school, he enlisted in the U.S. Air Force. He served for over four years as an Airborne Radio Operator aboard the AWACS E-3 Sentry, deploying for both Operation Iraqi Freedom (Iraq) and Operation Enduring Freedom (Afghanistan). There he not only met many people with the same affinity for cinema, but also took to heart their core values: integrity first, service before self, and excellence in all you do. He has since brought those values to Los Angeles, where since 2005, he has been working his way up the commercial and feature film ranks. After years of working as an independent producer, David joined Snowfort Pictures from 2015 until 2017. Then, along with long-time collaborators Justin Benson and Aaron Moorhead, he formed Rustic Films. His features include *Synchronic, The Endless, She Dies Tomorrow, Afer Midnight, Something in the Dirt, Trash Fire, 68 Kill, 24x36: A Movie About Movie Posters, Spring,* and *Resolution.*

ABOUT THE COVER ARTIST

OLIVER (OLLY) JEAVONS is a UK-based artist also known as *artofolly*. He works with many different medias and styles, and he is always pushing his creativity further. Comic book art, book cover art, and commissions of all types are included in his portfolio.

PERMISSIONS

Also Available or Coming Soon from Dark Matter INK

Human Monsters: A Horror Anthology
Edited by Sadie Hartmann & Ashley Saywers
ISBN 978-1-958598-00-9

*Zero Dark Thirty: The 30 Darkest Stories from Dark
Matter Magazine, 2021–'22*
Edited by Rob Carroll
ISBN 978-1-958598-16-0

Linghun by Ai Jiang
ISBN 978-1-958598-02-3

Monstrous Futures: A Sci-Fi Horror Anthology
Edited by Alex Woodroe
ISBN 978-1-958598-07-8

Our Love Will Devour Us by R. L. Meza
ISBN 978-1-958598-17-7

The Vein by Stephanie Nelson
ISBN 978-1-958598-15-3

Other Minds by Eliane Boey
ISBN 978-1-958598-19-1

Frost Bite by Angela Sylvaine
ISBN 978-1-958598-03-0

Monster Lairs: A Dark Fantasy Horror Anthology
Edited by Anna Madden
ISBN 978-1-958598-08-5

Chopping Spree by Angela Sylvaine
ISBN 978-1-958598-31-3

The Bleed by Stephen S. Schreffler
ISBN 978-1-958598-11-5

Free Burn by Drew Huff
ISBN 978-1-958598-26-9

The House at the End of Lacelean Street
by Catherine McCarthy
ISBN 978-1-958598-23-8

The Off-Season: An Anthology of Coastal New Weird
Edited by Marissa van Uden
ISBN 978-1-958598-24-5

The Dead Spot: Stories of Lost Girls
by Angela Sylvaine
ISBN 978-1-958598-27-6

When the Gods Are Away by Robert E. Harpold
ISBN 978-1-958598-47-4

Grim Root by Bonnie Jo Stufflebeam
ISBN 978-1-958598-36-8

Voracious by Belicia Rhea
ISBN 978-1-958598-25-2

Abducted by Patrick Barb
ISBN 978-1-958598-37-5

Darkly Through the Glass Place by Kirk Bueckert
ISBN 978-1-958598-48-1

The Threshing Floor by Steph Nelson
ISBN 978-1-958598-49-8

Printed in the USA
CPSIA information can be obtained
at www.ICGtesting.com
JSHW030225280923
49209JS00008B/209